B.J.,
Hope you and Kyle's story! ♡
All the best,
Denise A. Agnew

TREACHEROUS WISHES

Treacherous Wishes
By Denise A. Agnew
Exciting Sequel to Dangerous Intentions

Acknowledgements

Copious thanks goes to Susan Yarina for medical information and martial arts tips. Thanks, also, to Lara Britton, Tara Manderino, Victoria Rivers, and Candy Sams for information on martial arts. Mega thanks to Bev Kay for her valuable insight into the workings of a soup kitchen.

TREACHEROUS WISHES
Copyright © 2001
By Denise A. Agnew
All rights reserved.

Cover design:
Copyright 2000 © Lee Emory
All rights reserved.

Treble Heart Books
1284 Overlook Dr.
Sierra Vista, AZ 85635-5512

http://www.trebleheartbooks.com

The characters and events in this book are fictional, and any resemblance to persons, whether living or dead, is strictly coincidental.

All rights reserved. No part of this book may be reproduced or transmitted in any form by any means, electronic or mechanical, including photocopying, recording, scanning to a computer disk, or by any informational storage and retrieval and retrieval system, without express permission in writing from the publisher.

ISBN: 1-931742-35-9

Dedication

To the man of my dreams, Terry.

Chapter 1

Heavy, raspy breathing echoed in Tammy Carter's ears. Fear slammed into her gut, wrenching her so hard that nausea boiled in her stomach.

She closed her eyes and tightened her grip on the telephone as the breathing on the other end continued. A flash of red filled her mind's eye and she shuddered. She sank into the chair behind her desk. For years she'd feared the day the evil might return. She dreaded the inevitable when she would sense the malevolence that came once or twice in a lifetime. Now it came through the phone…reaching…reaching…

Oh, God. Not now.

Shades of blue and black mingled with the red behind her eyes, and she hoped the person on the other end of the line hadn't already committed some horrible crime against an innocent person. Then scarlet came as a hot wave over her body…the fever of illness. Azure pierced like the cold, sharp sting of an icicle stabbing her arms. Black left a deep, hollow well in her stomach.

No. No! She didn't want to see what the breather had done. Didn't want to know. She opened her eyes, denying the ability that gave her this horrible insight. As the breathing on the end of the line continued, she jerked her connection away from the person on the other side. Fear mutated into fury.

Tammy clenched the telephone receiver until it felt as if the plastic might break. She gave the breather five more seconds to speak, then she cursed and slammed down the receiver. As she shook from reaction, her body suffused with a cold sweat. Perspiration formed on her forehead and upper lip, and she reached for a tissue box. Dabbing a tissue over her cheeks, she took deep breaths and the fear eased minute by minute.

Nice thing about these episodes. Quick to come, quick to go.

Calm settled over Tammy. Whatever animal had called had disconnected from her, and she didn't want to worry about the creep anymore.

Must forget. Must let it go.

A sparkling tune about love flowed from the small radio tucked beneath the high counter of her desk. *Yeah, right.* She snapped off the radio.

What a fine way to end a day's work. First, several folders had disappeared and it had taken half the day for her to deduce where the temp had filed them last week. The young, inexperienced woman had wreaked havoc in the office with her incompetence.

Tammy would have been happy if only one thing had gone wrong with the day. But a client had made a sexual harassment complaint against one of Taggert Security Team's bodyguards that afternoon. Tammy had missed lunch, and two bodyguards on assignment had come down with the flu.

She never should have taken vacation for an entire week. Mrs. Taggert and several of the bodyguards had almost kissed her feet when she'd walked in the door that Monday morning. Sure, it was gratifying to be missed, but not when she found twice the work piled on her desk once she returned.

Hungry, tired, and downright hacked described her attitude to an inch. Mrs. Taggert might pay Tammy well as her personal administrative assistant, but today's events had strained Tammy's steel nerves to the limit.

The phone rang again.

The breather had called three times in ten minutes, and that last *connection* had about broken her. She hesitated.

She *should* say Taggert Security Team. She *should* take a deep breath and stay calm.

Screw it!

She picked up the phone on the third ring. "Listen you jerk, this is a business. Stop calling us!"

Silence on the other end shocked her. Finally the person spoke. "Tammy?"

She recognized the deep voice and a blush flooded her face. "Hawthorne? Damn it, I'm sorry."

"Hey, babe, are you all right?"

His silky, husky voice sent a wild fluttering into her stomach. Tammy swallowed hard. Kyle Hawthorne might be the most handsome man she'd ever met, but that didn't mean she needed to dissolve into gelatin at the sound of his voice. The jibes, barbs and teasing they'd traded for the last year meant nothing. Employees at Taggert Security leaned toward the wild side; their dangerous jobs made them less willing to follow convention. Hawthorne was no exception. He played the role of flirtatious, handsome charmer all the way. More than once friends of Tammy's speculated about his love life. But she tried not to imagine Hawthorne holding a woman in his arms. It gave her a headache.

"Tammy?" he said again, concern deepening his already low voice.

"Sorry. I...uh...I just thought you were someone else."

He chuckled. "What's the matter? Art forget to pick you up for a date?"

Leave it to Kyle to remember the one time Art Childress had forgotten a date with her. "He's working tonight. We had to cancel."

"Again?"

"What do you mean *again*? We've gotten together three times in two months. I'd say that's a record."

"If you were my woman, I'd make sure we *got together* several times a week."

With impeccable timing, her heartbeat accelerated, and her mouth went dry. Babe? His woman? It sounded primitive. Some might say chauvinistic. Yet she knew this man too well to believe he meant any irreverence toward her. He believed in equality of the sexes. Tammy reminded herself that he didn't mean anything and flirting came second nature to him. His woman indeed!

"Better watch out, Hawthorne. I could break your neck for saying something that suggestive and sexist."

"Chauvinistic?"

"Don't play dumb with me. *Your woman?* Hell, why not go all the way and call me wench?" His laugh soothed her skittish nerves. She sighed and rubbed the tight muscles in the back of her neck. "What are you doing calling the office at this hour?"

"What are you doing at the office at seven o'clock at night?"

Tammy fiddled with the small, brown plastic stegosaurus on her desk. "Answer my question first."

"Burke still working on the Alexander case?"

The stegosaurus tipped over, and she let it lie on its side. She stared at its underbelly. "No. He went home an hour ago. He thinks he's coming down with the flu as well."

"Great. At this rate Mrs. Taggert will have to quarantine the office."

She groaned. "I don't even want to think about it."

"Okay, so why are you still at work and who did you think was calling?"

"Today was hellish and I got behind. And I thought you were the breather. He's called three times in the last ten minutes. When the phone rang, I lost it."

"Obscene phone calls? That's a first at the agency. It must be your velvet voice."

"Right, Hawthorne. My voice is about as sexy as an elephant sneezing."

He laughed. "Did this creep say anything?"

"No. He wasn't original enough. Just a lot of heavy panting."

"Are you about ready to leave?"

"Just put away the last file. I need a cup of caffeine for the road."

"Stay put. I'm almost there."

"What?" She accidentally knocked the pencil cup over and writing instruments rolled across her desk.

"I'm calling on my cell. When I get there I can walk you to your car."

"You don't have to do that." She hated the shaky, nervous quality in her voice. Tammy righted the pencil cup and started dropping pens and pencils into the brilliant red holder.

"I don't have to. I *want* to. See you in a few minutes."

Stunned, she kept the phone to her ear for a moment before she realized he'd hung up. She slipped the receiver back into the cradle.

Staring at the pencil cup, she wondered if the breather had rattled her more than she wanted to admit. Tammy hadn't experienced a wave of revulsion like the one she'd experienced with the breather in…well…a good long time. Hell, it had been such hard work to keep her ability under wraps. So hard. For years she'd tucked away her psychic abilities, then six months ago she'd resurrected them for a case involving another bodyguard at the agency. Then she'd stuffed them back in the little niche she reserved for things she didn't want to think about. Why had her abilities reappeared now?

Memories ate at her, rearing their repulsive heads so that she recalled fifteen years ago with clarity.

Tammy closed her eyes and saw her older sister's smile, her long, red hair so much like Tammy's own. Then she saw her sister's blue eyes staring at the sky as Barb floated in the family swimming pool, her life throttled out of her by a madman.

Shivering, Tammy pushed away the memory. She hadn't thought about those horrific events for a long time.

The phone rang, and she jolted. It was probably Hawthorne saying he'd changed his mind about coming by the office. Good. She didn't need the distraction.

"Taggert Security. May I help you?"

"I see you."

The rough, guttural tone sounded like crunching gravel. Pure apprehension roiled inside her. Before Tammy could say a word or hang up, the voice came again.

"You can't hide from me. You're in my book of wishes."

She felt it again.

Pure, unadulterated evil.

Tammy opened her mouth but nothing would come out. The red wave started at the corner of her vision and she closed her eyes. Red. The color of violence and pain and sometimes the hot, overwhelming tide of love and sex.

No. Please not again. I can't do this again.

A hushed laugh echoed into her ear. "What's the matter, Sweet Magnolia? Cat got your tongue? Well that's no matter. I'll have your tongue before long."

She inhaled a sharp breath, revulsion sending a metallic taste to her mouth. She slammed down the receiver. Fear rocketed through her like a missile. Tammy rubbed her arms as goose bumps spread over her skin. Swiftly she turned on the answering machine. If the bastard called again she wouldn't have to tolerate his vile comments. Her only salvation came in banishing these visions once and for all.

Coffee.

Coffee cured everything. When Tammy stood she held on to the desk while she regained equilibrium. The aftereffects of these strong visions mimicked illness, and all she needed now was for Hawthorne to arrive and find her collapsed on the floor.

She headed for the lounge at the back of the large office space. Her footfalls made a soft swish over the carpet, and the minute sound made her feel vulnerable. Once inside the lounge, she grabbed her mug and poured a cup of mocha java. She tried a sip. A little bitter from too many hours on the hot pad. No matter. She loved mocha java no matter what its condition. Tammy switched off the machine and distracted herself by cleaning the coffee pot and the counter.

Sighing, she thought about Hawthorne's insistence that he stop by the office and walk her to her car. Earlier she wouldn't have hesitated to enter the parking garage alone. After that slimy call, her knees had weakened. No, she'd feel more secure now that Hawthorne would arrive any minute.

Immediately she pushed aside a feeling of helplessness. She had never come close to being a weak, defenseless female in all her twenty-nine years.

Her fingers trembled as she put down her mug and rubbed her arms again. The turtleneck sweater dress couldn't protect against the cold fright that skulked into the room and wrapped itself around her like a many- tentacled beast from a nightmare. Ice sank into her bones, digging deep like a dagger.

"Oh, God," Tammy whispered.

For the umpteenth time a shudder ran through her. No. She had to think of something else. Something pleasant.

Kyle Hawthorne.

She didn't even know whether to call him by his first name or his last anymore. For months she'd called him simply Hawthorne. She called all the bodyguards by their last names. But sometimes he became Kyle. Had become Kyle since that night six months ago when he'd suffered a bullet wound.

He might be a man of mystery, but Tammy had no intention of trying to decipher him. In the year he'd worked at the bodyguard agency, she'd seen his quick wit, his professionalism, and his cool, cocky side. He flirted and joked, but tonight she'd heard a difference in his voice. Or had she? Maybe the stress of the day had fried her brain.

For a second she got a vision of that famous commercial from the seventies.

"This is your brain. This is your brain on drugs," she said out loud, then a made a sizzling noise. Tammy laughed weakly. "Yep. That's me."

But he'd called her *babe*. He'd never called her anything other than her first or last name before.

Although Edith Taggert, owner of the agency, didn't have a stated policy on sexual harassment, Tammy had no compunction about trading witty repartee with the bodyguards. Flirting meant absolutely nothing. She knew that from long experience.

She wasn't getting involved in a romantic relationship again for a good long time, if ever. Her track record proved she couldn't trust her feelings in that arena. Tammy was engaged once, right out of college. Her lawyer boyfriend had discovered a beautiful brunette in the law firm suited him better. Second only to that painful discovery had been her other attempts at relationships.

Too many times men had flirted and romanced her until she lost control and believed herself in love. Each time she discovered the men not only didn't love her, they wanted to use her. She'd given her affections to men who had no intentions of returning her love.

The phone rang again, but Tammy let the machine get it. From this distance she couldn't hear the person leaving a message, and that was mighty fine with her. Let the bastard babble to a machine. Maybe he'd get off on talking to himself and leave her alone.

Less than two minutes later the phone rang again. Once more she ignored it.

Tammy thought of something that sent her heart into a rapid jig. Was the front door to the office locked?

Putting her mug on the counter, she trotted out to the front area. When she reached her desk she saw the door unlocked. Damn! This might be a secure building, but Tammy never left it unlocked when alone in the office.

Before she reached the door a blast of scorching, vivid red blinded her and she stumbled back, falling to the floor and landing on her butt. Tammy gasped, startled by the force.

Whoever or whatever had called her had come into the building and was close. Too close.

Tammy struggled to unscramble her senses as another wave of scarlet splattered across her vision. Power flooded her system and she stood, legs wobbly and step uncertain. Fear surged through her veins like electricity, and she knew she must reach the door and lock it before the fiend with the blood red aura could arrive first.

Now. Go. Hurry.

The crimson retreated, draining away like the lifeblood of the dying. She closed her eyes and the burning sensation left her body. Relief made her almost as dizzy as the vision, and Tammy took another step. *Must lock the door. The person may come back.*

She stepped forward and had just touched the knob when the door came open.

Tammy jumped back, a startled yelp leaving her throat. Her heart slammed in her chest as her heel snagged on the carpet and she started to fall backwards. Before she could make another sound, the big man in the doorway leapt forward and caught her in his arms. He hauled her against his chest.

"Tammy?" Concern drew Hawthorne's dark brows downward and his lips thinned into a frown.

"You," she said, sighing in total relief.

No red. No colors at all. She never saw colors when she was around Hawthorne.

"Were you expecting someone else?"

"No," she said weakly. "I was going to lock the door when you came busting in and scared the bejeebers out of me."

"You're trembling." He tucked her a little closer and the heat of his body warmed her.

"I think the air conditioning was up a bit high. I...I got cold."

Although stunned, Tammy couldn't ignore the fact she pressed against his tall, rock hard body. The soft, denim shirt couldn't hide the evidence of broad shoulders under her fingers.

She'd tried over the time she'd known him to disregard another disturbing realty; Kyle Hawthorne sent her libido into overdrive.

No, he'd never be model handsome, but perhaps that was what made him interesting. Most women found Hawthorne's dangerous air mixed with a sharp sense of humor almost mouthwatering. His face had a mixed-up perfection that belonged in the movies. Dark and deep, his brown eyes could switch from amused to frosty in a heartbeat. His almost too long nose matched well with his uncompromising jaw. Cocoa brown hair was cut close enough to his head to be neat, but not quite military length. Tammy had a notion if he let it grow much longer the waves would go wild. Despite his looks, his face could turn hard and unforgiving. No one could ever call him boyish.

"Are you sure you're okay?" he asked, his eyes narrowing.

His touch, his nearness had wiped away the terror of moments ago. "I feel good."

As she gazed up into Hawthorne's eyes and cursed the gods that gave some men long sexy lashes, she saw something change within him.

A sudden, shocking warmth ignited in his eyes and flickered into full flame. "You feel great."

Her mouth dropped in surprise. Was he flirting with her again? Hawthorne's mouth turned up in his trademark quirky smile. Between tender and hard, his mouth looked undeniably masculine. Suddenly Tammy was downright breathless. His warm, spicy scent had teased and tantalized her many times before, but now she felt every inch of him, every nuance. Something had changed and it sent waves of heat straight to her toes. Lean without being skinny, big boned and perfectly muscled, Hawthorne looked capable of kicking anyone's ass. His jeans slicked along narrow hips, tight butt, and long, powerful legs. Tammy licked her lips and swallowed hard as another fluttery sensation darted into her stomach.

Maybe she should say something before he thought she had lost her mind. Surprised by the instant reaction to his nearness, Tammy pushed against Hawthorne's chest and eased from his arms.

"Where are you off to in such a hurry? I thought you were waiting for me?" he asked.

"I got another one of those phone calls and I remembered the door wasn't locked."

It didn't help when he came close, standing so near she inhaled a whiff of his aftershave again. He cupped her shoulder. "You look a little shaky."

She realized that she'd been rubbing her arms. "I'm fine."

As if to contradict her, her body rebelled and a wave of nausea replaced the desire she'd felt moments ago.

"Can't fool me." His quiet voice soothed her senses. "You're pale as the dead."

Barb's grave. The caller had awakened the dead. "I'm okay, Hawthorne."

Hawthorne didn't look convinced. He shoved a hand through his already mussed hair. "What did the caller say?"

"Stupid things. It's nothing."
He looked doubtful. "All right. About ready to go?"
"Yeah. Let me get my coat."

But then the queasiness increased and as Tammy turned, she pressed her hand to her stomach. Before she could say or do a thing, dizziness assaulted her.

"Hawthorne—"

Darkness blotted every color from her vision.

Chapter 2

Tammy fell to the floor practically at Hawthorne's feet. "Tammy!"

He'd seen her wobble, and had stepped toward her when she'd uttered his name and collapsed without warning. A sinking, cold concern stunned him. Then instinct revived, and he raced toward her. She'd fallen on her right side. Without moving her, he felt for the pulse in her neck. Relief filled him; her pulse beat steady and strong.

"Tammy? Can you hear me?"

No response.

Gently he turned her onto her back. Her small, well-proportioned features looked young and defenseless and fired every protective instinct he possessed. Her ashen cheeks added to the false portrait. Her chin length, auburn bob was mussed and strands fell over her cheeks. As he brushed the hair from her face, he had to remind himself Tammy Carter didn't have a fragile bone in her body. A year of working with her had taught him that he didn't know a tougher, quicker, wittier, or more efficient woman. She ran Mrs. Taggert's schedule and the rest of the office with self-confidence. Seeing her vulnerable like this turned fear to ice in his belly. He placed his palm on her forehead and her frigid skin surprised him.

Shock? It didn't seem likely, but he couldn't take chances. Maybe she'd contracted the flu ravaging Taggert Security in the last two weeks. He leaned down until he could hear Tammy's breathing. Softly her breath touched his face.

"Come on, babe," he whispered. "Snap out of it. Open your eyes. You're starting to scare me."

When she didn't move or make a sound, he cursed. He started to reach for his cell phone to call for medical assistance when she stirred and a soft moan escaped her lips. Her eyelids flickered and opened. Soft, dazed green eyes gazed up at him. She appeared bewildered, like a child that had wandered into danger and didn't know which way to turn.

He placed his hand on her forehead. Her skin had warmed. "You all right?"

A smile flickered over her cherry lips, and he had an insane desire to press a kiss there to comfort her. "I can't believe that just happened."

He grinned to reassure her and took his hand from her forehead. "Well, it did. How do you feel? Are you in pain? Do you feel sick?"

She shook her head and sat up. He put an arm around her shoulders and kept it there. Inhaling deeply, he caught her unique soft scent.

Right, Hawthorne. What a time to notice how wonderful she smells. Get with the program.

"Easy. Just take it slow," he said.

She waved a hand as if to dismiss her condition. "I didn't get any lunch today. Maybe that's what's wrong."

Tammy didn't sound convinced, and his concern notched upward. "Are you sure that's all it is? Sure it's not this damned flu going around the office?"

"It's not the flu. I just need to head home and have some dinner."

As Tammy started to rise, he assisted her, half tempted to haul her into his arms so he could carry her to the couch. Her color hadn't returned yet. Putting his arm around her shoulders again, he brought her against his side as he headed to the lounge.

Under his arm her shoulders seemed delicate. "Is there anything to eat around here? You should eat something."

She paused inside the break room and eased from under Hawthorne's arm. Cocking one cinnamon-colored eyebrow, she said, "If you call breakfast bars something to eat."

He grinned. "How do you do it? I've seen you chow down and yet you keep that sexy figure."

Her eyes widened, and for a moment he wondered if he'd crossed the line. "Exercise. I don't crave sweets. Now popcorn and pizza. *That's* another story."

He headed for a cabinet next to the refrigerator and after some rummaging located the box of granola bars. He tossed her an apple raisin bar. "Now I know there's something wrong with you. I expected a snappy comeback after I told you that you have a sexy body."

Tammy threw him a sarcastic grin and he knew he hadn't upset her. "You're right. I just don't have the energy I had earlier when you called. Guess the day sapped it out of me."

Ripping open his granola bar, Kyle took a big bite and chewed. Until that moment he hadn't realized how hungry he'd become. She wasn't the only one who had endured a long day.

When she didn't start eating, he gave her a stern look. "Eat up, then you'll feel better."

After they sat at the little table on the other side of the room, he took in her appearance again. Freckles sprinkled across her nose contrasted sharply against her wan face. Only her eyes, highlighted with brown eye shadow, seemed bright. Nope, he couldn't let her head home without an escort.

"I'll follow you home." He crumpled the granola wrapper and tossed it into the trashcan across the room. He snapped his fingers and smiled. "Three points!"

"No."

"What? That was a perfect shot."

"No, I don't need you to follow me home."

Hawthorne had witnessed that stubborn tilt to Tammy's chin before, and the grim set to her mouth. The last woman he'd met this stubborn was Kiley Danger. Wife of Hawthorne's friend and former bodyguard Scott Danger, Kiley joked about her first name being similar to Hawthorne's. Hawthorne had been on assignment to protect her, and almost lost his life as a result.

As he took in Tammy's gentle features, a memory flashed into his mind. Tammy visiting him in the hospital as he'd recuperated from a bullet wound. Her worried eyes. Yeah, he'd seen something in her expression then that kept him curious to this day. Something he'd never seen in a woman's gaze before.

"Face it, Carter, you're not going home alone." He leaned on the table until he could see straight into her beautiful eyes.

Obstinate lines furrowed her brow as she took another bite of granola. "I'm capable of taking care of myself."

"I didn't say you weren't."

Tammy blinked, and he tried to read the expression crossing her face and couldn't. Aiming for the trash can, she missed and the wrapper landed on the floor. Tammy strolled across the room, snatched up the paper and deposited it in the can.

"Story of my life. Always missing the mark." She sighed and put her hands on her hips. "Time to go home."

He stood. "Are you going to tell me what really happened?"

She crossed her arms. "What are you talking about?"

He stepped closer until only a foot separated them. Tammy stood her ground. "Those calls bothered you more than you're letting on."

"Pranks don't upset me." She tucked her hair behind her ear and a small diamond earring winked at him. "Everything is okay."

"It might have been a prank, but I'd feel better if you let me follow you home. And maybe you should call in sick tomorrow."

"No way. If I do that the work will pile up even more."

"Mrs. Taggert will understand. I'll vouch for you. You fainted."

She passed a hand through her hair. "I have too much to do."

He followed her out to the front, and she retrieved her coat. When Tammy struggled with one arm of her light trench coat, Hawthorne helped her.

As she winked at him she said, "You're such a gentleman."

He drew her coat together at the lapels and held on. Her eyes burned warm and welcoming; the stubborn look she'd given him moments ago had disappeared. "I aim to please. In this case, though, I think you should take my advice."

"About what?"

"Following you home—"

"No—"

"Tammy—"

"*No.*"

Hawthorne flinched, then gritted his teeth. She looked more than headstrong; she appeared invincible. With any other woman he might have given in to her refusal long ago, but since he'd met Tammy, he'd forgotten how to back down. Everything within him refused to relent when she challenged him.

It was too much fun.

God, she looks good. Attractive. Hell, more than that. So damned pretty.

Every time her eyes threw off green sparks, or the air rang with her throaty laugh, his thoughts turned to sex. Not sex with any woman, but sex with her. It had happened from the first day he met her.

Warning, warning. Trouble ahead. Deep, inescapable trouble. He couldn't afford to obsess about her, sexually or otherwise. Friendship was one thing. A deep relationship fell into the no-can-do category. They enjoyed a flirtation, but Tammy made it clear long ago she didn't want to date him.

Hawthorne shrugged. "You can't stop me from following you, so why are you fighting it?"

She frowned. "You're crazy."

"Crazy maybe, but not stupid, babe."

"Why are you calling me that? You never called me 'babe' before today."

He always admired directness in a woman, but this time it took him by the throat and choked his words.

"What's the matter? You've never been caught with your pants down before?" she asked.

Her gaze tested him. Tightening his hold on her lapels, Kyle stepped closer. He inhaled that floral scent again, his senses dizzy with it. "How do you know?"

Touché. Her mouth dropped open. "Well...um...." A soft blush covered her cheeks.

Impulsively Kyle reached up and cupped her cheek with his right hand. "Tammy, please do this for me. As my friend. Or think of it as a professional courtesy. Hell, it's in my blood to guard your body."

A gentle smile curved her lips, and she leaned into his hand for a moment until she covered his fingers with her own.

"Why, Hawthorne, if I didn't know better, I'd think you might be worried about me."

"Me? Worried? Nah. You're tough as rhino skin, Carter."

She wrinkled her nose. "Thanks."

"Don't mention it."

He released her, well aware that she'd hit on the mark. He not only worried about her, he'd been tempted to do something pretty stupid. Like cup her face in his hands and give her a gentle kiss on the forehead. Yeah. A chaste, totally friends only type of kiss. Even doing that, though, could be misinterpreted. They might be good friends, but employees in the same company didn't kiss each other *anywhere* if they were just friends.

"Let's move out," she said, heading for the door.

Silent on the ride down the elevator, she looked composed. Not at all like a woman who had suffered harassing calls and fainted. She stayed quiet until they entered the parking garage and reached her red Saturn coupe.

Tammy unlocked the vehicle and climbed inside. "Thanks for the escort, Hawthorne."

A flicker of concern held him there. "Maybe you should see a doctor."

"I'm okay." Determination firmed her lips.

He put his hands up in surrender. "All right. All right." He turned away and started toward his Jaguar. "See ya tomorrow."

When she drove out of the parking structure, he sat in his car for several moments thinking about the odd events of the evening. Tammy was right. He'd never called her babe before. He shrugged. So he wouldn't call her babe again. He stared at the concrete wall in front of him and recalled how his sister Selina had called him a worrywart.

A fine sliver of pain wedged between his shoulder blades and he shifted in the seat. He'd worried about Selina obsessively when she had trouble with the law all those years ago. All the concern in the world hadn't saved her.

Another dagger stabbed him between the shoulder blades. "Look out hot tub, here I come."

Resolute, he shoved away ugly memories before they could swallow him. He started his car and drove away.

* * *

Salty tears touched the man's tongue as he licked his lips. Standing behind the concrete pillar like a human frozen by Medusa, he'd watched as Sweet Magnolia drove by, then as the bodyguard in the fancy car left.

The man touched his gun, fingering the soft leather of the hip holster. Closing his eyes, he imagined the cowhide was Tammy's soft, fragrant skin.

He'd been close to her so many times he knew she smelled like citrus shampoo and sometimes like roses. Tangy and full of fire, his sweet, Sweet Magnolia. A smile spread over his lips and he sighed. The cold concrete against his side seemed to disappear as he imagined her fragrance pouring over him like a wave. So many years had passed since he'd seen her, since he'd heard her laugh. But now he was close. Near all the time. He opened his eyes and cold reality seeped back to the surface.

The walls around him whispered that his mental sanctuary had vanished, leaving him to patrol the glass and steel building above. He realized that the parking structure had disappeared and been replaced by a long corridor. He didn't recall leaving the parking structure, or how he'd arrived in the hall outside Taggert Security Team.

As he stared into the darkness beyond the windows into the dim interior of Taggert Security Team's offices, elation triggered another grin. He'd found asylum in those odd moments when he lost contact with the world and became one with his fantasies.

He touched the glass and wondered if Tammy Carter had ever done the same. Had she looked into another place and wished she belonged? Again he closed his eyes and concentrated on a new fantasy filled with treacherous wishes.

* * *

The nightmares didn't come often. At least, not while Tammy slept. But she drifted into slumber that night with trepidation filling her soul. A long soak in a hot bath scented by rose oil had loosened her limbs. She'd almost dropped her book into the water as the relaxation lulled her into a zombie state.

Now, not long after, a dream crept into her night, threatening her shallow peace.

"Sweet Magnolia," the voice whispered.

Her sister's long red hair gleaming against her white shoulders as she'd waved goodbye to Tammy and her father. The dream shifted.

Walking with swift, purposeful movements, Tammy went into the house ahead of her father when they'd come back from the grocery store.

"Barb! Hey, where are you? I got the chocolate fudge. We can make those sundaes."

Her flip-flops made loud flapping noises against the kitchen linoleum, then the terra cotta tile leading to the sliding glass door. Somehow her feet slowed to a crazy, cartoon crawl, and she discovered that the whole house had turned to windows.

Windows with a pool outside each pane of glass, the green blue water reflecting diamond points. She stopped, her mouth dropping open as she saw Barb in each enormous pool.

Drifting. Floating. Stuck in the small waves the brisk wind blew across the water.

"Barb," she croaked. "No."

Seconds later she'd transported outside, and somehow she had Barb locked in her arms, towing her to the side of the pool. She heard her father's scream of denial. Then she stood beside the water, watching him perform CPR on Barb.

Numb, Tammy heard her own wail in her head. Nothing

mattered but getting that scream out, letting it blast from her chest like a horrible creature in a sci-fi movie.

Yet the scream wouldn't come, and she knew it never would. Tammy felt, as her sister must have, a breath that wouldn't come. Would never return to her brilliant, sweet, kind sister....

Tammy bolted upright in bed, her throat constricted with a need to yell her agony. Nothing came but terror.

Always this paralyzing fear. Never the needed release.

Sweat beaded her forehead and she glanced into the gloom. Shapes, obscured by night, hulked in corners like monsters. Irrational fear, born of the primitive side, flared. Tammy jolted, then reached for the bedside lamp, her breath rasping and short. Welcome light flooded the room and returned the chamber of horrors to a normal place.

Sinking back onto the pillows, she concentrated on the photo picturing her family as it had once been. Tammy, Barb, mother and father. Like a special protective talisman, the photo gave her peace whenever bad dreams assaulted. Discomfort traced her body like a hairy spider traversing her skin. She hated weakness and willed the fright to disappear.

Hours passed before she could close her eyes and sleep.

Chapter 3

"*Are you sure* you don't want more coffee?" Gregg Le Blanc asked Tammy.

Tammy settled into a red, hard plastic chair around one of the four break-room tables.

"No thanks, Gregg. If I have another cup I'll be running around the office like a jack rabbit."

The mocha java, supreme gourmet coffee had tantalized her nose all morning, and after two luscious cups, the high-test drink rattled her nerves.

She could blame memories of yesterday for her jitters.

Gregg's wide grin filled his hazel eyes as he leaned back against the break room counter. "That would be interesting to see."

Tammy laughed and took a sip of cooling java. "Better watch your step. I might take you seriously. Then where would you be?"

Tammy gazed at the handsome man and wondered if Mrs. Taggert specialized in hiring drop-dead gorgeous men for bodyguards. His smile had impressed more than one female client, and even a couple of male customers. With longish wavy blond hair that touched the collar of his shirt, and a wide jaw hinting at a younger Harrison Ford, Gregg defined good looking. Though his strong, tall body rippled with muscle, and he possessed a great sense of humor, she didn't find herself attracted. He didn't have that certain…something. He didn't make her long for romantic evenings by the fire, or nights full of wild sex and passion.

Red.

Before she could take another breath red, yellow and purple slashed across her vision. Immediately a small pain darted through her stomach. Putting one hand to her midsection, Tammy gasped.

"Oh, God," she whispered. "Not now."

"Tammy?"

She heard Gregg's voice, but it sounded far away, a tunnel hollow vibration that hovered on the edges. Taking a deep breath, she pushed the rainbow vision away. She shuddered as it receded as quickly as it had arrived.

Hands clasped her shoulders. Masculine, hard fingers pressed her skin. She started and wrenched away with a small sound.

Gregg squatted in front of her. He frowned. "Sorry. I thought you were sick or something."

Tammy shook her head and clasped the table where she sat. "No. I mean, I think I'm just tired. It's nothing."

Gregg's eyes narrowed as he assessed her. "You sure?"

"I'm great. Now you'd better get back to work, Le Blanc. Just because you've been working here a month doesn't mean you can slack off."

He stood up. "Right. See you later."

Grinning sheepishly, the bodyguard left the break room.

Great. He's bashful, too. Some unsuspecting young woman would fall hard for him.

Tammy uttered a nervous laugh as she went to the sink to rinse her cup. Okay, so any relationship needed to be rooted in more than lust, but a little heavy-duty male/female chemistry couldn't hurt.

Not that she wanted a relationship right now. No, sir. Besides, what man would want a woman who had visions of color dancing in her head? Ideas flitted around in her mind. If she did want to get involved with a man, what qualities would she require?

As water swirled down the drain, she murmured, "He's got to be special. Witty, full of life, and—"

"Sounds like me."

Tammy almost dropped her mug in the sink. She turned off the water and spied Hawthorne standing in the doorway. He crossed his arms and leaned on the door jam.

"Hey." A grin bloomed on his lips. "Didn't mean to scare you."

Embarrassed, she sagged against the counter and wiped her hands with a paper towel. "What are you doing here? I thought you were working on the Hamilton case."

"A fine afternoon to you, too, Carter."

Sighing, she tossed the paper towel into the trash. "Sorry."

"To answer your question, I'm all done with the case. They caught the man stalking her."

Stalking. The word haunted her, resurrecting memories of her sister's torment as a man pursued her relentlessly all those years ago. Before the law paid much attention to stalkers. Before anyone could have saved her.

I could have saved her.

Guilt stabbed her in the gut. If only she'd paid more attention. If only she'd believed her high-strung sibling's entreaties that someone shadowed her.

Tammy shifted, realizing the silence lengthened and Hawthorne stared at her quizzically. "I've got to get back to work. Alison isn't going to sit up at reception all day."

"Would do her some good. We'll get the last bit of work out of her before she goes on maternity leave."

Walking toward her, he smiled. It went with the casual

attire...the grin, that is. Her gaze took in his cowboy hat, red flannel shirt, slim-fitting jeans, and cowboy boots. She couldn't help admire his swagger and the way the new jeans loved his muscled thighs. Everything about his rugged exterior looked devastatingly handsome. Without warning female appreciation darted through her stomach. *Man, oh, man, Carter. Get a grip!*

"What's with the get-up?" she asked.

He reached for his mug, a tall, black job with white letters that said, "Marines have bigger weapons."

"Smells good. Is this mocha?" he asked.

"Yeah." The hell with how the coffee smelled. Tammy inhaled that special, masculine scent that defined Kyle Hawthorne. Impulsively she reached for his shirtsleeve and fingered the soft material. "You didn't answer my question."

"I'm going dancing at Cahoots tonight."

"Dancing? You? At a country-western bar? I never would have guessed."

As he poured coffee, he tossed her a satisfied grin. "There's a lot you don't know about me."

Unease filtered through her. "Amazing, isn't it? After knowing you a year, you'd think I had it all figured out. Now you're telling me you're a closet cowboy."

Hawthorne took a sip of coffee. "Hardly. I'm as far from a cowboy as you can get. City born and city bred."

"Chicago man through and through?"

"You got it."

She gazed at his profile, intrigued by his solid jaw, and the way his long lashes framed his intriguing eyes. "Taking a hot date?"

Mischief entered his gaze. "A sweet young thing. I think you'd like her."

Uncomfortable with the intensity in his gaze, she almost shifted away. Instead she felt drawn to him. For a moment she thought about trying to read his colors while she had him near. A second later she dismissed the idea. It had never worked before. Why start now?

The idea of him dating a nubile young woman didn't sit right. "I thought you didn't date much. You said your life was full enough already."

He winked. "I'll always make exception for the right woman."

Disconcerted, she tried to analyze why his statement made her itchy. He had every right to date. Tammy hoped the lucky lady would appreciate him. Then she turned her thoughts from dangerous speculation.

When she didn't speak, Hawthorne turned toward her, his gaze measuring. "How are you feeling?"

Shifting away, she put her mug in the dish rack to dry. "Good. Why do you ask?"

"You still look pale."

"Thanks. You know how to boost a girl's ego."

He sat his mug down with a thunk, his face clouded. "I'm serious."

"So am I."

"You're not ill?" Tilting her chin up, he brushed over it with his thumb.

Shivering with pleasure as his skin skimmed hers, she grinned. "Sick of people worrying about me. Mrs. Taggert has been hovering all day. Did you say something about last night to her?"

Looking guilty, he released her. "She asked me this afternoon if you were all right."

All her defenses fired, and she straightened. "What did you tell her?"

"I told her the truth. I said I wasn't sure if you were all right or not. I told her that you fainted."

Irritation trickled over her nerves. "Hawthorne, what are you trying to do? I just had a vacation. She's going to think I'm trying to get more time off or something."

He grunted. "Give me a break. She knows you better than that. I saw you last night. I can tell the difference between someone who has passed out and someone acting a part." Hawthorne's lips tightened with determination, his gaze turning grim. "It's you're imagination if you think she's hovering."

Putting her hands onto her hips, she glared. "My imagination? The only thing I hope I'm imagining is you interfering."

His mouth dropped open and he uttered a noise in disbelief. "What the hell's gotten into you? She asked me a question and I was honest about what happened. I don't plan on lying to her. And if I see you getting sick again, you can be damn sure I'll tell her about that, too."

Tammy's annoyance took on ridiculous proportions, but she couldn't stop. She poked him in the chest with her index finger. "Fine. Do me a favor and don't help me anymore, Hawthorne. I don't need your type of—"

He caught her hand before she could poke him again, and he brought her palm against his hard chest. "You sure as hell need someone to look after you."

Despite her indignation, her senses fixated on the heat under her fingers. Hard muscle flexed under her touch.

Oh, God.

Tammy's attention snagged on the hair peeking out the collar of his shirt, and primal impulses kicked arousal through her body. Her cheeks heated. When she caught his gaze, the temperature she saw there surprised her. Smoldering with intent, his eyes said one thing. Her breathing accelerated as she scanned the message. He was attracted to her. Very attracted. He looked as if he would kiss her any second. Stunned, she sucked in an astonished breath.

What was this man doing to her? Tammy jerked her hand from his grip and away from hazardous terrain. She might have seen this man's bare chest before, but that didn't mean a tantalizing glimpse or a fleeting touch couldn't fire her wayward hormones into overload.

Backing away, she headed for the door. "I can take care of myself."

Hawthorne berated himself all the way to the soup kitchen that evening. After pulling into the parking lot and entering the back door of Ascension Catholic Church, he took off his Stetson.

Playing games with Tammy would alienate her more, and her behavior in the last couple of days concerned him. Hell, he didn't *want* to worry. He didn't *want* to care about her, but he did. It did no good to deny it.

"Hey, Scooby Doo," a cheerful voice said as Hawthorne pushed open the swinging door to the kitchen.

"Hey, Davis, what's up?"

The older man's dark gaze perked with good humor. "A fine evening, that's what. Where you been? Carlotta's been looking for you." Davis took off his baseball cap and then settled it on his balding head again. He tugged the bill down, then set to stirring the soup in the big pot on the stove. "I've never seen a woman so ready to go dancing in my entire life."

"So why haven't you asked her out to dance?"

Davis's lined face wrinkled even more as he grinned. "Now I would if I didn't think she'd slap my face."

Hawthorne laughed. "Why would she do that?"

"I'm too old for her. She's only fifty-five."

Laughing even harder, Hawthorne surveyed the room. "Well, she didn't have any trouble asking me and Joe to go dancing. Maybe she doesn't realize you're interested."

Davis put a lid on a pot of stew. "You should talk."

"Huh?"

Heaving a sigh of disbelief, Davis crossed his arms and tilted his head to the side. "You're not dense, boy. I haven't seen you asking any of the young women who volunteer here out on a date."

"And you never will."

"Never?"

"I'm too busy most of the time to date. The only reason why I can go dancing with Carlotta is because I just finished a case."

Looking dubious, Davis returned to his work, tossing some carrots into the stew pot. "Ah, I see. And here I thought you just wanted to take an old man's chance away from him."

"You aren't old, Davis. Just crotchety."

Davis chortled and tossed an apron at Hawthorne. "Damn fool pup. Ain't you working on the line this evening?"

Hawthorne tossed his hat onto a bare counter and inhaled savory scents wafting around the huge kitchen. Several people worked steadily; the chop and slice noises combined with the clank of utensils.

"No. I'm working with you tonight."

"Then get your ass over here."

Hawthorne barely held back a laugh. He'd started chopping onions when the door swung open and Joe Cartolli strode inside.

Joe waved at him, but didn't come Hawthorne's way. Someone else had caught his attention. Every time Hawthorne saw the older man, he thought of six months ago when Old Joe had transformed from an untidy, unfocused individual to a man with a purpose. After the case that had almost cost Hawthorne his existence, Joe dedicated his life to helping the soup kitchen. Hawthorne had met Joe here many months ago, and Hawthorne admired him. A Vietnam vet, Joe had suffered...still suffered from flashbacks, mild depression and other mental problems. His association with people at Taggert Security Team, as well as his work with at the soup kitchen, had changed his life for the better.

"So, Scooby, did Carlotta tell you there's a new volunteer working tonight?" Davis asked as he tossed more ingredients into the stew.

"Nope."

"Name's Tucker Phelps. He's from Denver University. A student in psychology. Guess he thinks if he studies the homeless he'll write up a damned fine desert station or whatever they call them."

Hawthorne grinned and continued working. "Dissertation."

"Whatever. Anyway, he's coming in after I leave. Maybe you'll get to meet him before Carlotta sweeps you away."

Hawthorne wanted to laugh again, but he held back the impulse. Davis loved Carlotta, and yet the man refused to tell her. Kyle was certain Carlotta would date the skinny, pale man if he asked her. The sixty-five-year-old former gas station owner had gone down a hard road of drinking and bankruptcy and almost died on the streets. Instead, Carlotta had rescued him from ruin and welcomed him into her friendly church. Davis had once said Carlotta's non-judgmental friendship had changed him. If she'd preached or tried to convert him to "God fearing folk," Hawthorne doubted the older man would have responded.

Carlotta's life involved many church activities a week. One day she might make rosaries. The next day she worked in the soup kitchen.

Davis didn't attend a Sunday mass, but he liked the atmosphere here. He might not have much money, but he understood the people who relied on this church for survival, and he treasured Carlotta.

Hawthorne smiled, enjoying a sense of peace. He drew on the wealth of diversity and strength he sensed within these walls. Not because he practiced a particular religion. But because the people he met here, people like Carlotta Jones, and Davis Childress, had good hearts. They broke the rules that said people with problematic backgrounds couldn't pull themselves up from the dirt.

Hawthorne should know. He'd done the same not so many years ago.

Carlotta's vigorous laughter interrupted his thoughts, and he turned toward the doorway. With a few extra pounds circling her tall frame, she dwarfed the small man standing next to her. Her dark, curly black hair contrasted with her pale skin, and her brown eyes sparked with genuine happiness. The plain denim dress covered her like a sack, but her beauty came from within. She wore her goodness of heart like a tiara, true and without artifice.

"Joe Cartolli, this is Tucker Phelps from the university. He'll be working at the kitchen here four times a week," Carlotta said.

Joe shook hands and murmured a welcome. After introducing Tucker to Davis, Carlotta waved and came toward Hawthorne.

As Tucker came closer Hawthorne took stock of the smaller man. Tucker looked about forty, and the years hadn't served him well. His skin looked as saggy as a Shar-pei. Tucker's well-worn T-shirt pulled taut across his thin chest, and his jeans hung loose on his scrawny hips. If Hawthorne hadn't known better, he would have thought the man was homeless himself.

"Howdy, Kyle," Carlotta said with an attempt at a southern accent. "I can see you're ready for our hoedown."

He grinned and gave her a kiss on the cheek. "Hi." He held his hand out to Tucker. "Pleased to meet you, Tucker."

Tucker pumped Hawthorne's hand with a demanding grip. Tucker's smile reached his lips, but didn't ascend further. His mop of thick, brown hair hung over his silver eyes, and he brushed it back. "It's a pleasure, Hawthorne. Carlotta was just telling me you're a bodyguard with Taggert Security Team. Hot shot agency."

Uncertain whether the man intended to sound condescending, Hawthorne said, "That's right."

"You were hurt last year guarding that rich woman's body, weren't you? The one who owns the women's rag downtown?"

Tucker's tone sent irritation charging up Hawthorne's spine, but he smiled anyway. "Kiley Danger. She owns *Empowerment Magazine*."

"Danger? What kind of name is that?" Tucker asked.

"Comes from Danjureaux. A French name," Carlotta said, nodding toward Hawthorne. "She's a beautiful girl. Married that other bodyguard that used to work at your agency."

"Yeah, they married a few months ago," Hawthorne said, hoping his association with this man didn't last a minute extra.

Carlotta clapped a hand on Phelps's sloping shoulder, and the man jumped. "Let's go look at the other facilities. This is one big place and we've got a lot to cover. Kyle, I'll be back after awhile and we can discuss the boot scootin' boogie."

After they walked away, Hawthorne's warning signals flared. Other than the fact Phelps was obnoxious, he couldn't say why he didn't care for him.

Davis flipped off his cap and brushed at what little hair he had left. "So, you think she noticed my new apron?"

Hawthorne chuckled. "I think she noticed there's a lot of grease on it already. Stew, I think."

Davis looked down at the long apron. "All Billy hell." When Hawthorne grinned, Davis threw him a disgusted smile and a snort. "What you looking at? That's what aprons are for."

Joe sauntered up to the pair, his own apron dotted with bits of tonight's meal. "Are you two fighting over Carlotta again?"

"No," Davis and Hawthorne squawked at the same time.

"Sure sounded like it." Joe's wide grin made his world-weary face look far younger than his years. He cleared his throat and turned his attention to Kyle. "When is Tammy coming back to visit us?"

Hawthorne's insides did a tumble when he thought of her. He hadn't enjoyed their altercation back at the agency earlier today. *Except when she touched my chest. Oh, man. That had felt way, way too good.* "I don't know."

"Humph," Joe said. "Well, tell her to come on by and see me real soon. I miss her."

Hawthorne resurrected his sense of humor. "Maybe you should ask her out, Joe."

Davis laughed and waved a spatula in the air. "A pretty thing like her doesn't need an old coot like Joe."

Joe frowned. "Huh! I'm not as old as you. I won't reach coot status for several more years."

Joe's eyebrows twitched. "Say, why don't you ask Tammy out on a date, Hawthorne?"

Hawthorne pitched his paring knife onto the cutting board. "I'm not asking anybody out."

"Why not?" Joe and Davis asked simultaneously.

"You guys are worse than Carlotta. Do me a big favor and stop trying set me up."

His firm denial seemed to placate them, and they all returned to their tasks. But as he worked, he experienced a twinge down deep. Tammy had invaded his thoughts often over the last year, and he didn't plan on letting her dig a deeper wedge into his psyche. A long time ago his sister and his father had taken pieces of his heart with them. He'd never gotten it back. Sharing with a woman would mean caring far too much. He put his heart into his work, and some into this soup kitchen. Beyond that he didn't have any more to give.

Chapter 4

"*Hawthorne had a date?*" Mrs. Edith Taggert asked as she stopped at the high counter surrounding Tammy's desk.

Tammy looked up from the document she'd worked on for the last hour. "He said he was going dancing, so I assumed he had a date. But you know how he is always blowing things out of proportion."

"Kyle Hawthorne?" Mrs. Taggert chuckled, her stern but generous nature showing in her lined face. She looked older than her sixty-one years, but everyone at the agency knew she'd earned each wrinkle. Her black hair, cut trim against her skull, curled gently. She'd cut her long hair months ago and shortly after the cut it started to turn gray. Yet she hadn't done a thing to cover the evidence. "Are we talking about the same man, Tammy?"

Tammy fiddled with her cartoon mouse eraser. The mouse's ears, in fact, were all that remained of the little guy. "Oh, yeah, same man. Didn't you see him wearing that cowboy get-up on the way out yesterday?"

Mrs. Taggert shifted her petite form, leaning on the counter so she could look down at Tammy. Her grey eyes glinted with amusement. "I missed that. It must have been a spectacle."

Tammy heaved an exaggerated sigh. "Perfectly pitiful, if you ask me."

"Is he going out with anybody we know?"

Tammy shrugged and threw her eraser into a desk drawer.

"He just said she was a *sweet young* thing."

Mrs. Taggert's bark of laughter startled Tammy. She should be accustomed to Mrs. Taggert's new outlook on life. The older woman had a tough reputation, but her fairness garnered her a loyal following among the twenty security specialists that worked for her. In the last six months her renewed relationship with her daughter, Kiley, had brought Mrs. Taggert deep happiness.

"Hawthorne exaggerates?" Mrs. Taggert said as Tammy plucked a pen from her pencil cup. "I say again, Tammy, are you sure we're talking about the same bodyguard?"

Alison, heavily pregnant, waddled by on the way to the copier, but Mrs. Taggert's words stopped her. Her blasé expression changed into undeniable curiosity. "Kyle had a date? With whom?"

Tammy sighed, weary of gossip. "Some woman he met. Who knows?"

Alison swept her straight blonde hair behind her ears. "I saw his duds yesterday and told him he looked like he was ready for a rodeo."

Mrs. Taggert laughed, but Tammy's brain clung to the idea of Hawthorne dating. Period. Thinking about Hawthorne holding a woman in his arms had kept her awake most of last night.

"I thought he looked great," Tammy said impulsively.

When both ladies turned amazed looks on her, Tammy wished she'd swallowed her eraser and kept her mouth shut. "I mean it was something different. He kind of looked like a Marlboro Man." When the women's expressions turned to knowing smiles, she said, "Not as good looking as the Marlboro Man, mind you."

"Uh, huh." Alison's gaze glittered with enjoyment. "Not good looking at all."

Mrs. Taggert shifted away from the desk. "Well, as much as I would like to talk, I've got things to do. Back to work, ladies."

Alison left, and Tammy stared at the pink pigs gracing the ink blotter on her desk. She imagined Hawthorne dancing slowly with a nubile chick cradled gently in his arms. She turned back to her computer with a groan. Maybe if she imagined him dancing with Miss Piggy it wouldn't matter so much.

"Argh!" She clicked her computer mouse more forcefully than necessary when a file wouldn't cooperate.

As the office door swung open, Tammy turned, ready to assist a customer. Instead two familiar faces, one male and one female, greeted her.

"Hi, Tammy." The young woman stepping through the door smiled, her black hair shining under the lights as it fell about her shoulders. Her infectious grin brightened the whole room. "Working hard or hardly working?"

Tammy squeaked in delight and ran around the desk. She hugged Kiley, wife of the very tall, rugged man who strode into the room after his spouse.

Scott Danger smiled, and even Tammy's feminine instincts stirred at the sight of his handsome features, striking green eyes, and the wavy long hair that cascaded around his shoulders.

Kiley hugged Tammy and then released her so Scott could receive a hug. Tammy grunted as the big man squeezed her.

"God, Kiley, has he been lifting weights again?"

"Again?" Kiley asked as her husband released Tammy. "He never stopped."

"What's the matter, Danger?" Tammy eased into the old routine they'd shared as fellow employees. "Something caught in your throat?"

Putting his arm around his wife, Scott looked down on her with a soft, heated expression. Kiley gazed back, her teasing grin affectionate.

"I think being married has toned me down." One of his tawny brows lifted. "Besides, it was a long drive out of the mountains."

"Humph." Tammy noted the couple's glow. "A second honeymoon in less than six months of marriage. You'd think the two of you were in love or something." Their faces grew even more delighted, if that was possible.

Kiley sighed. "Actually, something did happen before we left the cabin this morning."

Even though they looked healthy and happy, Tammy's anxiety meter emerged. "What's wrong?"

Scott shook his head. "Things are going to be different soon."

Kiley beamed. "We have plans to make."

Tammy put her hands on her hips. "Will somebody tell me what's going on?"

"Yeah, what's up?" Hawthorne asked as he came around the partition. He gave Kiley a hug, then slapped Scott on the back in the greeting men had used since the Ice Age.

"They were just about to tell me when you interrupted." Tammy gave him a mock frown.

Hawthorne leaned close to Tammy, and the subtle scent of his musk washed over her. "Well, *excuse* me."

Tammy's eyebrows rose in half-disdain. "There's no excuse for you."

Scott laughed. "You two haven't changed a bit."

"You two *have*." Tammy shifted a couple of inches away from Hawthorne. "Fess up."

Kiley put her arm around her husband's waist as she smiled, and Tammy wondered what it would feel like to love a man that much, and to have his unconditional adoration.

"We're pregnant," Kiley said. "A month pregnant."

Tammy gasped, and before she knew it she'd hugged Kiley again and congratulations flowed. She turned away from her friend and before Tammy could protest, Hawthorne tugged her against his solid body.

In those few seconds time drew out, slipping slow and sensual as his quick embrace enveloped her in feelings. Before she could register more than stunned pleasure, he released her.

"Hey," she said. "What are you hugging me for?"

"He just wants to get his arms around you," Scott said, mischief brightening his eyes.

For the umpteenth time that day, heat reddened Tammy's face.

"Creep." Hawthorne gave his friend a crooked smile. "You're embarrassing the lady."

Tammy looked up at Hawthorne and his slow, simmering smile made her wish they were alone. She glanced away first, unable to bear it, and aware they had an audience.

Kiley's eyes widened. "Say, why don't we go out for lunch? We can celebrate."

Tammy pursed her lips slightly in disappointment. "Wish I could. I already had lunch."

"What about you, Hawthorne?" Kiley asked.

He agreed, and they announced the good news to Mrs. Taggert. Mrs. Taggert hadn't eaten yet, so she accompanied Scott, Kiley and Hawthorne out to lunch.

Tammy tried to concentrate on the table of figures on her computer, but weariness settled over her. Tonight she'd sleep well. No more nightmares. No more memories of her sister's demise at the hands of a killer.

All she could do was hope.

He watched her from the window.

Standing at the corner, he could see the reception area, but the angle would prevent her from spotting him. His leather holster creaked again, and he shifted, uncomfortable. Even though she smiled, he knew she burned deep inside to express her love. He'd seen it in her eyes the last few days. Sweet Magnolia had pined for him. Somehow he'd make her understand that if she'd look at him, she'd see all the love she'd missed.

The old song, one he'd heard Sweet Magnolia sing once as a child, played in his head like a nursery rhyme. A love song. Even then, as a girl, she had called to him with music. Her voice had been warm and wild, giving birth to fantasies that shocked and shamed him. He grinned. What would his old ma think if she knew how he'd wanted to touch Sweet Magnolia, to initiate her into those dreams until she screamed with ecstasy? Wailed with a need to give him everything he'd wanted but never had.

Though the song sounded chaste, his ma would say he'd burn in hell fire for singing a song like that...because love music inspired lust. Carnal needs cemented the road to hell as easily as other sins.

Discomfort burned his gut, lancing with unusual pain for acid stomach. He reached into his pocket and took out a packet of that medicine. Supposed to ease his heartburn or whatever the hell this crap was plaguing him. After chewing into the chalk-like pill, he leaned against the corridor wall and concentrated on looking at Sweet Magnolia again.

Her beauty hurt him, and he closed his eyes, his hand resting again on his belt. His fingers lingered over the leather piece holding the gun in the holster. Caressing it, he imagined her skin under his fingers again. He liked to play out this ritual at least once a day. Yes. Soft, hot skin filled with life and damnation fires. Oh, but the hell would come so sweet.

"Sweet, Sweet Magnolia." Barely aware that someone might see him, might hear him, he murmured her name. Her true name. "Tammy."

Tammy's sister hadn't needed him this badly.

He'd followed her while her love etched deep wounds in his body, tormenting him in a special Hades designed for sinners. Barb had paid for her sins, as Tammy would when the time came.

But she'd enjoy the pain. Enjoy watching him do to her what he'd done to Barb. For the ecstasy on her face would surpass Barb's wide eyes and open mouthed plea for more. Sweet Magnolia's agony would be her last, and would give him the most satisfaction he'd ever experienced.

He'd gladly burn for eternity if he could taste her sugar. He'd spread it over his skin and watch the glistening moisture touch him where he burned the most. Unsnapping the holster, he brushed his thumb over the cold metal of his gun. Sharp, stinging cold. Not flaming like the beautiful hair on his Magnolia.

Tonight he'd follow her again, keeping well back so that so she wouldn't know. Soon she'd feel his touch and comprehend that she wanted him as much as he wanted her.

Then she would be his forever.

Around seven the next day, Hawthorne strode into the office with a grimace on his face. Shoulder pain had interrupted his sleep several times last night. Painkillers didn't destroy the ache, and he wrestled with the thought that he should see the doctor again and have it checked. Instead, he let the sight of Tammy's pretty face bolster his piss poor mood.

As she spoke into her phone, her voice reflected the broad smile curving her lush lips.

Lush lips. His groin tightened with a vengeance and he wanted to moan. *Damn it, now was not the time to start fantasizing about her.* He pushed forward, letting his aching shoulder reclaim his thoughts. Seconds later she looked up. As he passed by her, he rotated his arm in a wide arc, attempting to loosen muscles. She finished her call rapidly, replacing the receiver and turning her chair.

"Hey, Hawthorne."

"Hey."

"Wait."

"I've got phone calls to make."

He heard her voice, but proceeded, heading for his office. Settling into his chair, he dug through paperwork on his desk looking for phone messages.

Before he could dial Tammy strolled in and planted herself in front of his desk. He shifted in his chair, dragging his gaze from the notes on his desk.

His gaze rested on the sensible blue Oxford shirt and her nondescript black pants. She'd never be a fashion plate. Instead she wore clothes that looked good on her, sexy styles that skirted the edge of business-like. His attention meandered to the buttons on her shirt. One had come undone in the center, and he fixated there.

Did she know a hint of lace showed? No. She'd never unbutton her blouse for me, so I'd better forget it. *"Jumping Jesus."*

"What?" Tammy's gaze pinned him like an eagle swooping in on prey.

Since he'd ignored their traditional morning greetings, he figured she'd give him hell. Pain lanced his shoulder and he winced.

Concern entered her eyes as she leaned on his desk to inspect him. "Are you all right?"

Rotating the offending limb, he grunted. "Old war wound."

Tammy smiled. "You've never been in a war."

He tossed a cockeyed grin her way. "Damn. I thought I had you fooled into thinking I was a hero."

Those lips he'd dreamed about last night continued to smile. "You help people every day. That makes you a hero."

He allowed his gaze to coast with heated attention across her body. "I think I've died and gone to heaven."

When his gaze met hers she blushed.

"Don't try and distract me with drivel, Hawthorne." Her brow knitted with worry again. "Did you hurt yourself?"

"That bullet wound from six months back has acted up again. Got any high-powered painkillers in the office? Aspirin has done diddly squat."

"Ran out yesterday." Tammy sank into the chair in front of his desk. "Have you seen a doctor?"

"It'll be okay later in the day." In a gesture that looked nervous, she tucked her hair behind her ears. "What if it's something serious?"

Standing up, he moved around to the front of the desk. Shoving files aside, he perched on the desk not far from her. "The doctor will tell me that it can't be helped. It may take awhile for the arm to feel better. It may not ever feel quite right."

Tammy's frown deepened and she looked at the floor. "I suppose you're right. This is a dangerous game you play, Hawthorne."

He shrugged, then regretted the sudden movement as an ache centered in his shoulder joint. "Why, if I didn't know better, I'd say you were worried about me."

One corner of her mouth arched in a sarcastic grin. "That's my line."

He willed her to look up, wanting to see her eyes sparkle with humor rather than concern. Their gazes tangled. For an unguarded moment, he revealed all in that look. A hunger to know the real Tammy Carter ate at him. Looking at her made him want things he'd never craved before. What would it be like to have this woman care about him for the rest of his days?

"Ever try a massage?" she asked, her tone a little breathless as she kept her gaze locked with his.

His mouth went dry. "Yeah. A long time ago. Why?"

"Maybe you need massage therapy on a continual basis."

Swallowing hard, he didn't allow her quarter. "Are you offering?"

"No. I…never mind. It was just an idea." She stood quickly. As she turned to leave, he stood as well. "Wait."

Turning slowly, she said, "Make it fast, Hawthorne. Paperwork awaits."

"Joe asked for you the other night."

Her creased brow smoothed at the mention of the man's name. "How's he doing?"

"He misses you. He asked when you were coming by the kitchen again."

Tammy shrugged. "I hadn't thought of it, really."

"Not even once?"

"Well...."

Hawthorne advanced and she took a step back. Her odd reaction spurred him onward. Suddenly she was a jumpy as a flea. "Why don't you stop by tonight? I might go by there, too."

Her small nose wrinkled in that disdainful way he'd grown to admire. The movement lasted a second. "Sure. I'd like to see him again since it's been awhile. I think I can fit it in my schedule."

Kyle let a sound of disbelief part his lips. "Your schedule? You mean Art doesn't have another hot date set up?"

Sincere irritation crossed her face. "Hawthorne, you are such a twit. Why the hell are you so intent on giving him a hard time?"

Tammy's question made him pause. "Other than the fact he's a wimp and doesn't appreciate you?"

Color stained her cheeks, but he couldn't be sure if anger or embarrassment caused the effect. She started away again, and he realized he'd acted like an ass. "Tammy, wait."

When she turned he came toward her again. If she didn't leap away like a frightened antelope, he could secure that freaking gap in her blouse that had tormented him since the moment she walked into his office.

He reached for her blouse, fixation making him act first and think later. Before Tammy could react he clasped the two halves of her blouse and buttoned it closed.

A gasp escaped her mouth. "What—"

"You didn't think I was going to let you show all the bodyguards in the office your hot pink lingerie, did you?"

Her mouth dropped open and it took her a moment to speak. "No, of course not. Thanks. I think."

He grinned, relishing her confusion and wondering what had gotten into him. "I wasn't coming on to you."

"Right. Uh…see you later."

She dashed out of the room, and closed the door with a definitive click.

Hours later Hawthorne still savored the glimpse he'd received of soft skin and lace.

Chapter 5

As Tammy stood close to the entrance of the huge soup kitchen, she wondered if she'd made a mistake. Behind her in the crannies provided by alleys and business doorways, homeless settled for the evening or waited for the next meal to be served. Some people ate here three times a day, especially if they signed onto a special program of rehab.

Tammy surveyed the room, marveling that volunteers sustained an operation this large. The bustle never stopped. College students received credit at the universities for assisting both in the kitchen and in counseling capacities. For the homeless who came in sporting a knife wound or an overdose, a hospital resided within walking distance.

Outside the sanctity and safety of the church, night hovered short hours away. Although it hadn't turned cool yet in the Mile High City, the shadows dancing around the downtown area made her twitch. Tammy shivered, drawing her light sweater closer about her. Summer days often ran hot, but in the Rocky Mountains warm days often turned into cool nights.

Get with the program, Tammy. What are you waiting for?

Sure she'd helped Hawthorne before. She'd met Joe Cartolli by assisting with food distribution, volunteering for Hawthorne when he'd been involved with a case. Unreasonable apprehension kept her from feeling confident this time. She couldn't imagine why. Maybe her reluctance stemmed from what Hawthorne had done and said earlier in the day.

When she'd discovered that his shoulder hurt, she *wanted* to massage the ache away. Nope. Activity like that in the office went beyond even Taggert Security Team's easygoing employee policies. The way he'd touched her had made her quiver with pleasant tingles. When Hawthorne had asked her to wait and came toward her, she couldn't imagine what he intended. Then when he reached for her blouse she'd been too stunned to slap his hand away. The man was too cheeky, and she searched her mind for a way to get back at him. Nothing materialized, unfortunately.

"'Scuse me missy, but have you turned into a doorway?"

The voice made her whirl around. "Joe!"

Hugging the thin man close, she noted his usual body odor had been replaced by a soap fresh scent. Pleased, she pulled back from his embrace.

Joe grinned. His dark eyes, widely spaced and intelligent, defied anyone to believe he lived on the streets not long ago. He'd trimmed his hair close, reducing the frizzy look.

"What's for dinner, missy?"

Tammy sniffed, then turned to look at the supper line. "Smells like chili."

Joe wrinkled his long nose as he stepped farther into the room. "Didn't they have that yesterday?"

"I heard someone say they had beanie weenies."

He moved aside as three large men swept by him and headed for the line. "Same idea. It's beans, isn't it?"

A wide grin teased her lips. "You've got a point. Come on, I've got to see Mrs. Traynor. Hawthorne's shoulder is acting up and he can't be here tonight. I told him I'd deliver the message."

"Damn, tomorrow this place will stink."
Wondering what that had to do with anything, Tammy walked onward. "Just tomorrow?"

"Beans. All those beans."

Tammy released a bark of laughter as she pushed through the swinging doors leading to the kitchens. "You're awful Joe."

"It's the one thing people say I'm good at...smelling stuff." She laughed again. As he shuffled along, she wanted to tell him to pick his feet up. But she couldn't fault him. He'd progressed a long way from a year ago.

"Of course those beans won't stink as bad as Tucker Phelps," Joe said.

"Who?"

"Tucker Phelps. He's volunteered here for about a week. Getting his degree or something and figured he'd check us out. See if all of us are crazy."

The noise of pots and pans clanking and the sizzle of frying mixed with scents of butter, onions, and spices.

Tammy paused. "What's wrong with him?"

"You'll see. Man's got a rotten smell."

Great. Joe and his psychic smells. So what if he'd saved Kiley last year by using his abilities to locate her? Tammy didn't care about the volunteer's odor. She didn't want to discover if she could see the man's colors, either.

"What kind of B.S. are you feeding this young lady?" a booming voice asked from behind them.

Tammy jumped, startled. She wondered if the man had heard their conversation. Tammy and Joe turned to greet the stranger.

About five four, the small man's bony body looked gaunt in comparison to Joe. Heavy eyebrow ridges, sharp nose, and pinched lips added to his skeletal appearance. His threadbare sport coat didn't fit his narrow shoulders and his slacks flopped around his stick legs.

"Tucker, this is Tammy Carter, a good friend of mine."

Tucker pushed his shaggy mud brown hair back from his eyes. His youngish haircut appeared odd on a middle-aged man. He held her hand as if he might kiss it. Tucker's intent gray gaze reminded Tammy of silver chips of ice.

A cold tingle darted from his fingers through hers and then a slow, chilled blue intruded on the corners of her eyesight. Tammy wanted to draw away. Hoping he didn't notice her reaction, she forced a smile. The blue flared in her vision, covering her view of him and the room.

Oh, no. No. Not again.

Apprehension tightened her throat and she yanked her hand from his.

"So pleased to meet you." His voice sounded raw and nasal.

The royal blue dropped from her sight and she sighed in relief. "Nice to meet you, Mr. Phelps."

His grin split his narrow mouth to reveal widely spaced teeth worthy of a jack o' lantern. "Just Tucker, please."

Tammy nodded and grinned, trying not to shiver. She hated the emotionless vibrations his touch revealed. So he was a bastard of the first order. No reason to get riled.

Sure the man's appearance gave her the creeps. She wanted to tell him to indulge in sweets and add some weight. Then she chided herself for judging on appearance. A quick glance at Joe revealed nothing. His face had gone tight as a mask.

"You're a friend of Kyle Hawthorne's?" Tucker asked, shoving his long fingers into his pants pockets.

Tammy nodded. "We work together."

His eyes narrowed to slits, the result disapproval. Before he could launch into more questions, she commenced her own query. "Joe says you're getting your degree."

Phelps puffed up, his chest expanding a bit. "My doctorate. I'm volunteering here to study many aspects of human depravity, hard luck, mental illness, and substance abuse. I think I can get examples here without going to a ghetto."

Lovely. Uncomfortable, she slapped on a fake smile. "What's your field of study?"

"Psychology."

Tammy wondered if he minored in acerbity. "Very interesting. My minor in college was psychology."

His gorilla brows twitched. "Where did you attend school?"

"University of Colorado, Boulder. Bachelors in Business Administration."

"Where do you work?"

Tammy flinched at his request for her resume. "Taggert Security Team. I'm an administrative assistant."

Phelps' nod said in action what he wouldn't say aloud. He sniffed. "How interesting. I'd think you could find a more promising career with a bachelors degree."

Her ire reached higher. "Where do you work?"

"I'm a security guard for Dunwell Security a few blocks from here."

"That's the security company that works at my building."

He nodded. "I know. I've never had the pleasure of working at your building."

Thank goodness.

Joe put a proprietary hand on her elbow. "We need to find Mrs. Traynor. You seen her anywhere, Phelps?"

With a twitch of his head Phelps indicated the hallway outside. "I think she was doing paperwork in her office."

Glad to be away from Phelps, she hurried away with Joe. "That was fun, Joe. Thanks *so* much."

Joe led her down the hall, keeping his grip on her elbow. "I figured you'd want lose from him. What a bastard. I don't trust him as far as I can throw a howitzer."

Creep of the first order. The words spun in her head again as she headed for Mrs. Traynor's office. "He's so…I don't know.

That comment he made about my degree and my job was tacky. What a turkey."

"Like he should talk. Working as a security guard is no big honor. In my Army days I could have kicked his ass with both hands tied behind my back. Like I said, he stinks."

She recalled the smell Joe had described when he spoke of evil in its darkest form. "Sulfur?"

He shook his head. "Not as low as that. I'd say it's as much a taste as a smell. You know. Somewhere between that gross ice maker ice and an old box of baking soda left in a fridge too long."

A reluctant smile parted her lips. "I'm not even going to ask how you know what the baking soda tastes like."

They arrived at the closed door to Mrs. Traynor's office, and he released his grip on her arm. Joe's gaze filled with dim memories of bad times, and she knew that digging deeper would be a mistake. "I'd stay clear of Tucker if I was you, missy."

She nodded. "Don't worry. I think we're safe to say I'm not spending any time alone with that man."

Tammy waded into the flow, instructed by the head of volunteers, Mrs. Margie Traynor. Tammy had experience in the cooking end of the operation, and worked for an hour before changing to the front lines.

Tucker Phelps, thankfully, kept his distance. Maybe he thought he was too good for her. Let him think that if it meant he stayed away. She didn't want to encounter his glacier blue soul again.

Fully equipped with hair net and plastic gloves, she served the line of homeless trickling into the soup kitchen. Her nose wrinkled. It took time to acclimate to people with cesspit body aroma, and Tammy wondered how Joe withstood the scents that assaulted a person from all sides. Of course, he'd lived with those scents so long it probably didn't faze him.

Hemmed in on one side by volunteer Millicent Craigmoor and on the other by Stephen, a young man with a dark ponytail, she worked steadily.

As she dished mashed potatoes onto one man's plate, Tammy asked, "Gravy sir?"

The old man, stick thin and bald, shook his head. He gave her a gap-toothed smile. "No, thanks, sweetie. Gotta keep my girlish figure." He chuckled and moved onto the vegetable area. "See ya later, girly."

Missy. Sweetie. Girly. Babe. What was it with the men in her life?

"So, are you staying with us?" Millicent asked between putting bread on someone's plate and dishing corn onto another.

Tammy nodded. "Absolutely. I've enjoyed it." Her stomach gave an embarrassing growl. "Oops."

"Sounds like you need a little food yourself," Stephen said. "When your shift is over you're welcome to a plate."

"Oh, no. I couldn't. I've got a pizza waiting at home with my name on it."

Millicent grinned, showing her tobacco-stained teeth. Her brown gaze warmed. "Well, if ever you *don't* have a pizza waiting for you, take something home from here. It's the least the church can do to thank you for your time."

"I wouldn't feel right taking food." Tammy put potatoes and gravy on another plate. She flicked a concerned glance at Millicent. "I don't mean that anyone who does take food...I mean..."

"We got ya. No offense taken. I don't take anything home either. My wife is a better cook," Stephen said.

Millie bust out laughing, the sound somewhere between a baying hound and a donkey. Warm and contagious, the loud noise made people all up and down the line pause to look.

Tammy joined in the laughter, enjoying her experience here even more as time went by.

Close to the end of Tammy's shift, a young girl of about sixteen came through the line. Her straight, bird's nest brown hair fell about her shoulders. The girl's pretty, oval face was decorated by showgirl makeup. Sparkling lime green eye shadow and heavy black liner ringed her dark eyes. Long lashes, undeniably false, flapped liked ridiculous bird wings every time she blinked. Clownish blush dotted her cheeks, and her blood red lipstick matched the polish on her short nails. The polish looked chewed.

A tight black leather bustier pushed up her generous breasts, and the matching black spandex Capri pants showed every curve to advantage. The girl hadn't been on the street long, or she'd eaten here every day. Nothing undernourished about this kid.

"Hey, Jeannette." Millicent plopped two pieces of bread on the girl's plate. "Looks like you're doing well. Those new duds?"

Jeannette lifted her nose and peered down the well-chiseled length. Her eyelashes flapped again. "Got them yesterday."

Tammy wondered if Jeannette had Joe Cartolli's skill for finding perfectly good clothes in trash bins.

Jeannette moved to Tammy's station and held her plate out. "Potatoes. Extra gravy."

Tammy smiled, injecting as much warmth as possible into her grin. "Coming right up." As she plopped the potatoes onto the girl's dish, though, a bit of potato went wild and splattered Jeannette's leather top. "Oh, God, I'm sorry. Here—"

"Bitch!" Jeannette slammed her plate down on the counter so that more potato flew in all directions. "You did that on purpose, didn't you?"

Tammy's mouth dropped open, shock holding her speech prisoner. She noted that Jeannette's sudden outburst had quieted a good portion of the dining hall.

Before Tammy could utter another word, Millicent put her broad hands on her meaty hips and glared at Jeannette. "Don't be ridiculous, Jeannette. You know better than that. Tammy didn't do it on purpose. She said she was sorry."

Jeannette's cute features reddened under the makeup as she transferred her glare from Tammy to Millicent. "She did it on purpose."

"Jeannette, if you're not going to keep calm we'll have to ask you to leave," Stephen said, his voice quiet.

"Backin' up the line," the man in line behind Jeannette said. "Backin' up the line."

Jeannette's gaze flashed bonfire hot as she tilted her nose at Tammy. "You just don't like me because I've got a better ass than you do."

The girl's assertion was so absurd that Tammy smiled. "Gee, I don't know. I can't see your ass and you sure as hell can't see mine."

The man next in line glanced without compunction at Jeannette's shrink-wrapped derriere. "Sure looks good from here."

Jeannette turned on the man and spat. The glob landed on his nose and slid down. He wiped at it and growled, "Now who's a bitch?"

Tucker Phelps entered the commotion. "What's going on here?"

"This whore is holdin' up the food," the man in line said as if he might be discussing the weather. "Been trollin' too long for a John."

"Bull shit," Jeannette said evenly. She placed her bejeweled hand on her hip. "This one can't keep his dick in his pants. I think you ought to throw him out for indecent exposure. Call the cops."

The man in line broke ranks and headed for the girl. Jeannette reared back and tottered on her "screw me" black platform shoes. She landed on her butt with an indignant yell. Tucker grabbed the man by the shirt collar and yanked him away.

Tammy reacted without thinking, dashing around the corner of the long serving area.

Jeannette pulled herself up, then yanked at her top, rearranging her cleavage. Tammy arrived at her side. She guessed that without skyscraper shoes Jeannette's stature came in at about five four, an inch shorter than herself. When she took in the girl's tremulous lower lip and the suspicious moisture in her eyes, Tammy wondered if Jeannette's attitude amounted to bravado rather than genuine moxie.

People flowed down the serving line again as Jeannette moved aside. Tucker hauled the loudmouth man to the other side of the room, reprimanding him all the way. Tammy gave Tucker credit for intervening.

"Are you okay?" Tammy asked.

Jeannette's space alien gaze took in Tammy. "What do you care?"

Tammy decided to try a soft touch again. "Because I'm a nice person. Just ask anyone here. I didn't mean to get potatoes on your outfit. Besides, leather is expensive. It must have cost you a lot."

Jeannette's raccoon gaze calmed down. "Didn't have to buy it. It was a gift."

"Then it's probably even more special."

"Not really." Jeannette curled her carnal red lips.

"Say, why don't we get your food and sit in that quiet corner." Tammy nodded toward the far edge of the room.

"We?"

"Yeah. We can talk."

"About what?"

"Anything. Besides, I'm almost done here tonight. I need a break. I've been standing a lot and it's killing my feet." Tammy looked from her athletic shoes to Jeannette's feet. "Aren't those things uncomfortable?"

Jeannette smirked. "You ever wear these kind of shoes?"

Tammy shook her head. "I try to stay away from them. But I

once had a leather mini-skirt that would have matched your top perfectly."

"You're shittin' me." Jeannette's grin looked real, sarcasm hinting around the corners. "*You?*"

"Sure. I was fifteen once."

"I'm sixteen." Jeannette almost snarled the words. "Bet you wouldn't wear a mini-skirt now."

Tammy recalled that she had a black clingy mini-skirt somewhere in the closet. "Would black spandex do?"

Curiosity replaced the hostility in Jeannette's eyes. "I dare you to wear it while you're at the soup kitchen."

Tammy flinched internally, but plunged ahead. "You're on. What days are you here?"

Jeannette glanced behind Tammy and smiled. Her unspoiled white teeth transformed her face from teen to grown woman. "I'll be back here Tuesday and you better be wearing that skirt."

"What skirt?" a deep, mellow voice asked.

Before she could swing around, Tammy knew the voice belonged to Hawthorne. No wonder the girl had smiled. "Hey, Hawthorne."

"Hey, Carter."

Tammy eyed him curiously. "What brings you here tonight?"

"My shoulder is much better. Thought I'd stop by and see if you were keeping out of trouble." Amusement gleamed in his eyes and twitched his mouth. Hawthorne planted his hands on his jean-clad hips. A blue polo shirt stretched over his broad shoulders. "I can see you've met Jeannette O'Connell."

Tammy's gaze swiveled to the teen. The girl shifted her stance, tilting one hip provocatively. Her smile was part seduction, part innocence.

"Hi, Kyle," Jeannette said, her tone whispery. She licked her lips.

Tammy didn't know whether to be amused or disturbed by the girl's behavior. "We were just going to eat. Care to join us?"

"I've already eaten, but I've got time to visit with two beautiful ladies." Hawthorne took in Tammy's appearance in one sweep.

"Well this outfit is not exactly glamorous." Tammy held up her gloved hands and glanced at her stained apron.

Jeannette glowered at Tammy. "Don't you have to work?"

Tammy realized she'd shirked her duties long enough. "You're right. I've got to finish up."

"Why don't you stop by our table after you finish?" Hawthorne asked.

Jeannette threw Tammy another defiant look, but Tammy ignored her and started away. "Sure. See you in about fifteen minutes."

Tammy apologized to Stephen and Millicent for leaving her post.

"No problem, my dear. I commend you for trying to get the girl calmed down." Millicent served another person in line. "She's got an attitude two miles wide. I tried talking to her once for all the good it did. She's been thrown out of here more than once for disorderly conduct."

As dinner shift finished, Tammy observed the teen and Hawthorne as they conversed on the other side of the room. Hawthorne smiled often, his grin apparently pleasing the girl. Jeannette moved her hands in an animated fashion and preened like a fancy bird.

Shortly afterward, Tammy left the serving area with a cola in hand. Stephen had pressed the drink onto her, telling Tammy she looked tired and thirsty. Jeannette's pleading voice gave Tammy pause as she arrived at the table.

"I need your help," the girl said to Hawthorne. "My pimp is trying to kill me. Can I stay at your place?"

Chapter 6

"Your pimp?" Surprise overran Tammy's ability to keep her mouth shut. This little girl had a pimp? Tammy's stomach jumped and rebelled.

Jeannette's smile turned to a scowl as Tammy sat on Hawthorne's side of the table. "Butt out. This is none of your business."

"Jeannette." Hawthorne's voice wore an undertone of steel. "Drop the queen bitch of the universe act and apologize."

To Tammy's amazement the girl's expression changed to remorseful as she lowered her gaze to her empty plate. "Sorry."

Tammy decided to use the old honey rather than vinegar approach. "If you need help, you've come to the right place."

"She needs to go to the police," Hawthorne said.

"I'm not going to the police. They'd arrest me and Blade would still be on the streets." Jeannette tossed her head and slicked her hand through her mussed hair.

Tammy noted that Jeannette wore a ring on each finger. She even wore bubble gum machine trinkets on her thumbs, and the fake gems sparkled under the fluorescent lights like valuable jewels.

Genuine worry stirred in Tammy's gut. "Why does this Blade fellow want to hurt you?"

"He says I haven't given him all the money for my tricks," Jeannette said, talking to her plate.

Hawthorne's mouth formed a grim line. He pushed away his glass and leaned on the table. "If you don't go to the police, I will."

Jeannette reached out and grabbed his forearm. Her eyes widened in alarm. "No. Please don't. I can do it."

Hawthorne remained silent for some time, doubt marring his face. "You can, but you won't."

Jeannette pouted, her lower lip protruding a tad. She probably knew how pretty that lip appeared.

Tammy had an idea. "Isn't there somewhere you can stay where he can't find you?"

Shrugging Jeannette said, "I suppose."

Tammy continued in a more adventurous vein, realizing her next idea would be rejected. "You could stay with me until the danger is over."

"What?" Hawthorne and Jeannette echoed at the same time.

"Are you crazy?" The teen asked, giving Tammy another glare. "You don't even know me. I could be an ax murderer or something."

Tammy grinned. "I doubt it. Tell me, Hawthorne, is she an ax murderer?"

His shocked expression had faded to amusement. "I can guarantee she's little more than a pain in the ass."

"Well, thanks a lot...you...you..." Jeannette sputtered, obviously hovering between telling the man where to go and still wanting him to like her.

"Jerk?" Tammy asked, nudging him with her elbow.

Hawthorne turned toward Tammy, that damnable grin flirting with his mouth again. "I love you, too."

The words, uttered in a soft, but undeniably husky voice, turned her inside out. A sharp pang of longing made her flush. She wanted to run before he could see the effect of his teasing.

Before she could retaliate, Jeannette took control. "I want to stay with you, *Kyle*. You can protect me."

Hawthorne shook his head. "Jeannette, you know I can't do that. It wouldn't be appropriate—"

"Why not?" Jeannette's question formed into a whine.

Hawthorne's face turned from good humor to exasperated. "I'm not having a sixteen-year-old girl in my house."

"Why not?" The girl persisted, more tenacious than a cat pursuing prey. "Plenty of other men your age have me over to their places."

Hawthorne's calm expression darkened, leaving him with a dangerous look Tammy couldn't recall seeing in some time. "Well, they're wrong. You're jailbait and these men are sick. It's one thing for a man to pick up a grown woman, but you're almost a baby—"

"Baby!" The girl's voice reached a strident tone, and once again people in the room watched as she launched into another terrible twos tantrum. "I'm a woman!" She pointed at Tammy. "It's her fault you aren't asking me to go home with you. If you weren't so hot for her you'd let me come home with you."

"Jeannette—" Hawthorne said.

"Screw it." The teen stood and backed away from the picnic style table. "I thought I could trust you."

Hawthorne's hands went up in a sort of plea. "You can trust me."

Jeannette stalked off. When Hawthorne would have followed her, Tammy grabbed his arm and pulled him back down in his seat.

"Leave her alone for now."

He pushed his hands through his hair, a deep sigh carving lines into his forehead. "Guess I screwed that up royally."

"Well, the baby comment was a little much."

He blew air out of his mouth. "Yeah. I should have known better." "It's not your fault the girl has the temperament of a spoiled toddler. Is she always like this?"

"This is the worst I've seen her. I think fear is driving her right now. This Blade bastard threatening her started last night. If she'd go to the police I could help her." Hawthorne ran his hand over his chin. "She was here the day I started volunteering, and she's changed in that short amount of time."

"How?"

He clasped his hands and looked at them as if they'd give him the answers. "From acting fairly sweet and innocent to a little hellion. Kind of like you."

She grinned. "I wasn't sweet and innocent when you met me."

His gaze absorbed her, drawing her closer with a warm intensity. "I suppose not. I don't know anybody who'd be cheeky enough to bring their cartoon character desk accessories with them on the first day of work."

Tammy remembered when Hawthorne first strode into Taggert Security Team. Immediately she'd admired his rugged good looks. But most of all she'd noticed his irreverence, as if part of him still believed in recess. "This is the man who wore a Daffy Duck tie after one week of work."

He held up his index finger. "Only on casual Fridays. You're a bad influence on me, Carter."

As he tossed her a sexy grin, a snap and crackle energy moved through her, as if she'd been seized by something chemical and fierce. She looked away.

Part of Tammy didn't want to know the answer to the next question, but her curiosity about Jeannette propelled her onward. "How long has she been a prostitute?"

"Around two years. But it's hard to say. She wasn't dressing in those hooker get-ups when she first came in the shelter."

Tammy lifted her hands in amazement. "Where are her parents? How did she get into this crazy predicament?"

Hawthorne's troubled gaze swung across the room. "She ran away from Connecticut after her parents were killed in a freak car accident. In fact, I think she blames herself that they were killed."

Stark sympathy stung her like a scorpion. Tammy understood far more than Hawthorne could know, how guilt could eat at a person's soul and litter their life with sorrow. "God, how awful."

He lifted his glass and took a long, slow swallow before he answered. "She was in the car with them. Her parents were going through a divorce and fighting over who would get custody of her."

Tammy muttered a mild obscenity. "How long ago was the accident?"

"About two years ago. She went to live with her aunt, but less than three months after that she ran away and made her way across country to Denver. Said she wanted to see the mountains."

Tammy groaned. "A rotten way to get a vacation to the Rockies."

"I think there's something more there. Something really nasty beyond the accident happened to her. I tried to get her to talk about it, but she acts like I'm crazy and flaps those bat wing size eyelashes at me."

She wanted to laugh, but the teen girl's predicament made her heart ache. Perhaps that was why she'd offered the girl a place to stay. Maybe she'd seen decency deep inside Jeannette.

Tammy thought about her color visions and realized that she hadn't seen any colors around Jeannette. Could Jeannette be one of those rare individuals, like Hawthorne, that she couldn't read?

She inhaled deeply. "You're worried about her, aren't you?"

"Of course. You shouldn't have offered her shelter. It's dangerous."

"Is that why you don't offer her a place to stay? Because of the pimp?"

Hawthorne's gaze traced her face closely. "You heard what I told her."

"Yes, but I didn't know if that was for my benefit or not."

Disbelief covered his face. "You think I...no don't even think it."

"I wasn't insinuating you'd do anything inappropriate."

"Then why would you have to ask?"

"Maybe you want the other snoops listening to the conversation to know you wouldn't do anything inappropriate."

"People around here know what kind of man I am."

In an odd, aching way, Tammy envied the people at the soup kitchen. Perhaps they did know him better than she did. Part of her wanted to experience Hawthorne on some fundamental level. She longed to crawl under every defense he possessed and learn each side of him.

His shoulders had turned rigid with tension, and she put her hand on his forearm again. "It's obvious she has a case of puppy love for you. Did you see the daggers she was sending my way? That's at least part of the reason she wants to stay with you. She thinks I'm some sort of rival, though I can't imagine why."

The unease lifted from his face, and he looked down at where her hand clasped his forearm. Hawthorne covered Tammy's hand with his and the warm, mild pressure sent tingles of pleasure radiating up her arm. "Have you ever had a case of puppy love?"

His question startled her so much she yanked her hand out from under his. "Of course not."

He laughed gently. "I don't believe you. Everybody gets a crush at least *once* in their lifetime."

"Okay, maybe when I was seven. Tobias Cranberry."

"Cranberry?"

"Unusual name, I know." Mischief twitched her lips. "And you want to know the real scandal?"

"Give me the juicy part." Hawthorne leaned closer and she once again drew in his fresh, masculine scent.

"Tobias, or Toby as everyone called him, was a younger man."

"So you started breaking hearts at a young age."

She nodded solemnly. "Yep. Toby was six years old."

Hawthorne's full-bodied laugh made her simmer with a newfound perturbation.

"My first crush I was eleven," he said.

"Late bloomer."

"Hormones finally kicked in."

"So did you fall in love with a younger woman?"

Slipping an irreverent grin into the occasion, he said, "Older. She used to babysit me and my sister when I was little."

Surprise tipped her. "You have a sister? I mean, you've never said much about family."

Tammy thought she saw pain flicker through his eyes, but it disappeared and he continued. "Yeah. Anyway, Diana Borkowski was a young woman that left our neighborhood and went to New York with aspirations. Within three months she'd signed on with a modeling agency. Everyone in the area admired her."

She wanted to ask him more about his family and his crush, but intuition told her now was not the time to probe his past. No one at Taggert Security Team knew about Barb, and that suited her fine. Some things shouldn't be revealed. But knowing that he had a sibling gave her an idea.

Excitement trilled through Tammy. Instead of letting it percolate, she said, "I know a way I might be able to help Jeannette." She snapped her fingers. "And Mrs. Taggert just might go for it."

His face turned suspicious. "Go for what?"

Grinning conspiratorially, she said, "My secret for now. You'll know in good time."

"You're too damned sneaky for your own good."

"Survival, Hawthorne, survival." She finished the last of her drink. "Besides, I like keeping you off balance."

Tammy enjoyed the curious, off-kilter look in his eyes.

Before she could blink, a red streak filled her vision and made her lean forward with open-mouthed shock. Spirals of brilliant red battered her, translating into hot, undeniable hate. She shuddered under the force.

God, where is it coming from?

"Tammy?"

Hawthorne's voice sounded far away, a strange down-the-tunnel resonance that reminded her of two cans tied together by string for communication. Child's play, but this time the color boiled in her mind with wrath and discontent. Whoever resided on the other end of the communiqué sent blazes of fire and destruction in increasing waves, and it made her lightheaded.

Must not faint. Not again.

Warm hands clutched at her, but Tammy couldn't see anything but the crimson slashes.

"Tammy. Babe, are you okay?"

The voice, concerned and pleading, brought her to the edge of breaking away from the color. She resisted the scarlet, which drew her toward a darker place. Slowly it receded, leaving a red ring around the edge of her vision.

Tammy could see Hawthorne through the dazed pattern in her mind. His hands brought her closer and he touched her cheek. Worry imprinted his face.

"Come on, Tammy. Speak to me."

"Hawthorne?"

"That's better. Are you all right? Do you feel ill?"

"I'm good."

"Good?" he asked incredulously. He took away his touch. "You looked like you were ready to pass out. Are you sure you're not coming down with something?"

Pinning on an indulgent smile, Tammy nodded. "I'm fine. Perfectly fine."

Treacherous Wishes

She registered the doubt lingering in his face. He grasped her upper arm gently. "Come on. I'll walk you to your car."

As the man walked by Sweet Magnolia on the way to his table to eat, he congratulated himself on fooling her. Fooling everyone. None could know his disguise, his supreme art. Hiding from everyone in plain sight wasn't his ultimate goal, but it felt good. The definitive objective remained ahead.

He glanced over and watched her speak with Hawthorne and put her hand on his arm. Arousal stroked his skin like moth wings, and he wished she touched him instead of Hawthorne. So many men in her life, but not much longer if he could help it.

A red haze flowed into his vision, and he dropped some soup on his shirtfront. The homeless man across from him chuckled like a turkey, warbling and gasping.

He wanted to wrap his hands around the old creep's neck and squeeze and squeeze until the codger's eyes popped out, staring and lifeless. Instead he took a deep breath and waited while his fury slowed to a dull, throbbing rush in his ears. Oblivious, the old creep slurped his soup with disgusting, irritating sounds.

His annoyance climbed like ivy and wrapped around to choke him. He shoved it back, and sweat ran down his forehead. Two droplets. This time, as always, he felt and saw and heard every detail, every sound and sight.

No.

Must concentrate on Sweet Magnolia.

When she shifted and came closer to Hawthorne, pain filled his breast.

With her keen senses she'd easily discover him if he didn't remain vigilant. Seconds, minutes, hours, days, months he'd waited in the shadows for her. She grew closer to Hawthorne and the idea sent another red blur into his brain. The pain and blood and eternal punishment. He bubbled inside with need.

With perverse pleasure he slurped his soup in a loud parody of the old bastard across from him. The dick weed didn't even look at him, so he gulped and sucked louder and suddenly all he could think about was sucking and licking Sweet Magnolia.

Done with his soup, he walked past Sweet Magnolia and the bodyguard man.

Bodyguard man. He wouldn't personalize the bastard by speaking his true name. From now on he would always be *bodyguard man*. Yeah, he could tell bodyguard man wanted to guard her body all right. Safeguard her day and night and do things with her—

No! He would never get the chance. Never be allowed to foul her skin the way Barb's divine flesh had been soiled by another.

Barb had paid for her indiscretion.

If bodyguard man fell for Sweet Magnolia it might not be such a bad thing. Then when he killed bodyguard man, she would see the love drain from his dead eyes.

Hawthorne kept a firm grip on Tammy's arm, and the heat seemed to sear right through her light denim jacket, through her T-shirt and into her flesh. He'd want to follow her home, she was certain. But she couldn't let him. Tammy didn't want him to feel obligated, and his protective nature would force him to act chivalrous.

"I'm okay, Hawthorne," she said as they arrived at her car a block down from the church.

He released her arm, but as she leaned back against the vehicle, Tammy saw the grim set of his mouth.

She crossed her arms in defense. "Out with it. I'm ready for the obligatory lecture."

His frown grew severe. "I'm following you home."

"No."

"What is wrong with you?" Hawthorne stepped close. So what else was new? To hell with personal space requirements. "Did you plan on coming out to your car tonight without an escort?"

"Of course not. It's dark by this time of evening and Mrs. Traynor told me Joe could walk me out in the evenings."

He nodded, and some of the tension left his face. A dark fire remained in his eyes. "Tell me what happened in there. You went into this weird trance and you looked ill. I've never seen you so pale. Not even the other day when you passed out in the office. If you're not sick, then what is it?"

She shook her head. "How many times do I have to tell you I'm okay before you get that through your stubborn head?"

Revelation flashed across his face. "Oh, man."

"What?"

"Are you pregnant?" he asked, his voice a whisper in the cool night.

Shock slipped through her and Tammy gasped. "Of course not. What kind of question is that? And even if I was, it wouldn't be any of *your* business."

"It *is* my business." He leaned closer, lines forming at his mouth as his jaw clenched visibly.

As heat blazed in his eyes, she knew she'd never seen him like this before. Curiosity drove her. "Why? Why would it be your business?"

His Adam's apple worked as he swallowed. Uncertainty flickered over his stubborn face. "I wouldn't be your friend if I didn't worry about you."

Her anger eased with the placation, but her voice stuck in her throat and she couldn't speak.

"Are you going to tell me what really happened in there, or am I going to have to force it out of you?" he asked.

"Exactly how do you plan to do that?"

As he took another step they almost touched, and she looked up into his blazing eyes. *Oh, man. He's just so...intense. So passionate. And he frightens the hell out of me because he reads me so well.*

Tammy's heart thudded in her chest and she took a quick, almost gasping breath. Tension tightened her limbs and sealed her in place. Gently, before she could protest, he cupped her face in his hands. Then Hawthorne pressed an almost chaste kiss to her forehead before releasing her and stepping back.

"All right," he said huskily. "You win for tonight. But if I hear about any more strange fainting spells or that you're sick and haven't told me, there will be hell to pay."

She had to take another deep breath to get her lungs working again, and tearing her gaze from his, she unlocked the car and slid inside. As she pulled away from the curb, Tammy thought her heart would never slow down and that she'd never stop shaking. For one heart-stopping moment she'd thought...

No, she didn't want to think about it.

It came anyway, flooding her with pure, sexual heat.

As he'd stalked toward her tonight, as he'd moved toward her in the office and buttoned her shirt, she'd thought he intended to....

Kiss her.

Chapter 7

"*You want a teen prostitute* to work part time helping you?" Mrs. Taggert asked Tammy at the front desk.

Before Hawthorne started around the partition, Mrs. Taggert's words bonded his feet to the floor. He eavesdropped without remorse.

"I know it's a reach, Mrs. Taggert. But if this girl can make money the legit way, maybe we can turn her around," Tammy said.

"We?"

"Well...I mean, I want to help her, and the best way is to get her into legitimate work. Sooner or later the cops will catch up with her. I'm surprised she hasn't been arrested before."

Mrs. Taggert's heavy sigh reached Hawthorne. "Not only is this a risky idea, it's highly unlikely the girl would go for it."

"It's worth a try."

As Tammy continued to push her idea, Hawthorne admired her conviction. It might be a crazy plan, but an honorable one. He hovered, unwilling to let them know he could hear the conversation. Instead he thought about how Tammy had looked trying to calm Jeannette. Composed, quiet, and a pro. Figured.

Handling people at the front desk made her an expert. Or perhaps she always possessed the ability to influence people.

Then he recalled when Tammy had asked him about letting Jeannette stay with him. He fell asleep last night, her question haunting him. One item bothered him more than anything else. He had to investigate and discover what made Tammy almost faint again.

The little devil on his shoulder taunted him. *So talk to her.*

First thing, he wanted in on the current conversation. As he cleared his throat, he headed around the partitioned area.

He started to speak, but his boss said, "Hawthorne, maybe you can shake some sense into Tammy."

Tammy sighed. "It's just an idea, but I know it could work."

"I heard." Hawthorne leaned on the counter. "I suppose it's worth a try."

Tammy's grin grew as wide as the Grand Canyon. Mrs. Taggert's frown went as deep as Loch Ness. One woman was happy with him, while the other was not. Great. He was caught between a cliff edge and a lake inhabited by a monster.

Mrs. Taggert pinned them with a dubious look. "I trust both of you, but I warn you, if it doesn't work…."

"It'll work. Now we just need to convince Jeannette she should do it," Tammy said.

Hawthorne straightened and ran his hand over his tie. "I'll talk to her, but I think she'll balk."

Tammy put her hand out, and he stared at it for a second. Touching her would create that crazy lightning again, and he didn't want Mrs. Taggert getting the wrong idea about them.

"Well, go ahead and shake on it," his boss said, breaking any idea about not touching Tammy.

Reluctantly he did as told, and the heat of Tammy's touch simmered inside him. After that he rushed back to his office, eager to flee from gut-wrenching need and treacherous wishes.

* * *

Tammy finished her time in the serving line at the soup kitchen Friday night, eager to discover if Hawthorne had talked to Jeannette. Tammy found her outside smoking a cigarette, standing with a group of tough looking men. One man, tall, dark, and ugly, leaned over Jeannette possessively. Probably Blade the pimp.
The girl's almost bored expression surprised Tammy. How could she stand associating with dirt bags? Wasn't she afraid the taint would cling to her like lint?
Tammy almost went forward to greet Jeannette, but self-preservation said safety came first. She didn't want the pimp to see her, so she remained in the shadows near the doorway, quivering as cold air and nerves traveled her skin. After the pimp and the heavies around him left, Tammy approached Jeannette.
Tammy half expected Jeannette to bolt, but instead the girl gave her a mocking smile. Tammy couldn't believe Jeannette's new outfit. A riot of fuchsia and lime paraded over the body-hugging spaghetti strap dress. Tammy smiled and looked right into the girl's eyes.
Jeannette blew a perfect smoke ring. "Kyle says you need my help."
"He's right. Can you help me?"
"I don't know. Why should I?"
"Money."
Jeannette blew another smoke ring, then gazed into the dark sky. The plastic gems on Jeannette's fingers gleamed under the lamplight as she brought the cigarette to her lips again. Thunder rolled in the distance as sheet lighting blanketed the sky with white. "I already make money."
"It's enough to buy you cigarettes, those clothes and a place to stay. But do you really *like* what you do?"

Jeannette dropped her half-smoked cigarette on the concrete, crushing it out with her barely-there startling green spike heel sandal. "And I suppose you love your job? A freaking secretary?"

"If you're trying to insult me, Jeannette, it isn't working. This isn't about me. And to answer your question, I love my job. I'm good at it, my boss gives me lots of recognition, I'm paid very well, and I get a large bonus at Christmas."

"So?"

"So, it's one of the best things that ever happened to me. I did a lot of drifting around trying to discover what I was good at. I decided managing people wasn't for me. I don't like the stress that goes with that responsibility."

Jeannette leaned against the wall, and Tammy shivered just imagining the cold stone underneath her naked back. "I like my job, too."

Tammy couldn't hold back a sound of derision. "Right. Flat on your back getting screwed in more ways than one. Haven't you wondered what it would be like to make money legally? No need to run from the law? No need to wonder if your pimp might kill you on a whim? Was that him I saw with you moments ago?"

"Yeah."

"I thought you said he wanted to kill you."

Jeannette shrugged. "He said if I was a good girl and let one of his clients keep me for this whole weekend that he'd forget about it."

"All weekend?"

"The John has a lot of money. I'll bet I can make more money this weekend than you do in a week."

"Do you want me to say it's all right to throw your life away? I won't say it because I don't believe it."

A bored expression grew like fungi on Jeannette's face, spreading outward until it covered her eyes with an indifferent glaze.

Everything within Tammy rebelled. She must get to this girl somehow. "If you come to work with us, it'll be part time. And you'll get to see Hawthorne more often."

Interest flickered in Jeannette's eyes, building momentum. She glanced Tammy's way, disengaging from her trance-like state. "Oh, yeah? Do I get paid as much as you?"

"Yes. Think of it as your bonus for helping me. It's been crazy around the office lately. My boss is willing to trust me and give you an opportunity. Would Hawthorne ask you to do it if he didn't think you needed help?"

Proud of herself for bringing Hawthorne into the picture as bait, Tammy waited while the girl churned the information. Tammy observed that everything about this girl seemed otherworldly. Her speech, her mannerisms all said adult, even though she'd barely cleared sixteen. So much had happened to Jeannette in a short time, it didn't surprise Tammy that the girl's innocence had been crushed. Yet under the bluster she was still a teenager.

Jeannette studied Tammy. "You sent Hawthorne to ask me because you were afraid I'd say no."

Not willing to give in, Tammy said, "Look, I've got ulterior motives. It hurts me to see someone with your intelligence throw away her future."

"Why should you care? Why should *he* care?"

"Because I know deep inside you want out of the hooker business. You've got more to offer. I wouldn't be doing this if I didn't believe in you."

The cocky, know-it-all grin returned. "You don't *know* me."

Tammy put her hands out in a pleading gesture. "Then let me know you. Show me I'm wrong. Do this work. I know you're smart enough to pull it off."

Jeannette laughed and straightened away from the wall. "That's a joke. I'm not listening to your goody-two-shoes preaching about what's good for me. I'm sick of adults telling me what's good and what's not. My mom and dad didn't know what was good. They couldn't even stay together."

Tammy saw the sheen of tears prick Jeannette's eyes and wanted to hug her. Instead she kept the distance between them. "Hawthorne told me about your parents. He said your aunt wanted you to live with her."

"Oh, yeah. Right. Her and her stupid husband. The prick."

Above the Denver downtown skyline, lightning forked the sky, bolts reaching and arching. Roaring above their heads, thunder punctuated the girl's words. Tammy flinched.

Tammy sensed there was more to the girl's story. "I'm sorry about what happened to your parents. But this is your life now. You're not stupid and you're very strong. You wouldn't have survived two years on your own if you didn't have guts. So what'll it be? Do you have the backbone to try something new? Or have you given up?"

Jeannette rubbed her arms, but the look in her eyes said she wasn't conscious of the movements. "All right. I'll do it."

Weight eased from Tammy, and she smiled. "Great."

"Monday. I'll start Monday after this last…job." When Tammy started to speak, Jeannette cut her off. "And only because Hawthorne asked."

Without another word, the girl strode away, her hips swaying. Seconds later Jeannette turned and grinned. She cupped her hands around her mouth and yelled, "By the way, great spandex skirt!"

Tammy grinned, pleased. Mission accomplished. Or at least part of it. Rain started to dot the sidewalk, and she turned back for the front door. Quick steps behind her made her tense, and she whirled around just as Tucker Phelps grabbed for her arm.

"Hey, what's your hurry?" he asked.

She looked down at his grip on her arm, surprised. Rain splashed against her short-sleeved top. "Hi Tucker. Uh, let's go inside and get out of this rain."

He kept his paw clamped onto her. "What I have to say can't wait."

Crawling revulsion meandered up her spine and a green slice of color spread around the outside of her vision. She fought the impulse to sink into the yawning crevice as the color threatened to banish all else from her mind. His touch transferred disturbing emotions, filling her with a desire to run.

"Got some things to do before I leave." She pulled against his grip. "Please, Mr. Phelps."

His scarecrow grin stretched his thin lips, but he didn't release her, his fingers biting painfully into her arm. "Stop fighting me. I'm not going to hurt you. I just wanted to warn you."

Tammy shook her head and a little of the color in her vision receded. "About what?"

"Hanging around these...these people isn't a good idea." He looked around the area at the bedraggled populace slumped in surrounding doorways. "I heard you talking with that girl. I know from experience that they can pollute you. I say you should stay away from her." He licked his lips. "That, and I wanted to see if you'd have a cup of coffee with me. I think we could have some interesting conversations."

His grip didn't loosen, and she let her anger free. "Obviously you have a poor concept of etiquette, Mr. Phelps. Didn't your mother ever tell you it was rude to grab people?"

Phelps laughed. "My mother perfected the art of grabbing people. She did it all the time."

Determined he wouldn't get the best of her, she twisted her arm and pushed away from him.

Muttering a curse, he stared at something behind her. Startled panic wiped away his supercilious smile. She glanced over her shoulder and saw Hawthorne striding their way. Hawthorne's expression defined pissed. Relief weakened her legs, and she stepped away from Tucker.

"What the hell is going on here?" Hawthorne asked, stopping next to Tammy.

Tucker's cocky confidence dropped clean away. "Nothing's going on. I was just telling Miss Carter she should watch out for these people. They can be dangerous."

Tammy started to retort, but Hawthorne beat her to it. "It didn't look like a friendly conversation, Phelps."

"It wasn't," Tammy said as her rain-soaked body shivered.

Phelps' wild grin returned. "Some people sure overreact."

"Don't touch her again." Hawthorne gently slid his arm about her shoulders and brought her against him. His warmth obliterated the cold rain and Phelps' icier stare.

With a shake of his head, Phelps turned and vanished into the night, the rain and darkness swallowing him. The olive drab green in her vision retreated, leaving her dizzy and her heart slamming. Lightning arced overhead, making her jump as the blue bolt sliced the air.

"Did he hurt you?" Hawthorne asked, looking at her arm. "You okay?"

Glancing at her arm, she wondered if there would be bruises tomorrow. "Let's get out of this rain."

Inside one of the back offices, they located some towels and tried to dry off.

Tammy couldn't get warm, and when she shivered, Hawthorne wrapped a towel around her shoulders. "Tell me what happened out there. What was that all about?"

"Wish I could tell you." She enjoyed his body heat as he held closed the towel draped around her. Anger darkened his gaze, showing he was far from placated. "He's just weird. I handled him."

A grin curved his mouth, surprising and delighting her. She hated it when he got that grim expression full of doubt and worry. "Yeah, you did. I was ready to kick his ass if he didn't let you go, but you were too tough for him."

"The hell with his ass. I almost kicked him in the nuts. Let's just forget about it, okay?"

"I don't think we should forget. We need to tell Mrs. Traynor."

"We'll just have a big to do on our hands and I don't feel like dealing with that right now."

His eyes narrowed. "Okay." Hawthorne drew in a deep breath and pulled his gaze away. Then he stepped back.

Damn. The price of getting his cooperation meant losing his heat. And she wanted that warmth in a way she couldn't define. When he touched her she didn't see colors, but she did receive security. A blanket that smothered the psychic visions she didn't want in the first place.

"Did you talk with Jeannette?" Hawthorne asked.

"Yeah. She's going to do it. We'll see her Monday."

Hawthorne grunted. "Wow. I never thought it would work."

"I know. You've said that enough times."

He ran a towel over his hair, ruffling it. "Sorry."

Sighing she pulled her towel from around her shoulders and dropped it on a chair. "No need to be sorry. Thanks for coming to my rescue."

He tossed his towel and it landed on top of hers. He reached out for the arm Phelps had gripped. "Anytime."

Gently he ran his fingertip over two red impressions on her skin, and another area that had started to bruise. He cursed. Hawthorne's touch made her flesh tingle, and Tammy had no wish to leave his tender grip. Instead she shifted a tad closer.

His gaze turned hot. "When I saw him restraining you I wanted to kick the crap out of him. The guy just makes me boil. I can't seem to control it."

Hawthorne gave her a searing look that traveled across her face and stopped on her lips.

How the mood changed from serious to sultry she didn't know. A soul-deep, knee-knocking desire held her transfixed, and she ached with a need to kiss him.

"My, my, Hawthorne," she said breathlessly. "I didn't know you were such an animal."

She'd thought he'd laugh, but instead his grip slid up to her shoulders.

"I have a lot of animal instincts. That's just *one* of them."

He was so close. So close she could just—

A shadow crossed the doorway, startling her. She stepped back.

Joe came into the room. "So that's where you're hiding out. I thought you'd left."

Hawthorne shook his head, as if wrenching himself from a daze. "We got caught in the rain." He picked up the towels on the chair and headed for the door. "I'll put these in the washer."

Tammy let out a tension-filled sigh.

Wow. She wanted to relive those moments before Joe had interrupted. She wanted to close her eyes and imagine what it would feel like if Hawthorne's incredible mouth touched hers. Tammy had kissed him once when he'd lain in the hospital six months ago. Even that minute brush of lips against lips had tingled through her like static.

As lightning illuminated the windows, she knew a real kiss between them would hold more electricity than a storm.

Joe cleared his throat, and she realized she'd drifted into a daydream.

"You okay, missy?"

She grinned. "Everyone's asking me that today."

Joe's troubled expression deepened. "Something I have to tell you. I should've said something earlier, but I got busy. It can't wait any longer."

"What is it?" She walked toward him, apprehension replacing earlier turmoil.

He fidgeted with his frayed collar, his eyes downcast. Then he pulled at his cuffs, trying to yank the too short sleeves into submission. Finally he looked up.

"You're being followed, missy. By an old evil."

Thunder reverberated in the old church and added a dramatic intensity to his words. Her heart picked up a frantic beat, fear adding to her shakiness. "Followed by evil. I don't understand."

Joe shook his head. "I don't know either. I just feel it. Always learned to trust my feelings better. And you know you can trust me, right?"

Her nerves tingled, firing with uneasiness. "Of course. But you're scaring me here. Give me more information."

Joe put his hands to his temples, and rubbed as if he could smudge away an image or a thought. "I almost didn't take that damned medication today."

"You should take it," she said gravely.

"I know, I know." He let his hands drop to his sides. "Sometimes, though, it takes away my seeing and smelling different things. If you know what I mean."

"I can imagine."

Rain pounded the windows, rushing with the wind gusts as the storm increased its fury. As lightning illuminated the windows again, she started.

Joe's voice went down to a whisper, and he started to pace. "You know this job is the best thing that's ever happened to an old bastard like me. And I don't want to lose it."

"That's understandable." She wondered why his thoughts jumbled even with medication in force.

"I didn't want to do this job. I wanted to be away from people where I couldn't smell them. Now I can sense their fear and pain. Can't shut it out. That's what happens if I don't take the pills. But this smell I got today…before the pills…"

Tammy rested a hand on his shoulder. "Tell me, Joe, before you lose the thought."

"It was that sulfur smell. I got it clear as the stink of garbage on the streets. Foul."

At his low, straining words, cold flooded her gut, then moved through her body.

He shuddered, as if he'd picked up her fearful, feathery afterthoughts. "There's someone out there you must watch out for, missy. Someone bad." He started to walk away, then turned back. "When you're ready to leave, I'll walk you to your car." He inhaled deeply. "And tell Hawthorne about those funny colors you been seeing, or I'll tell him myself."

Tammy's mouth opened in protest, but he left. She didn't need to wonder how Joe knew she'd seen about every color in a rainbow's spectrum. The longer she knew Joe, the more she realized he didn't just smell people's intentions; his psychic abilities reached farther than that. She also knew part of what the doctors called hallucinations amounted to psychic visions. She knew, as did his other friends, that he might have some personality problems, but his abilities far outweighed annoying traits. She forced her thoughts back to what Joe had said. How could she tell Hawthorne about the colors, and why did Joe believe it important?

Tammy wrapped her arms around herself as a deep trepidation mingled with caution. Realizing she stood alone, isolated from the pack, she rushed to the dining hall and to the comfort of other people.

Chapter 8

Jeannette strode through the doorway Monday morning wearing skin tight blue jeans and an electric pink T-shirt that said, "Just do it, baby."

Alison stood next to the front desk, and her mouth dropped open when she saw Jeannette's clothing. She hadn't liked the idea of Jeannette taking over lunchtime phone answering duties. Tammy didn't know whether to be amused or angry at Jeannette's idea of work clothing. Tammy noted thankfully that she'd toned down her makeup.

"Well, would you look at this," Jeannette said, distracting one bodyguard as he walked by. He stared at her T-shirt. "I finally get to see Hawthorne's pad."

Tammy wondered if Jeannette realized that the word pad had vanished with the seventies. "He's allowed to use the place, when he's good."

Sashaying over, Jeannette slung her big black plastic hobo purse onto the counter. "Oh, I'm sure he's very, very good."

The innuendo in her voice made Alison's eyebrows rise. Tammy ignored the insinuation and headed around the counter.

"Let's find a place to put your stuff."

Jeannette followed Tammy to the employee lounge. Tammy reached for Jeannette's purse to put it in a closet, but the teen pulled the huge bag away.

Jeannette held the bag to her chest. "I'm not leaving my purse there."

Tammy sighed. "It's all right. No one's going to steal it. I keep my purse in here and so does Alison."

"No way." Defiance set her face in concrete.

"You're really going to carry that heavy thing with you all day? What have you got in there anyway, the Taj Mahal?"

"The what?"

"Never mind."

Jeannette's eyes mirrored suspicion and lingering fear. Tammy softened her approach. "I realize this is all new to you, but the whole thing's a learning process. The first thing you need to realize is that you can trust everyone here."

The girl's apprehension appeared to ease, and she started to stuff the bag in the closet when it slipped from her hands. Jeannette gasped as it landed on the floor with a solid thud, the contents spilling out. An economy pack of condoms tumbled from the bag.

Jeannette cursed and stuffed the large package back into the purse. "Look what you made me do."

"Industrial size," Tammy said, amused.

Jeannette smirked. "Just the number, not the *size*. Believe me, most men don't need the large. One size basically fits all."

"Yeah, I know."

Jeannette pulled a doubtful expression as she finished reloading her bag. *"You?"*

"Me." Instead of getting mad, Tammy smiled. "I'd say you're one smart girl."

"Huh?" Clearly unused to compliments, Jeannette jammed her bag into the closet and shut the door.

"The condoms. I'm glad you have them...considering your profession."

A flush stained Jeannette's cheeks, and Tammy marveled at the girl's embarrassment. "You're not gonna say anything to anybody are you?"

Grinning, Tammy patted Jeannette on the shoulder. "This isn't junior high, Jeannette. What's in your purse is your business, unless it's something illegal. Then it doesn't come in the building."

They completed paperwork to get Jeannette started on work, then introduced her to the bodyguards. The employees kept a straight face when they saw Jeannette's T-shirt. Tammy had warned everyone that Jeannette might try something or wear something over-the-top.

When Jeannette and Tammy entered Hawthorne's office they found him getting off the phone. Jeannette sat on the corner of his desk.

"How's it going?" he asked as he put a pencil into an electric sharpener on his desk.

"Peachy," Jeannette said before Tammy could answer. She blinked slow and seductive. "'Course it'll be so much better if you take me to lunch."

Hawthorne's eyes widened, then he glanced at Tammy. She simply pursed her lips slightly and then grinned.

"What, you have to get permission from her?" Jeannette asked with a sneer.

His jaw tightened, then relaxed, and Tammy wondered how he'd handle that question. "The only person I have to answer to around here is Mrs. Taggert. And she usually lets me have lunch when I want. Today, though, I'm having lunch with Tammy."

Tammy's mouth dropped open, surprise choking her response. Jeannette's disappointment, if she had any, didn't show.

Hawthorne gave Tammy an unflappable look that asked her to participate in the charade. She didn't know what he had in mind, or why, but decided she wanted to discover the answer.

"Oh," Jeannette finally said, sliding off his desk and crossing her arms.

"We've got a lot to finish," Tammy said, nodding toward the door. "We're outta here."

Once outside his office, Jeannette gave a frown worthy of a two-year-old in a conniption. "You've got a date with Kyle?"

"No date. Just lunch." Tammy put her hand on the girl's shoulder. "We're just friends."

The teen stepped out from under her grip. "Yeah, well he may think you're just his friend, but you've got other ideas."

Tammy's blood pressure elevated, but she held her voice down to a whisper. "Think what you want."

"I think you're hot for his bod."

Time for a little discipline.

Tammy kept her comments low so that no one else could hear. "I didn't ask Mrs. Taggert to hire you because I wanted a laugh. If you think you can get me to yell at you or fire you because you have no sense of professionalism, you can forget it. I'm giving you a lot of slack because I think you've had it tough and you don't have any business experience. I'm not giving up on you, Jeannette, just so you can claim no one ever did anything for you."

Jeannette shielded her gaze by looking down at her cartoon-covered sneakers. Perhaps she wasn't used to anyone believing in her, especially when she tried so hard to sabotage herself.

When she didn't say anything, Tammy took a deep breath. "Hey, neat feet."

"Huh?" Jeannette wrinkled her nose.

"Your shoes. Notice the stuff on my desk?"

"Yeah. It's pretty cool. Where did you get it?"

"Variety of places."

Jeannette looked at her feet again but said nothing. Tammy wondered if the girl was finally stumped. Maybe Tammy could reach the girl by keeping her off guard.

"So, are you going to keep out of trouble while you're here?" Tammy asked.

"What if I don't?" Jeannette's nose rose as she tilted her head.

"Just think, if you stay here, you'll see Hawthorne Monday through Friday."

That did it. The teen grinned. "You think?"

"I think."

Lifting her hand, Jeannette gazed nonchalantly at her short fingernails. Today she'd chosen to wear only two rings on each hand. "What do you think of him?"

Tammy shrugged. "He's nice. A pain in the ass sometimes, but otherwise he's okay."

Jeannette stopped inspecting her fingernails. "You're kidding right? Just nice? He's a hunk. Gorgeous. Sexy—"

"You guys talking about me again?" Gregg Le Blanc said from his office door behind Jeannette. He leaned against the door jamb in a casual pose. As he gazed steadily at Tammy, his attention felt more intrusive than welcome.

Tammy attempted a smile that failed. "Mel Gibson. We're talking about Mel Gibson."

Jeannette winked at Gregg. "Ever consider wearing a kilt?"

Gregg grunted. "I don't wear skirts. Besides what's he got that I don't have?"

"I don't know. You wanna show me?" Jeannette asked, swaying her hips as she walked toward him.

"Whoa." He held up his hands and stepped away from his door. He walked backwards down the hall. "See you later."

Before Jeannette could reach him, he disappeared around the partition. She turned back, a self-satisfied smile giving her a look far older than her years. Tammy wondered how far Jeannette would push. How long would Mrs. Taggert endure her antics?

"Isn't that sexual harassment or something? Can't he get in trouble for that?" Jeannette asked.

"We've got work to do." Tammy decided to ignore the girl's continued attempts to rattle her. She walked past Gregg's door. "Let's get to it."

The red came without warning, burning into Tammy's skull with a fire terrifying and unexpected. Sucked into a madman's dream, her ears and eyes and nose became the repository for new sensations. A sizzling pain filled her ears. She gasped and put her hands to her ears.

"Hey, what's wrong with you?" Jeannette's voice sounded far away.

"Uh…oh…I think it's a migraine or something." She'd never experienced a migraine in her life, and she didn't believe the red slashing across her sight had anything to do with headaches.

Instead of disappearing, the colors swam over Tammy's vision until she felt nothing but hot waves of pain.

"You don't look so good," Jeannette said.

Tammy closed her eyes, swayed and reached out with both hands. The red receded to the corners of her vision, but in front of her Tammy saw the corridor outside Taggert Security Team. Someone stood there watching. Waiting. *Oh, God!* Inside the person's body the heat and hatred flowed like a miasma. Every second the heat increased and blended with images of what this man wanted to do. A man. Yes. He needed. He planned.

She knew without a doubt he wanted her. Wanted her in vile and hideous ways that sent cold crawling over her skin and deep into her soul.

"No," Tammy gasped.

He is here in the building.

Dread shuddered through her in great waves. As the vision faded she saw that Jeannette had disappeared.

"Come on." Jeannette's voice came from behind her and she turned toward the sound, her limbs trembling. "She looks like hell."

Nausea flooded her stomach and she shivered. She couldn't get sick. *Must sit down.*

Yet her body wouldn't listen to her mind and she stumbled against the wall. Hawthorne and Jeannette came toward her, Hawthorne's expression marked by deep concern.

With relief she started toward him. Hawthorne caught her shoulders as she sagged against him, her legs unwilling to support her.

He lifted Tammy in his arms. "Did you have another one of those damned spells?"

"No," Tammy whispered, allowing him to stride with her down the hallway toward Mrs. Taggert's office. "Where are you taking me?

"Mrs. Taggert's couch where you can lie down. Jeannette, there's a blanket in the closet in the break room. Get it."

Tammy moved in his arms. "No, Hawthorne, I'm all right."

"Be quiet for once."

Indignation managed to break through the sick feeling. "How dare you?"

"You're not going to ignore this, Tammy. You're either going to the doctor or I'm calling an ambulance."

Drained and unwilling to fight with him, she put her arms around his neck and laid her head on his shoulder. When he reached Mrs. Taggert's office, the door was ajar. He nudged it open with his shoulder and went inside.

"What on earth?" Mrs. Taggert's alarm punched through Tammy's foggy state. "What happened?"

"I think she's having another one of those spells," Hawthorne said, his voice husky with worry.

Tammy's eyes popped open and she lifted her head from his shoulder. Her head felt as heavy as a bowling ball. "I just need to eat something."

Hawthorne settled her on the leather couch, and Jeannette rushed in with the blanket. Tammy welcomed the fleece cover and Hawthorne tucked it around her body, the softness comforting and warm.

Hawthorne cursed under his breath. "This is the second time in a week. Last time she passed out right in front of me."

"Damn it, Hawthorne," Tammy said. Some spunk filled her veins now that the color vision had lost its grip.

Mrs. Taggert's face creased with curiosity and consternation as she stood at the foot of the couch. "You fainted last week?"

"Monday." Hawthorne knelt by the couch and pulled the blanket closer around Tammy's neck. His long fingers brushed against her chin and neck as he arranged the blanket, and she wanted the reassurance in his touch. Embarrassment threatened at the edges.

"This is ridiculous. I'll be all right in a minute." Tammy started to sit up, but Hawthorne's hands held her down.

"Stay put." His stern expression gave a dire warning. "Now are you going to the doctor, or do I call the ambulance?"

She could see determination in his eyes and knew resistance, in this case, wouldn't help. "All right. I'll go to the doctor."

Mrs. Taggert went to her desk and lifted the telephone receiver. "I'll call Dr. Jacobssen. I'm sure she'll see you as soon as possible."

Tammy and Mrs. Taggert happened to share the same doctor. When Tammy had first moved to Denver and started work with the agency almost five years ago, she'd signed on with Dr. Jacobssen's new practice.

Hawthorne's gaze swung to Jeannette. "Jeannette, go see if Alison needs help. Let her know what's going on and that I'm taking Tammy to the doctor immediately."

Tammy's equilibrium had returned, and she was surprised to see that Jeannette not only looked concerned, but that she didn't argue.

Tammy sighed. "I'm not sure this is necessary. I appreciate it but—"

Hawthorne threw up his hands. "She *must* be all right if she can still be a stubborn, mouthy wench."

"Wench?" she asked, unsure whether to laugh or snap his head off. "What's this wench business?"

He brushed her hair away from her face, then cupped her cheek. Tammy shivered with pleasure at his warm, gentle touch. He leaned down to look in her eyes. "Look at me. That's good. Your pupils look okay."

Tammy grinned again. "Thank you, Doctor Hawthorne. Can I sit up now? Alison is going to kill me. I haven't trained Jeannette."

"Forget about it. Your health is more important," he said.

Mrs. Taggert hung up the phone. "Dr. Jacobssen says come on in. She'll see you right away."

Hawthorne stood and held out his hand to Tammy. "Come on. Sit up."

"Yes, sir," Tammy said wryly. "Did you know you were hiring a bossy man when you interviewed him last year, Mrs. Taggert?"

"Absolutely." Mrs. Taggert grinned. "It's a requirement for a bodyguard at this agency. And in your case, I think you need someone bossy taking care of you."

That stung. Tammy didn't want coddling. She'd done well for almost thirty years. "I'm not a piece of china, you know." She made a gasp of surprise as Hawthorne picked her up in his arms. "I can walk to the car, damn it."

Hawthorne gave her an indulgent grin. "You're not walking."

Argument over, they retrieved her things and he carried her down to the parking structure. All the way there she savored the warmth and power she felt in his arms, drawing strength from him. At the same time, she knew Dr. Jacobssen wouldn't find anything wrong and she'd be right back to work the next day.

But as hard as she tried, Tammy couldn't forget the horrible, crimson death she felt hovering close. Despite the safety of

Hawthorne's arms, the danger lay somewhere near. Perhaps not close. Perhaps not even in the building at this moment. Yet it watched, waited for the opportunity to...what? Kill her?

Why now? Why had these visions come to her and why had depravity found its way into her life again? Hadn't Barb's death been enough punishment?

Disgusted with herself for her lack of control, Tammy wondered how she would explain her mysterious illness. Evil hovered close, threatening her sanity, pecking and ripping at her nerves like a vulture.

"Are you going to tell me what this is all about?" he asked as they reached his Jaguar.

"What?"

"There's a lot more to this than just your illness. Something is very wrong. And you're going to tell me all about it. Or else."

Chapter 9

As Hawthorne pulled into the driveway of Tammy's condo complex, her expression remained set like a stony mask.

He shut off the car and turned toward her, sliding his arm onto the back of the seat. Her hair fell about her face in disarray, so close to his fingers he could almost touch it. A wild impulse to bury his face in the softness of her hair and to cover her stubborn mouth with his rocked him to the core. His groin ached in response.

Control, Hawthorne. Now is not the time to get horny.

She gazed at the thunderclouds rising in the west, and he wondered what clever thing she'd say next. What excuse would she have for this mysterious malady? The answer came quicker than he thought.

"I told you Dr. Jacobssen wouldn't find anything wrong," she said.

"A fever isn't normal. You've passed out twice in one week. I'm not sure I trust the doctor's take on this." When she stayed silent, he said, "Maybe you should get a second opinion."

"They'll say the same. You know Dr. Jacobssen is one of the best."

Hawthorne couldn't deny the doctor had an excellent reputation, but that didn't mean she couldn't be wrong. Leaving the car, he headed around to the passenger side. Before he could get there, Tammy opened the door and slipped out. When she stepped onto the blacktop, her eyelids fluttered and she grabbed the car door.

"Whoa." He clasped her shoulders. "Easy. Just take it easy."

Automatically she clutched his shoulders. The movement brought her close against his chest. The desire to pull her close and hold her made his breath stagger. Tammy's fresh floral scent teased him and brought dormant need firing to life. He shook his head to realign his thoughts.

Hawthorne smoothed his fingers from her shoulders down to her upper arms. "Tell me something. Do you have a problem with trust?"

A puzzled expression creased her face. "I'm used to taking care of myself. It's hard to relinquish control."

"I understand. I have the same problem."

"No kidding."

A grin tipped his mouth, and when Tammy responded by smiling he drank in the sight of her vulnerable mouth.

He could dip his head, devour her lips, discover once and for all if she tasted as hot as she looked. Instead he cleared his throat. "Let's get you inside."

Tammy didn't protest this time when Hawthorne lifted her in his arms. People coming in and out of the complex stared as they passed, stopping to ask Tammy what had happened. She introduced him as a colleague, and the knowing glances they tossed his way made him wonder. Hawthorne shrugged off the irritating idea that people thought something was happening between them. He'd probably never see these people again.

Hawthorne set her down when they reached her condo, then kept a steadying hand on her arm as they walked inside.

Immediately he noticed what made this place unique and screamed one hundred percent *Tammy*. She might wear short skirts and own tons of cartoon character memorabilia, but her furniture taste leaned toward conservative and classic. Inside the front door sat a huge mahogany hall tree with attached mirror. As he glanced in the mirror, he thought he looked pissed off. He rotated his shoulders to loosen up.

As she headed for the living area, Tammy asked, "Like something cold to drink?"

"That would be great."

"Iced tea okay?"

"Sounds good."

While Tammy rummaged in the kitchen, Hawthorne surveyed her living room. He saw Tammy's personality here. Clean but not stark.

Large and airy, the condo had high ceilings. Three enormous skylights in the broad living area allowed plenty of light into the room. Sky blue walls calmed. A dark blue couch shared the room with a matching love seat and recliner. The whole place had harmony and peace written into it. Hawthorne grinned.

A matching blue rug decorated the floor near the red brick gas fireplace. As he walked toward the hearth his imagination kicked into high gear. He saw her lying on that long, oval rug, her naked curves shadowed and defined by firelight.

Hawthorne sucked in a deep breath. He must banish crazy ideas about her before she saw through him and realized how he felt about her.

How did he feel about her?

Shoving away dangerous thoughts, he switched his attention to the fireplace.

Various size photographs graced the fireplace mantle. One large black and white photo showed a plain-faced man with a pretty woman standing outside a ranch and adobe style house. A pixie-faced girl that he assumed must be Tammy wore a gingham dress and stood in front of the adults. The woman resembled Tammy through the jaw and mouth, but her hair flowed down in waves around her shoulders. Another girl of about fourteen stood next to the man, her hand on his shoulder. The teen took after the father.

Tammy's sister? She never talked about her family or any siblings.

"Here you go."

He started, guilt pouring into him for staring at her photographs and wanting to invade her privacy.

Smirking, she handed him the tea, generous chunks of ice floating in the glass. She sipped her own tea. "Didn't mean to scare you, Hawthorne."

He leaned back against the mantle. "You didn't scare me."

"Did too."

"Did not."

She smiled again. "No one's going to win this game."

He winked. "I could win it."

"Huh!"

Tossing her a grin, Hawthorne turned back to the photographs. "Your family?"

Her gaze scanned the photos. "Yes."

When Tammy turned away immediately and headed toward the love seat, Hawthorne followed. He settled next to her and put his drink on a coaster. He glanced at her expression and saw things there he didn't like. A bleak mien. Mistrustful.

"Is that your parents and your sister in the photograph?" he asked.

She looked into her drink, as if the contents worked like a crystal ball. "A long time ago."

"How come you never talk about them?"

The glass slipped through her hand, splattering cola as it went down. "Damn it!"

Hawthorne went for paper towels, then returned from the kitchen to hand her a bunch. They sopped up the mess and she squirted carpet cleaner onto the upholstery and rug.

Tammy headed for the kitchen with the sopping towels and he followed her.

Remorse tugged at him. "Did I upset you?"

She grabbed a sponge near the sink, then gazed into the garbage disposal. "Do you really want to know?"

He crossed to the kitchen counter island. "Yeah, I want to know."

Tammy inhaled deeply, then released it slowly. She left her gaze to his. "My sister, Barb, was murdered fifteen years ago."

Shock held him speechless until he could force another breath into his lungs. "Oh, Jesus."

Pain filled her eyes, and she closed them. Hawthorne moved closer, a desperate need to comfort her gripping him. He reached for her, caressing her cheek. She opened her eyes, and Hawthorne knew the agony of her sister's death had never left Tammy.

"Tell me," he whispered.

"It's...I can't. Not now."

"When?"

Tammy eased from his touch, and he wished he'd folded her in his arms. "I...never. Never."

Final. Certain. Damn! He'd pushed too hard, too fast. "Never is a long time."

Tammy stiffened, straightening her shoulders. "Well, it's the way it's going to be."

Realizing he wouldn't extract more information from her tonight he said, "All right. I'd better go so you can rest. Thanks for the drink."

As he started for the door, she followed him. "Thanks for looking out for me."

Tammy touched his shoulder, and the embers that seemed to burn between them traveled up his arm like a firestorm. Was he crazy or did she feel the same thing?

Before she could take her hand away, he clasped it in his own. Her long, delicately fashioned fingers felt cool in his palm. Without thought he brought her hand up and kissed the back, holding it against his mouth. Tammy's lips parted, her mouth forming a little O of surprise. God, she was so soft. He wanted her mouth under his, and the idea made him crazy with longing.

No way, Hawthorne. You've fallen over the edge. Time to climb up the mineshaft and forget the treasure.

"You handled Jeannette well today." He dropped her hand and shoved his own in his pockets so he wouldn't be tempted to touch her again.

Tammy clutched her hands together, too. "She's not easy to deal with. Maybe I shouldn't have hired her."

"That's the first sensible thing I've heard all day. I don't think she's going to work out."

Tammy rubbed the back of her neck. "She's only been at work a day."

"A day is long enough for some people. Her clothes, her manners, her snide remarks; the list is infinite."

"I told her about appropriate wear for the office. Then I gave her a few dollars to buy the right clothes."

"What? That's not a good idea. You don't give people like her and Joe money."

Hawthorne knew he'd stepped in deep cow patties when her lips compressed and her hands balled into fists at her sides.

"I can give money to anyone I want, Hawthorne. I don't need your permission or your approval."

Scrubbing his hand through his hair in frustration, Hawthorne wondered how things had transformed from comfortable to rough in a heartbeat.

"I know that. I'm saying their chances of succeeding in the world are low. Joe has therapy and medication, but eventually he goes off both. He may end up back on the street at any time.

Jeannette won't turn into little miss cooperative anytime soon. She's too headstrong. You can't change her with just a snap of your fingers."

Her features turned hard. Almost unforgiving. Hawthorne had never seen Tammy as angry as a wet wasp before. A flush tinted her cheeks and nose, as if she'd stayed in the sun too long.

"Maybe because everyone tells them they can't succeed. I know how it works. I've been told often enough and long enough that my choice of career means I'm dumb, stupid, and an idiot. If you hear that enough times, you start to wonder."

He felt his gut sour. "Dumb, stupid, and idiot mean basically the same thing."

Tammy looked at the ceiling and sighed before returning her defiant gaze to him. "No shit, Sherlock."

Hawthorne's eyes widened and his eyebrows lifted. Tammy might be feminine and sexy. She might look so edible he wanted to nibble on her and kiss her senseless. She was strong and insightful and had depths he could only imagine. But Tammy also suffered from an obstinate streak. He wished he had a thermometer to gauge her irritation.

Hawthorne shifted away from the door, ready to stay longer. "Tell me why you believe Jeannette and Joe have a chance."

She headed for the couch. "Sit down."

"Yes, ma'am."

When they'd settled side by side, Hawthorne moved so that his right ankle hitched over his left knee. He turned toward her. "Okay. Shoot."

"Joe should be obvious." Tammy's obstinate, tilted jaw said she'd defend her position as long as it took. "Look how far he's progressed in a year. He takes his medication, he's productive at the soup kitchen, and he's happy." She leaned toward Hawthorne and dropped her voice. "Why even the other day he told me he could scent—"

She stopped, reining in like a horse team.

"What?" Hawthorne asked. "Has he been saying he can smell evil again?"

Reluctance stained her face, then she nodded. "Yes."

Scoffing, he inclined toward her. "He can't be taking his medication if he's smelling odd things again. According to the medical center, Joe has schizotypal personality disorder. He has oddities of thinking, perception, communication and behavior. One of those behaviors is thinking he can smell evil. He's not severe enough to be schizophrenic, but it's bad enough."

Tammy looked at the floor and sighed. "I know."

Silence covered the room for a significant time before he spoke again. "When he's on his medication and working at the church, he's great. All I'm saying is these smells he talks about are a part of his illness. Nothing psychic."

"I still don't see how you can say that after he helped us with that case last year. If it hadn't been for him—"

Hawthorne held up one hand. "I know what everyone said."

Her expression didn't alter. "And you chose not to believe one of your best friends, his wife, Joe, and myself?"

"I believe that *you* believe it." He knew she wouldn't change her viewpoint on the subject. "I don't believe in psychic powers. Never have. Never will. Life is complicated enough without people adding mystery where there is none. Joe's mental problems can't be explained away by saying he smells people's true nature. It's…." He gestured with one hand. "Unrealistic."

By now Tammy's face registered irritation. "I don't believe that. It's not all black and white. Frankly, I'm surprised at you. I thought you were more openminded."

"I'm not when it comes to psychic stuff." Sensing the strain building between them, he softened his voice. "Look, we can agree to disagree about this right now, can't we?"

Tammy inhaled deeply. "Of course."

After another awkward silence, he stood and headed for the door. "You need rest. But we need to talk about those fainting spells. Tomorrow."

She trailed him to the door again. "Maybe tomorrow."

Exasperation spiked up his spine, but he held back a retort. "I'm holding you to it."

A suspicious smile touched one corner of her mouth. "And how do you plan to make me talk?"

"Don't worry. I'll think of something. Call me if you need anything."

As he walked to his car through the dimness of a cloudy twilight, wind ruffled his hair. No rain. The threatened precipitation hadn't materialized. But Hawthorne's senses felt skewed and battered as if he'd weathered a storm.

When he reached his car, he knew he'd messed up by demanding she talk about her sister. Not many people would call him subtle. It seemed he needed to learn and learn quick. He also wanted to learn more about the most exasperating woman he knew.

He hopped in his Jag and roared off. Soon the steady sound of the engine purring and the heavy metal CD playing stirred his needs.

I could get to know Tammy outside the work environment.

No.

If he stayed near her in a social setting, God knew how he'd resist that sweet, hot mouth of hers. His physical reactions to her would be impossible to ignore.

And yet he wanted her trust with a gut-wrenching force.

Cursing, he turned the music up a little louder and hoped the screaming strains of the electric guitar would blast his rebellious thoughts into outer space.

Across the street from Tammy's condo, the man watched from his VW Beetle. Outside storm clouds hovered, waiting for the right time to strike. Inside the car he watched, betrayal eating at him like a maggot feasting on carrion. He wished now was the right time. The right time to bring her little games to an end. To bring bodyguard man down like the dirty, inhuman creature he'd become when he'd looked at Sweet Magnolia. Tasted her. Oh, God. He'd probably licked her, too.

Like a serrated knife, hatred and jealousy slid sharp and jagged over his nerves. Sweet Magnolia had committed *the* sin letting Hawthorne into her home. If she had screwed him she would forever be soiled. The images came then, drowning him in heat and light and accusing voices. Through the windshield he saw the women he'd had killed standing on the pavement and they hounded him. Begged him for another woman to complete the circle. His tormented Sweet Magnolia would be cleansed and anointed when she joined the others.

The man's fingers tapped the steering wheel over and over as he hummed and chanted. "Sweet Magnolia will be dead. Sweet Magnolia, I'll have her head."

Giggling hysterically, he threw his head back and let the jovial sound reach over him like a blanket, insensate to all but his own world.

Then, as if someone had popped a balloon, his laughing halted.

He stared at the condo, wishing that bodyguard man had stayed. Maybe he would have done them both tonight. Just the thought of her messing with bodyguard man made his heart cringe...crumple like cellophane. What was a little girl like her doing with a man like that anyway? Bodyguard man couldn't give her what she needed. She'd have to be punished for her unfaithfulness. Then she would know the meaning of love. The love only *he* could provide.

* * *

Hawthorne's phone rang late that evening while he stepped out of the shower. Dripping with water, he sprang out of the bath and into his bedroom.

"Yeah?" he grunted into the phone as he fell stomach-down onto the bed.

"Joe here."

"Hey Joe. What's up? Everything okay at the shelter?"

"Everything is cool. Groovy."

"Groovy?" Hawthorne grinned. "Aren't you a little behind the times? Shouldn't it be something like 'totally rad'?"

Joe chuckled. "I think you're behind the times, son. I think totally rad was ten years ago."

Hawthorne laughed and rolled onto his back. He stared at the ceiling with its swirling, repetitive pattern. Joe was great, even if he had serious problems. Hawthorne wished he could believe Tammy's assertion that the older man had paranormal abilities.

"Did Tammy tell you about the evil?" Joe asked.

Hawthorne immediately wondered if Joe had taken his pills. "I don't know what you're talking about."

"Tammy's in danger, boy. She's being stalked by someone, I'm sure of it. I can smell him around sometimes when we're at the soup kitchen. But I think he's everywhere."

"Come on, Joe, you know I don't believe in that."

"Damn fool kid. You got a brain in your head. Use it." Joe's belligerent tone surprised Hawthorne into silence. "You're like a mule, Hawthorne. She's in trouble. I told her if she didn't say something to you about those episodes she's been having then I'd tell you."

Hawthorne sat up, easing off the bed. "How did you know she's fainted?"

"She almost fell on her face here at the soup kitchen the other day. Didn't pass out, but she looked ready to."

Hawthorne spilled a virulent curse. "Damn her cute little ass! I knew this was more complicated than that."

"Usually is with that girl."

Worry roughened Hawthorne's voice. "I tried to talk to her tonight but she wouldn't listen."

"Do something, Hawthorne. This evil is real bad. If you think young Kiley and Scott had a bad time of it a few months back, you haven't seen anything yet."

Chapter 10

"There are pens missing from the supply cabinet."

Mrs. Taggert's words were laced with a steadfast tone and punctuated by a frown as she walked up to Tammy's desk.

The day had been long, busy, and filled with minor mishaps. Tammy had arrived at work early, determined to make up for leaving early yesterday after the fainting spell. Jeannette had come to work on time. Hawthorne had worked on an assignment outside the office and when he'd called ‚Jeannette purred into the phone like a milk-sated kitten.

Now, everyone had left with the exception of Gregg Le Blanc and Mrs. Taggert.

"Pens?" Tammy asked.

"Not the one or two you'd expecte when someone needs a new pen. Your last order had ten boxes on it and now there is only one box left."

Tammy didn't know what to think. Her nerves had tingled all morning, anticipating another vision to explode her world. "But that doesn't make sense. We just got those supplies last week."

"Exactly. And the only person I know who might take them is Jeannette."

Tammy's stomach sank. "Oh, no."

"Oh, yes." Mrs. Taggert watched as Tammy fiddled with her plastic dinosaur. "Keep that up and you'll rub a hole through the plastic." Her eyes narrowed. "Is there anything else wrong?"

Tammy couldn't admit that her muscles knotted with tension and her insides felt like jambalaya. "Of course not."

"No ill effects from yesterday?"

"I'm great. Maybe a little stress."

"Then perhaps we need to decrease your work load."

"No," Tammy blurted. "With Alison about ready to shoot out that baby, I can't afford to slack off now. Soon she'll be on maternity leave."

Mrs. Taggert tilted her head to the side like a curious bird. "Most people would jump at having their work load decreased. Now that Jeannette is here, maybe you can relax a little."

Pushing her dinosaur back in a niche in her desk, Tammy picked up a bright fuchsia pen and doodled. "You know me. I like to work and I don't expect you to treat me any differently than anyone in the office."

"Very commendable, but if you work yourself to death, where will I be then?"

Tammy dropped the pen on her desk. "I'm sorry. I've been a bit distracted. Maybe a little nervous trying to get Jeannette up and running on this job."

"I understand completely. Promise me, though, that you'll ask for help if you need it? You practically scared us to death yesterday by almost keeling over like that."

Feeling foolish, Tammy said, "I didn't mean to cause so much trouble."

"Of course you didn't." Mrs. Taggert smiled and straightened the bright green silk scarf anchored about the collar of her suit jacket. "You're an excellent employee, and I'm more than glad to have you working with me. If we lost you for any reason, it would be devastating." Her smile faded slightly and became rueful. "I'm concerned about your welfare. We all are. The look on Hawthorne's face when he carried you in the office was very telling."

Startled, Tammy peered at Mrs. Taggert as if she'd never seen her before. "He was just being a good friend. Overreacting, but a good friend."

A knowing smile crossed the older woman's lips. "Hmmm."

"What?" Tammy asked warily.

Mrs. Taggert shook her head. "That was more than worry I saw in his eyes." She looked around, then lowered her voice. "Normally I wouldn't say anything because it's my policy to keep out of my employees' personal lives. But Hawthorne seems like a man in love."

Tammy's gut clenched again, this time with frigid denial. "With whom?"

"Pfft. You, Tammy. You."

Everything stilled within Tammy. Her breath, her heart, her lungs, her thinking processes. This time she couldn't blame it on a vision. "Me."

"That's what I said."

Tammy shook her head. "That's over the top. We haven't dated. We barely know each other."

"Hah!" Mrs. Taggert threw up her hands. "If that isn't the lamest excuse I've ever heard."

Spellbound with amazement, Tammy let her mouth drop open. She'd never seen her employer like this before, letting out her feelings on a subject like love. Since Mrs. Taggert had confessed six months ago to having a daughter, and Kiley Danger had reentered her mother's life, Mrs. Taggert *had* become more sentimental. Still, Tammy's astonishment lingered.

"Pardon me, Mrs. Taggert, but you're not only wrong, you're dead wrong."

Now it was Mrs. Taggert's turn to look surprised. "Have it your way."

Tammy's throat felt parched and she swallowed the ache lodged there. "Maybe he's in love with someone we don't know. That would explain the goofy expression on his face sometimes."

Mrs. Taggert smiled and crossed her arms. "It's possible."

"It's *probable*."

"The man's good at hiding his feelings most of the time, but believe me they were clearly visible yesterday."

Tammy didn't want to think about Hawthorne and love. "Getting back on our original subject, do you really think Jeannette took the pens?"

"There's a very good chance."

Taking her newly acquired bifocals from a pocket inside her jacket, Mrs. Taggert plopped them on her nose. She looked like a disapproving school administrator. "We'll keep a close watch on the situation. If anything else goes missing, I'm afraid young Miss Jeannette may be without a job."

Shortly after Mrs. Taggert left the office, Tammy gathered her things, ready to head home. As she put away paperwork, her thoughts centered on the very idea that Hawthorne harbored anything more then friendship for her.

Ha! Preposterous!

Hawthorne might flirt with her and she with him, but that didn't mean he *loved* her.

She closed her eyes a moment and fantasized. Hawthorne tugging her close as they moved about a shadowed dance floor. His intent gaze devouring her with obvious desire.

Tammy sat down in her chair with a thump. He would move her around the floor with sensual, sure movements. He'd—

Stop! Thinking about him like this would lead places she couldn't…shouldn't…want to go.

She switched gears and wondered if Jeannette had dared to steal the pens. If so, why? To annoy her or Mrs. Taggert or both of them?

Third, Tammy understood why her nerves had jumped all day. When would the next vision come? How could she defend herself against the man...the fiend that threatened if not herself, then other people? How could she control these visions so they wouldn't interfere with her job? Quandaries raced in her mind and blocked even thoughts of Hawthorne in love with her.

Helpless feelings welled inside and made her angry.

Helpless, my ass. I'll never lie down and expose my underbelly.

Footsteps intruded on her thoughts, and Gregg Le Blanc appeared from his area. He looked ready to leave for the night, but he leaned on the counter. "Hey, aren't you ready to go home?"

"Just about."

One of his brows twitched. "You don't make a habit of this staying late thing do you?"

Tammy put away the last paper in a file cabinet. The metal drawer rattled as she closed it. "I have lately. Don't worry, I'll get over it."

"Come on. I'll walk you down to your car."

She made certain her gaze held his, wanting him to know she couldn't be talked into it. "No, thanks. I've got a little more to do."

Gregg shrugged, his frown clear. Unease danced along her spine like a feather touch.

"Suit yourself." He headed toward the door without a parting smile or wave. Once the door closed behind him, she shook her head.

"Great," she muttered as she reached for the drawer with her purse in it. "Just what I need. A pouting bodyguard with an ego the size of the Astrodome."

The phone rang, and she about jumped free of her chair in surprise. She grabbed for the receiver and gave her usual announcement. "Taggert Security Team. How may I help you?"

"Hey, Tammy." The deep, familiar tone sliced through her defenses like a knife.

"Hawthorne." Her voice wavered, and she wanted to curse. "What are you doing calling at this time of night?"

"I think we've had this conversation once before."

The amusement in his tone lightened her mood. "If you've called for Mrs. Taggert, you missed her. I'm the last one in the office."

"Again? Tammy—"

"Spare me the lecture. Mrs. Taggert already told me to take it easy. Maybe when…correction…if Jeannette works out, then I can use her to help with the load."

"*If* she works out?"

"It's up for debate right now. Mrs. Taggert noticed pens taken from the storage area and I just ordered ten boxes. Did you scarf up pens?"

"Nope. I've got more than enough in my desk drawer. So Mrs. Taggert thinks Jeannette took them?"

"She suspects. Damn thing is, I don't blame her. I suspect the little nincompoop, too."

"Little nincompoop?"

Tammy started fiddling with her pencil cup. "You know what I mean. That's probably way too mild a descriptor for Jeannette."

He chuckled. "Did she act up today?"

"Well, she didn't wear the obnoxious T-shirt again, thank you very much. She wore a blouse and skirt she'd bought from the money I gave her."

"I'm surprised."

"Sometimes you have to give people an extra chance. Have faith." Silence entered the line. "Hawthorne?"

"Sorry. I was just thinking that you're a pretty amazing woman." Thankful he couldn't see the blush cover her face, she made a dismissing noise. "Right."

"Great way to accept a compliment, *Carter*."

Perturbation added to the heat in Tammy's face. How did he get to her so easily? The longer she knew him, the less she could talk to him without stumbling and bumbling. "Sorry. Now did you call for something in particular?"

"Yeah. When I called your apartment and didn't get an answer, I figured you were still at the office. I'm checking up on you."

She didn't know whether to feel gratified or mortified. "You didn't need to do that. I mean call me."

"You're right. I didn't need to. I wanted to."

Mrs. Hawthorne's assertion that Hawthorne loved her bled through Tammy's mind, but she dismissed the idea again.

"I wanted to see if you were all right," he said.

"Thanks, but I'm okay."

"I don't like the idea of you being there alone."

She almost blurted out that she wasn't helpless. Instead Tammy swiveled her chair and looked at the utilitarian office clock across the room. "I'm about ready to leave."

"Give me a call when you get home."

"Why?" she asked cautiously.

"I want to make sure you're safe."

"I'll be fine. I'm leaving right now."

"Just call me," he said sternly, his voice deepening. "Or I'll come looking for you."

"But—"

"No buts. I'm serious. Talk to you later, babe."

"But—" A dial tone stopped her. Tammy growled and put down the phone with more force than necessary. She glared at the phone, then took a deep breath. "Babe! I told him not to call me that."

Tammy closed her eyes and sighed. Okay, so maybe she overreacted. Hawthorne offered her friendship and she balked at his concern. What was wrong with her? A dawning answer attempted to tiptoe into her thoughts, but she shoved it aside. She didn't want to analyze Freudian thoughts. A hot bath and herb tea would settle her nerves and give her all the answers she needed.

Tammy headed to the parking garage less then five minutes later. The elevator seemed to take forever to reach the underground parking structure. As the elevator opened on the lowest level and she took several steps into garage, it hit her.

Light flashed across her vision, and the sudden pain throughout her body made her flinch and step back against a concrete pillar close to the elevator. Taking gasping breaths to relieve the pain, she became aware that savage hatred dwelled in this place. Calling to her. Warning her.

Danger.

It skulked like a living entity, as close as the breath in her lungs.

Weakness melted her muscles. Nothing prepared her, even yesterday's vision, for what she experienced then.

Heat gathered in her body like a volcano's pyroclastic flow. Sweat broke out on her body as nausea washed through her. Tammy tried to move away from the pillar, but her legs trembled.

Dread splintered her into fragments, allowing a kaleidoscope world of pain and evil to intrude. She tried shoving the tide away, but it flowed back, a miasma that clogged her senses. Her heart thumped wild and strong, her breath rasping in her throat.

Pressing against the pillar, she experienced the chill air in the concrete dungeon. Red and black stripes covered her vision. Quivers slipped across her skin. Powerless against the invasion, she closed her eyes to shut out the image, knowing her resistance meant nothing.

Seconds later the red became a crimson frame around a black hole. A vision poured into her mind.

Barb walked in the kitchen, smiling back at the person watching her, grinning at her killer. The killer's glee as he looked at Barb moved through Tammy. Hideous need, akin to savage pleasure, rushed through the killer's veins. Barb gestured toward the pool area, her lips moving in silent conversation.

Barb opened the sliding glass door. She stepped into the brilliant light near the forty-foot kidney-shaped pool. Light reflected a thousand diamonds off the water. Everything within Tammy rebelled, fighting against the visualization. Instead, it worsened.

Barb's expression changed as she turned to look back once again. Stark surprise altered her from happy to terrified in seconds. A silent scream parted Barb's lips as she tried to back away from the unseen horror. Hands came toward her. Hands reaching for her neck. Male hands.

"No!" Tammy screamed.

She refused to see her sister's murder.

No, no, no!

The mental picture broke with a gasp from Tammy's lips, the color frame dissolving at the edges like skin exposed to powerful acid. She jolted from the vision as she slid down the pillar and collapsed sitting up, legs straight out. Tammy's heart thudded like a drum, her breath rattling until she cleared her throat.

"Oh, God," she rasped, her mouth dry.

Chills traversed Tammy's limbs as she opened her eyes. Hyperawareness assaulted her and she shuddered. She thought she heard water dripping along pipes in the building. The scuttling of insects and rodents in the walls. Traffic roared, horns honked and people chattered on the sidewalks outside. The night wind shifted against the walls. Scents intruded, prickled her nose. The garbage in the alleys, the sour stench of unwashed bodies, rancid breath. Evil's sulfurous reek.

All sounds coalesced until they thrummed in her ears. All scents blended until she almost gagged.

Tammy looked around the parking structure and saw no one. But she knew *he* lurked near.

"No," she whispered again.

Panic fluttered in her stomach, and she rummaged through her handbag for her cell phone. Retrieving the small instrument, she hoped it would work under all this concrete. Tammy dragged herself to her feet, her gaze searching the area around her for signs of danger. She couldn't see it, but she could feel it so deep in her bones that it hurt. Frantically she tried to remember Hawthorne's number. She stumbled away from the pillar and headed for her car. Her legs reacted like sticks, barely bending as she rushed forward.

Only two rows away. Must get to my car. Lock myself in. Eyes watching me. Oh, damn. They're watching me!

Tammy reached her car and used her automated key to unlock just the driver's side. She jumped in, and immediately locked the door, her heart slamming against her ribs with enough force to make her breathless. Dizziness floated through her head, and she struggled to remain conscious. She grabbed the steering wheel for a moment, using it like a life preserver to keep her afloat.

Reaching for her day planner, she opened the company roster and found Hawthorne's number. While looking around the parking structure for signs of an attacker, she waited for the cell phone service to engage. Weakness threatened to swallow her, and she shook her head.

"Come on. Come on!"

To her amazement the phone rang twice. Three times.

"Hello?"

Hawthorne's welcome voice eased some of her fear, but she continued to look around the garage. "Hawthorne?"

"You can't be home already," he said, a smile in his voice.

Static dimmed his voice, and she cursed under her breath.

"I'm at the parking garage at the office. I need…." Her voice cracked. "I'm in the garage and something weird has happened. Please—"

"Tammy? I can barely hear you. What's wrong?"

"I need you Hawthorne. Please help me!"

More static intruded, snapping and popping.

Seconds later she fell down the long slope of unconsciousness as her eyelids flickered closed and all faded to blackness.

Chapter 11

Tammy heard a tapping noise and the hum of voices. She struggled against the morass that held her under, her fear enlarging as she wondered if the horrific vision had returned.

Then she thought she heard, "Tammy? Tammy, can you hear me?"

She pulled her eyelids open and willed the drugged sensation to leave. She jumped as movement outside the driver's window attracted her notice.

Hawthorne and a security guard stood outside her car. Hawthorne's worried expression melted into some relief. Immediately she unlocked the car, and Hawthorne opened the door, pulling it wide so he could squat in front of her. He reached in and put his hand on her shoulder.

"Are you all right? What the hell happened?"

She shook her head, deep trepidation destroying her composure. "I need to get out of here." Tammy trembled, her hands shaking.

Immediately, he took her hands in his. "Are you hurt?"

"No. Nothing like that."

He frowned, his dark eyes conveying more anxiety than she'd seen in Hawthorne's face before. "Your hands are like ice and you're trembling."

"I'm all right now that you're here."

He glanced over his shoulder at the guard. "I'll take care of her now."

"You sure?" the guard asked.

Tammy didn't recognize the security guard. "I'm okay."

When the guard relented and left, Tammy savored the warmth of Hawthorne's fingers against hers. His contact acted like a balm and relief seeped into her. Like it or not, she needed him. When he touched her face gently, tears filled her eyes. Her limbs shivered and she wanted him to hold her. Just this once.

"Come on. I'll take you home," he said gently.

Surprised he didn't demand an explanation for what had happened, she slid out of the car. She grasped his arm for support, relishing the heat and strength under her fingers. Her legs wavered like liquid.

"I'm sorry," she whispered.

He peered down at her and frowned. "For what?"

"For calling you." Her voice trembled as she kept tears at bay. "For putting you out."

He cursed. "You're not putting me out. I'm glad you called."

Hawthorne's rough tone cut into her dwindling barriers. She sniffed and gulped and even a deep breath didn't help. "Damn it."

Tammy's face crumbled and the tears flowed. Control lost, she didn't resist when he mumbled another soft curse and drew her into his arms.

"It's all right." He slid a hand into her hair, holding her head against his shoulder and pressing his cheek against her hair. "It's all right."

God, it feels so good to be held.

Not by just anyone or just any man. By *this* man.

Melting into his care, Tammy allowed the confusion and terror to ease in his tender embrace. His arms felt wonderful. Hard. Powerful. Safe.

His fingers caressed her hair, his other hand warming her back as sobs shook her entire body. "It's all right, babe. I'm here."

The tenderness in his tone enthralled Tammy and broke her tears. Slowly she raised her head. Worry covered his strong features. He probably thought she had lost her mind and didn't know where to find it. She'd just stood in his arms and sobbed and babbled like a crazy woman.

He pushed a lock of hair away from her face. "Feeling better?"

"Yeah. Sort of."

"Sort of?"

"Can we get out of here?" When he kissed her forehead, she gasped. "What was that for?"

"GP."

"GP?"

"General purposes. Come on. I'm driving. You're not up to it."

As they gathered her tote bag from the car, she contemplated the vision and its implications. How could she hide what was happening to her after this?

Once in his car, Tammy fidgeted, worried he'd see too much in her expression and deduce what had occurred. Denver lights passed by as he drove toward her neighborhood, and some part of her wished she hadn't called him.

Once at the condo, he parked and turned off the ignition. "We need to talk about what happened."

Bingo.

"I knew you'd say that."

Hawthorne's brow furrowed. He put his hand on the headrest behind her and turned toward her. "I'm not leaving here until I make sure you're all right and I get an explanation."

Wanting company, she nodded. "I could use some coffee. Come inside and stay awhile?"

He looked surprised that she didn't argue.

Once inside the condo he volunteered to make coffee and she went to her bedroom and changed into navy sweats. She savored the soft pile carpet under her bare feet, and decided not to wear socks.

Looking in her bathroom mirror, she saw dark circles under her eyes that hadn't resided there earlier. Another deep shiver hit her. Shell shock. She'd felt like this after finding Barb floating in the pool, so it stood to reason she'd feel the same after having a vision of Barb's last moments.

Why now? After all these years the scene emerged to torment her with no warning. Rubbing her cold hands together, Tammy knew she had to tell Hawthorne what had happened. One thing could be said about him; he could wrangle a confession from a mute monk.

Now or never, Carter.

The aroma of mocha java teased her nose as she walked down the hall to the kitchen. When she entered, Hawthorne reached high in a cabinet to retrieve big mugs. Muscles flexed under his green T-shirt, and she admired the taper of his back where wide shoulders narrowed to his trim waist. His jeans molded without remorse to his fantastic butt.

Man-oh-man. She was loosing her gourd thinking about him this way at a time like this.

Now she'd discovered how protected she felt in his arms, she had to admit it had fired her senses with pleasure as well as comfort.

Face it. The man turns you on whether you want him to or not.

Hawthorne turned around, his expression sober and curious.

Tammy moved farther into the kitchen. "Thanks for making coffee. It smells great."

He leaned back against the counter. "So you really are a mocha java fan."

Tammy attempted a smile. "You've found me out."

"I haven't found out everything I want to know."

So he'd decided to head right for the point. "Let's go in the living room."

Settled on the couch, they sipped the strong beverage in silence.

Finally she put her mug on the coffee table. "You want to know what happened tonight."

"Wouldn't you want to know if you were me?"

Tammy nodded, and when he turned toward her again, she knew she had Hawthorne's full attention. She stared at a snow-capped mountain scene framed on the wall across from her. The scene had always soothed her; she could almost sense the wind blowing icy over the tall crags, the fresh, chilling scent of winter touching her nose.

"Tammy?"

"Sorry. I zoned out."

He glanced at the picture. "You want to be there?"

"Anywhere but here."

"What's wrong with here and now?"

"I don't want to talk about this."

"But you will."

"You're not going to believe a word of it."

"Why not?"

"It's too strange. Too weird for you."

Hawthorne's gaze pinned her. "You know I'm not leaving until you tell me why you called me, terrified, asking for help."

Guilt pricked at her again. "I shouldn't have called you."

With an exasperated groan, he slid closer on the couch and put his arm around her. The sudden movement startled her. "I already told you I was glad you called. Spill it, Carter, before I do something drastic."

Tammy wanted to push him. She wanted to experience his extreme measures. She saw his ruthless side in his eyes, demanding immediate answers. She took a solidifying breath. "I had a vision."

That formidable frown hardened his features again. "A what?"

"You know how Joe picks up people's scents?"

Wariness entered his eyes. "I know he *believes* he picks up scents. But scents are all around us all the time, and we get so used to it sometimes we don't smell it until much later." He sniffed. "Right how I can smell the mocha java, and your perfume. Subtle but enough for me to recognize it. That doesn't mean what he smells came to him psychically."

"Can you reserve judgment for one moment?"

Reluctance lined his face, but he nodded. "All right."

Using his arm around her to secure confidence, Tammy said, "Last year when Kiley was kidnapped, and you and Joe were in the hospital…there was more to finding Kiley than just Joe and Scott. I helped Joe find her."

"What? How?"

"The scents that Joe picks up usually come at random. But that night he tried to control his abilities and to some extent he succeeded. When he told Scott that Kiley was being kept in a place that was similar to a dungeon, I was the one who came up with that hypothesis. We worked together."

Hawthorne held up one hand. "Let me get this straight. You can do this psychic mumbo jumbo?"

His tone irked her. "I helped him find Kiley. Most of the time I can't control the visions. They come when they want."

Tilting his head to the side, he asked, "So why haven't I heard about these visualizations before?"

"Give me a break, Hawthorne. You said it was crap. Why would I tell you when you've got an attitude?"

He grunted. "An attitude?"

When she gave him a stony face, he relented. He squeezed her shoulder and his gaze turned from incredulity into understanding. "I'm sorry. I really want to know. Please tell me."

Where to start?

"Since I was a kid I've had visions of things that have happened before I could possibly know about them. Precognition. Most times it came upon me without warning. I didn't cultivate it. I didn't want it."

"Seems it would be an asset to know things beforehand."

"Imagine it, Hawthorne. Imagine your parents having a child who could tell them someone was good or bad by looking at their colors. Imagine the fear a child would have seeing and hearing things that had no reasonable explanation. Especially when your parents didn't support you and you had no one to turn to."

His fingers caressed her shoulder. His puzzled expression increased. "Colors?"

She looked at her hands. "It doesn't happen much anymore. I mean, it didn't happen for years because I pushed it away. Lately, when I'm with people, I see colors. Those colors sometimes surround them like an aura. If the person is in the area but not in my sight I'll see the colors around the edge of my vision. Like a tunnel."

"Uh-huh."

His doubtful utterance amplified her discomfort. Even his arm around her didn't reassure. Tammy plunged onward. "That day you called and I was still at the office, I'd just had a vision. The phone call...I saw hues of red."

"What does red signify?"

"It depends. Sometimes blood. Maybe death. Or passion."

"Three big differences."

"I didn't say it was an exact science. With the colors I get a feeling, so I can usually tell which of those three things the red represents. That time, when I answered the phone, I felt death and depravity. Before you got to the office, I felt it again and knew the man was in the building."

When he didn't speak she said, "You came in seconds later."

His arm shifted, and she looked up at him. Implacable, his mouth showed displeasure and astonishment. "You think I'm the man who was harassing you?"

"Of course not. What I don't understand is why I felt that red...that hot and powerful death and hatred. There must have been someone out in the hallway a short time before you arrived."

Hawthorne shook his head. "None of this makes sense to me. I hear what you're saying but it sounds incredible." He rubbed his chin in a classical masculine gesture. "I want to believe you, but..."

"But?"

"Tell me the rest."

Disappointed, yet knowing she had to continue, Tammy looked away again. "The visions drain my energy, pulling my resources outward into the atmosphere like a sponge."

"You're saying it makes you physically ill?"

"Almost every time." When she glanced at him his expression remained unreadable. "I hate the images. I don't want to feel this way. I don't want to know these things. They're horrible."

Hawthorne's hand slid from her shoulder to the back of her neck. Heat filled her face as the strength and warmth in his fingers made her shiver in reaction. Tammy knew enough about male-female interaction to know she treaded a high wire with Hawthorne. They'd flirted and sent sparks off each other. A touch to the head conveyed intimacy. He took his arm from around her, and the withdrawal came emotionally as well as physically. Putting his elbows on his knees, he leaned forward and covered his face for a moment.

Hawthorne shook his head and sighed. "I think this calls for more coffee."

As he took both their mugs back to the kitchen, Tammy wished she could make him understand. Instead it was happening again. Every man she'd met freaked if he discovered her secret, so she'd learned to hold that covert information deep inside. Only her trust in Hawthorne had made her speak. Now, as he moved about the kitchen, she couldn't be sure anymore.

Restless, she left the couch and entered the kitchen. He turned and gave her a fresh cup of java. She looked at the mug and its cartoon mouse design.

"Maybe I should start looking for new mugs. Seems like I have way too many cartoons in my life," she said.

As Hawthorne's gaze lightened, she appreciated his calmness. Even if he didn't believe her, he didn't ridicule her the way her father had done more than once when she'd had a vision. He hadn't turned away from her like other boyfriends.

Other boyfriends. Oh, no. Come on, Carter. Hawthorne is your buddy. Not a maybe boyfriend, not a real boyfriend, not a lover.

"I like your cartoon collections. Do you have matching plates?"

Sheepishly she nodded. "You got it."

His grin went wide and relief filled her deep inside. "Next you'll tell me you've got matching wine glasses."

Grinning, Tammy let him wonder.

"You're kidding?" he asked.

"Champagne glasses. I have Mickey and Minnie Mouse champagne glasses."

Hawthorne laughed, throwing back his head and revealing the strong column of his throat. He put down his mug before he spilled coffee.

"Wanna see 'em?" she asked playfully.

"No, that's okay. You can show them to me some other time. I'll bring the bubbly."

His suggestion fired her confidence. "You're on."

His jovial grin faded. "Tell me more about these so-called visions."

The camaraderie she'd experienced moments before blinked out like a light bulb. "There you go again, Hawthorne. So-called visions? And you expect me to spill my secrets to someone who ridicules me?"

He sighed heavily. "Damn it, Tammy, that's not what I'm doing."

"Sure sounds like it to me."

He threw up his hands. "All right, all right. So every time you get these visions, you get sick?"

"That's right. That's why I was saying I didn't have the flu and why Dr. Jacobssen wouldn't find anything wrong with me."

Pacing to the middle of the room, he put his hands on his hips. "That's what Joe was talking about. He called me the other night."

Surprised, she asked, "What did he say?"

"He said you're in danger."

Dismay made her sigh. "He said I should tell you about these visions before he did. I guess he couldn't hold back."

"I didn't believe him."

She shrugged. "Why should you? According to you the scents he smells don't exist."

Hawthorne glared. "You're twisting my words. He smells things, but they're not because of psychic ability."

Deciding to take another strategy, she said, "He's crazy."

"You were the one defending him the other day, saying he's not insane."

Tammy thought about telling him more, about revealing what she'd seen of her sister's death. She hovered in that indecision zone for a millisecond, and it passed before she could take the leap.

Instead she said, "He's mistaken that I'm in danger." Tammy leaned back against the counter. "In that case I'd say he did overreact. The visions and the fainting aren't dangerous in themselves. Inconvenient maybe."

Her shift caught his attention, and Hawthorne's gaze fastened on her with an intensity that infused her with a wild heat. "What aren't you telling me?"

"I'm not backpedaling."

He moved closer. "I don't believe you."

Tammy shrugged, injecting as much apathy into the movement as she could. "I've told you everything."

When he edged closer she became aware of all those scents and sights and sounds he'd mentioned moments ago. Her heart beat a tremulous, crazy rhythm, her breath coming shorter. Tammy drew in the spicy, masculine scent that defined Kyle Hawthorne.

His T-shirt molded his pecs, and each slow stride he took made her heart accelerate. His boots made soft thuds on the floor. No used denying it. Hawthorne had charisma. Right now that mind-bending formula completely foiled her concentration. What had they been talking about?

When he progressed to within inches of Tammy, his frown unnerved her almost as much as his nearness. Why was he looking at her that way? As if he wanted to eat her up in one swallow. With his hands. With his lips.

She'd gone over the edge. Certifiable.

Heat flushed her cheeks and spread down her neck.

Tammy couldn't stand the knee-buckling electricity that arced between them. "Hawthorne, what are you thinking?"

"I'm thinking you're headed for trouble."

She decided to assume he meant her visions. "So you believe Joe that I'm in danger, but you don't believe in how he knows that information?"

"Whether you have visions or not is irrelevant. If you're in danger, I want to know it."

Irritation made her clutch the counter behind her. "If you don't believe me, then this conversation is pointless."

He groaned and closed his eyes. "I knew it. I knew it would come to this."

"What?"

"That you'd deny it once again. Damn it, maybe I'm wasting my time."

That hurt. "Thanks."

"I mean wasting my time asking you questions."

"I'm surprised you've given up so soon."

"Your safety isn't a game."

"Thanks for caring. But if you can't understand what's really happening, then what difference does it make?"

He leaned his hands on the counter on either side of her, and she thought she might die. His nearness did overwhelming, crazy things to her equilibrium, as powerful and unnerving as any vision.

"Because you can trust me, Tammy. I'm your friend. Promise me you'll come to me if you need help. Call me if you ever feel afraid. Don't hesitate." His gaze turned serious and almost frightened. "When you phoned tonight and then the call cut off, I thought something...I thought you'd been assaulted. Robbed or who knows what else. It scared the shit out of me, babe. I was shaking so badly when I got in the Jag that I couldn't get the key in the ignition on the first try."

Hawthorne's admission stunned her. The look in his eyes told all. Real fear. Genuine concern.

With barely a breath between them, the air hummed with energy and each pulsation in her body beckoned her closer. "Why, Hawthorne, I think there's a tender heart under all that tough guy bravado."

His eyes narrowed, and she knew she'd said the wrong thing. "Just remember what I said."

"Okay," she said softly, daring to keep eye contact with him. What she saw there frightened and excited her so much, she could hardly suck in a breath. "Where do you go when you're afraid?"

"I go to friends. I'd like to think I could come to you. Could I?"

"Yes, of course." She swallowed hard. "Anyone else? Any special...woman?"

"There hasn't been anyone special in years. When I was in the military I moved around a lot and didn't find many woman that interested me."

"Wow."

He chuckled. "Wow?"

"I mean…well…are you saying you didn't date much?"

"Not much."

Incredible. Women of the world get a clue! "That's nuts. You're—"

Tammy managed to stymie the stream of words before she did serious damage.

He hadn't moved away an inch, and thoughts of stalkers and visions departed. Turmoil roiled within her, forcing her to acknowledge the facts. Hawthorne defined prime male sexuality. No, even that wasn't a good enough descriptor.

"I'm what?" he asked huskily.

Tammy licked her lips and admitted it. "You're funny and nice and interesting and—" She gulped. "Sexy."

Chapter 12

Hawthorne's eyes widened and his mouth popped open. Then his gaze settled into an inferno that sent Tammy's pulse rocketing.

She saw his shield go up, and when he moved back a couple of steps, Tammy knew she'd said the wrong thing yet again. Hawthorne sexy. *God, now he knew she found him attractive.*

His rueful grin looked like her old buddy Hawthorne, not the sexy, incredibly handsome man who had almost kissed her. *He'd almost kissed her before.* She'd wanted him to kiss her. Damn it!

"Thanks," he said finally. "No woman's ever said that to me before."

"You've got to be kidding?" She almost squeaked the words in her amazement. "A woman would have to be completely blind not to—"

She cut herself off again. *Maintain, Carter. You're going into the deep end of the ocean without a breathing apparatus.*

His smooth chuckle came from deep in his chest, a low rumble that sent her libido strumming again. How ridiculous. She'd never felt this attracted to a man in her life, and it frightened her. Why now? Because he'd rescued her from the bogie man and held her close?

"Where were we?" he asked when she said nothing for several moments.

"Friends," she mumbled.

Did she see a smug look twisting his lips? Perhaps her admission had stroked his ego and he'd gotten his jollies from her clear confession that she found him attractive.

His dubious expression disappeared. "Speaking of friends, there are some people I'd like you to meet. Are you free Saturday night?"

Tammy's heart almost did a back flip. "Yes. Why?"

"I've known Lincoln and Sandy since I was a kid back in Chicago. They moved to Colorado several years ago. They invited me over for a barbecue this weekend."

His suggestion, coming from nowhere, surprised and pleased her. "I'd love to meet them."

"Great. I'll pick you up."

She wanted to ask him if this qualified as a date, but the words lodged in her throat. Better to play it cool.

Silence pressed in, and she looked away, finding the quiet awkward. Hawthorne came toward her again, and for a breathless time she thought he might gather her close. Man. How she wanted that. Her need disturbed her deep in her gut.

He reached out and cupped her cheek with his big, warm palm. "Are you going to be all right?"

Tammy wanted to tell him not to go. "I'm feeling great thanks to you."

His hand left her face. "Make me another promise. I'm giving you space now, but someday you'll tell me everything. What's really happening and what frightened you tonight."

Two things had frightened her. The knowledge he cared for her, and the realization that Barb's killer lurked near.

Launching into an explanation wouldn't resolve anything at this point, and so she nodded. "I'll tell you some other time."

When he left she sank onto the couch and trembled, the entire evening's events shattering her to the core. Tears came again, but this time no one was there to comfort her.

Hawthorne didn't hesitate. Following deep-seated instincts, he made sure he parked out of sight on the street, but close enough he could observe Tammy's condo. The late hour didn't matter. He wouldn't leave her.

Sheet lightning blanketed thunderheads in the east as they drifted away from Denver, an eerie background for the full moon as the luminescence covered the ground in a silver glow.

Figures. Weather like this and a full moon riled up weirdoes with regularity. But even if the moon hadn't been full and the weather rocky, he'd still have guarded her. Tammy needed protection, whether she knew it or not. Hawthorne's instincts fired, raising the hair on his arms. Danger stalked Tammy. She wouldn't admit it, and for some reason she cloaked the real reason.

Deep inside he knew he must keep her safe, and he'd do it without her permission. Something spooked her tonight in that parking garage.

Visions. Right. He wouldn't question Tammy's cleverness because he knew her intelligence came razor sharp. Why would she concoct stories about visions?

Face it. She's got you worried big time.

He'd almost suggested that he sleep on her couch, but he knew that wouldn't work. Number one, she would have laughed and told him to leave. Second, if he'd stayed in her presence any longer, he would have kissed her. In the kitchen he'd been drawn to her, almost out of control with a desire to pull her into his arms and kiss her until they both went up in flames. Yep. He danced on the edge, amazed and aroused by the chemistry. When he confessed that worry for her had made him fumble for his keys, he hadn't lied. Hell, no.

Hawthorne watched her house through the night, a yawn or two cracking his jaw. As the hours passed he craved another cup of coffee, needing the caffeine to boost his sagging energy.

He didn't fall asleep, his concern and his military training too ingrained. He could stay up forty-eight hours without faltering. When her bedroom light came on in the middle of the night, he almost went to her door to see if she was all right.

Instead he waited, and an hour later the light went off. Soon he'd call Mrs. Taggert and tell her what he wanted to do. Mrs. Taggert might say no, and as his employer she'd have the right. But once he explained, he didn't think she'd flinch. Tammy was his new bodyguard assignment, and he wouldn't take no for an answer.

Sweet Magnolia. Ah, the wonderful, gentle, sweet girl.

As he watched the video of Sweet Magnolia made all those years ago, he wondered what she'd think if she knew how much he craved her. Craved her *then*.

Yet he knew she wouldn't care. Too wrapped in that bodyguard man. Just the thought of her messing with that man made his heart crumple like ashes.

But last night he enjoyed seeing her fear. When he'd gotten to a safe spot he'd let the pleasure gush. Almost as good as killing. Almost as hot and tasty as blood. He'd grunted and groaned and left his mark on a concrete pillar like the one she'd leaned against.

The same one she leaned against when she'd gone all nutty. He'd watched her eyes go big and horrified. Staring into space like a dummy in a store window, she'd gawked, mouth open, unblinking. He wondered in that moment if she'd died. He'd almost gone to check, but then she'd twitched and moved.

The video flickered off and caught his attention. Damn it! He'd missed the whole thing dreaming about Sweet Magnolia. Rewinding the tape, he played it again. Again. Again. Again. Until he memorized the words as he had learned it before. As he had memorized her sister's plea for mercy. Each time he played the tape, he pretended he'd never seen it before. Each time the tape stopped, the pain of its ending ate at him like a million hungry beetles biting his flesh. Sadness would engulf him. Depression and self-anger would return. He pressed the rewind button on the remote until the tape reached the beginning. He touched the play button. Watching the tape for several seconds, he realized he felt a need.

Putting the tape on pause, he went to the minuscule kitchen and rummaged in the fridge. It was back there somewhere. The cold wisped out, touching his fingers like death. He thought that must be what death was like. Cold. Hard. Forever. And he'd rather other people die because he wouldn't. Everyone else first because it would take a hell of a long time before everyone died. It would mean he'd live for billions of years.

He realized his hand touched a milk carton. As he opened the container a sour stench penetrated his nose. He tossed it at the open trashcan and it missed, spilling milk on the floor and across his new leather loafers.

He screeched, spilling foul words. He stomped on the wet floor, splashing more milk onto his shoes. Milk footprints littered the cracked, dirty linoleum. Red split his vision, purple and black along the edges. Rage boiled, filtered, trembled, and needed an escape.

Someone would pay.

Sweat ran down his face, and he searched in the fridge again as his breath rasped in his throat. Had to be there, behind the rotten lettuce. Gotta be there behind all this crap. Finally he saw it. The beer bottle.

He took the brown, long-necked bottle and fingered it. He'd peeled the label off long ago. Been keeping this one for the right time. Felt like now was right.

Maybe. Possibly. He didn't know.

A growl issued from his parched throat. So much want. Yet nothing satisfied. Gently, slowly, he put the bottle back in fridge. Not now. It wasn't the right time.

Soon he'd know when.

Going back to the tape, he saw the video player had started again because it exceeded the pause time. Sweet Magnolia cavorted on the screen with her bitch sister. Splashing in the cleansing water. The water would always cleanse the wicked. As it had purified Barb Carter, so it would bathe Sweet Magnolia one day.

Tammy bolted out of sleep, fumbling for the bedside lamp. Whimpers tumbled from her lips before the blessed light destroyed the darkness. Three o'clock in the morning. Shoving her hands through her hair, she shivered with vague memories of monster men walking through her dreams. They lingered, attached to events of last night like leeches. Such dreams drained her of security and energy. Tomorrow she'd feel as if she'd been run over by a tank.

On the edges of her dreams she remembered a man's rage. Crying over spilled milk? Tammy shook her head. A cliché. He'd screamed. Pure anger had launched through his brain until he'd seen the red. Until she saw red.

She reached for her journal, the one she wrote in when the mood struck. She hadn't written for several days, and now the words poured, as the pen seemed to gain life and dumped words almost faster than her hand could move.

When her hand cramped she closed the journal and headed for the bathroom. Tammy moaned as fear paled her cheeks and dampened her eyes. Okay. So the dread hadn't disappeared with the writing this time. She saw the distress measured in every line of her face, in her wild, rumpled hair. Splashing her face with cold water, she wondered if the chill could awaken her from this living nightmare.

People wouldn't accept her if they knew what she saw. They'd thought Barb was loopy for having visions. The disapproval and knowing looks had hurt Barb deeply.

Back in bed, Tammy switched off the light. Must get sleep. Must forget the horrible sights popping into her vision whenever she closed her eyes.

As exhaustion threatened to drag her into sleep, she remembered Hawthorne. What would he do if she called now?

No. She couldn't. Weakness would get her nothing but heartache. Besides, why entrust him with her deepest fears when he hadn't believed her? Shivering, she closed her eyes and tried to remember what Hawthorne's arms had felt like. The heat and comfort lulled her to a fitful sleep.

Tammy woke to the jarring jump of rock and roll as her mouse clock played a Jimmy Hendrix tune.

"Shut up!" She reached for the clock and it fell on the floor and stopped shrieking. "Blast it!"

Less tame words followed.

Pressing her palms against her temples, Tammy flopped to her back and took several slow, deep breaths. She knew why a throbbing headache dogged her. Residuals from yesterday's experience in the parking garage.

Slowly, as every bone in her body protested, she slipped from bed and started for the bathroom. She got no further than washing her face and brushing her teeth when the doorbell rang.

She muttered a curse, her heart tripping in her chest. Maybe yesterday and last night had rattled her far more than she had admitted to Hawthorne. "Coming!"

The doorbell rang again as she patted her face dry and headed to the front door. She looked out the peephole. "Well, I'll be. Surprise, surprise."

She unlocked the door and swung it wide. "What do you want so early in the morning, Hawthorne?"

He leaned against the door jamb and winked. "Now isn't this a hot picture."

She glanced down at her short, baby blue sleep shirt with the red heart over her left breast. Three buttons had come undone down the front, giving him an excellent view of the shadow between her breasts. If he looked closely enough, he'd see more than that. Hastily she buttoned the shirt and stepped back.

"Get your butt in here." A small smile touched her lips. "And stop trying to flatter me."

He grinned as he strolled inside. "Aren't *we* grumpy today?"

"Humph."

As Tammy headed for the kitchen, intent on a cup of coffee, Hawthorne followed. "What's wrong?"

"I have a mother of a headache and I almost broke my mouse alarm clock."

She'd just scooped the coffee into the filter basket and added water to the coffee maker when his hands came down on her shoulders. Stiffening, she started to turn around. "Hawthorne, what—"

"Wait." He kept his hands firmly on her shoulders. "I can make you feel better."

The low, warm huskiness in his voice made her skin tingle, as did the gentle pressure as he massaged her shoulders.

"I've got a headache, not a shoulder ache." Tammy closed the basket on the coffee maker and flipped on the switch.

The steady, soothing heat of his hands relaxed her, and she wanted to sink back against him. But no. That wouldn't do. Not at all. Instead, Tammy allowed Hawthorne to continue, and she realized seconds later he'd worked his hands into the collar of her shirt and now touched bare skin.

"What are you doing here?" Tammy's senses thrummed as his fingers stroked. "It's early."

"Checking up on you."

She made a disgusted noise. "I told you last night I'm fine. You're worse than a mother hen with new chicks."

"I called Mrs. Taggert and told her you wouldn't be in today."

She broke out of his hold and whirled around. "What?"

He held his hands up in surrender. "You need rest. You're not well."

"I'm fine. I thought we covered all this last night"

Hawthorne put his hand to Tammy's forehead, and his palm cooled her skin. His touch made her realize how hot she was. Even with nothing more than a sleep shirt and panties on, the room seemed warm.

"I'm not sick." *At least not the way you think.* "It's a reaction from the visions. I always run a low fever after the visions."

"If that isn't sick, I don't know what it is."

Once again his hands dropped to her shoulders. Outside the sun barely peeked above the horizon, and the landscape sparkled with dew as first rays of light hit the windows. Tammy should have been cold with naked legs and feet, but instead the intensity of Hawthorne's gaze kept her burning.

What woman wouldn't go nuts for a man that made blue jeans and a T-shirt look the way he did? Hell's bells, he looked good enough to nibble. Tammy wanted to stay right here and absorb the stable, comforting glow. Even stubble along his jaw looked gorgeous in a cocky, hard-edged way.

"Wait a minute. Aren't those the clothes you were wearing last night?" she asked, peering at him closely.

"Yeah."

"Don't tell me—" She halted, the implications sinking in quickly now that she was half awake. "Did you stake out my condo last night?"

Deadpan, he crossed his arms. "Yep."

"Why?"

"Because I've got a feeling, and I know better than to go against my gut."

"I thought you were starting on that new case...that floozy socialite."

Hawthorne chuckled. "Adelia's pretty nice. She's funny, bright, and pretty."

A slow burn of something possessive welled within her, and she didn't like it. "Funny and bright. Pretty."

"That's what I said." The grin on his wide mouth notched her "crazy meter" up another centimeter.

Mimicking his stance, she crossed her arms. "She's also rude, opinionated, loud, and aggressive."

"You and I are opinionated. Sometimes we're rude, loud and aggressive with each other."

"Well...not with other people. I mean, not usually. Only with people who deserve it."

Hawthorne's eyes sparkled with a wicked light. "Maybe she thinks the people she's rude, loud, and aggressive with deserve it."

She let her head fall back as she stared at the ceiling for a moment. Sighing she said, "Why do you always have to be the devil's advocate?"

He didn't say anything until she looked back at him. "Because it's fun. It keeps people moderate. We all need a little reality check from time to time." Slowly he eased into a serious look. "Otherwise we spend too much time locked in our own little world.

It's cozy and sweet in there. It's safe. But we start to lose touch. Pretty soon we're blind to everything but our own pain."

Hawthorne's words sank into Tammy like heavy cream, rich and full of meaning. Yeah. As if she understood him because of a simpatico between them.

No. Maybe it's your freaking imagination. Ever think of that, Carter?

His smile regenerated. "Darrel is guarding Adelia."

"What? Why?"

"I'm working for you instead."

"What?"

"You sound like a parrot, babe."

"Don't call me babe. I get a little vision of that talking pig."

"Hey, Babe is cute. You should be flattered."

"Oooo," Tammy groaned, stepping up to Hawthorne as if she might smack him one. Practically nose-to-nose, anger grilled her guts. "You don't mean what I think you mean?"

"After the incident at the office yesterday, and the calls you've been getting, Mrs. Taggert is worried."

"And?"

"I'm your bodyguard. I called her this morning and told her I wanted to be assigned to you."

Hawthorne's confirmation doubled her fears. She couldn't let him put his life in danger for her.

"But that's crazy." She threw her hands up. "That would mean you'd be living here. We'd be together twenty-four hours a day."

"Exactly." He brushed her nose lightly with his index finger, as if punctuating a sentence. "Starting right now."

She groaned and put her hands up to her temples.

"Come on. It won't be that bad."

But it could be very bad. Very bad if Hawthorne finally understood what it meant that she could see into the twisted imaginings of a killer.

"It's nuts. I don't need a bodyguard because I fainted."

"You called me last night with terror in your voice. I heard it and I saw you unconscious in your car. I'm going to figure out what the hell is going on and I'm going to protect you."

Tammy worried the end of her sleep shirt.

Hawthorne glanced down, and she realized her action had pulled the shirt farther up her thigh; he had a clear view of a lot of skin. Primordial male appreciation flickered in his gaze.

"Stop that," she said.

"What?"

"Starring at me like I'm a…a…"

"Yeah?"

"Like I'm…"

"Spit it out. My feet are growing to the floor here."

"A side of beef," she sputtered.

"I see. You're doing this to distract me from what we were really talking about."

She gave his chest a mild push with one hand. "You're the one staring at my legs!"

Hawthorne caught Tammy's hand and held it to his chest. Slowly he reached up with his other hand and cupped her cheek. Soft tendrils of need trickled over her skin as he caressed her.

"Hey, I'm sorry. If it makes you uncomfortable…." He released her and stuffed both his fists into the pockets of his jacket.

"Of course it does."

He moved away and the heat of his body left with him. She wrapped her arms around herself and shivered. Suddenly the floor was icy cold, and a draft touched her legs.

"I was out of line and I apologize," he said from several feet away.

Hawthorne's contrition came through loud and clear, and Tammy realized she'd overreacted. "It's okay. I know you…I know you didn't mean anything."

One corner of his mouth went up. "Oh, I meant something all right. But I'll keep my hands to myself if that's what you want. I'd rather do that than have you think badly of me."

That did it. Her heart stuttered, then went into rapid fire. Everything within her softened like pudding.

Hawthorne took a step toward Tammy, and she pushed her hands through her hair to keep them from fluttering nervously.

"Let's get one thing straight, Tammy. You're stuck with me—"

"I have to work. I have to volunteer at the shelter. I have responsibilities."

"I'm not talking chances with your life. Pack a bag. We're going to my place."

"What?"

"You're staying with me until this is over. I've got a security system. And unless someone is following you, they won't know where you are."

Resigned that she now had a bodyguard, she said, "Two conditions. I go to work today and continue my volunteer work. I'm not dropping out of life."

For a moment he looked as if he might object. With a reluctant nod, he conceded. "You're on."

Chapter 13

"*Lose the gum,*" Tammy said to Jeannette as the phone rang at the front desk.

The teen made a face and tossed her gum into the trash before answering the phone. "Taggert Security Team. May I help you?"

Tammy sighed and relaxed in her chair positioned next to Jeannette's. Through numerous interruptions, the teen's training had gone well. Earlier that morning people had stopped by to chat and inquire about Tammy's health, and the attention made her uncomfortable. Even Jeannette had acted concerned.

To Tammy's amazement, Jeannette progressed throughout the day, her phone manners and customer service skills surprising. Maybe this hare-brained idea to reform the girl had worked. At least Jeannette possessed a work ethic. Somewhere deep within, she could find and use her strength to survive beyond her turbulent childhood. All she needed was this chance.

Even the teen's clothes choice reflected an attitude change. She'd taken the money Tammy had given her and purchased a couple of five-piece suit combos.

Satisfied and feeling better about the future than she had

earlier, Tammy watched as Jeannette handled some paperwork.

Jeannette slanted a curious look at Tammy. "So, Hawthorne is your bodyguard?"

Tammy put her finger to her lips. "Quiet. That's not for mass consumption."

"Everybody knows. What's the big deal?" Jeannette put her papers down and swiveled her chair toward Tammy. "God, what I wouldn't give for him to guard *my* body."

Gregg Le Blanc came into view. His gaze targeted Jeannette with a predatory gleam. "I can guard your body anytime you want."

Tammy bristled, but she managed to halt a blistering retort. Instead, she stood slowly. "Le Blanc, can we talk in the back room for a moment?"

Jeannette's gaze darted back and forth between them, her eyes wide.

Le Blanc nodded, grin in place. "Anything for you."

"Take over here until I get back," Tammy said to Jeannette.

Tammy hadn't realized until that moment exactly why she felt unease around this man. He'd answered that question in one revealing sentence.

When they reached the back room, she closed the door. Le Blanc's grin grew to ridiculous proportions. For a startling second a blanket of red started at the corner of her vision and nausea pushed at her stomach. It blinked out like a broken light bulb.

"What's up?" he asked, injecting a husky nuance into his voice. That voracious gleam now focused on her.

Taken aback by her vision of his colors, she almost faltered. Instead, when he came close, she didn't retreat. She lifted a finger as she spoke. "Keep away from the girl."

"What?" he asked with a disbelieving laugh.

"Jeannette is a minor and you're a grown man. Figure it out."

He lifted his hands in a halting gesture she'd come to associate with him. "I didn't mean anything by it."

"Joking with me is one thing, Le Blanc, but what you said out there was highly inappropriate. If you do or say anything like that to her again, I'll report you to Mrs. Taggert and your job here will be over. I'm also going to instruct Jeannette to report any suspect action on your part to Mrs. Taggert or me. Do I make myself clear?"

Anger flared in his eyes, and his mouth flattened into a hard line. "Yeah. Real clear."

When he turned and left the room, Tammy's breath escaped her lungs in a rush. She sank into a chair, her legs weakening. Nausea invaded her stomach again, but she ignored it. Nope. This wouldn't do. One way or another, she would get control.

Back at the front desk, she found the area quiet. Jeannette was reaching into her hobo bag when it slipped from her fingers and flopped onto the floor, spilling its contents with a clatter. Jeannette whispered a profanity, and leaned down, panic altering her young features. Then Tammy saw the boxes of pens. Disappointment and a slowly building irritation moved her toward the desk.

She squatted next to Jeannette, and the girl looked up.

Tammy picked up a pen box. "This looks awfully familiar."

"What?" The girl snatched the box from Tammy's hand and jammed it into her bag.

"Let's just cut to the chase, Jeannette." Tammy grabbed Jeannette's purse.

"Hey—"

Tammy kept the bag out of her reach. "Stolen supplies."

Jeannette's features hardened, no remorse evident. "So what?"

"You have the money to pay for what you've taken?" Tammy took three boxes of pens out of the girl's mammoth bag and placed them on the desk. "What exactly did you need the pens for?"

Jeannette shrugged, slumping back into her chair. Petulance gave her a little girl air.

Sighing, Tammy sank into her own chair. She glanced around, hoping no one had heard the conversation and chastising herself for reacting strongly. Waiting until they had privacy would have made more sense.

"If you wanted a pencil or pen, you could have asked me for one of these." She reached over to the pencil cup and held up a pencil with cartoons cavorting along the side. I bought this for myself. I would have gladly given you one or more. What do you need all these boxes for?"

Jeannette colored. "Writing."

Surprise darted through Tammy, and she relaxed, leaning back slightly. "Writing what?"

The girl pulled a sheepish expression and looked down at her naked fingers. She wasn't wearing the plastic rings. Not even one. "I write in my journal every night. Well, almost every night."

Impressed, Tammy said, "That's wonderful. Journal writing is great to relieve stress. Good therapy."

"I don't need therapy."

Tammy shrugged. "And you don't need to steal. You're making money here. You can buy your own pens for home use."

Jeannette's face pinked again and her jaw tightened. "I ain't even making as much money here as I do on the street. What good is this job?"

Resisting the urge to rap the girl on the head with one of the pilfered pen boxes, Tammy sighed. "It's better than getting money for allowing a bastard to use your body."

Jeannette's knuckles turned white as she gripped the sides of her secretarial chair. "Did you scare Gregg away?"

"I hope I did. If he does anything like that again you're to tell Mrs. Taggert or me. Do you understand?"

"What's the difference between Gregg flirting with me and Hawthorne flirting with you?"

Tammy's mouth opened, then closed. She had to word this carefully. "Hawthorne and I are adults. You're a minor and Le

Blanc is a grown man. There's a *big* difference and don't you forget it." Jeannette's tiny shrug and dejected expression surprised Tammy. Where was that fire the girl usually displayed when confronted? "It's not healthy for a grown man to be interested in young girls."

"You going to get him in trouble?"

Tammy shook her head. "I'm not saying anything for now."

Jeannette finally looked up at Tammy. "Thanks. I don't want to get jacked up for it."

"Why would you get into trouble for what he did?"

Jeannette's eyes filled with tears, taking Tammy off guard. Her own throat tightened in empathy.

She leaned forward to press the girl's hands. "What is it?"

"I always got into trouble with my momma when I told on daddy. He…uh…didn't seem to know about it being unhealthy to like little girls."

Tammy's insides roiled, comprehension tilting her world. As her fingers tightened over Jeannette's, a deep blue descended into her vision and she shuddered. *No!* She shoved away the colors, a symptom of empathizing with the girl's feelings. She took a deep breath.

"I'm so sorry, Jeannette."

Jeannette stiffened and drew her hands from under Tammy's. When she said nothing, Tammy decided now was not the time or place to discuss something this personal.

"Jeannette, if you want to talk about this later—"

"No."

Tammy nodded. "All right. Promise to tell me if Gregg does or says anything inappropriate. And you shouldn't lead him on, either." She put her hand out. "Give me the rest of the pens."

The girl excavated the boxes and handed them over. "You gonna tell Mrs. Taggert?"

"Not this time. If it happens again, I'll string you up by your toenails."

Jeannette's girlish smile resurrected, a sincere relief glowing from her gaze.

Tammy's heart lightened as the girl turned back to her work. In the back of Tammy's mind Le Blanc's actions troubled her. She considered mentioning what had happened to Mrs. Taggert, but Hawthorne appeared at the front desk. He announced he had some errands to run at lunchtime, and made Tammy promise not to leave the office without him.

Later that afternoon, after Tammy finished eating lunch in the employee lounge and Alison had the phones, Mrs. Taggert stopped by the lounge.

After summary greetings, the older woman asked, "Did Jeannette own up to stealing the pens?"

"How did you know?" Tammy asked, stuffing her half-eaten sandwich back in the paper bag.

Mrs. Taggert's countenance went grim. "Gregg told me. We can't have Jeannette stealing things and getting away with it. Why didn't you tell me she really had stolen those pens?"

Tammy's blood heated. "Le Blanc is a jerk. I didn't know he'd heard my conversation with Jeannette. I should have waited to talk with her, but the pens had fallen out of her purse, and then he came by and made that indecent remark—"

"What conversation? What indecent remark?"

Tammy closed her eyes and put her hands over her face for a minute. Might as well tell Mrs. Taggert everything now. After relaying what had occurred, Tammy waited.

Mrs. Taggert's unreadable face transformed into disappointment at what she heard. "Seems we have two problem employees here."

Tammy tried for a weak smile. "Hopefully I'm not one of them."

Her attempt at levity failed as Mrs. Taggert flatted her palms on the table. "Jeannette has one more chance. If she steals again, I'll have to release her."

Tammy nodded. "That's only fair. What about Le Blanc?"

Mrs. Taggert's eyes hardened, her lined face weary. "I'll give him another chance as well. He's a highly qualified bodyguard, Tammy."

"But that doesn't supersede what he did, I hope."

"Of course not." When Tammy didn't respond, Mrs. Taggert moved away from the table and poured a cup of coffee. She sipped it before speaking. "I'm surprised you didn't balk when Hawthorne decided he was going to guard you."

Tammy turned around in her chair. "I did, believe me. I wish you'd kept him on that other assignment. With *that* woman."

Mrs. Taggert chuckled. "*That* woman? I take it you don't like her."

Tammy shrugged. "She's always devouring Hawthorne with her eyes."

"And that bothers you?"

Afraid she knew the direction the conversation was going, Tammy said, "All that flirting in public. It's just not appropriate."

Mrs. Taggert almost choked on her coffee. Coffee dripped over the side of her "boss lady" mug and she wiped it with a paper towel. "Sounds like I need to take you and Hawthorne aside and discipline you."

That got Tammy's attention. "What?"

A mischievous smile darted around the corners of Mrs. Taggert's mouth. "The heavy artillery you've been firing at each other lately. I swear on some days you *couldn't* cut the sexual tension with a chain saw it's so thick. Now that he's guarding your body, I expect it to get worse." As she walked out the door she tossed back, "Keep the flirting out of the office environment."

Stunned, Tammy stared at the open door. Her boss, the woman who ran a tight ship but didn't mind humor in the work place, had never insinuated that Tammy had done anything inappropriate with Hawthorne in the office.

Wrinkling the napkin on the table in front of her, Tammy groaned. Wonderful.

Fine. She wouldn't have the entire office thinking she'd done something indiscreet. From now on the so-called sexual tension between her and Hawthorne would be non-existent.

Tammy stood at the sink in the back room when Hawthorne approached her at the end of the day. After five o'clock, most everyone had gone except for Hawthorne, Le Blanc and Mrs. Taggert.

"Been avoiding me?" Hawthorne asked.

Tammy about left her skin. She whirled around and glowered. "Don't sneak up on me like that."

Not looking the least contrite, he closed the door and came forward. "You ready to leave? I'm starving and I've got a steak in the fridge with my name on it. I've also got a great bottle of Merlot—"

"Open that door."

"Why?"

Without fail his proximity petrified what brain cells she had left. "Don't."

With a massive frown he asked, "Don't what?"

"We shouldn't be in this room alone."

Hawthorne put his hand on the cabinet behind her. His movement, naturally, brought him way too close. Her heart started that undeniable flutter.

"Out with it. Did something happen today to make you edgy? Did you get a threatening phone call?" he asked.

"Nothing like that." She explained about Jeannette and then about Le Blanc's inappropriate comments to the teen.

"I thought the guy was a bit weird, but that's way over the line." Hawthorne's frown increased. He chewed on his lip for a second, his dark eyes storming. "I'll talk to him. I think he's still here."

He started to walk away, but she panicked and grabbed his arm. "Don't you dare, Hawthorne. Let it be." Her action drew him near, and she lowered her voice. "Enough stress for the day. Let's just get out of here."

Hawthorne's gaze trapped hers as she kept her hand on his arm. "Something else happened today that I don't know about."

Nervous, she licked her lips. "We have to watch our own behavior in the office."

"What do you mean?"

"Mrs. Taggert said that she's noticed...um...sexual tension between us." Tammy felt her stomach tighten. "Her exact words were that the tension is so high she couldn't cut it with a chain saw."

She expected him to laugh and deny it. Instead his gaze went thermonuclear, snatching her breath and her senses along with it. "Damn."

"Exactly," she said a little breathlessly.

"What do you think?" His gaze did a slow thoroughfare over her face. "Do you think there's something going on between us?"

Heat surged from somewhere deep inside and she trembled. "We can't stand here like this. What if someone came in?"

One corner of his mouth twitched. "Don't you ever take a chance?"

"Not in the man and woman game. It's too risky. I've had enough tag team sports to last several life times."

A smug, slightly superior expression brightened his face. "Could have fooled me."

Indignant, she put her hands on her hips. "I beg your pardon?"

"If there is sexual tension between us, it isn't just me participating."

"We don't have sexual tension." Tammy's body stirred, languorous and lazy, refuting her words. "This thing, whatever it is, it can't be sexual. We're...you and I are just friends. Good buds."

As his hands slid up to cup her elbows, her hands landed on his chest. Whether to hold Hawthorne away or to draw him nearer, Tammy couldn't be sure. His warmth, the heat of his rock-hard muscles under her fingers about drove her wild.

"You can deny it all you want, babe, but there *is* something between us and it sure as hell has nothing to do with being just friends."

Flustered she said, "Then we need to rein it back and get control. With these visions of mine I don't need any more raging colors running through my mind." When he said nothing, she continued. "We can't flirt, we can't touch, and we need to keep this professional."

His face tightened. "I said I'd stay away from you back at the condo, even though the sight of you in that shirt about gave me a heart attack. And I will. At least you can stop denying what you feel."

"I don't feel anything," she said firmly.

"Are you afraid of me?"

Her brow furrowed. "Of course not. I always feel very safe when I'm with you."

Hawthorne's deep chuckle vibrated into her body. "I'm not sure if that's good or bad."

"Danger is always bad, Hawthorne." She considered his life. "Peril is a part of your existence. When you were in the Marines it was, too. I don't want that for my life."

"As your bodyguard I'm keeping danger away from you. Unless that's not what has you worried here."

"I'm not really that adventurous a person. In any arena, if you know what I mean."

"As long as you don't close your feelings off to those who care about you."

"I'm telling you how I feel right now. You've been great. A fantastic friend. You're even working for me."

One of his thick, dark brows angled upwards. "I suppose you want me to call you boss lady now?"

Tammy managed a smile. "Yeah, and I'll have to do some serious damage to you."

His answering smile faded and he took a deep, almost shuddering breath. "But you're right. We need to step back. And if the real boss lady says enough is enough, we'd damn well better listen. Agreed?"

Disappointment and relief mingled inside Tammy like two opposing chemicals promising a chain reaction explosion.

"Agreed," she whispered.

Gently he slid his hands up to her hair, cupping her head in his powerful hands. "Just one thing and then it's hands off."

Hawthorne's touch, warm and tender, unraveled her control. "What's that?"

Tammy knew the answer as his head lowered.

"I'll be damned if I won't know exactly what I'm giving up."

Excitement danced in her stomach. Her legs lost strength and turned to elastic. Dumping pretense, her eyelids fluttered closed as his mouth found hers.

Chapter 14

Tammy had heard all the adages about the earth moving and stars falling. She'd heard it and hadn't believed a word.

That was until Kyle Hawthorne kissed her.

His touch came sweet, almost chaste. But the taste of his mouth, the desire behind it twisted her world and inflamed her imagination for more. How long had she wanted this? How long had she pretended to the outside world that she *didn't* want this?

Tammy recognized that Hawthorne leashed his primitive desires, and now he showed her but a tiny part of the whole.

God help her if he ever released all he had to give.

Her hands cupped over his. Hawthorne's lips feathered across her mouth in another touch so gentle it might never have existed.

Every brush of skin against skin heightened her needs. Tammy's breath escaped in an excited rush, quickening. Desire licked secret centers in her body. Back and forth his lips caressed, not demanding, but presenting a gift. Tears sprang to her eyes. Warm. His mouth lingered so warm.

Every tight, aroused fiber in her body released, sinking into the moment and destroying other considerations. She ached for

Hawthorne until she hurt. Who cared if someone might walk into the room? This kiss was worth any price.

Before she could respond properly, he pulled away, taking several steps back. Hawthorne's eyes gave new meaning to scorching. To her delight and terror it looked as if he wanted to yank her into his arms, smother her mouth, and stake a much stronger claim. Primordial wishes flushed his face and his mouth parted as his chest rose and fell.

"Now I know what I'm missing," he rasped. Shaking his head, he started for the door. "I'll be in my office when you're ready to leave."

When the door closed behind Hawthorne, she tottered to a chair and sank down.

"Oh. My. God." Covering her hot face, she relived the kiss again.

No doubt about it after that mind-melting kiss. The chemistry she'd ignored since she first met the man could not be denied.

More than anything else, she pondered *what ifs*.

What would have happened if he'd yielded to the desire she'd seen etched across his face moments ago?

The last two days defined hell on earth.

For Hawthorne, two days in Tammy Carter's presence...in the same house with her day and night...yeah, that qualified as purgatory.

As Hawthorne drove toward Lakewood, Tammy said nothing. She stared out the window where infinite space seemed most likely to exist, caught up in her own world. He was glad. Overjoyed she hadn't said much to him the last two days and had stayed clean away from touching him. She spent time in her bedroom reading. He exercised, channel surfed and read. Still, for the entire two days he'd experienced that ripple. The unmistakable knowledge that by kissing Tammy he'd unleashed yearnings he couldn't capture and confine.

If Tammy had touched him once, even accidentally, he might have finished what he'd started in that back room in the office. Imagining what might have happened if they'd been alone in the office drove his temperature into the stratosphere. He would have tasted her deeply, explored. Not some light kiss but—

No. Time to get a grip.

Hawthorne tried not to replay those moments. Remembering the hot, incredible softness of her mouth hardened him to stone in seconds. Hawthorne's jaw ached from gritting his teeth too often, and his heart thumped wildly whenever she entered the room.

Hormones.

That's all it was. Nothing more complicated or less. Yeah, that was it. The danger of discovery had sent him over the edge and he'd kissed her.

This is getting too damn serious. Way too complicated. Once Tammy is safe, I'll turn my back and forget that I want her.

Problem was, he didn't know if he could turn his back when the time came.

He returned all his thoughts to driving. The land rippled with hills as he neared Lincoln and Joyce Gillman's home. As usual for the Rockies, thunderheads already crested the mountains. With the temperatures predicted to peak in the upper 80's he'd worn a tank top with his shorts. If Lincoln and Joyce suggested they sit on the back porch and enjoy the summer, he'd be ready. Tammy wore a purple dress with three-quarter sleeves, and it skimmed her body down to her trim ankles. His gut clenched whenever he looked at her feet encased in white sandals. How could a woman so simply dressed send his blood pressure skyrocketing?

When they reached the house, he anticipated great conversation and good food. He hoped visiting with his old friends would distract him from obsessive thoughts about Tammy.

Pulling into the circle in front of the stucco Southwest style home, Hawthorne turned off the Jag and climbed out of the car. He rescued the food basket from the trunk; Tammy had insisted on making peanut butter and butterscotch chip cookies.

He sniffed, the aroma of the barbecue cooking in the back yard making his taste buds fire to life. As Tammy followed him up the sidewalk, her expression seemed subdued, and he wondered if she'd remain quiet all evening. He rang the doorbell, and seconds later Joyce greeted them. Grabbing him in a bear hug, Joyce planted a fat kiss on his cheek. Her sixty-five-year-old face looked remarkably unlined for her age, her grey eyes sparkling with good humor, her rounded body garbed in a denim dress with short sleeves. Her curly salt and pepper hair tossed around her shoulders as wind gusted under the porch.

Joyce pulled back from his hug. "We haven't seen you in over two weeks. Some big case keeping you occupied?"

Hawthorne didn't have to force his grin. "You got it. Joyce, this is my colleague Tammy Carter."

Joyce's expressive face broke into a wider grin. She shook Tammy's hand warmly. "I'm so pleased to finally meet you."

Tammy's eyebrows winged up, and he wondered if she caught Sandy's reference to "finally" meeting her. Had he talked about Tammy that much?

Joyce led them into the living room just as Lincoln entered the room from the backyard. "'Bout time you got your butt over here. Joyce and I thought maybe you'd gone on some slippery assignment."

Hawthorne grinned. "Sorry, I should have called you." He glanced at Tammy. "Things have been busy."

Lincoln's speculative gaze volleyed from Hawthorne to Tammy. "All is forgiven if you've brought dessert."

In his friendly way, Lincoln slapped Hawthorne on the back, then hugged him. Lincoln's enthusiasm and looks reminded

Hawthorne of a happy Afghan dog. Long silver hair fell about his shoulders. A short beard, gold trimmed glasses on his long nose, and his spare, tall body added to the illusion. True to form, he also wore cut off jeans with holes in them and a peace sign emblazoned on the ass. His T-shirt proclaimed, "Bite me."

"Lincoln, this is Tammy Carter," Hawthorne said, impulsively touching her shoulder.

Lincoln shook her hand with enthusiasm, accepting her compliment on their house with a grin. "Thank you, dear. Say, Kyle, come out in the back with me. I've got something to show you."

Hawthorne had no choice but to follow the high-energy man through the sliding glass doors to the back.

The older man held his hands out and turned in a circle in the middle of the large yard. "What do you think?"

They did this every time he visited. Never idle of hand, Lincoln always kept a house project in progress. Hawthorne gazed about the yard with the impeccable lawn and high fence. Lincoln and Joyce had planted shrubbery around the fence and various flowers grew in beds dotted about the yard.

"You've got me. That bird fountain was here the last time, the hummingbird feeder the time before that. What's new?"

Lincoln slanted a disbelieving look at him. "Give me a break. You don't see it?"

Hawthorne surveyed the yard again. "Nope."

Sighing heavily, Lincoln moved to the flaming barbecue and tossed another burger on the fire. "You're hopeless. I put in a brick row around the flower beds."

"You did all that in two weeks?"

Flipping a burger, Lincoln said, "Retirement gives a body time to do what it wants." He dug around in a cooler. "What'll you have?"

"The usual."

Lincoln tossed him root beer, then grabbed a can of cola and popped the top of the can. "Speaking of doing what you want, have you asked that young woman out yet?"

Hawthorne stiffened, the abrupt change in topic unsettling him. "What young woman?"

"Don't be dense, boy, you know who I'm talking about." Lincoln gestured with his spatula toward the closed sliding doors. "Tammy. I'm glad you brought her by."

He really had talked about her too much if Joyce and Lincoln had picked up on this incorrect idea. As a delay tactic he took a long sip of his drink. "She's just a friend."

Groaning and closing his eyes, Lincoln tossed the spatula down on a paper napkin on the table next to him. "If I hear one more person use that overworked excuse I'll scream. Just a friend? That's what we used to say back in the sixties, man. That's what they say in Hollywood. Get over it."

Hawthorne sniffed. "Uh-huh. Well I was barely out of diapers when you were using that excuse, but in this case it's true. Tammy and I *are* good friends."

Lincoln said nothing for a moment, and then he reached in his pocket and took out a hair tie, sweeping back his grey hair. "That's what I used to say about Joyce, you know. When she hightailed it to that women's college I hadn't told her how I felt about her. I figured after all those years she already knew." He put his cola by the spatula and stuffed his hands in his pockets. "We didn't see each other for a year. Pretty soon her letters came less and less. I felt like hell. I was loosing her."

"So you danced around the subject too long. Why?"

"We were damned fools. She thought I didn't love her and I thought she didn't love me. We were so afraid the other one would reject us if we said how we felt."

Sharp suspicion worked into Hawthorne like a splinter. "Let me guess. One of you finally confessed your love."

Lincoln nodded. "I dated others, she dated others. It took almost two years for us to get it through our thick skulls that we were meant for each other."

Hawthorne didn't know where the conversation would lead, but it made him uncomfortable. Suddenly the root beer tasted flat. Hawthorne put the can down on a plastic table near the grill. "How did you come to your senses?"

"I realized that I missed her like hell and arranged for us to meet again over a weekend. I knew when I looked at her that I'd always loved her. Even if she rejected me, I had to take that chance."

Hawthorne stared at the cooking meat. He grabbed the apron off the table and slipped it over his head, using the motion as an excuse to think.

He took the spatula from Lincoln. "Give me that. Never did know how to cook hamburgers. Always did burn the hell out of them."

Lincoln chuckled. "Hit too close to home, did I?"

Lincoln wasn't usually so glib. Correction. He didn't talk about gooey subjects. In other aspects he came right to a sharp point. "I'm not an idiot, Lincoln. I know there's a reason why you're telling me this. Spit it out."

Lincoln's grin exploded on his face. "I can tell you've got deep feelings for Tammy. All I'm saying is don't make the mistake I almost made. Give in to it, man. If you love her, tell her."

"Tammy and I aren't in that type of relationship." Hawthorne inhaled deeply. "And we aren't going to be."

"What's stopping you?"

"You're ruthless."

"And you're avoiding my question."

Hawthorne slanted a warning glance at his old friend. "If you weren't such a good friend and like a father to me, I'd tell you to get your ass out of my business."

Lincoln chuckled. "Okay, okay. I get the hint." He nodded toward the house. "Don't let her get away because you're afraid."

"Me? Afraid? Hell, I've done about everything. Jumped out of airplanes. Rappelled out of helicopters. I've been shot, shot people, been in a car wreck." He muttered a curse. "I'll be busted up by the time I'm your age." He shrugged. "What's there to be afraid of?"

Lincoln snatched the spatula out of Hawthorne's hand. "Sometimes there are dangers that have nothing to do with getting busted up. Maybe you should get out of this business."

"Most of the danger was while I was in the Marines, not my current job."

"I'd call almost losing your life last year pretty damned dangerous. Still…maybe that's why Tammy hasn't approached you. Maybe that's why she doesn't want to get involved."

"She's not interested in me that way. Where is all this psychology coming from? I've never seen you like this."

Lincoln put a hand on his shoulder and grinned. "Sorry, buddy. I was just thinking this week about when I first met you."

Hawthorne didn't want to think about his teen years. "Why? What's that got to do with me and Tammy?"

"Back when you were a kid you didn't make decisions based on your gut. Remember how much trouble you got into?"

Hawthorne walked to a cushioned lounge chair and sank into it. "You've got it backwards. That's what used to get me into trouble. My gut. My 'do it if it feels good' attitude."

"Those are two different things. You were doing what you thought everyone else wanted you to do. Now you're doing the same thing, but this time the topic is love."

Amazement made Hawthorne pause. He almost laughed. "Are you trying to tell me to get in touch with my feminine side?"

Lincoln laughed. "I'm just telling you to trust your instincts. They're probably right on the mark."

Meat juices sizzled, filling in the gap left by ceased conversation. Wind blew tumbleweeds over the fence. While Lincoln chased the weeds, Hawthorne stared into space and contemplated. Through the sliding glass doors he saw Tammy and Joyce sitting in the family room conversing with serious expressions.

Doubts and confusion battled for supremacy. In the end, he knew, he'd come to the same conclusion he always did. Gut feelings or no, Tammy could never be his woman.

Tammy saw Hawthorne looking at her through the sliding glass window, a strange intensity in his eyes. She didn't know what he saw when he looked at her, but the attention gave her unmistakable pleasure. She held that stare for several seconds, aware that Joyce noticed the exchange. Then Tammy looked away, her heart thundering with a strange excitement.

So far she'd kept her mind off him by enjoying her conversation with Joyce. Friendly and cheerful, the woman's sense of humor acted as a balm on Tammy's sore heart. When she'd entered the house she'd felt a warmth and goodness that permeated her soul. Joyce's colors had touched the outside of Tammy's vision, a gentle pink and green. Lincoln's bold yellow and orange colors came stronger, but neither person's hues made Tammy in the least ill. She felt comfortable here.

Now, if she could train her thoughts away from her disturbing relationship with Hawthorne.

"More lemonade?" Joyce asked her from the leather love seat.

"No, thanks." Tammy slid one hand over the couch she sat on, admiring the butter soft dark green leather.

The other woman's soft voice eased any apprehension Tammy might have experienced. Her curiosity about the Gillmans overflowed. "Hawthorne didn't tell me how you all met."

Joyce smiled and took a sip of her lemonade. "He's quiet that way. Always has been. I told him once when he was a teen that he'd drive the girls nuts when he grew up. He leaves people hanging until they can barely stand the suspense."

"That describes him perfectly," Tammy said. She winced, afraid of her own impulsive words. "I mean, he's the proverbial silent type. Sure, he jokes and he's friendly, but there's something...something so deep about him that a person just can't touch."

Tammy stopped, realizing that she rattled onward without considering what she said or how it would sound. Embarrassed, she clamped her lips shut.

Joyce's gentle expression altered to big smile, and she leaned forward. She put her sweating glass on a coaster. "Go on. Don't worry about giving offense."

Tammy shrugged. "He's a mystery to me in so many ways. I think he likes it that way."

"I'd say he's so used to protecting himself from pain that he doesn't even realize he's closed himself off." Joyce hesitated, as if unsure how much to reveal.

Tammy didn't want to enter forbidden territory, but her curiosity shifted into gear. "Some mysteries are never solved."

"Ah, yes. But in his case, I think he *needs* to be opened. There's a great man in there, Tammy. Trapped and wanting to get out. He's like a son to me. Did he tell you that Lincoln and I were foster parents to him and his sister for awhile?"

"No," Tammy said softly. Astonished, she continued in a rush. "Never. He's never said anything about his family."

Joyce nodded. "I think you've become as close to him as anyone."

Surprised by the woman's assessment, she swallowed hard. "Me? We're just co-workers. We pal around a little."

Disbelief curved the older woman's lips into a doubting smile. "That's what I mean. Most people don't pal around with him. He has to trust you. If you're joking, having a good time with him, that's about as deep as it gets. Sometimes I'm afraid for him."

Feathery alarm tickled somewhere in Tammy's psyche. "Why?"

"He's got so much love to give. Lincoln and I know he loves us, but Kyle needs more. We want to see him happier than he is. Fulfilled."

Tammy's discomfort must have shown. Amazing that Joyce would tell her this much, expose this much to someone she didn't know. At the same time, Tammy's gratification and pleasure came full circle. With a deep, profound sense of destiny, she knew she must understand Hawthorne. Had to decipher the motives behind the man who had given her the most tender, soul-shattering kiss she ever received.

Joyce shifted so that she faced Tammy. "Am I scaring you with all this, dear?"

Tammy nodded, clasping her hands in her lap. "A little. I shouldn't invade his privacy."

"He's talked so much about you I just assumed..." Joyce shrugged.

Pleasure rocked Tammy. "I didn't realize he talked about me at all."

Joyce stared at her half empty glass. "He's never spoken about a woman the way he has about you. That's why I don't mind telling you this." Joyce heaved a sigh. "He's come through the proverbial school of hard knocks." She pointed to the fireplace mantle. "Take a look at those photos up there."

Tammy rose and walked to the mantle. Among a tangle of pictures of Joyce and Lincoln on various adventures, a photo of Hawthorne as a younger man caught her attention. Even years younger, Hawthorne commanded respect. Garbed in the dress uniform of a Marine, he looked proud and defiant. Another photo showed him as a preteen, his face scrubbed clean of adulthood but tinged with unusual maturity.

Fascinated, Tammy touched the corner of his Marine photograph. "Something's missing. No other family."

"It's a long story, dear. When he was ten his mother died during her third pregnancy. Toxemia."

Tammy pressed her fingers to her mouth. "Oh, no."

Joyce's eyes saddened. "After that his father went wild. Drinking, taking up with prostitutes. Then his father disappeared one day. Went crazy with grief apparently. Kyle lost his father only six months after his mother."

Tammy's stomach clenched in sympathetic agony, tears stinging her eyes. She gazed at the photographs again. She saw it now. That indefinable ingredient that reached out from his teen picture. "I can only imagine how abandoned he must have felt."

"That's only half of it. He'd adored his father. This was back in Chicago. He and his sister Selina—she was eight at the time—were placed in a foster home until their father could be found." Joyce rose from her seat and joined Tammy at the fireplace. "Problem was, no one could find Abraham. Kyle got into fights at school and the foster parents didn't want him or Selina. The kids were shunted off to another family."

Tammy couldn't imagine Hawthorne as a juvenile delinquent. "Please, go on."

Joyce's eyes glittered with sadness. "Selina was the vulnerable one and Kyle tried to protect her. When he caught their foster brother molesting Selina, he beat the boy. The foster brother probably would have raped her if Kyle hadn't heard her scream and came to her rescue."

A wound opened in Tammy, burning as she heard Joyce's words. Chills assaulted her and she rubbed her arms. Stepping away from the fireplace, she retreated to the couch. "Oh, my God. That poor girl."

Joyce closed her eyes, shaking her head. When she opened them she looked at the photos on the mantle. "Kyle was about fifteen by that time. The family didn't want either Kyle or Selina and neither Kyle nor Selina could prove the other boy had tried to rape her. Before they could be moved to another foster home, Selina ran away."

"Hawthorne must have been frantic."

"He searched everywhere. The authorities couldn't locate her." Joyce leaned back against the mantle. "We found her first. You see we used to volunteer at the St. Patrick's Catholic Church soup kitchen many years ago. That's where Selina turned up one day. Here in Denver. Cold. Tired."

Joyce rubbed her arms, as if she felt that cold now.

Tammy's attention hung there, waiting to hear more. Finally Joyce spoke again.

"We saw something in the girl, even under all her defiance and surliness. Unfortunately, before we'd met her, she'd turned to prostitution."

Tammy frowned, a deep ache eroding her heart. "I know a girl like her. She's only a teen and she's now working at the security agency with me."

Joyce nodded and moved back to the love seat. "Hawthorne told us about her. I think she reminds him of his sister."

Had Jeannette's appearance at the soup kitchen brought horrible memories back for Hawthorne? "But what happened to Selina?"

"We took her in to live with us with permission from social services."

"Thank goodness."

Joyce's features saddened, and for a moment Tammy thought the gentle woman would cry. "For a time it was good. Selina was out of prostitution. She finally told us about Kyle and we located him in Chicago. By that time he'd located his father. What he found was devastating."

Before Joyce could continue, Hawthorne opened the sliding glass door and stepped inside. His gaze danced from Tammy to Joyce with curiosity. "Hamburgers are ready."

Joyce and Tammy held an awkward silence.

Lines formed between his eyebrows. "Everything okay?"

Tammy stood and injected a happy mood into her face, even though her mind remained staggered by all she had learned. She headed toward the sliding glass doors.

"About time, Hawthorne." She slipped her arm through his and he had to follow her. "I'm starving."

Chapter 15

Much later that evening, long after the sun had retreated, Tammy and Hawthorne arrived at his place.

As they slipped through the garage door and into the utility area, Tammy stifled a yawn. She headed for the living room, flipping lights on as she went. Though weary, she was filled with an edgy anticipation she didn't understand.

"Tired?" Hawthorne asked softly as he trailed behind her.

"Two glasses of wine," she said through another yawn.

"Did you have a good time?"

She removed her light cardigan. "Great time. Joyce and Lincoln are a hoot. And very sweet. I can see why you love them."

She headed toward the kitchen, intent on a glass of water and an excuse to avoid his gaze. Unfortunately, he followed. "They've been good to me."

As she opened the refrigerator and removed a jug of purified water, she smiled. "Did you know you're following me around like a puppy, Hawthorne?"

He shrugged, and his muscles rippled in ways that excited her. His grin looked rueful. "I wanted to ask you some questions."

Tammy took a plastic tumbler from a cabinet and filled it. "Water?"

"No, thanks." He watched her put the container back into the refrigerator.

"Fire away. What's on your mind?"

He crossed his arms, his gaze uncertain, almost exposed. She figured that this strong, gritty man had a marshmallow core deep inside. Part of her wanted to reach for him and forget consequences. The damn man had wedged his way into her thoughts and desires until she connected with him far more than she liked.

"What was Joyce telling you about me before I came inside the house and announced that the chow was ready?" he asked.

Oh, oh. "How did you know we were talking about you?"

One dark brow tweaked upwards. "Gut feeling. Lincoln told me I should use it more often."

He meandered closer. Hawthorne up close and personal. *Not a good way to keep your sanity, Carter.*

"Tammy? You're not answering my question."

Retreating to the breakfast nook, she sat on a small, white wood chair. He slid into the one next to her, his big frame swallowing the space. This close his fresh, musky scent tantalized her. *Why couldn't he have sat across the table?*

Tammy swallowed hard. "She told me about your early years. Up to a point. When you came inside the house she hadn't finished telling me all about it."

His startled expression deepened into something close to resignation. He passed a hand over his face and sighed. "Joyce told you."

"I was very surprised that she did. She hardly knows me."

Another half smile tugged at his mouth. "Joyce is a good judge of character. She must like you very much."

Tammy decided bold was better. "She said that you talk a lot about me."

He closed his eyes for a few seconds, and when he opened them, his gaze showed indisputable interest. Maybe, if she stretched the meaning, she could imagine his face revealed affection. "I guess I do. I talk about all the people at the office."

Slam-dunk.

So much for being special.

Tammy cleared her throat, trying to dislodge her disappointment. "Are you angry she told me?"

"No. I trust you."

She grinned. "Thanks. Coming from you, that means a lot."

Amusement brightened his gaze. "Don't push it, Carter."

"Joyce was about to tell me what happened after your sister told them you lived in Chicago. After Selina was molested and then ran away to Denver."

Tammy saw fresh pain enter his eyes. "I'd been in juvenile hall awhile after beating that bastard that hurt her. I was enraged. Selina and I were very close."

"You lost control when you beat the boy."

"You got it. I was stupid. Even though the asshole had punishment coming to him, I screwed up. Instead of trusting in the system, I took things into my own hands." He shifted in his chair again, as if nervous. "Months of my life disappeared, and I couldn't be there to protect my sister."

Stunned by his assessment, she shook her head. "You were young and made a big mistake, but how did you harm your sister's life? You were only trying to protect her."

"I understood the repercussions. I *chose* to do wrong. I allowed my anger to dictate my actions for a long time."

"That doesn't explain how you hurt your sister."

"If I hadn't been in juvenile hall, I could have protected her from herself. She ran away because she had no guidance."

Tammy could see guilt eating away at him like a rot. What torture his guilt must have caused him. Watching him berate himself wounded her as well.

"Hawthorne, you can't blame yourself. Ultimately it was her decision to run away, just as it was your decision to beat that boy. Like you said, you understood the consequences. Selina must have, too."

Deep in his dark eyes she recognized a similar culpability within herself. Hadn't she been responsible for Barb's demise? Maybe not directly, but through her own disbelief, she drove her sister into an early grave.

"You still have remorse all these years later?" she asked, wanting to connect in a small way.

Hawthorne leaned way back, so far he could prop his head on the back of the chair in the ultimate casual pose. He gazed up at the ceiling, and Tammy thought he looked like a little boy. Amazing how this incredibly masculine man could turn from raw to tender. Hurt and anger sped through his face.

"It's not all black and white. I try not to think about it much. My childhood wasn't exactly the greatest experience."

"You're a well adjusted man."

A big smile spread over his face. "I've got my moments."

Ever the mystery man. Tammy wanted to crawl inside his skull and learn those secrets one by one.

"After I left juvenile hall they wanted to put me with a new family, but by that time Selina had run away and had a head start. It made it harder to find her."

"She must have felt so alone and helpless when you were locked away. How long were you in juvenile hall?"

"Six months." He shifted in his chair, his eyes murky with recollections. Sprawling with his legs apart and his hands clasped, he stared vacantly at the table. "By the time I got out she'd already made her way to Denver. While I looked for her, I started searching for Dad, too."

"That's incredibly brave for one so young."

"I'd matured some. While I was locked away my outlook

changed. I wanted a chance to make good. I stayed with the foster family while I looked for my real family."

"Were they good people...the new foster family?"

Hawthorne's shrug said it all. "They were all right. Most of my searching for Dad and Selina I did on the side. Then, right before Joyce and Lincoln located me in Chicago, I found my dad." Leaning forward, he put his arms on the table. "When I found him he wasn't really my dad anymore. Not the man I remembered. He was well on his way to oblivion. Cirrhosis of the liver had set in. I had two weeks with him at the hospital while they tested and poked and prodded. He had multiple things wrong. Malnutrition, organ damage. You name it, he had it. The street hadn't been kind to him."

Empathy threaded through her like needles, pinching and burning. "He was homeless. That's why you volunteer at the soup kitchen, isn't it?"

She touched his forearm and his hard muscles stiffened under her fingers. Hawthorne looked down at Tammy's hand, then covered it with his own. His skin felt deliciously warm, the silky hair on his arm caressing her palm. Linking with his gaze, Tammy relished learning this complex man's secrets even as her stomach tightened with sympathy.

"Dad blamed himself for everything that had gone wrong in the family. In the end he died from disease and no desire to live." Hawthorne inhaled deeply, and she saw his vulnerable side emerge again, a bottomless hollow. "I begged him to fight for his life. I told him I'd help him. You know what he said?"

Almost afraid to ask, she watched as he took another shuddering breath to bulldoze his emotions into order. "No."

"He said he'd done enough damage and that life was too painful for him. He didn't...he didn't want to burden my life."

"He didn't cope with life, he ran from it." Tammy shifted her fingers under his grip and when he took his hand away, she automatically removed her own fingers from Hawthorne's warm forearm. "He must have been a good man when he wasn't in that state. Before the alcohol and other things took him from you."

His intense gaze assessed her, as if he couldn't believe how open they'd become. "How did you know that?"

"Joyce said you loved your father very much. I can't picture you loving someone just because of blood relation. He had to be a great dad at one time."

Hawthorne closed his eyes again, and she wondered if he imagined his childhood in color, scent and sound as she often did. "I have memories of good times. Mom was wonderful—"

He fell into silence.

She headed back to guilt, needing to talk about it as much for herself as for Hawthorne. "Isn't that what you're doing, Hawthorne? You're repeating your father's mistake by blaming yourself for other people's actions. It explains your need to help at the soup kitchen and your cynicism about Jeannette and Joe."

Hawthorne shoved his fingers through the short strands of his hair. "They're examples of the same neglect. But they're different people from my father and sister."

Tammy nodded and leaned back. "Agreed. But I've never experienced what you have and it's freed me to believe there is hope for Jeannette and Joe. You've decided they're doomed."

He hit her with a laser point stare. "You've got secrets of your own, honey."

Even his endearment, said in a silky warm voice, couldn't distract her for more than a second. She tossed him a grin. "We're not talking about me here."

"You're relentless, Carter."

"It's one of my better traits."

A chuckle rumbled from deep in his chest. "I'd say there are a lot of fabulous things about you."

While pleasure darted through her, she said, "Back to the subject at hand."

When his smile disappeared, Tammy experienced a moment's regret for pulling him away from flattery. "You're paying a sort of penance for not saving your family. Unlike your father you've survived that penance. Yet you're determined to pay for this perceived wrong for the rest of your life."

His gaze came back to her with a comprehending light. "You have to know it all, don't you?"

"Everything."

Once again Hawthorne shielded his eyes, putting his hands over his face. "My sister was out of prostitution for some time. She even started helping me at the soup kitchen. Then she...." He swallowed hard, moistening his lips. When he lowered his hands, a spasm of incredible pain rippled over his features. "Selina and I had a stupid fight. You know how siblings can be."

Oh, yes. She knew. Knew and didn't want to remember, but understood that by sharing with him she'd move closer to understanding her own demons. "Of course."

"She ran out of the soup kitchen in a huff. I thought she'd gone into another part of the church." Hawthorne moved again, dropping his clasped hands between his knees, his head hanging down slightly in supplication. "I never saw her again." He made a scoffing noise. "And you know what? I don't even remember what the damned argument was about. Can you believe that?"

Unable to bear seeing him in pain, Tammy rested her hand on his shoulder. Her sensitive nature couldn't hold against his emotional onslaught. Moisture trembled on her lashes and fell on her cheeks, but he didn't see her tears.

"They found her...they found her body in a dumpster a block away," he said hoarsely.

"Oh, no," she murmured, more tears flowing free.

"She'd...she'd been raped and strangled by her former pimp. He was never tried or convicted."

Tammy knew words wouldn't help. Hawthorne's muscles under her fingers felt hard with tension. She started a caressing motion on his shoulder, soothing and hoping he'd relax. She'd discovered his heart wasn't made of granite. Tammy suspected all along that he possessed depths of feeling she'd never witnessed. Now that she saw them, felt them, it roused her interest to greater heights. Frozen in place, he looked dejected and hurt. The woman in her wanted to kiss him senseless, hold him in her arms and tell him all would be well.

Dangerous thinking. Very dangerous thinking about him this way. Although disturbed by her feelings, she pressed onward.

She took a shuddering breath and tried to curtail her tears. "What did you do then?"

"Joyce and Lincoln kept me from losing it. I didn't even cry," he rasped.

Tammy felt his ache, his memories bombarding her as if she could absorb them into herself.

He continued. "I graduated from high school. My grades weren't good, so getting into a college straight away was out of the question. I joined the Marines and with tuition assistance managed to get my bachelor's in History."

"You did good," she said with a sniff.

Hawthorne looked up and obviously he could see the sadness moistening her cheeks. "God, Tammy. I'm sorry. I didn't mean...."

His stood with a jackknife quick move, the chair scraping against the floor. The noise jolted Tammy from the web their intimate conversation had wrapped around them.

He moved to the kitchen window, leaning on the edge of the sink with his palms. "I didn't mean to make you sad."

"I know you didn't, but it couldn't be helped. I sometimes do that. My empathy comes on strong." Trying for a lighter mood, she stood and joined him at the window. "Don't blame yourself for that, too."

The house went quiet. Outside a warning roll of thunder heralded a storm building in the night. Tammy wondered if he experienced the same tension she did. It drew around them, an entity, curling up her spine, tightening her muscles and fluttering in her stomach. Fear? Uncertainty? A latent desire? She couldn't say.

Hawthorne turned toward her and a smile played with the corners of his lips. "You're really something."

Glad for the mood change, she eased into their old pattern. "Is that a compliment?"

"A very big compliment. You look tired. You've had a hard week."

"Yeah. It's been a bitch."

He laughed, and the genuine amusement in his eyes removed lingering traces of sadness. Silence came again before Hawthorne spoke. "You know you're going to have to tell me what's happening with you. I'll get it out of you one way or another."

Fatigue and emotional burnout made her waver. Despite her tiredness, she managed a smile. "Do you want me open a vein right here and now?"

She saw the thought race through his expression, but then he shook his head. "I'm letting you off the hook this time. Why don't you get some sleep?"

Before she could do something stupid like reach up and kiss him, she moved toward the kitchen door. "See you in the morning."

As she headed down the hallway to her bedroom, a lightness of heart descended on her. Hawthorne had shared a piece of himself. She was approaching an abyss, knowing if she grew closer to him she could fall. And fall very hard indeed.

Outside Hawthorne's house, the man hid. So many other nights he hid outside Sweet Magnolia's condo, waiting in case she ventured out.

He watched the night. Time moved with archaic slowness, generated by the persistent progression of thunderclouds pushing across the mountains. Deep in his bones he felt it come across him. The need. The want.

Every compulsion he experienced clawed forward. He wanted to crawl, walk, run to the house and break down the door.

Sweat trickled from his armpits, the salty pain worrying his thoughts. Yeah, he'd even dreamed about doing Sweet Magnolia's little whore friend. Jeannette O'Connell, little Bo Peep in wolves' clothing, had hoodwinked Sweet Magnolia into thinking she'd changed. But he knew. He'd had her once…had screwed her deep and decided to let her live. Lucky, lucky girl.

Rolling down the car window, he drank in the heady ozone of approaching lightning. Above almost anyone he'd met, he could smell storms. Not the water. The energy. Cloaked in darkness, he watched as the storm boiled overhead. Lightning illuminated roiling clouds, and he laughed. He'd tried to hold the ritual within for years, his impulses to destroy the unworthy held in check until he found Sweet Magnolia.

Failing always hurt.

Every time he bungled he cried, then went to his house and broke one or two things. He drank from the beer bottle and the water of life after the screaming and breaking. Drinking from the bottle cleansed from his soul what had lurked in the women. By touching them he'd polluted himself. By killing them he saved himself. By killing them he also failed. A double-edged sword if ever there was one. But the compulsion never ceased.

So he messed up, but he rejoiced in the heady agony of the screaming, breaking, and drinking. Kill Sweet Magnolia too soon and he'd lose whatever chance he'd established to break the cycle. All his planning, from his first kill to his last, would fail.

The need gnawed, twisting his intestines with nervous jumbles. Her scent, her shape, her silk warm looks, the cinnamon in that red hair...all gave him sinister desire. All tantalized him to the precipice, calling him to jump. Destroy and renew, kill and let live.

He smiled, drinking in the rain, fast approaching. Power rammed through his veins. Omnipotent, he could defeat his own desires and destroy anyone else's lust with his decree from higher powers. He chuckled in triumph. There'd never been a man like him before nor would there be again.

As thunder chased behind a broad lightning slash, he opened his car door and headed across the street toward bodyguard man's sinful den.

Tammy saw the red obscure the night, turning her dreamless slumber to nightmare.

Once again her sister went through the motions of inviting the killer into the house. Tammy wrestled with her terror, hoping to shake the dream. Everything within her screamed to run, but she followed in the path of her sister's murderer.

Roaring filled her ears, and she looked through the executioner's eyes and saw thunderheads spit lightning. A bolt headed straight for Barb.

Tammy jerked from slumber, a shriek parting her lips.

Seconds later a form burst into the room, and another scream ripped her throat.

Chapter 16

"Tammy!"

Light blazed from the ceiling fan light in the guest room.

Relief hit her as she recognized the man standing in the doorway, his weapon held in front of him. Semi-crouched, Hawthorne scanned the room.

"What's wrong? Are you all right?" he asked, his frown fierce as he straightened.

Trembling, she nodded. "Nightmare."

He strode across the room and laid his weapon on the bedside table. Settling on the edge of the bed, he assessed her with a worried gaze. Clad in a denim shirt and jeans, his hair rumpled, he looked as if he'd slept in his clothes.

Lightning brightened the room, and the lamp overhead flickered. Thunder growled.

She jammed her hands through her hair. "I'm sorry I woke you up."

"I fell asleep on the couch. That scream scared the hell out of me."

Another tremor shuddered through her body. "I'm sorry. I'm fine now."

"Tell me about it."

Tammy shook her head. "It's ridiculous."

He reached out, touched her face. She realized tears dampened her cheeks, and a burning sensation assaulted her throat.

"Come on. What was the dream about?" He swept his thumbs across her cheeks to remove the tears. "You'll feel better if you tell me."

"I need a cup of tea or something to calm me down." Tammy realized her stalling tactics wouldn't last long with this man.

He stood, and as she climbed from bed Tammy remembered that she wore a spaghetti strap tank and matching tap pants. His gaze slid down to the tank top. Settling on her breasts, his gaze traced the rounded fullness with unmistakable interest.

"Hawthorne," she said softly, half reprimanding, half amused. "What the hell are you doing?"

He winked and then perused the tap pants and her bare legs. "Okay, you caught me. I realize this isn't the time or place to say this, but you look great in those tiny scraps, Carter."

Aroused and amused by the compliment, she made a scoffing noise and headed for the door. "Tiny scraps my ass."

She thought she heard a stifled choking sound coming from behind her, but ignored it. Acknowledging that he found her attractive made her nervous in about a dozen ways.

Tammy settled on a glass of water, deciding the caffeine in tea would keep her awake. She knew, though, that recalling the dream would do far more to keep her wide-eyed.

They went into the living room, sinking onto the couch. As she sipped the icy water, he remained quiet.

"You don't have to stay up with me. You must be tired," she said.

Hawthorne slipped his hand behind her neck and kneaded tight muscles. "Tell me about the dream."

Startled by the intimate touch, she almost spilled her water.

She didn't protest, though. His touch created pleasant stirrings of excitement.

How could she confess the dream without explaining the visions? "I dreamt about my sister, Barb."

Lines formed between his brows and his mouth dropped into a frown. He nodded, keeping up the stroking rhythm of his fingers.

She'd struggled for years not to discuss her sister in any way. Giving in to his request hurt like a tooth extraction. "Barb was older than me by a few years. She'd be thirty-five now."

After swallowing more sips of water, she put the tumbler on a coaster and turned toward Hawthorne, effectively removing his touch. On a roll, she decided to divulge more information before he could ask. "I coped with the grief by going to college. I moved into my own apartment, paid most of my own way. I couldn't bear to be in our house...where it happened."

Tammy pushed a strand of hair behind her ear. "She was in the house alone one Saturday. Mom was visiting friends. My dad and I had gone out for ice cream. We even brought some back for her—" She cut herself off, her throat closing around the painful memory.

"Why was she home alone?"

Tammy shrugged. "She said she had homework to do. She was training to be a vet, and she always had assignments. I think there was more to it. But I couldn't prove it at the time and I can't prove it now."

Hawthorne reached forward and took her hands in his. His hands gave her strength. "Evidence?"

"Intangible evidence."

She was aware she skirted the edge. Much more and she'd tell him things he wouldn't believe. She wanted to tell him everything but she couldn't. Withdrawing her hands from his, she rubbed together the fingers he'd touched.

"What do you mean by intangible?" Caution and uncertainty laced his voice.

"She'd told me that someone new had come into her life. A man. Barb told me this a week before she died. She didn't tell me how or when she'd met him, and my life was so busy I didn't ask." Tammy sighed. "I wasn't interested. Barb flirted outrageously and she dated heavily."

"So you figured this was just another one of her flings?"

"Exactly. Now I know if I'd taken the time to find out who this man was, she might be alive right now."

He leaned forward, his gaze hardening. "Now wait a minute. There's no way you could have known—"

"Yes, I could have." She shivered. Remembered sorrow, fear, and the coolness of the room combined. "Looking back days after she died, I had clues. I could have prevented her death. No doubt in my mind. My mother was devastated and never really recovered. She was like your father. She ran from her pain rather than dealing with it."

"What happened to her?"

"The stress ate her alive. A series of health problems stored up over two years and she died on the anniversary of Barb's death." Though she'd hoped spouting the information would keep emotions at bay, buried anguish buffeted her with powerful waves. She sucked in a painful breath. "Pneumonia brought her down. I saw her waste away."

Raw and aching, her feelings flowed, moving her to say more. "She didn't want to live. I begged her, just as my father did, to fight on. Like your father she chose not to and the pneumonia destroyed her far more easily than it should have for a woman that age."

Hawthorne tilted his head. "I thought I'd seen something more than sympathy in your eyes. You really do understand what I felt about my father."

Tears threatened again, backing up in her throat. "Oh, yes. Unlike you, I *am* responsible for my sister's death. In ways you can't even imagine."

"That's impossible. How could you be responsible for her murder?"

"Because I saw it before it even happened."

Shock covered his face, then he made a disparaging noise in his throat. "Oh, come on. You're not serious."

"Deadly serious. I had a vision of her death. It's the same vision I see in my dreams. The same dream I had tonight."

Silence blanketed the room until another flash of lighting and horrific thunder vibrated the area.

Tammy continued. "And the only reason I can imagine why I'm having these dreams and these visions is that the killer is out there again. He was never caught. I'm not sure why he's back, but I can feel his power. His hatred. It scares me to death, Hawthorne."

Tammy saw the doubt and confusion entering his eyes. She wanted to trust him. She did trust him. But if he wouldn't accept the paranormal as an aspect of her life, how could he help her?

Better to go it alone.

Isolation burrowed within her. "I'm going to bed."

She stood, but the pain in her soul ignited, and before she could leave the room, a sob escaped.

Hawthorne caught up to her, grabbing her arm gently and turning her to face him. "Hey, it's all right."

Tammy saw his concern and was grateful for this small gift. As his hands slid up to grasp her shoulders, tears fell down her cheeks. "It's not all right. It's never going to be all right as long as that monster is out there. He killed my sister. Now I think he wants me."

Hawthorne made a sound of concern and drew her into his arms, holding her tight. His hand slid into her hair, cupping and holding her head against his shoulder.

She shuddered and the wrenching sobs took her by surprise with their force. Tammy absorbed the heat in his muscular body, revealing in the strength and reassurance his powerful arms provided. Perhaps she'd never resolved the grief. Maybe the renewed dreams and horrific visions were a symptom. The storm outside increased, the wind driving against the walls and battering the windows. The maelstrom sounded like banshees demanding entrance, and the thought sent hideous imaginations into her mind's eye. Tammy felt she might never stop crying. Her tears dampened the material of his shirt as she crumpled the fabric in both hands.

Hawthorne kissed her hair, softly caressing the nape of her neck, trailing his hand up and down her back.

"It's all right. You're all right here with me. I won't let anyone hurt you," he whispered. His husky rumble vibrated through her body more powerfully than the thunder.

Soon her body surrendered, nourished by the tenderness she felt in Hawthorne's arms. Sweet, heady warmth filled her heart where raw pain had resided moments before. Tammy lifted her head and looked up at him in the dim light and saw her own agony reflected back at her in his midnight eyes.

"I'm sorry," she said, gulping. Aware of how good his embrace felt, she moved from his arms. "I'm acting like a complete fool and you're being so nice. I—"

"Shhh." He pushed her hair back from her face and smiled tenderly. "I'll be here with you. I promise I won't let anything happen to you." His eyes turned hard with determination. "They'll have to get through me, first. And I guarantee that isn't going to happen."

A deep, primitive feminine reaction stirred inside. He might stand here in rumpled hair, denim shirt, jeans, and bare feet, but he looked like a dangerous, seasoned warrior. Tammy believed him when he said he'd fight for her.

"Thanks, Hawthorne," she said softly.

He took her arm and started for the kitchen. "I know just the cure for sleeplessness."

"What?"

After he flipped on the light, he opened the freezer and held up a large carton of double fudge ice cream. "High test, sinful ice cream. In a chocolate cone, no less."

Tammy laughed. "At this time of night?"

"Absolutely. Greatest cure in the world for insomnia is a calorie overload."

"You're nuts."

"Sorry, I don't have any nuts to put on your ice cream. Might have some of those chocolate whatcha-ma-call-its."

"You mean chocolate sprinkles?"

"Yeah, those things." He waggled his eyebrows. "Real men don't say sprinkles."

Groaning, she watched him retrieve cones from the pantry and scoop ice cream. "Lunatic."

"I think we've already established you think I'm crazy. But what I want to know is…two scoops or one?"

"Gawd." She sighed. "One. Just one please." She'd never admit that the idea of double chocolate sounded divine. "I never know what's going to happen around you."

He threw her a cocky grin. "Is that good or bad?"

"I haven't decided yet. Both, maybe." Hawthorne handed her the cone and she moaned. "Damn it, I said one scoop."

He laughed. "Eat it. No complaining."

She glared at him, then the cone. "You're bossy."

"Since when?"

"Since forever."

"Bull," he said amiably. "Hold this."

Grinning, Hawthorne handed her his double cone and then put the carton back in the freezer. After he retrieved his ice cream from her, he tasted the chocolate and managed to get some on his nose.

He wiped at his nose with a paper towel and smirked.

"Serves you right," she said, grinning.

"Why?"
"Because."
"Because what?"
"Just because."

He grunted and took another big bite. It wasn't long before he'd devoured his treat.

"Jeez, Hawthorne, think you ate that fast enough?"

He stayed silent and smiled.

"This is delicious." Tammy closed her eyes, licked the cone, and whimpered in ecstasy.

"You shouldn't do that." Hawthorne's voice lowered as she opened her eyes.

Warm and intense, his gaze held hers. She licked her lips free of chocolate as a tingle spiraled through her stomach.

It was the ice cream. It had to be.

"Do what?" she asked.

Hawthorne reached for the cone and snatched it from her. "Eat this."

"Hey!"

As his tongue gathered chocolate into his mouth, a spark ignited in her lower stomach and spread everywhere in her loins. "Give it back. No fair you having two ice cream cones."

Tammy reached for the dessert and bumped into his hand instead. Ice cream went flying, and as she gasped in dismay, the delicious concoction landed smack dab on the front of his shirt, then hit the floor with a splat.

"Oh, no!" She gaped at him, horrified.

"Why, you little sneak." Hawthorne grinned as he reached for another paper towel.

She helped him clean up the floor. Giving him a wobbly smile, she tossed the remnants of the late night snack in the trash.

"I didn't mean to—" she started.

"Uh-huh." He dabbed at his shirt. "That'll cost you."

Hawthorne started to unfasten his shirt.

As his shirt came open, her brain turned to soggy cereal. Damn, she had to think fast. She was gawking like the village idiot.

"Planning to torture me with the sight of your ugly chest?" she asked.

Amusement crinkled the corners of his eyes and curved his mouth. Hawthorne pulled the shirt off and revealed his muscled torso and powerful arms. "I'll toss this in the wash."

Her gaze flicked over his incredibly sexy chest, then she looked away. He turned and headed for the utility room.

As he retreated she perused the arousing, mind-boggling sight of broad shoulders and muscled back.

She stood for a few seconds, still shocked.

The last time she'd seen his chest six months ago, it had been swaddled in bandages that covered his bullet wound. She'd been far more worried about his health than his physical attributes. Obviously Hawthorne worked out.

Hard, carved biceps and forearms. A generous covering of dark, curling hair over fine, sculpted pectorals that trailed down and over well-defined stomach muscles. Lean waist and hips.

Perfect.

"No." A little breathless, she trotted after him and into the hall. "I...uh...let me take that. I'm the one that made the mess."

Hawthorne turned suddenly, and Tammy collided with him. He clasped her upper arms. His musky scent and nearness sent an unprecedented shock wave through her.

His lightly tanned skin tempted her. Hell, a woman would have to be half dead not to appreciate this sheer male beauty. Heat filled Tammy, and the glow reached her cheeks.

A man like this didn't come along every day. Slowly, intently, Hawthorne's gaze caught and held hers until her breath trapped in her chest. His lips parted as if he would speak. Oh, God. He was so, so close. Snapping from the trance, she stiffened and he released her.

Tammy reached for the shirt he'd flung over his shoulder and brushed warm skin overlaying steel.

"I've got it," she said softly.

"You certainly have." The teasing but sultry tone in Hawthorne's deep voice made her shiver with anticipation.

She headed for the utility room, brushing by him quickly. He followed, trailing close behind.

"So what's my punishment?" Tammy opened the utility room and headed for the washer. He didn't answer as she put the shirt in the machine. *Ouch! Bad question to ask, Carter.*

He leaned against the dryer and crossed his arms. *Man, did he have to do that?* Hawthorne was simply the most exciting man she'd ever known. If he hadn't been so kind...so darn human with his idiosyncrasies and quirky humor, she wouldn't have been so attracted to him. But she was, damn it. Hopelessly, irretrievably engrossed in Hawthorne. Most important, these crazy feelings she had for him scared the hell out of her.

As Tammy put in detergent and turned on the washer, he came closer. She turned toward him.

"I want my payment now," Hawthorne said.

Warmth...no, more than warmth burned deep in his eyes. Desire. A pure animal need entered his expression, tempered by his gentleness.

"Not until you tell me what you want," she asked.

Slowly, without touching her anywhere else, he leaned down and kissed her nose. A chaste kiss that didn't match his expression in the least. Close enough to feel his body heat, she put her hand out to touch his biceps. The hot, hard strength beneath her fingers made her want more. So much more.

Desire simmered, and Tammy had a feeling if she made a move toward him all bets would be off. The passion would spiral out of control.

"Was that my punishment?" she asked, her voice hoarse.

"Payment. Unless, of course, kissing me is a punishment."

She shook her head. "Not even close." As soon as the words came out, sounding breathless and needy, she wished she hadn't opened her big mouth. "I mean—"

"You liked it?"

"I...." Tammy took her hand away as he uncrossed his arms. He clasped her fingers and brought them to his lips and kissed her fingers. "What are you doing, Hawthorne?"

"What does it feel like?"

Feather light kisses landed on her fingers again, and the wild fluttering it created in her stomach made her gasp. "Don't."

He released her immediately, but he didn't look away. "Is kissing me such a bad thing?"

As Hawthorne shifted closer, her gaze fell to his lips. Tammy leaned back against the washer.

"Of course not. I mean, you've kissed me on the forehead and the nose and the...."

When she drifted off, he leaned both hands on the washer, bracketing her inside his arms. "And the lips. Don't forget the lips."

"Uh, I think we've been in this position before."

"Does this frighten you?"

She wanted to say yes, but then she'd be lying. Tammy had never experienced the raging need, the desire that surged inside her now. Oh, yeah. She was losing control and couldn't stop. Didn't want to stop.

"No. I trust you."

"Maybe you shouldn't." His voice rippled over her, his breath scented with chocolate.

"Why?"

"I said back at the office that I wouldn't touch you again. I thought I could handle it. But you're driving me crazy. I want...."

When he stopped, Tammy waited, her breath halted in her lungs, her pulse thrumming out of control.

"To hell with it," he said hoarsely.

Hawthorne's mouth came down on hers, and the world did a crazy tilt. He leaned into her, pinning her to the washer. The hardness of his arousal pressed against her. Searching her mouth, he consumed her lips with ravenous need, his tongue coaxing her to open. A soft moan parted her lips, and he plunged and retreated with a rhythm that sent wildfire vibrations through her. Nothing sweet or tentative about this kiss. Warm and insistent, blatant and without remorse, he ignited her hidden needs for this virile, electrifying man.

She arched against him, arms circling his neck, holding him close. Responding to his consuming kiss, she enjoyed the repeated slide of his tongue against hers. Hawthorne uttered a soft growl of masculine appreciation, and the sound fired her craving to new heights.

Tammy couldn't believe how wonderful kissing him felt. All her attempts to stay away from Hawthorne's potent masculine appeal had failed. Every outline of his body molded to hers, his hands moving along her back in searching caresses, his kisses driving her to want more and more.

Swift desire bolted through her like the storm outside. This man had given her so much, and she wanted to absorb his strength. Perhaps she could give him something in return. Her understanding. Her affection.

Slowly he caressed her, magnifying the throb that centered in her breasts, her belly, in every increment of her body. Hawthorne's mouth left hers as he reached behind her and closed the washer. He lifted and settled Tammy on the edge. Before she could speak, his lips claimed hers again. Long, drugging kisses made her world narrow to wonderful sensations. His hands slid down to her knees, the heat of his palms against bare skin startling and thrilling. He parted her thighs so that he stood between them. Just the right height to….

Oh. Her gasp was followed by his groan as he fitted his hips tight against her, letting her feel the hard, unmistakable evidence. Pure, erotic wishes gathered tight in her stomach and settled between Tammy's legs. Unable to remain still, she arched against him. Without hesitation he pressed forward, establishing a tempo that accelerated her breathing and brought her mindless pleasure.

Tammy tested the strength in his shoulders, smoothing over his naked skin. She savored his scent, drinking him in until she was dizzy. Running her hands over his chest, she reveled in the sound he made as she found his nipples.

Finally Hawthorne moved to her neck. Sharp tingles passed over her skin as his lips explored, his tongue caressed.

As he found Tammy's ear, his palm discovered her breast, and this time she gasped and arched against him. Only a little more and she'd come apart in his arms. Only a few more strokes of his hardness between her thighs and she'd fall forever.

"Hawthorne."

"Mmmm?" He continued his tender assault on her ear.

"I…we…." She didn't know. He was driving her out of her ever-loving mind.

Hawthorne shuddered as he passed his thumb over her nipple. The stinging pleasure made her writhe. Then his hot hand slipped under her tank top and cupped her bare breast. The jolting pleasure propelled her into reality. His thumb flicked over her hard nipple. Her head dropped back, a soft groan ushering from her lips.

"Oh, God, Hawthorne."

If she didn't stop…if they didn't stop…he'd make love to her here and now.

Chapter 17

Reality dumped freezing water on Tammy's desire for Hawthorne. Panic jumped close behind. She couldn't make love with him. Couldn't make love to a man who desired her but didn't love her.

She avoided another of his kisses, pulling back against his embrace. She gasped. "No."

Startled, his brow furrowing, he kept her loosely within his arms. His cheeks held a flush, his gaze unfocused with arousal. He cupped her face.

"What's wrong?" he asked.

Tammy allowed herself to caress his shoulders one more time before pushing against his chest. He stepped back, removing his heat and the wonderful feeling of his arousal pressed against her.

"I'm sorry. I think we...I just think we're out of control. We need to think about what we're doing. Maybe this is all an illusion, Hawthorne. You're my bodyguard. This isn't a good idea."

She knew she was babbling, and the arousal in his eyes hadn't diminished. Her gaze dropped. *Oh, man.* His body betrayed its intentions. He still wanted her.

Hawthorne backed up until he leaned against the opposite

wall. She slid off the washer and rested against it, uncertain her legs would hold her otherwise.

"You're right," he said, his expression cautious. "I'm sorry."

She flapped her hands in a dismissing gesture. "It was as much my fault. It's been a crazy few days with the visions and the dream."

"I'm glad you stopped us. A few moments more...."

She didn't need to hear more to know what he meant. A few more minutes and the inferno would have raged. Right then and there he would have had her. *On the washer.*

As much as the idea of making love to him excited her, it frightened her. Tammy knew that coupling would have changed their relationship. They would have been linked by desires they hadn't the strength to deny. But he didn't love her and she didn't love him. Tammy wouldn't give in to the physical without that emotional equivalent. Too much was at stake to pretend that she could make love with him and act later as if it didn't matter.

Deep inside she feared one thing. If she made love with him, she might fall in love with him. The last hurrah in an emotional landslide.

Tammy saw memories of their passion grip him, returning desire in his gaze. Did the same wishes show in her eyes?

Her alarm reared up again. "I...I think I'm going back to bed. Goodnight."

She turned and left, her doubts riding hard on her heels.

"Afternoon, Kyle." Jeannette's purr made Tammy flinch.

Hawthorne walked up to the front desk after a meeting with Mrs. Taggert.

Jeannette handed him pink slips of paper. "We've got messages for you. One from Mrs. Traynor at the soup kitchen.

She wants to know if you can work an extra night this week. Stephen and Millicent are both down with a virus." Jeannette, wearing a proper blue business suit, sank into her chair, managing to hike her skirt so a generous amount of thigh showed. "I'm going to be there tonight, too."

Tammy watched a devastating grin lighten his face as he smiled at the teen, then flipped through the messages. "I don't know if I can work tonight. It depends on what Tammy has planned."

Tammy answered automatically. "Tell Mrs. Traynor I'll be there, too."

Jeannette smiled rather than giving Tammy her usual snide comeback. "Cool. I think it's pizza night."

Hawthorne flashed another grin, and Tammy found her heart thudding uncontrollably. *Get over it! So you almost did the hunka chunka with the man. Big deal. Wrestle those hormones into submission!*

"I've got work to do. Talk to you later." Hawthorne sauntered off, and Tammy watched him until he disappeared around the partition.

"You've got it way bad," Jeannette said softly. "When are you gonna admit it?"

Tammy almost opened her mouth to agree, then it dawned what she'd reveal. "Uh...no. He's a handsome man, and he's...uh...my bodyguard. But that's all there is to it."

Needing fresh air to clear the wild thoughts shouting in her head, she stood.

"Where are you going?"

Jeannette's hard question brought Tammy up short as she rounded the front desk on the way to the door.

Frowning, Tammy turned and put her hands on her hips. "I'm going down to the parking lot. I just realized I left my lunch cooler in the car."

"But you're not supposed to go anywhere without Kyle—"

"Uh, uh." Tammy held her index finger up and wagged it. "My lunch is waiting. I'll be back in a few minutes."

"But—"

Tammy ignored her protest. On the way down in the elevator, she inhaled stale air. As the metal container moved down the floors, her stomach twisted until it formed into a dozen knots.

No. Claustrophobia hadn't gripped her before and she wouldn't allow it now. Moving from Hawthorne's protective watch for a few moments brought relief. After the weekend and the combustible quality of their relationship, she'd decided to keep her distance. Sure, she tried and failed one time to manhandle her feelings and desires into check. This time she would succeed.

That morning, Tammy was surprised and delighted to hear that Jeannette had jumped into the front desk job with gusto. Alison praised her as a quick study, and Mrs. Taggert reported that Jeannette hadn't stolen anything else from the supply cabinet.

The morning had progressed well, even though Jeannette had given her the cold shoulder. Tammy knew the teen didn't like Hawthorne pulling bodyguard duty for her. The girl's crush on him wouldn't diminish. Despite the seriousness of the situation, Jeannette didn't understand. Then again, Tammy wasn't entirely sure she needed Hawthorne's protection. After all, other than a few calls and some frightening visions, the murderer hadn't attempted to hurt her.

Yeah, Carter. Keep telling yourself that.

The elevator opened and Tammy stepped into the lot. The heels of her sensible pumps clicked on the concrete, a hollow echo ringing out. In this underground environment the air brushed cold over her short sleeved blouse, prickling her skin with goose bumps until she shivered.

She'd insisted that she drive her car to work, Hawthorne following in his Jag. The arrangement afforded her some autonomy. She reached her car and opened the passenger door, bending to retrieve the lunch cooler.

Footsteps sounded behind her.

She whirled, key held in defense, ready to stab.

Gregg Le Blanc strode toward her, dressed in tie and expensive suit. As he approached, blue and purple formed at the edge of her vision. Sucking in a deep breath, she forced the colors away. A shudder rolled through her body, icy and hot all at once.

"Hi," he said, waving.

Tammy managed a smile. "Back from your assignment already?"

He stopped in front of her, way too close. He put a hand on her car, and she almost told him to take his greasy palm off the paint job. Gregg's obsequious smile made her edgy, and fire yellow flickered at the edges of her vision. She blinked.

"Yeah. The politician had his own bodyguards. I was just a supplement. As long as I'm paid, what do I care?" He took a step closer. His heavy cologne tickled her nose and she sniffed. "Besides, now I've got you alone."

I've got you alone.

Alarm bells panicked and rang full strength in Tammy's head. "I'm expected back at the office any minute. What's up, Gregg?"

She didn't care how unfriendly she sounded. So be it.

"I wanted to discuss our little misunderstanding the other day."

"I don't think there was any misunderstanding. You screwed up with Jeannette and I called you on it. She says you've been a good boy lately. Keep up the good work."

His gaze caught and held hers. Marauder eyes. The man spotted his dinner and went after it with gusto. Nothing had changed. Her instincts told her to remain cautious around this man. She wouldn't run screaming, but her hand tightened on her keys in reflex.

"I wanted to say I was sorry I made that statement to Jeannette. I didn't want it to influence our relationship."

"Sorry, but it already has."

Did anger flicker in his eyes? She couldn't say for certain, but his mouth tightened. "It doesn't have to be that way."

"Yes it does. I can't respect a man who would come on to a teen like that. I can't trust you."

Gregg's innocent look deteriorated into peeved. "And yet you can trust a man like Hawthorne? That putz?"

She shook her head and slammed the car door. She put her lunch box cooler on top of the car. "I trust him. It's none of your concern."

"You mean if I asked you out for a friendly drink as a co-worker you'd say no?"

Annoyance gathered inside her. "I'm not mixing business with pleasure these days."

His leer increased, and her imagination exploded as she saw him as an old man...a lecherous old man one day.

"What do you call shacking up with Hawthorne? Looks like playing house to me. I don't believe this crap about you needing protection because of obscene phone calls."

Tammy couldn't believe she'd ever thought he looked innocent and beguiling. "It's not your concern if I'm shacking up with him or not, now is it?"

"I've seen the way he looks at you. He'll take you and use you."

Her temper flared. "And you wouldn't?"

"I know how to treat a woman."

"I'm not going to dip to your level, Le Blanc. What do you hope to gain by this conversation?"

"A little cooperation."

"For what?"

"Go out with me."

"What a monumental ego you have." She started to turn away, appalled. "You've got to be insane if you think I'm going to buckle. I'm giving you one more chance before I report you for sexual harassment."

Before she could about face, he grabbed her arm and dragged her against him. Tammy's heart leapfrogged.

"Let her go!" A couple of choice expletives issued from Hawthorne's lips as he started toward them, his strides eating up ground.

Relief jounced through her and she yanked from Le Blanc's grip. Hawthorne's stony stare laced with pure anger and when he reached them, he stalked past her and got in Le Blanc's face. Le Blanc shrank back against Tammy's car.

"Don't you touch her again, or I'll personally see to it that you lose your job." Hawthorne's throaty growl left no doubt he'd do exactly as he threatened.

Tammy felt the air crackle, the intensity of the testosterone skyrocketing. She knew something would happen in seconds as the men glared at each other.

The tension exploded.

Le Blanc swung at Hawthorne with a right hook. Hawthorne sidestepped cleanly, countering with a punch to the man's stomach. Le Blanc gasped for air and doubled over, reaching for the car as support. He stumbled and landed on his knees, gasping for air.

Hawthorne stood over Le Blanc, his hands clutched into fists, his chest rising and falling with each inhalation.

"Oh, my God," Tammy whispered. "I can't believe you did that, Hawthorne."

Tammy had never seen Hawthorne look this way before. Feral. Ready to detonate again.

"What the hell was this bastard trying to do to you?"

Her anger boiled "He was asking me out. What he did isn't a butt kicking offense." Lunch box in hand, she stepped out smartly, heading back to the office. "Men. Irrational, stupid, Neanderthal—"

"What did you call me?" Hawthorne asked, striding alongside.

"A Neanderthal." She stopped and turned to him as more vitriol poured into her veins. "No. Maybe *that* doesn't even describe it. I'm doing a disservice to the Neanderthal. Hitting Le Blanc was uncalled for. Do you realize this is the second time you've come to my rescue like this? Except you didn't punch Tucker Phelps."

"For your information, I wouldn't have punched Le Blanc if he hadn't taken a swing at me first."

Tammy shook her head, ready to screech with indignation. She strode away again. When she reached the elevator, she switched directions. Maybe a good jaunt up the stairs would clear her mind.

She opened the door to the stair well. Unfortunately he followed. "Stop it, Tammy."

Tammy reached the first flight of stairs, her breath rough from adrenaline. "Don't tell me what to do."

"Wait. We've got to talk—"

"You don't want to talk, you want to lecture. Well, let me tell you something, Kyle Hawthorne, I'm not a baby. I don't need your advice or your brawn."

As she climbed up the steps, red seared her vision and she almost stopped. It receded instantly, and fear gathered in her throat.

What was this? Not anger, exactly. Not passion.

Determined, she ignored the color, hoping it would disappear.

When they reached the second floor he grasped her arm, much as Le Blanc had done. He turned her around, gripping her shoulders firmly. "No. You're not a baby. You're a grown woman who drives me insane in more ways than one."

"So we annoy the hell out of each other. What else is new?"

He laughed, the sound devoid of amusement. "We used to like each other. At least I think we did. What's happened to us?" His expression saddened, shocking her down to her shoes. "We can be friends again, can't we? Hands off like we used to be?"

"I...I don't know." Something resentful reared inside her again. "That's no reason for you to come charging like a bull. *I am not your possession*. I will never be any man's possession!"

Continuing to hold her shoulders, he said, "Did I say you're my possession? What I did say was that I reacted instinctively, like a bodyguard. Like I'm supposed to. And if you were using your brain, you wouldn't even think of going anywhere without me."

"Thanks so much, Hawthorne. Now you're calling me stupid."

They glared like to gunfighters ready for a show down. In a perverted way she enjoyed sparring with him. Before it had meant flirting. Tammy couldn't say what it translated into now. Yet she didn't feel right arguing with him this way. This time it hurt and hurt badly. The red still hovered at the edge of her vision, and she decided it was caused by the argument.

His fingers pressed her arms, but not enough to hurt. "You're just not thinking. If you keep it up, you'll end up dead."

He had her there. The conviction in Hawthorne's voice said he believed it down to his bones. *Crap, but she didn't want to be wrong.* It ate at her to submit to his protection, to admit vulnerability.

Tammy asked the next thing that came to mind. "Why were you out here in the parking lot?"

"Jeannette told me you'd snuck out to get your lunch."

Figures. "What a little—"

"I'm glad she told me. She's only worried about you."

"Come off it, Hawthorne. She isn't concerned about me. She's got a crush on you. She wants to make points with you."

"So? I'm your damned bodyguard, Tammy." His gaze slid over her body in a sweltering, all encompassing survey. "I'm sticking to your pretty little ass like glue from now on. Even if I have to sit at the front desk to make sure you don't try this stunt again."

Tammy made a little noise, half protest, half disbelief. "Why you arrogant...my pretty little ass?"

"That's what I said." One of his eyebrows lifted in a sardonic display. "This isn't the time or place to mention it, I suppose, but I like your ass. That should have been evident when I had you up on the washer."

Heat flooded her body at the memory. As his gaze snagged hers, she inhaled. Tammy saw the recollection of their passionate encounter register across his face. His pupils dilated, his nostrils flared slightly.

Swallowing hard, she stepped away from his disturbing heat and the grip of his hands. "It was a mistake. I just want to forget it."

"I've never seen you run away from anything until now. You and I have a powerful attraction, Tammy, and you can deny it until you turn blue, but it did happen."

Tammy trembled, bombarded by desires. Desires to flee. Desires to grab him and kiss him until they sent each other over the waterfall. "I don't want a relationship with you. Not a…not a sexual relationship."

To her surprise his gaze softened. Unbidden attraction for this man licked at her once again, like flames threatening too close. His heat, his undeniable power drew her toward him a step.

"You're absolutely right, Carter. We need to keep this relationship strictly professional."

Silence stretched and she wanted to escape. Dash from the wild, almost irrepressible urges that provoked her every time she was near this man.

"I shouldn't have left the office without you. You know I'm not used to being dependent on anyone," she said.

Hawthorne's gaze didn't alter. "I want to keep you safe and I can't do my job if you're undermining me." He shrugged. "But I'm not sorry I kicked Le Blanc's butt. He deserved it."

"He's probably in Mrs. Taggert's office right now telling her what you did."

"Let him. She'll want both sides of the story. She has to know how I feel. If anything happened to you...." He took a deep breath, then nodded toward the stairs. "Come on. Let's go back to the office."

All the way back, Tammy wondered what Hawthorne had almost confessed.

He waited until their voices faded before he departed the parking garage. He got into his car and left.

Between his own hot anger and the stimulating echo of the argument, he didn't know whether to be euphoric or infuriated. Blood bumped through him like a river, waves crashing onto the banks, splashing hot, red fury into his system. He drove faster. Faster. Pushing the car to take the streets aggressively, he knew police might stop him. Of course, he'd flash his identification and they'd let him off. Maybe.

Pricks. They'd probably give him the ticket anyway, because they all imagined themselves better than him. Stupid cocks. Heady laughter burst from his lungs as he turned a corner.

Sweet Magnolia and the bodyguard man's angry words hung in the air like miasma, coating his body in happiness. Ah. Felt so good to know they squabbled. He'd heard Sweet Magnolia declare she didn't want a sexual relationship with bodyguard man. Sweet Magnolia understood Hawthorne couldn't be the man for her.

Hot on the heels of his pleasure came disappointment. Somehow he had to regenerate his courage, or he'd have to drink from the beer bottle again and taste the sourness of sin. He'd rinsed the bottle last night, hoping he wouldn't have the urge to fill it again. Yet the compulsion had engulfed him forcefully until he couldn't deny it.

Well, it was his fault. If he hadn't chickened out the other night and decided *not* to kill bodyguard man while he fornicated with Sweet Magnolia—

Still, he should have broken into bodyguard man's house, while the storm rattled and raged outside. The screams would have sunk way under. Way, way down under the cannon blasts of thunder.

He groaned as moisture-laden wind blasted through the open window into his face. Water tapped his skin as gentle white clouds released rain into the atmosphere. He licked at the water on his mouth, and imagined Sweet Magnolia doing the same for him. Soon. Soon…within days. She would know her master, her true lover…the only man for her.

Chapter 18

"What's wrong with you, Scooby Doo?" Davis asked, his smile wide and knowing. He served mashed potatoes while Hawthorne ladled pork and beans. "You've been acting weird all evening."

Hawthorne glanced at Tammy, several people down, serving apple pie. Hawthorne knew what ate at him, but he wouldn't blurt it out in the food line. "Nothing's wrong. I've got a lot on my mind."

The old man scratched his chin with his rubber glove. "Any fool can see that, Scooby. What I want to know is when you're wiping that Grand Teton size frown from your puss."

"Maybe never."

The last person in line moved by them and headed for the apple pie. Hawthorne took another gander at Tammy, damning this obsession to watch her. Before she slid pie onto the homeless man's plate, she caught Hawthorne's gaze long enough to glare. She looked…smug? Bored?

Mrs. Traynor slapped both him and Davis on the back. "Time to clean up. Get busy, boys. No time for chat."

"Slave driver," Davis said with a smile. "She's a slave driver. No relief in sight."

"Shut up," Mrs. Traynor said with a face-splitting grin. "Or I'll handcuff you to the food line table."

"Would you please?" Davis turned toward her with his pan of food. "That could be mighty interesting."

Blushing clear to the roots of her hair, the woman puffed her cheeks until she looked like a blowfish. She let the air out with a puff. "You are sick. Very sick, Davis."

As she walked away, Davis turned his self-satisfied smile onto Hawthorne and then laughed. "I think she likes me."

"Don't be too sure." Hawthorne peeled off his gloves. "Never can tell with a woman."

As he walked with the older man to the kitchen, he saw Joe gesture at Tammy, and she went over to talk to him.

"Do I detect a little skepticism?" Davis asked.

Hawthorne used one shoulder to open the swinging door to the kitchen, and Davis followed him inside. "You detect full-blown, one-hundred percent skepticism."

"Oh, oh. Woman trouble."

Hawthorne just grunted, then went on to help Davis with clean up. But the jovial attitudes of those around him couldn't break his strange mood. Instead the clatter of dish washing, the disposal grinding, glasses clinking together almost drove him mad.

Tammy had avoided talking to him or looking his way, though an overwhelming compulsion to watch her refused to release him. Time and time again he told himself his bodyguard instinct explained the need to stare at her.

There was more, of course, if he took time to admit it.

Tammy's kisses, hungry and deep, had rocked him down to his boots. Without a doubt, if she hadn't pushed him away, he would have had sex with her in the utility room. His body had reared into action, burning to sink deep and hard and fast into her softness. He flushed, remembering that bone-melting need. Silently he cursed his affliction. One way or the other, he would protect her without becoming physically involved. He feared it was too late to stave off emotional involvement. Way too late.

"Joe, it just isn't practical," Tammy said, keeping her voice low. She took Joe's arm and they slipped into the hallway. "I can't control these visions any more than you can control yours."

Joe smirked. "Now you know that isn't true, missy. Remember when you helped me find Kiley? That wasn't an illusion. You focused and you got answers, just like I did when I tried. You know that doesn't happen with most psychics. We've got a gift. Some people laugh at us. Some people try to tell us we're nuts." He shrugged. "In my case they're at least half right."

Tammy grinned at his last sentence. Though she knew he spoke the truth, the idea unsettled and disturbed her. She didn't want to control her so-called powers. "If I could control this then...then I'm even more responsible for my sister's death than I thought."

Joe frowned fiercely. "What? Where did you get a fool idea like that?"

She toyed with the edge of her cotton tunic. "Barb had visions that she didn't heed."

"Sort of like you're doing now?"

"Like I have sometimes, yes. Colors. Just like I have recently. I didn't take any stock in them. I refused to direct those visions to see her killer before he struck. Or to find him afterward."

"You listened to too many of those clinical bastards like I did at first. I knew my smelling things wasn't my upper lip." Joe propped against the wall, staring at the church bulletin board. "You were afraid of all the horrible things you'd see. Things you'd find out."

She, too, turned toward the bulletin board. Maybe if synchronicity arrived tonight, something on the board would prompt her. Give her ideas on where and what to do next. Tammy's gaze floated over wedding and engagement announcements. Her thoughts drifted to the happiness these couples would enjoy on their wedding day.

"What are you thinking, missy?"

Tammy leaned heavier against the wall, as if it could support her drifting thoughts. Could she anchor herself if she used her visions to see the stalker? "I'm thinking I should get back to work instead of talking about psychic stuff."

Joe straightened, jamming his hands into his ratty jeans pockets. "Maybe. But you and I both know hiding away from problems never solved anything. I did that way too often. That's why I was homeless. I was running from what happened to my daughter and my wife. I was running from all the things I could hear and see so much better than other people. But you're smarter than that."

Joe's concern warmed her, and tears stung her eyes. She couldn't look at him, for if she did she'd bawl like a baby. Instead she gave the bulletin board more attention than it deserved.

She sniffed. "I don't know what to do, Joe."

"Hawthorne can't be your bodyguard forever. You've got to do something. Find those demons and eat them for lunch. Or maybe dinner."

His humor gave her strength to look at him. "I know you're right. I just don't know how to go about it. The regions I'd have to explore. It's scary."

"Talk about it to Hawthorne."

Tammy put her hands up. "I've tried that. He doesn't believe in psychic abilities. He thinks these visions are something else. When I passed out in the office that day he was sure Dr. Jacobssen would find something physically wrong."

"That would be what most folks would think right off. But you've got to think of a way to prove it to him."

"I don't *need* him, Joe. He's a bunch of thorns around my neck. He's—"

"Shame on you. Hawthorne's a damn good friend to you." Joe's eyes narrowed, anger quickly replaced by dawning awareness. "Wait a minute. It's happened hasn't it?"

Afraid she knew what he referred to, she didn't speak.

Joe's mouth split into a full-fledged grin. "I knew it. I knew the two of you couldn't last much longer around each other."

Heat filled her face. "I don't know what you're talking about."

He winked. "Yeah, right. Well, missy, I've got work to do." He clasped her shoulder and squeezed gently. "You think about what I said. Hawthorne's a good man, and you need his help. I know it won't be easy going trying to make him understand, but you must try again."

Before she could comment, he headed down the hall, his lanky walk transporting him quickly.

Seconds later she heard a noise two doors down. The door was open a sliver, but no light flooded the interior. Tammy waited. Her breath tightened, inexplicable fear sliding through her like a drug.

Come on, Carter. You don't know who is in there. Back to safety.

With a fortifying breath, she emerged from her fearful trance and retreated to the kitchen.

Latching onto Hawthorne's arm, Jeannette pulled Hawthorne outside the kitchen door as clean up finished.

"What are you doing?" Hawthorne asked, annoyed at the girl's insistence. He reined in his impatience and asked, "Is something wrong?"

"Yeah, something's wrong. I heard the weirdest crap."

"What?"

"Tammy and that old creepy guy were talking."

"You mean Joe?"

"Yeah, *him*."

"He's not creepy."

She flipped back her hair with a shrug. "Whatever. Anyway, I overheard them talking awhile ago."

He groaned. "Jeannette, you weren't eavesdropping?"

Sheepish guilt passed over her face. "Well, yeah. I was…uh…in this other room when I heard them come out to talk. I turned the light off and listened. But that's beside the point. They were talking about all these psychic powers. Are they really psychic? Or are they both just flipping out?"

"Joe has had problems in the past, but he's under supervision and medication."

"What about Tammy?"

"She's fine. Perfect mental health."

Tilting one hip and crossing her arms, she pursed her lips. "Well, I think she needs help. I'm not saying you're the one to do it. I just wondered what was going on. Do you believe in psychic powers?"

"Hell, no. And don't eavesdrop again. It's not polite. Come on, let's finish up and get out of here."

Trotting to keep up with him, she asked, "Since when am I polite?"

Hawthorne smiled. "Mrs. Taggert tells me you filled in for Tammy very well and that you're polite on the phone. That's a big compliment. Not many can do that job well."

"Better than Tammy?"

He threw her a cautioning look mixed with a smile. "Don't get too cocky. You've got a ways to go yet."

The smug look disappeared from Jeannette's face. "Did Miss Goody Two Shoes tell you that?"

"Who?"

"Tammy. She's so clean she squeaks."

He stopped dead in the hall. "Cut the crap, Jeannette."

Jeannette's lower lip almost stuck out. The effect might have looked endearing on a three-year-old, but on the teen it looked petulant. "She can't do anything wrong. According to you and, like, everyone else in the office, she's a saint. I've seen how you are around her. Like she is the…I dunno…bloody Queen of England or something."

Hawthorne wondered how parents dealt with nonsensical teens. He decided blunt was the way to go. He cleared his throat. "Jeannette, she's human. She's not perfect. But she's also a fantastic person. Tammy has a big, soft heart in many ways. Apparently she sees potential in you."

When Jeannette retained her ridiculous sulk, Hawthorne rolled up the sleeves on his sweatshirt. Time to dig in. "She offered you the job. She convinced a highly skeptical Mrs. Taggert that you deserved a big break. No one else I know would have given you this chance. I know I sure as well wouldn't have."

Jeannette's sulk transformed to pure hurt. "Why wouldn't you have given me a chance?"

"Because I lost someone very dear to me once. My little sister. When I first got to know you, I realized you and Selina were a lot alike. Smart, tough, and reckless. Her ego was smaller than a pinhead, yet she still made it through tight spots. But she had a fatal flaw."

Tears moistened her eyes. "Fatal?"

Emotions clogged his throat, but he forced himself onward.

"She was murdered by her pimp. I've seen this happen before, so I was certain you'd fall into the same trap. You might still fall into that hole and never climb out." He held his hands up in supplication. "If you listen to Tammy and take her direction and if you keep your job at Taggert Security Team, I think you'll survive. But if you throw away the chance Tammy's given you, then you deserve everything you get."

Hawthorne knew his words had punctured her leather hide, because the tears fell, dampened her cheeks and rolled down her chin.

"I'm sorry," Jeannette whispered.

Taking a deep breath, he let it out slow and easy. "Just remember what I said. Come on. Let's get back and finish up so we can go home."

Tammy used her new dachshund shaped eraser to fix some paperwork Jeannette had done incorrectly. Her mouse eraser had bitten the dust earlier, falling apart between the ears. She'd perused the shelves of her favorite supply store looking for a new mouse eraser, then decided it was time to change pace. The weenie dog eraser had called to her and she'd bought it, feeling a bizarre sense of completion in the act. *Life's little pleasures. Yes, indeed.*

Maybe she needed to do the same in the rest of her life.

She sighed as she fixed Jeannette's mistake. Tammy had no intention of reprimanding her for it. The weekend had almost arrived, and she didn't want to ruin either her Friday night or Jeannette's. Jeannette, unfortunately, would probably choose to play hooker. The thought made Tammy wince. She worried about the girl daily, wondering if Blade the pimp would decide to hurt her.

Too many things to worry about anymore. Would she ever get a break?

"Hey, Tammy. 'Bout time to close up shop."

Damn him. Hawthorne had changed into his western shirt, jeans, and boots again. His cowboy hat didn't grace his head, though. Tammy's heart did a thump, a stutter, and almost came to a screaming halt. As usual, her reaction metamorphosed into defense. As he leaned on the counter, she gave him an old, familiar smile.

She hid the eraser in a cubbyhole, certain he'd have a comment to make about the little creature. "I didn't know you were going dancing again tonight. So *that* was what was in the duffel bag this morning."

"I'm surprised you didn't ask me about it earlier."

She shrugged as nonchalantly as possible. "I'm trying to keep out of your affairs."

"I noticed. Ever since the...." he lowered his voice to a husky nuance, "....the utility room."

Tammy's memories animated. With staggering clarity she saw them in the utility room. Images of his naked chest, the feeling of his hands as they coasted over her, the mind-numbing pleasure of his kiss. The staggering intimacy of Hawthorne pressed between her thighs, hard, hot and—

Jerking herself from the fantasy, she glanced around. "Keep your voice down."

When he chuckled, Tammy glared. Then it dawned on her that his cow daddy outfit meant something. "Wait a minute. If you're going dancing, that means *I'm* going dancing."

He straightened. "You got it."

"But—"

"No buts. We both need to get out of the house, and a little recreation won't hurt either of us."

Another idea came to mind. "But if I'm dancing with someone and you're dancing with someone, how are you going to *bodyguard* me."

Tammy recognized the heat she saw in Hawthorne's eyes, and the intent behind it intrigued her. "We'll dance together. Exclusively."

She moaned. "I don't know...."

"It'll be fun."

"Yeah, well, lying on a bed of nails or walking on hot coals is supposed to be fun, but you won't catch me trying it."

Her comparison made Hawthorne laugh. He hooked his thumbs into his belt loops. "That bad, huh? What are you afraid of?"

Double damn him. "Dancing. I'm not very good at it."

"We'll stick to the slow kind. That way we won't have to bust any fancy moves."

Slow dancing with Hawthorne would mean playing with nitro. "I don't think so."

Hawthorne's eyes sobered. "We've got some things to talk about. Very important."

"Can't we talk here?"

"I don't want anyone listening in."

She adjusted the collar on her short-sleeved blouse, nervous as a day old kitten. "This isn't a good idea."

"Jeannette gave me important information. I need to talk with you about it. Serious business."

Relenting, she pushed back from her desk. Tammy's nerves fired with anticipation, and she had to acknowledge apprehension about dancing had little to do with it. Cuddling with Hawthorne on the dance floor would be nerve-wracking enough, but imagining what Jeannette had told him worried her more.

"Lead on, MacDuff," she said.

Following bodyguard man and Sweet Magnolia became ball-busting work. As they headed into downtown Denver, the VW strained to keep up with bodyguard man's Jaguar.

He wondered at his glorious luck, his ability to arrive in the right place at the right time. To take opportunities where so many would fail to venture. His ego swelled, and he felt it like a sunrise.

His dawning would improve human kind, as it already had. People had no idea, in their stupidity, what he did for them. He cleansed the earth, he renewed it. All his hard work would bring the earth improvements it had never known. Certainly others had done similar things. But his contribution surpassed those men and women by far.

He shifted the car into a higher gear, screaming through a yellow light. Chuckling, he slapped the steering wheel. Worth it. Worth the possibility a cop would stop him for speeding. It didn't matter if a cop saw his face. People didn't pay him much heed. He blended, and he prided himself on that chameleon aspect. He needed no disguises, no camouflages. He simply "was." Long ago he'd been told he looked good. Handsome, if women could be believed. When he looked in the mirror he doubted it. Only the devil looked handsome, and the eyes staring back at him in the rear view mirror didn't look attractive. They appeared divine.

"Never you mind," he said to the empty interior of the car.

He wanted a storm to boil over the Rocky Mountains and bring relief to the ninety-degree weather. Even more he wished for frightening flashes of electricity, the power-filled rumbles that made him flinch and then smile in ecstasy. The rapture that filled him during a thunderstorm was almost as delightful as taking a woman. The women knew when he "finished" them, the true state of his power.

As he followed Sweet Magnolia and bodyguard man, he smiled. Soon he'd know her taste and he'd glory in the bodyguard's blood. Tonight might be the night.

His mother had always said she'd beat him until he reached purity. She'd hit him so often he was sure she'd propelled him into sanctity dozens of times. And all his sips from the beer bottle, all these years, had given him the wisdom and power to defeat anything and everyone he chose. He was invincible.

Chapter 19

As Tammy stepped out of Hawthorne's car, the sound of country-western music pumped through the doors of the restaurant and bar. Rock-a-Billy's combined rock music with country-western, a truly unique experience in the Mile High City. Not a bad mixture, especially if they played oldies.

Cool night breezes floated from the mountains down into the city, whispering between the buildings. Heat inversion had covered Denver earlier in the day, blocking in pollution. Now the mountain winds had blown away many noxious fumes.

Hawthorne laid his palm on the middle of her back as they walked, his possessive touch warming her clear through. She'd wished she'd worn a heavier top. Maybe then she wouldn't feel his heat so intensely. Her suit skirt covered her legs down to mid-calf. Yet with Hawthorne she felt exposed.

She glanced at him. "Where's your hat, Hawthorne?"

"Decided not to wear it. Can't dance with it." He looked down at her and winked. "At least not slow dancing. It gets in my way."

"Gets in your way how?" Curiosity pushed the edge when

she knew she should keep her trap shut. "I've seen other guys wearing hats while dancing."

Under the dim illumination his gaze flared. "Keeps me from getting as close as I'd like. Hard to kiss a woman with the brim hitting her in the forehead."

Tammy's heart rate went up. Did that mean he planned to kiss her tonight? *No way. She couldn't take it. She'd combust. Explode.* The litany flowed in her mind as she recalled their last knee-melting kiss. One more time would do it. She'd simply puddle at his feet.

Music blared through the door as Hawthorne held it open for her. Loud, yes, but at least they wouldn't need to scream to be heard.

They maneuvered through the doors and into the thick crowd. Tammy hadn't danced in ages, and she knew slow boogie with Hawthorne bordered on insane. She wanted to know what Joe had told him, though, and hoped Hawthorne would fess up if she caught him in an unguarded moment.

Hawthorne grasped her hand as he plowed through the crowd. He led her toward a booth cloaked in semi-darkness. Couples moved about a dance floor in the center of the room, but back here the music seemed muffled, giving intimacy to the surroundings. Suddenly Reba McIntire's "Lighter Shade of Blue" smoothed over the speakers.

Hawthorne came to a sudden halt, and she almost ran into the back of him. Without relaxing his hold on her hand, he leaned down and whispered into her ear.

"Let's dance while we talk."

His warm breath on her ear and neck made her shiver with excitement. Smiling sardonically, she said, "What? No buttering up first? No drinks?"

"Nope." He grinned and pulled her to the dance floor, wedging his way to a spot in the middle.

Tammy's stomach fluttered, a heady contradictory mixture of exhilaration and unease that made her feel lighter than cotton candy. "Hawthorne, I don't know about this...."

As he encircled her waist with one arm and held her other hand, her disinclination narrowed. Hawthorne wasn't dragging her up close. Keeping a "professional" distance should remain possible. Maybe. She took a deep breath, hoping it would cleanse her fears.

Reba's mellow and compelling voice drew Tammy into the rhythm as they moved slowly around the dance floor. Moments passed and Hawthorne said nothing. She didn't look at him. Couldn't look.

Finally she spoke first. "So, what's up? What did Jeannette say? Something to do with that awful pimp?" Apprehension gripped her and she stopped dancing. "Is she in more danger?"

Hawthorne's arm tightened, bringing her a tad closer. He started the dance again. "No, I think she's all right for now. I'm starting to think she exaggerated the pimp's anger."

Tammy sighed. "That's good. I mean, that it was only exaggerated."

Hawthorne brought her closer yet.

So much for keeping distance. In rebellion she shifted, putting more distance between them. She had to keep this tantalizing man at bay.

If he noticed her moving away from him, his expression didn't change. "Last night she told me she eavesdropped on your conversation with Joe. She heard you talking about those colors again."

Tammy wanted to throttle the girl, then hang her by her toenails from a hundred foot bamboo bridge. "Damn that girl. I hope you told her not to eavesdrop?"

"Yeah, I told her. I don't know if it'll do any good. You know how stubborn she is."

"So what do you care about this conversation I had with Joe? You don't believe either of us has psychic abilities."

"I've been thinking."

"That's good news. Warn me the next time that happens."

Amusement and annoyance warred in his eyes, and he tugged her nearer as a new song flared to life over the speakers. "Has anyone ever told you what a brat you are?"

Tammy gazed into the dim lights overhead. "Hmmm...let me see. Why, I think it was you."

An ironic smile traced his lips. "I say again. You're a brat."

"But you like me anyway."

"I'm trying to keep an open mind about this psychic...."

"Stuff?"

"Yeah. I've decided that if you can prove this 'color' sensing ability I'll know it's real. I'll even believe Joe might be able to...scent certain things."

Surprise rocked her. The curiosity in Hawthorne's eyes pleased her. That his endorsement meant that much to her also drove her batty. "What brought on the change of heart?"

He shrugged and stepped them around a couple that seemed intent on wearing a hole in one section of the floor. "If I'm going to keep this bastard away from you, I've got to have weapons at my disposal. That and...."

"And?"

Reluctance covered his expressive eyes and mobile mouth. Gently he shifted closer, as if he could hide the encroachment. "I trust you, Carter. And if you say you're having visions and they're connected in some way to your sister's death...I want to believe that."

Using equal finesse, she put space between their bodies. "But I have to prove it?"

His hand cupping her fingers tightened. "Give me something to go on. I deal in facts."

"Not in emotions," Tammy said matter-of-factly. "Mr. Granite."

His nose wrinkled. "Mr. Granite?"

"You're hard to figure. Difficult to read. Like a smooth stone."

"In this business I'm not sure it's such a bad thing."

"True, but with friends it's not always the way to communicate."

Hawthorne's compelling gaze altered to that intense, absorbing attention that made her insides quiver with sensual longing. "What's my expression telling you now?"

"I...." She licked her lips. "I don't know. I'm not getting any colors."

"Who says anything about colors? Just look into my eyes and tell me what you see."

"I'd be wrong, Hawthorne. Even if I can see colors doesn't mean I'll understand your expression or the meaning behind the colors. It's not that black and white. When I see colors there's often an emotional content with it."

He held her gaze. "What do you see?"

Her head felt fuzzy. *Crap. This was it. She was going down for the last time.*

The waters closed over her head, and Tammy lunged to the surface, gasping for purchase on the unforgiving, rocky shore. "You're enjoying holding me. You keep bringing me closer."

They'd moved almost to the edge of the dance floor, and she wondered if she could relocate them to a table. All around her the music pulsed, the air inundated with leather, cologne, and probably pheromones.

His deadly as sin smile inflamed the sensual light burning inside her.

"Very good. Very damn good." The husky, sexy quality to his voice aroused her intensely. She almost squirmed with need.

She parried his thrust. "How do I know you won't just say yes to whatever I say?"

Hawthorne slid them back to the center of the floor, and Tammy groaned inside. The man was too clever. "Why would I say yes if you weren't right? Why would I tell you I want to hold you close if I didn't?"

Is it hot in here? Am I melting?

"Body language has nothing to do with psychic abilities," she said quickly.

"So prove it, then. Read my colors."

Tammy made a disgusted noise in her throat. "This isn't going to be easy. Joe and I also talked about controlling my visions."

"Both you and Joe controlled the visions when you were looking for Kiley, right?"

"He directed his scents better than I did the colors. I haven't tried anything like it since."

"Not even when you had the last couple of visions?"

She shook her head. "I'm not sure I can do this."

"Try it with me. That's all I'm asking."

Reba McIntire's duet with Vince Gill, "The Heart Won't Lie," came over the speakers. The heart-felt love song wouldn't decrease the crazy spell Hawthorne had conjured. Instead it stoked her fire. Her body yearned to snuggle him while her mind screamed for her to put distance between them.

"All right," she said. "But I can't be held responsible for the consequences."

His chuckle rumbled up deep from his chest. "That sounds interesting. I promise I can take whatever you dish out."

"Are you sure? What if I uncover some hidden, Freudian desires?" she asked sarcastically.

His dark, thick lashes flicked up so that he could stare deep into her eyes. "Mine? Or yours?"

Hawthorne's insinuation made her body flush.

Tammy fumbled. "Either. Both."

"I like the sound of that, too. How can I help?"

"You can't. I've got to relax."

"What can I do to *help* you relax?"

"You can't. Now shut up and let me concentrate."

Hawthorne's laugh vibrated and rippled across her skin. How could a man's laugh be so sexy?

Feelings surged through her in colossal waves she couldn't stop. He'd loosened every defense she'd had and brought it down stone by stone. The last wall came down as she dared to look into his eyes one more time.

Oh, God, she couldn't stand it.

She was intoxicated.

Sighing, Tammy flowed with the music, allowing it to ease into her one note at a time. Slowing her heartbeat. Slowing her breathing. She closed her eyes. "This is crazy."

"Bring it on."

As she allowed music and rhythm to unite, she experienced a change. A parallel world yawned. As male and female voices joined, proclaiming a love everlasting, Tammy realized that she'd never felt this sensation of being cherished, this warm, this alive. Something about this man freed her.

The music changed, flowing to a throaty sax that whispered and throbbed. Tammy shifted, looking up at Hawthorne. The low light shuttered his gaze. Yet his eyes said everything. His mood matched the music, hot and wanting. As his arms slipped tighter around her again, Tammy knew she couldn't deny what she saw. His need. His desire. Life filtered from him to her like water. Giving. Receiving. Responding.

Rock hard chest to breasts. Hips to hips. Thighs to thighs.

All around her the music flowed, undulating like a sensual river.

"So much for country music," she said.

"This is better. Fits the mood."

"What is the mood?"

"Highly dangerous. Something could happen at any time."

Tammy shivered, then swallowed hard. When she didn't speak, he smiled slowly, conveying a teasing note. "Cold?"

"No."

The sax tune molded them together until a piece of paper couldn't be wedged between them.

"Can you see my colors?" He slipped his hands up and down her back.

"Not yet. But I will. By touch perhaps. Being this close to you...."

"Yeah?"

She couldn't answer because the music's flow caught and enthralled. Instead she put her head on his shoulder. Moving against him like this, with constant friction, material over material, his hands sliding to her hips...almost touching her buttocks....

Her skin prickled, ultra sensitive, her breasts tingling, and nipples peaking tight.

Red exploded, obliterating her vision, and she closed her eyes. But instead of frightening her as the other red had in times before, the heady color blended with deep blue, whispering over her senses. Tammy didn't perceive the colors of a killer this time. But of a lover.

Lover.

The red faded to the corners of her vision, but didn't disappear. *Hawthorne wanted to be her lover.*

Tammy finally dropped her resistance. She'd fought her attraction to Hawthorne for what seemed an eternity. Now that his colors came to her after all this time, she sank into them more willingly than she would have expected.

"Red," she whispered, keeping her head on his shoulder.

His hot breath touched her right ear, sending shivers of delight rocketing through her. He pushed her hair back from her neck, exposing tender flesh.

"Did you say something?" he asked into her ear.

His lips brushed her earlobe almost too softly to notice. Sweet tendrils of need went through her skin.

Tammy released a moan. She tilted her head so she could speak in his ear, half hoping he'd experience the same amazing thrill she had seconds ago. "Red, blue. Even some purple thrown in for good measure."

Hawthorne pulled back a little and looked into her eyes. He looked dazed, as if he'd experienced a new awareness. "Something strange is happening."

What she saw in his eyes told her he hesitated on the edge, ready to fall into trust.

As they continued circling on the dance floor, the sexy saxophone music didn't fade. Instead it continued, lulling like a hypnotist's persuasive voice.

His mouth hovered over hers. Tammy wondered if the entire room could sense the heavy power between them. Red poured into her vision again, then retreated, settling into every place they touched.

"Let's get out of here," he said, his voice rough with need.

Excitement pooled in her belly. "Go where?"

"My place. Your place. Anywhere we can...talk."

"Talk?" She let her desire show in her eyes, knowing he had to see it, feel it all.

"Communicate," he whispered.

He released her, and she missed his arms. Seconds later he slipped his arm around her shoulders and they moved quickly, eager to leave the music and the crush of people. The music followed them outside.

Once outside Hawthorne drew her down the sidewalk toward their car. Before they reached it he pulled her to a small alleyway. His arms came around her and he pulled her against him. Surprised delight parted her lips and she made a small sound.

His palms coasted over her buttocks. Cupped her. She gasped as Hawthorne brought her flush against him.

His lips touched her nose in an utterly endearing kiss. Fire coalesced, drawing her tight, sending undeniable flutters of desire to places that burned for his touch. Hawthorne's mouth tantalized her with promise, remaining inches from her lips. Just enough to keep the tension humming like a tuning fork.

"If you don't tell me what the colors mean, I'll do something desperate," he said.

"Like?"

"Do what I'm dying to do."

"Such as?"

Hawthorne pushed his hand through her hair, cupping the back of her head. "This."

Before she could speak his lips brushed hers. A tiny touch. So tender. So light.

Tammy moaned softly. "Oh, God."

"There's more where that came from. The colors?"

She'd tell him. She had to before she went insane. "I told you I saw red."

"As in hot?"

"As in passion."

His grin returned. "You're right. And it's making me crazy."

Tammy couldn't take it and closed her eyes. Pleasure permeated her at his admission.

"What am I feeling?" he asked.

His mouth pressed hers tenderly, infusing her with desire. She shivered and responded. When he retreated she managed to speak.

Her arms slid around his neck. "You want me. But I could tell that from other things, not just colors."

His muscles moved against her, rubbing in a sensuous concert with her curves. "I do want you, Tammy. I want you so much I ache. And I'm sick of denying it."

Before she could speak, his warm, exciting mouth took hers. He searched, betraying the heady passion she felt in his hard body.

Tammy answered, parting her lips for his tongue as he pushed deep inside. Heat surged. Everything within her responded as his mouth caressed hers hungrily. His need flared inside her until she moved against him and matched his ardor. She traced her palms over the taut muscles of his arms and shoulders.

She heard heavy breathing, a soft moan and knew it was their excitement ready to tumble over the precipice.

As his hand cupped her breast, caressing the nipple with gentle brushes of his fingers, she shuddered in staggering desire. Pleasure thrummed, hardening her nipples and causing her hips to move against his.

Oh, yes. There was more than a pounding need to strip him bare and love him until he couldn't stand. Way more. Happiness coursed through her along with wonder and hope.

She'd fallen in love with him. Deeply. Irrevocably.

Sweet heaven. I want to be with him forever.

Maybe something in her body language told Hawthorne. Gently he pulled away from their kiss, his breath hissing out. His hand remained over her breast, but he stilled all movement. His chest heaved with each breath, and in the shadows she could barely see the unrestrained desire on his face.

"Tammy. Sweetheart—"

Red slammed into her vision without warning, causing her to arch against him. But not in passion.

Fear.

"Hawthorne," she gasped.

Darkness passed near, leaping from the shadows. Tammy's heart lurched in terror. "Hawthorne, look out!"

Chapter 20

Tammy's warning came almost too late.

Hawthorne saw the panic in her eyes and dodged to the side, pulling her with him.

The attacker's growl sounded like an angry beast.

Pain cartwheeled through Hawthorne's head and arm as something hard landed against the side of his head and his right shoulder. Another blow to his right side made him stagger with searing pain, the motion sending him reeling against Tammy. She fell against the wall. Hawthorne landed flat on his face.

He heard Tammy release a sound halfway between a gasp and a scream.

Without pause, Hawthorne flipped onto his back, instincts firing to life.

Fight. Survive. Live.

Hawthorne kicked the attacker's legs out from under him, sending the man crashing to the ground onto his right side. Metal clinked over the ground.

"Tammy, get outta here!" Hawthorne heard her scramble toward the end of the alley. He heard her call for help, a desperate plea.

There, in the semi-darkness of the alley, Hawthorne had a second to see the attacker wore all black and a ski mask pulled over his features. A large knife lay on the ground near the man.

Before Hawthorne could reach for it, the man snapped up the knife in his black-gloved hand. Hawthorne rolled, grabbing the attacker's wrist and applying pressure with his thumb. The attacker grunted and dropped the knife, lunging to his feet as Hawthorne lost his grip. Hawthorne responded, jumping to his feet, poised to fight. The man swung out with his right fist. Hawthorne ducked.

As Hawthorne landed a sharp punch to the dark form's midsection, Hawthorne heard a gasp and the attacker stumbled back.

The attacker came again, and Hawthorne dodged as the man swung at him. Hawthorne executed a punishing right hook to the man's jaw, then another to the attacker's stomach. The man fell back against the alley wall with a groan.

Far in the distance Hawthorne thought he heard sirens. A side door attached to the bar opened and light spilled into the alley.

"Hey, what the hell's going on out here?" a man's gruff voice asked.

The shadow man took off in the opposite direction that Tammy had gone, darting around boxes, trash, and a dumpster. Hawthorne started to charge after him.

"Hawthorne, don't!" Tammy's desperate plea halted him.

Immediately he stopped and turned back.

What if she's hurt?

As he turned he saw her trotting toward him.

"Are you okay?" he asked through one heaving breath and the next. He knew he sounded anxious as hell, and he didn't care.

"I'm fine." Her voice trembled, her breath coming heavy with fear and exertion. Her eyes were wide, her features etched in shock.

More voices came into the night as two huge men stepped from the doorway and into the slash of light that now illuminated part of the alley.

"I said," the man with the harsh voice asked, "what the hell is going on? Are you bothering this lady?"

Tammy glared at the bouncer types. "No, you don't understand! The other man attacked us. He's getting away. I called the police."

Hawthorne ignored the other men and clasped Tammy's shoulders, peering into her eyes. Tears trembled on her lashes, but she looked unharmed. He saw courage in the set of her jaw. One part of him wanted to hold her close and the other wanted to chew her out for sticking around.

One of the bouncers leaned down and picked up a black object. He pulled on the short stick and it lengthened. "Hey, this is one of those telescoping batons. Like the police use, you know?"

Hawthorne took a deep breath and winced as pain throbbed through his head and his right side. "Yeah, I'm pretty sure that's the weapon he cracked me with." Hawthorne turned his attention to Tammy again. "You should have run when I told you."

"Are you kidding? It all happened so fast."

The thought of a gun or a knife taking Tammy's life made him feel ill. He released her and turned around to scan the alley. He saw the knife on the ground not far from him and leaned down, wincing in pain as he retrieved the weapon.

Blood stained the blade, and now his fingers. Suddenly he felt shaky and weak. Maybe a let down from adrenaline. His stomach flopped and he swallowed hard.

He turned back to her, blinking hard as his vision went fuzzy. *What the hell?*

"Oh, no," she gasped, reaching for his right side. She turned to one of the men from the bar. "Hurry, get me a towel. He's bleeding."

Disbelief mixed with the throbbing in his temples. "The guy barely touched me."

Annoyed at his own weakness, he started to pull back from Tammy. He looked down at stain spreading over his shirt near his lower ribs on the right side. He cursed violently and put his hand over the wound. Pain shattered his side and he inhaled sharply. His world wavered and he cursed again.

"The bastard stabbed me."

"Hawthorne." Tammy's cry of distress made him withhold his temper. She reached for him and held her hand against his side. "You could have been killed."

"I'll be all right." He pulled her against his other side and pressed a kiss to her forehead. "You're safe. And that's all that matters."

He'd failed to release Sweet Magnolia from the devil's grip.

Staggering into the night, he wanted to wail and shake his fists, screaming into the heavens. He wanted to scream. Scream. Scream again. Instead his breath rasped his throat, hoarse and hurting. Sweat ran into his right eye and he blinked, swiping at it with his right hand. His fingers twanged, painful, swollen. The bodyguard man had done something to his hand when he'd taken the knife away.

He made a frustrated gurgling, then cursed vehemently. The bodyguard man had surprised him with power and a will to survive. He'd been sure the time was right. Time to attack with baton and knife. Now the police probably had the evidence. He ripped off the mask that had at least kept his features a mystery. Jamming it in a pants pocket, he continued to run.

Then his feet skidded on slimy concrete, and he landed on his stomach. Air left his body in a rush, and he groaned. He lay stunned.

He heard footsteps but couldn't move.

"Hey, Mister, you okay?" a rough voice asked and a hand landed on his shoulder.

He growled as he caught his breath and surged upwards, bumping into whoever had stopped to help him. He shoved, sending the other man backwards onto his butt. Running onward, he kept his face away from the man that he'd pushed. No need for a witness.

All around, the night mocked him. High above the heavens threw scattered clouds across the face of a full moon. Horns blaring and the stench of gasoline and refuse permeated his senses, battering his head as he dashed from another alley onto a street.

He raced toward his car parked not a block away. Once he glanced back to make certain bodyguard man hadn't followed him. When he reached his car he fumbled with the keys, well aware that time would run out soon if he didn't get away. The cops would look for him. Inside the vehicle he started the motor and raced away into a night he hoped would cloak him from danger.

As the tires ate up miles, his mind cleared, bringing fear under control and desire's renewal. He'd find a way to get her. It wouldn't take much longer. So he'd failed and would pay with a drink from the bottle in the back of the fridge. Licking his lips, he imagined the revolting flavor. Still, though it sickened him, the tang wouldn't leave. Over and over he licked his lips, wishing to banish the bitterness.

Sweet Magnolia betrayed him. All this time he believed bodyguard man had pursued her, influencing her. Now he knew she hadn't fallen under bodyguard man's spell just tonight. She'd wanted the man all along.

For that infidelity she would pay dearly.

Pain pierced his side and he remembered that he'd sliced bodyguard man at least once with the knife. He hoped he'd gone deep. Deep into the man's ribs and had taken the breath from him.

The idea made him smile. Maybe the night had merit after all.

Tammy's hands shook as Joe handed her a cup of coffee. She noted the calm expression on his face as he smiled. He settled next to her on the hard, plastic couch in the emergency waiting room.

Inside she trembled. "Thanks. That was fast."

He nodded and smiled again, clasping his hands over his stomach. "Least I can do. You've been shivering like a kicked pup. And it isn't cold out."

"I can't seem to stop shaking."

"Shock, I'd think."

She tossed him a sarcastic smile. "Not every day I get to see someone beaten and sliced right in front of me."

To her surprise, the sometimes-taciturn man looked sad and sympathetic. "'Specially when it's someone you love."

Startled realization rocked through her. Yes, she'd acknowledged to herself that she loved Hawthorne, but how did Joe know? She didn't want to say it out loud and admit it to anyone else.

Before she could fumble a reply, he said, "Glad you called me."

She didn't know why he was the first person she thought to call. Worry for Hawthorne had translated into an anxiety she hadn't felt in some time. Not even the odd visions she'd experienced had prepared her for the fright of seeing the flash of a knife cutting into Hawthorne, nor the blood seeping from the wound. She'd thought of Joe. She needed an anchor right now, someone extra to depend on if needed.

"I really need to see him," Tammy said, not caring what Joe thought about her confession.

"Just relax a moment and drink that coffee."

She mumbled around a sip, wincing as the liquid burned her tongue. "Amazing. I didn't think coffee out of a machine could taste this good."

What a horribly inane thing to say, Carter. She couldn't believe she sat here discussing coffee as if nothing happened an hour ago. Joe's scrutiny unnerved her.

"Maybe the doc should have checked you out, too?" he asked.

"I'm just worried about Hawthorne. What's taking them so long?"

"Don't think it was too serious."

"But he almost passed out, Joe."

"A little shock, letdown from adrenaline rush. He was fighting for your lives. I don't think he lost that much blood."

Deep inside Tammy's gut twisted with remnants of fear. Though she had control of herself, she teetered on the boundary. She wanted to run to the front desk and ask again if she could see Hawthorne. She took another gulp of the cooling coffee. She'd gone through this once, when he and Joe had been shot at and Hawthorne had taken that bullet to the shoulder. She'd felt balled up inside. Now, though, the feelings came stronger and harder.

Realization seeped into her. *I was crazy in love with him then and didn't recognize it! How stupid I was. I wish I'd told him.*

She rallied and hoped words would push away these feelings. "I saw the colors while he was there, Joe. It wasn't any random attempt at mugging. The man who attacked us was the madman who's been tormenting me."

Joe nodded. "I believe you. Now it's up to you to try and stop him."

"What?"

"No one else can stop his madness but you, missy."

The horrifying thought poured into her blood like ice.

He slid down on the uncomfortable seat. "Here comes the nurse."

Tammy nearly spilled her coffee as she put it on a side table and popped out of her chair. She rushed toward the nurse. Nothing mattered but Hawthorne's condition.

The nurse reported that they'd patched Hawthorne's wound. "It wasn't that serious, and he's insisting he wants to go home."

Tammy glanced at Joe and then to the nurse. "You mean you're not keeping him here?"

"Not if he doesn't want to stay. We patched his head, too. He had a cut from being hit with that baton."

Tammy recalled the wicked-looking telescopic weapon, and figured the police had bagged it for evidence just as they had the knife. The attacker had worn gloves, so she doubted prints would be found to identify their assailant.

When they saw Hawthorne moments later in the partitioned area of the emergency room, he lay looking pale and worn. His hair was matted, his eyes closed, his lips flat as if he'd fallen asleep. He was shirtless, but he still wore his jeans. She hesitated at the foot of his bed. Before she could back away, Hawthorne's eyes opened. To her relief, a wide smile parted his lips. Even now that grin made her stomach flutter.

"Hey," he murmured. He sat up, a small wince marring his features. "Haven't we done this once before?"

"Wait a minute." Tammy came to his side and reached for his biceps. She wanted to slide her arm around his shoulder, but the table was too tall. "Are you sure you're suppose to be sitting up?"

"The doctor says I can go." He slid his legs off the table. "Besides, I'm not staying here while you go home alone."

"I would have managed."

"Uh-huh." Grit underlined his voice as he glared. "I'm not

leaving you alone. The stakes are way too high at this point." He moved off the table, but she kept her grip on his arm.

"But you're hurt."

He shrugged and she released his arm. "I'm a little bruised and I might be stiff in the morning, but I've had a lot worse."

Unbidden tears surged to her eyes. "I remember."

Tammy's words seemed to have an effect on Hawthorne. She knew he could see the tears threatening to fall. His gaze turned lambent, and he reached up to caress her face gently. Tammy saw many things in his eyes right then. She might want him with a potent desire that stunned her, but she also recognized admiration and tenderness in his face.

It warmed her cheeks, her throat, and her entire heart in the process. He cared about her. Even if he didn't love her—

Someone cleared their throat, and Tammy and Hawthorne shifted to see Joe standing patiently at the end of the table. They'd completely forgotten him. Joe grinned and stuffed his hands in his pockets.

"Hey, Joe. What are you doing here?" Hawthorne asked.

"The missy here called me." Joe winked. "I think she needed a shoulder to lean on after that mess."

Hawthorne looked back at her. "It wasn't that bad. The wound, I mean."

A tiny piece of Tammy cracked, breaking like fine china in her heart. She'd thought she was stronger than this. Instead, when the cards had landed on the table, she gave in to fear and worry. Tammy knew stress did odd things to people, but that didn't prevent her reaction. When she'd seen Hawthorne's wound she didn't cry, nor had she cried on the way to the hospital, riding along in the ambulance.

Instead the tears she'd restrained came surging to her eyes. Saying anything became impossible; the lump pushing its way into her throat threatened to choke her.

The tears flowed, and embarrassed, she murmured, "Excuse me."

She dashed from the area as Hawthorne said, "Wait. Where are you—"

She trotted down the hall and didn't stop until she reached the automatic sliding glass doors leading out of the emergency area. She leaned against the wall outside, drinking in the cooling air and letting the tears come. Self-recrimination burst to the fore, and she reached into her pocket for a tissue. Sniffing, she dabbed at her eyes.

Less then a minute later Hawthorne appeared through the sliding doors, his stride quick. He'd put on his torn and stained shirt. When he saw her leaning against the wall, he scowled. *Great, here it comes. A lecture on safety.*

He stopped in front of her and glowered. Her tears dropped steadily, and she wouldn't look at him.

When she did venture to peek over the tissue, his eyes had changed, back to that soft, warm glow that made her insides quiver.

"What's wrong?" he asked softly.

"What's wrong? What's wrong?" She straightened. "You almost got killed because of me, *that* is what is wrong."

"It's my job, Tammy. I'm a bodyguard, remember?"

"Yeah, but that's not all." When she realized what she'd said and how it sounded, she rushed to cover her slip. "I mean, I can't have that on my conscience. You're hurt and bleeding and if you'd been killed, I don't…I can't…." She sucked in a breath as the tears flowed again. "Damn it! I hate being this out of control."

"Hey, hey, it's all right." He cupped her face with one hand again. "I've had the crap kicked out of me before. I always bounce back." He kissed her nose. "Come on, babe, you're making me ache watching you like this."

"Ache how? Does your wound hurt?"

"I ache because I feel rotten when you cry." His next kiss

landed on her lips, soft and sweet and way too short. "Besides, it's not safe to stand out in the open like this again. I'm packing my weapon from now on. I was careless."

His rueful smile helped some, and she sniffed. "Let's go back to your place and barricade in."

Hawthorne slipped his left arm around her shoulder. "Sounds like a deal. I don't think he'll try anything again tonight. But he will come back, Tammy. And when he does, we'll be ready for him."

Tammy watched Hawthorne set the alarm system and noted he moved slowly. Did he hurt all over like she did?

Not just her body. Her mind. Her heart.

He moved to the window, peeking through the curtains. "Peterson just pulled up across the street. Looks like he's settling down for the night."

"Extra protection sent by Mrs. Taggert? Do you think the creep is nearby?"

Hawthorne pulled away from the window, letting the curtain fall back in place. He sighed and looked at her. "Wouldn't you feel him close? Wouldn't you see his colors?"

She didn't want to think about that, but circumstances said she must. "I think so. I never expected…."

"What?"

"I never expected the creep to come after us like that, Hawthorne."

"We let our…we let other things get in our way when we should have paid attention to things around us."

Part of her wanted to cry again. Could he be saying, in some small way, that he regretted their kisses?

Automatically she turned the dimmer switch so the glare in

the living area was reduced. She couldn't stand seeing too many details right this minute.

His poker face eased into a rueful grin. "Don't look so serious. You'll be safe here with me."

Tammy didn't respond, and then he walked toward her until he'd stepped into her personal space. She inhaled deeply, enjoying the scent of man and musk. As she looked into his eyes she realized he bristled with a forceful maleness that thrilled her on all levels. She ached, responding to his raw physical power. The undeniable male within him captivated everything female within her.

But that wasn't it. That wasn't what made her wild for him down deep inside.

She loved everything about him. His professionalism, his determination to do the job right garnered her admiration and deep respect. His ability to joke, to make things light when the going got too tough warmed her inside. His caring for people, his deep, undeniable goodness. And his heart-stopping gentleness unraveled her like thread on a spool. All of it added up to the man she knew she would love for the rest of her life.

She wanted to grab him and kiss him until the sun rose. Fear grappled with desire until she wanted to scream. "I can never repay you for keeping me safe."

"What makes you think you have to repay me?"

"Guilt. It's not every day a man gets hit with a baton and stabbed for me."

The hint of a smile around Hawthorne's mouth disappeared, replaced by that searching quality in his eyes that always stripped her naked. Struggling between wrenching need and a drive to run, Tammy caressed his beard-roughened cheek.

His hand came up to capture hers. "Don't. It's making me…think things maybe I shouldn't."

So the truth came forward. He did want to back away from what they'd started on the dance floor and continued in the alley. Her heart felt like it might stop. "I see."

"No, you don't see. If I'm this close to you it's going to be damned hard to keep my hands off you."

A thrill pulsed through her body. She turned away from him, hoping her pounding heart would slow.

He stepped up behind her and talked over her left shoulder. "It's too strong, Tammy. This…this thing I have for you won't stop."

"You're saying you regret breaking Mrs. Taggert's rule?"

"Screw her rule."

She laughed. "I thought in the bar when we danced…the things we said…."

"I'm saying I want to be with you." His voice went low and rough with something she dare not name. "And not just because it's my job."

His words softened her heart when she wanted to harden it like stone. "You're my friend. That's why you want me safe."

"No." Hawthorne's warm breath whispered close to her left ear, his voice dropping into a husky tone. "Not just that." He clasped her shoulders and pressed softly. "You're all I think about. All I worry about. If anything happened to you…."

The color came then. It formed as pure, magical pink and red, slipping across her vision and filling her with sweet languor. Not the rage red of the madman, but the brilliant shade of love and a staggering passion.

Tammy turned her head toward him, tilting back until her throat felt bare for the taking. Color surged like a flame, scarlet and undeniable. He still wanted her. The tension pulled tight across her senses, the tempo of breathing quickening. Dry air stung her throat and she swallowed hard.

Hawthorne turned her toward him. When she looked into his eyes this time, she let her love for him spill. He cupped her face in his hands and drew her so close they touched all along their bodies. She laid her hands on his chest and felt the strong beat of his life under her fingers.

"Hawthorne?"

"Yeah."

"You scared the crap out of me tonight."

Tiny lines appeared between his eyebrows. "In what way?"

"When we were in the bar and we danced and I realized you wanted me. I...I never confessed. I never said it out loud. And I've got to now."

"What?" he whispered, his gaze smoldering.

"Oh, damn." She couldn't wait. Didn't want to say it when she could show him.

Tammy grabbed the front of his shirt with one hand and slid her other hand behind his neck to pull him to her.

When he simply searched her gaze, she swallowed hard. "I'm sorry you were hurt for me. But I'm not sorry I'm in your arms."

Hawthorne's gaze went thermonuclear, and before she could say another word, he kissed her.

Chapter 21

Exquisite. Impossibly wonderful.

Tammy had never tasted him like this. Not even their encounter in the laundry room matched her desire to dissolve into him.

Their lips met again and again, attracted by a flame that had burst to life from the first day they'd met. Each exquisite encounter went on and on and the world around them faded.

Hawthorne's arms encircled her and brought her tight against him. Warmth filled her stomach as he found her buttocks and cupped and caressed. Heat rose faster than a firestorm.

He reached for the button and zipper on the back of her skirt and with three quick movements the garment fell to her feet. She toed out of her pumps. Her half-slip slid down over her pantyhose, pooling around her ankles. Before she could utter a word, he kissed her again. Surrender formed deep in her heart as he teased her with his kisses, making each a testament to his desire, but never giving his *all* to her.

Gently she pulled away from his kiss. "Oh, man. This is—"

He kissed her. "I know." Their lips came together, then parted. "I know."

"I'm sorry about—"

Hawthorne kissed her again. Then he stripped her hose down her legs and helped her to step out of them. When he stood back up he slid his hands into the back of her panties. She gasped into his mouth, her skin jumping and tingling as he pushed the material down and it joined her slip.

Cupping her butt, he hauled her up and her legs came around his waist. His muffled groan of satisfaction fueled her onward. She knew this night would be the most insane and satisfying of her life.

Insane all right. Insane with love for him.

She didn't want a sweet, sensual joining. Not this time. Too much had happened between them, too many risks pushed this desire to the limit and built inside her with staggering strength.

Seconds later, Hawthorne walked down the hall with her wrapped around him. Heat accumulated, her senses erupting into a riot so clear she could hear her own pulse. Feel the thump of his heartbeat against her breasts, his harsh breathing.

She swept her fingers through his hair, exploring the short strands like a sensual diagram, her nerve endings exposed to commotion with startling clarity.

He stopped in the hallway for a moment and twirled like a slow top, making her dizzy with desire and a playful sense of inevitability. She giggled, more alive than ever, giddier than a first blush of discovery. He sampled her neck, and tingles swirled through her body.

He hefted her up higher, finding a snug grip. He walked through the bedroom door and seconds later fell to the bed with her. She giggled, joy rippling through her. Without a doubt Hawthorne gave Tammy this feeling of renewal, of experiencing the first time all over again. She hadn't realized until that moment that her love for him could multiply, but it did.

Hawthorne had never wanted a woman more than he wanted

Tammy. Her sweet laugh set his heart free, mixing with the driving need to love her hard and deep until they both went blind with the pleasure. The tug of her fingers at his jeans made him grit his teeth in desire. He reached to help her, finding the buttons and flicking them open so that she could touch him. When she caressed him he jerked with ecstasy, his body taut. He saw her eyes widen in appreciation as she stroked him.

I'm going to die. Right here, right now.

Tammy wanted him. He could see it in the flush in her cheeks, the rasp of her breath strong in his ears. She licked her lips, and her gaze flicked up to his eyes. His heart jumped, more than physical pleasure sweeping through him. They struggled against their remaining clothes, tossing each piece away. He yanked off his boots and they thudded to the floor. His jeans went flying and hit the bedside table, knocking the alarm clock onto the floor.

It started to ring.

He cursed, reached down, and slapped his hand over the off button.

She laughed and he stifled the sound with his mouth. When he lifted his head, he took a moment to look at her incredible breasts and he moaned. Her grin widened.

"You," he gasped, "are beautiful."

Without taking time to see her reaction, he pulled the hospital scrub top over his head.

Damn good thing I'm not still wearing that Western shirt and bolo tie. I'd have strangled by now.

"Hawthorne, your wound—"

"If you think that is going to stop me now, sweetheart...." He left the sentence hanging as he gave her a smile. He watched her eyes widen in appreciation as he pulled down his briefs and they fell to the floor.

"Hawthorne...." Her sigh came out raspy with passion.

He leaned over her and she pushed her fingers through the

hair on his chest, her gaze simmering with a sensual side he'd never seen in her eyes before.

This was Nirvana, and he sighed as she explored him in ways that made him gasp. Her hands trailed through the hair on his stomach. "Honey, you keep doing that, I don't know how much longer I'll last."

"Me neither."

Seconds later he rolled on top of her, growling when she touched him again.

"Oh, God, Tammy don't." She did it anyway, a wicked, yet somehow shy smile etching her full lips. "Wench."

"Wench?" Mock indignity covered her features. "I'll show you a wench."

She stroked along his hard length and he inhaled sharply, the sound coming like a hiss. He leaned down until his mouth hovered over hers. "You're gonna pay for that one."

She'd pay all right. He'd wring every last drop of passion from her until she screamed for mercy. Urgency pushed him on, unforgiving and unrelenting.

Seconds later his hands found her breasts, detouring over them with a fever Tammy relished like a starving woman. He licked and seduced until she arched. His tongue was fire, and she didn't think she could stand another minute. When he suckled her, a rhythm that tugged deep inside her, she released whimpers of pleasure. For what seemed forever he devoured her until she thought she'd die from the torture. Her body arched as screaming pleasure seemed to race from one end of her body to the next. Passion seared her, driving all thoughts from her mind but the final goal. Loving Hawthorne to the end.

He settled his hips between her thighs.

A last semblance of control tried to reassert itself. "Hawthorne."

"Mmmmmm." His tongue inspected one stinging, hard nipple.

She gasped and moved against him. Hawthorne kissed her

deeply, giving her the taste of his tongue in continual strokes. She'd been dying for him to kiss her like this. *Finally. Finally he's putting me out of my misery.*

Surely she'd die of pleasure, and they'd find her lying here, an exposed mess, her hair tangled like Medusa, and her lips parted in a grin that told all.

As his hands traced an urgent path down her body, he reached the part of her that ached the most. Moaning a soft appreciation, he touched slick folds. Sweet, sharp pleasure rocked her as he inserted two fingers deep inside. She clenched against him, a shocked delight rippling through her. He instigated a steady cadence until she arched and moaned. Then he found a special spot, pausing over it, then touching, then retreating…a caress that drove her to the edge. He stopped.

"Babe," he managed to rasp.

"Yes."

Struggling for control, he found the foil packet in his bedside drawer and seconds later he slipped between her thighs again.

This was it. He paused at the entrance to heaven. She writhed, tortured by feelings both emotional and physical.

Unexpectedly, tears gathered in her eyes. "I've waited so long for you."

"And I you," he whispered, his tone husky with need.

Their gazes locked, then eyes closed as they kissed and he brought himself home. Hot, and hard he stroked, shoving deep the first thrust.

Somewhere she'd heard that making love could be like a dance. A waltz that started slow with each violin building and adding until every instrument demanded the swirling movements to go faster and faster. Now she knew it was true. With Hawthorne she'd found a love that filled her heart and body. A dance that would never leave her soul.

Another hard thrust brought her up against him, and she lifted her hips, eager to take all of him. His muttered satisfaction aroused her as much as each powerful movement of his hips.

She clasped his buttocks, sliding her fingers over territory that made him inhale harshly. Tammy savored the power she had to bring this extraordinary man to this primal joining. She'd never experienced such heady excitement before, and she wanted to hold onto it for as long as possible.

Sensations inside her spiraled to a tremulous height, propelled by a desire that refused to wait for tenderness or time and wouldn't let her go. Everything was now.

Tammy reached for Hawthorne as he kissed her, swirling through a maelstrom of exhilaration. Nothing mattered but the continual movements, the impact of him against her. It took her up, threw her skyward, made her realize that this man would always be the one she loved. No matter what happened from this point forward, she would remember the slide of Hawthorne's flesh against hers, the incredible reality of his body within her.

She couldn't believe the fiery pleasure that beat against her body with every hard thrust. She met him head on with the roaring in her ears and the stinging in her blood.

He picked up the pace, hammering deep. She trembled as ecstasy built too high to contain. A storm approached, clawing its way up as the clouds burst and rained upon her. She gasped and gasped again, each breathy exhalation a testament as ecstasy found her at last. The stinging, unbelievable burn of pleasure drove her upward against him.

Tammy looked up at him and saw it all in his eyes, in his face. The rush to completion was almost upon him. A desperate wildness hovered out of his reach, and she saw it flash through him. He looked amazed. Beyond heaven.

Hawthorne knew a blinding need, a desperate love that came to him like a tremendous tornado, screaming through his veins. With each immersion inside her he knew that love had never existed before for him. He opened his eyes, aware of the heat of their breaths, the scent of their passion and the taste of her on his tongue. Her snug warmth drove him to this side of insanity.

Hawthorne caught her gaze, his arms trembling. Moments away from a second explosion, she trembled, her mouth open on a moan.

So he gave her all of him.

Again. Again. Again.

Almost there.

Almost.

And the night went nova, all thoughts of yesterday and tomorrow lost in the now.

Yes.

Denied once again. Deprived of Sweet Magnolia.

He reached for the refrigerator door, cursing the ground he walked on and the oxygen he breathed. Frosty air slid through the crack of the open door.

As he reached inside the fridge and shoved aside a milk carton for *the* bottle, he sank into his dreams where Sweet Magnolia knew him intimately. Where she touched him as she must have caressed bodyguard man.

He stood with the door hanging open, billowing cold air touching his legs. Finally, after staring at the open door for a considerable time, he slammed it shut and took the bottle to the living room. The amber glass bottle looked black in the dim light.

As he sat in his recliner and reached for the television remote, he realized the bottle was only half full. Several curses issued from his mouth, then he put his hands over his lips. His momma would wash his mouth out with soap. He cackled. Damn. Wasn't that the truth? At least it would be, if the old bitch had lived long enough to see this.

The snow on the television reminded him he hadn't switched on the VCR. He aimed the remote like a weapon, starting the VCR and the tape that held permanent residence there.

For a startling second, as Sweet Magnolia's image came across the screen, he wondered if anyone would think him strange for watching this tape two hundred times and counting.

No. Three hundred and sixty-five times this year alone. Last year...well last year he'd watched it at least twice a day. His obsession had seared his brain like a brand, reminding him of the day his cousin had caught him looking in Sweet Magnolia's house...looking in her slut sister's window and watching Barb the Bitch slip from her clothes piece by piece.

God, you're such a faggot.

His cousin's words had made no freaking sense. Faggot? He was watching a woman. How could he be a fag?

Then his rage had gone volcano, piercing his skull like an ax. Something had flickered in his cousin's expression. Fear? How he'd relished that trepidation as his cousin had left.

But he'd followed his cousin home.

He closed his eyes and the scene replayed, much like the images flickering across the television. But to his disappointment the fantasy didn't come clear. Instead it moved and jumped like worn videotape. Parts of the plot didn't make sense.

Bad editing. Very bad.

He grinned as he saw himself hitting his cousin's jaw, and he'd heard the sickening crack as the force had split the bone. His cousin's wails as he'd flailed at him echoed in his head. He laughed remembering the stricken look rolling across his cousin's expression.

His aunt and uncle had cursed him, telling his mom and dad they should send him away.

And they had. For a long, long time.

But when he'd come back to the United States he'd shown them. He'd shown them all.

He cursed. Screw them. They didn't understand him, didn't know how powerful he'd become since he'd exorcised the demons inside him and learned his true purpose on earth.

To be with Sweet Magnolia and savor her as no man could. Then to kill her to save her from the sin of her womanhood.

She may have escaped his blade this time, but she'd see into his eyes before she died. When she felt the parting of her flesh under his weapon, she'd know that he was her true master.

He opened his eyes, replete from the daydream. His stomach burned, and he reached for an antacid. After chewing and swallowing, he took a swig from the bottle and drifted into the heaven and the hell.

Morning inched under the drawn curtains, a pale strand of light that alerted Hawthorne to a new day.

He groaned. He didn't *want* to think about a new day.

Tammy sighed. When she shifted in his arms and kissed his cheek, he brought her nearer. He remembered when he'd wakened her in the dead of night with his kisses and caresses, loving her with a fierce possessiveness that caught them both by surprise. The heat between them had roared up like a firestorm, burning them to cinders. Recalling how she'd fallen into a screaming, writhing climax made him grin with male pride.

He loved her. God, how he loved her.

Each little movement of her body made him want to love her again. Sliding his palm over her smooth back, he traced the indent of her spine and she shivered. Possessively he cupped her bottom, then let his other hand fondle the side of one breast.

Silence cloaked the room, and a dream like state drew a haze over his awareness.

Tammy propped up on one elbow. "Morning."

He answered her by way of a kiss.

When he didn't speak, she asked, "What are we going to do?"

Through dazed eyes, he tried to focus on her. "About what?" His voice sounded rough, and he cleared his throat.

"We broke that fraternization rule—big time." Her wistful tone made him take her seriously.

He shook his head. "I think Mrs. Taggert was worried about having a little too much closeness in the office. She can't dictate our relationship out of the office."

"You don't think she'll fire us for being involved?"

That woke him up. "Why would you think that?"

She shook her head. "I don't know. Just a silly worry, I guess. Everything that's happened in the last few hours…."

"Yeah." He reached for her, pulling her on top of him and kissing her deeply. "We've plunged in the deep end, eh?"

A small smile made its way across her mouth. "I think I need a little mouth to mouth. Please save me."

One teasing kiss led to another. Even their wild encounter last night, when he'd thought the top of his head would explode, couldn't match this.

Slow and tender he found her, showing her with lips and tongue and fingers everything he could do for her. When he reached her toes and gave them special attention, she practically vaulted off the bed.

"Oh, God!" She shivered. "I never knew. Hawthorne you are…"

"Yeah?" He nuzzled her big toes and then her little toes, then every toe in between. She had evenly spaced, shapely toes on long, narrow feet. He'd never found feet sexy before. Until now.

She closed her eyes and shook and shivered, each pant divulging her stimulation. His touches and kisses found their way along her flesh until they tested the heat between her thighs. She flowed warm and musky, and he couldn't get enough of her, exploring until she wiggled and gasped.

She begged for him to stop, then to start, then to take her over the top. Yet he didn't want to. Not yet. Not until they both lost their minds and could forget the outside world held a madman bent on their destruction.

With deliberate caresses he charted her stomach, his mouth joining the adventure in seeking her breasts. After molding, shaping and driving them both to the edge of madness, he reached for another condom. Then he rolled over onto his back.

He urged her to take him. She rode him, sliding deep and hard. It went on forever, yet not long enough. Her cries of need escalated, and he thrust upward, demanding and giving with his body and his words.

Then she shuddered and her eyes closed and her head fell back exposing her long throat. A primitive cry escaped her and she clutched around him, rippling in release.

The day grew white hot as his pleasure shot from deep inside. His body pulsated, jetting a scalding release as he cried out and his body melted under the force of her sun.

The rapid cadence of their breathing eased as they cooled. They lay silent, as if dazed. His brain had liquefied and he didn't plan on thinking again anytime soon. A sharp ache entered his side, a muscle protesting.

She sighed. "That man who attacked us. He's not going to give up, is he?"

"No." He couldn't keep the inevitable from her. Didn't want to. Knowledge would act like ammo. "It's got to be someone you've known in the past."

Tammy disengaged herself from his arms and sat up. When she arranged her legs Indian style, he about choked.

Hawthorne cursed softly. "Babe if you sit like that for much longer I might just die of a heart attack."

She grinned, evil intent clear. "Uh-huh." Her gaze slid down his body, pausing at his chest, his stomach, and regions below. A conspiratorial smile covered her lips. "I think it's too late for me. I've already died and gone to heaven."

Her words made his chest feel tight. *Lord save him.* He wanted to say the words that burned his esophagus, but he couldn't. *I love you so much I ache.*

What if she didn't love him?

The idea stopped his confession cold.

He couldn't tell her now. The time had to be right. After this nasty stalker business had ended he'd tell her everything he felt.

Switching gears to halt his misery, he said, "Think about anybody in your past that could have a vendetta against you. Anyone at all." Tammy leaned toward him, and his gaze riveted to her breasts. He swallowed hard. "An old boyfriend? Someone you dated in high school?

Tammy's eyes widened. "High school? No way."

"Way."

She shrugged. "I didn't date much when I was a teen, Hawthorne."

"You're kidding, right?"

"I'm not. I was as ugly as the back end of a mule." She sniffed. "You should see my yearbook pictures."

Anger surged forward in him and he sat up. "Damn it, don't put yourself down like that. I don't believe you've been ugly at *any* time in your life, so don't give me that crap."

She didn't look fazed by his vehemence. "It's not crap. It's reality. I just wasn't the type of girl boys lusted after. I was bony as hell and almost didn't get breasts until I was eighteen. I also had braces. How many teen boys fall in love with girls who wear either braces or glasses and have a chest as flat as an ironing board?"

His eyes narrowed. "You wore glasses? I thought you have twenty-twenty vision."

"I do." She shrugged. "For all the attention boys paid to me, I might as well have worn glasses. I was the invisible woman through and through." When he didn't reply she chuckled. "I'll prove it to you the next time we're at my place. I'll show you my senior picture."

He clasped her wrist and pulled her on top of him. He used his arms and his legs to trap her. He let her know with his intent gaze how much he admired her. His hands drifted over her buttocks.

"Bony my ass," he said.

She pursed her lips and sighed. "And what does this really have to do with mad stalkers?"

"Nothing. Are sure there isn't an old boyfriend out there who doesn't want to make your life miserable?"

"No. No. I can't think of anyone."

They stayed silent until something else occurred to him. "Wait a minute." Gently he shoved his hands through her mussed hair. "When we were in the alley you didn't pick up the attacker's colors. Why?"

She kissed his nose. "Easy answer. I got a flash of red right before he attacked us. Just enough for me to warn you. I might have felt something earlier, but I can't experience more than one person's colors at a time. I was too busy wrapped up in your passion." Tammy smiled gently. "You melted me right into my shoes."

"I think I like the sound of that." After taking her lips with a kiss, he turned back to serious. "Maybe we need to analyze all the times you remember seeing the red color, when you weren't around me."

She nodded. "All right. But what are we looking for?"

"Who was around you the first time you saw the red?"

"The first time no one. I was in the office. I got the colors when the creep called me."

"You don't think that could have been some other jackass and you picked up on his aura?"

Tammy's brow creased, concentration clear in her gaze. "That's it."

Trepidation rode his spine. "What?"

"That's it." She snapped her fingers. "How stupid could I be?"

"What?" he asked impatiently.

"I'd forgotten that the colors I see are individual to the person. Like a fingerprint. If I think back on each time I saw the red, there are times when the color signature didn't match with the original phone call. People's colors are subtle enough that when it's a different person I know whether I've experienced that color before."

Comprehension made him sit upright and she tumbled off him. "When *did* it match up?"

"The phone calls all matched, and he called me Sweet Magnolia more than once. I saw the colors once when I was in the garage…the time I called you. I saw the colors when I was around Le Blanc, but even though he had red in his colors it didn't match that of the caller or the time in the garage. His red was from lust."

"So that just means Le Blanc isn't the man."

"Right." Her expression flickered from concentration to another revelation. "Oh, man. I saw the same color signature more than once while I was at the homeless shelter."

Tammy's words chilled him. "Do you remember who was around at the time?"

She shook her head. "One time there were dozens of people around. The other time I was in the back room after talking to Joe."

"We know it's not Joe."

"Of course not." When her gaze went intense and determined, he knew she'd had a revelation. "But I have an idea of how I can find out who it is."

Chapter 22

Hawthorne put down his coffee cup with such force some of the liquid sloshed onto the kitchen counter. "I still say it's a crazy idea and you're nuts for even considering it."

Tammy's disappointment took an upward spike as she stared at him across the kitchen. She turned away and fluffed the eggs in the frying pan with a spatula. "Thanks so much, Hawthorne. Glad I can count on your confidence."

They'd argued about this all morning. She'd suggested she work at the shelter this evening, hoping the creep would appear and she'd see his signature color pattern.

"This has nothing to do with confidence in you." His voice went rough with irritation. "It's about you not getting dead."

Blast his logic. What could he do? Tie her to the bed? As intriguing as that might sound in other circumstances, she wondered how he thought he could stop her.

"It's too dangerous," he growled.

"You've already said that about a dozen times."

"I figured if I said it often enough you'd come to your senses." She continued to stir the eggs, unwilling to allow his skepticism to ruin her breakfast. "How else do you expect us to find this dirtball?"

Tammy heard him move around the counter until he stood near her, but she didn't turn around.

"We can let the police do their jobs."

Tammy shrugged. "We don't know how long that will take."

"I'm not letting you use yourself as bait and that's final."

She shut off the stove and scooped scrambled eggs and sausage onto two plates. She handed him one. "You take risks every day. What's the difference?"

Hawthorne's faced turned hard and unforgiving. "You know the answer to that."

He strode to the breakfast nook and sat down at the table.

Closing her eyes for a moment, she took a cleansing breath. When she opened her eyes, he was tucking into his breakfast with relish.

She grinned. "Guess the last couple of days made you hungry."

When he looked up from his breakfast his gaze reminded her of searing kisses and the sensation of him driving deep within her. "Especially last night and this morning."

The sheer magnetic force of his attention made her flush from head to toe. Keeping her winsome smile, she joined him at the table and sipped her grapefruit juice.

"So how long should we hang out here at your place, Hawthorne? Until we're ninety-five? Never knowing when this guy will strike?"

Reaching for his coffee Hawthorne took a long sip, contemplating her over the rim of the cup. "Sounds reasonable to me."

Frustration nipped at her. "I can't live like that. And I think if you're honest with yourself, neither can you."

"I'm not letting him get that close to you again. Ever."

"And I can't imagine wondering for the rest of my life when this nut case is going to show up." She chewed a sausage and swallowed hard. "You can't protect me for the rest of my life. You've got your own life to live."

His lips compressed. He put down his fork and leaned his arms on the table. "We'll find the bastard before then. You won't need protection for that long."

Tammy nibbled on her eggs, chewing slowly. "Can you guarantee that?"

"There are no guarantees in life."

"Exactly. That's why I've got to take the risk."

He closed his eyes for a moment, and when he opened them, he shoved back from the table. He headed into the kitchen and came back with the coffee carafe.

After pouring himself more coffee, he gestured at her empty mug. "You want some?"

She nodded and he poured. When he retreated into the kitchen again she tried not to think. Instead she put creamer into her coffee and stirred.

"Inaction is almost as dangerous as no action," she called out.

When he didn't respond she sighed. He returned moments later, and Tammy started in again. "Maybe if we have extra backup I could still do this. I'll be at the shelter, surrounded by people like Joe. The guy isn't going to try anything in the middle of a crowd."

"How can you be sure?"

"Do creeps like this usually go in for attacking people in front of crowds? No, I don't think so."

After several moments of silence, he nodded. "You're right—"

"Ah-ah!" She gestured at him. "You admit I'm right."

"Only in that it's not the usual MO for this type of person. If he's the one who killed your sister, then he's probably killed others. We're most likely dealing with a serial killer. There's got to be a safer way."

Tammy wanted to scream. Instead she started tearing her paper napkin into little pieces and littering the table. "You know,

Hawthorne, I think your stubbornness was one of the qualities that attracted me to you in the first place."

One of his eyebrows twitched and a corner of his mouth tilted up. "What? Not my staggering good looks?"

"And your overwhelming modesty." She tore the rest of the napkin and it fluttered to the table. "Okay. You're a disgustingly attractive man."

His grin came small and tentative. He took a sip of coffee. "Thanks."

"You're also infuriating."

Hawthorne's smile widened to full scale devastating within seconds. "Isn't it amazing how the very thing that attracts you to a person can drive you nuts the next moment?"

Deciding she could use an ego feed, she leaned closer and asked in a whisper, "What attracted you to me?"

This time amusement reached his entire face and brightened his eyes. "Everything. From the first day I saw you."

Warmth spread from her heart to the rest of her body. "The first day?"

He shoved his plate away. "I knew you were special when I saw your cartoon desk accessories. Especially when I spied that plastic dinosaur."

She laughed. "He's my favorite."

"I could tell." He leaned forward, giving her his full attention. His voice lowered. "I knew there was an independent spirit wrapped inside that…" He paused to peruse her with mind-melding thoroughness. "…that incredible body. You wore that red dress and it clung to all the right places. Very sexy."

The blushes kept heating her face. Incredible. She had no control over the way he made her feel. None whatsoever.

Hawthorne continued. "It snowballed from there. The cocky way you teased me. The snappy comebacks. Your obvious warmth and goodness. I think I…."

When he faded out, her curiosity rose. "Yes?"

He cleared his throat and pushed back from the table. He crossed his arms. "I knew then I was in big trouble. But I denied it. For a whole damn year."

The admission made her breath stop. Was it possible for her to fall even more in love with this man? On one level the depth of her feelings for him frightened her. How could she tell him? The words wouldn't come. Shame rocketed through her. She vowed to tell him she loved him, and yet the words kept lodging in her throat.

When she stared at him but didn't speak, his gaze came up. "I can't let anything happen to you."

"You won't."

"Tammy—"

"You know we've got to do something and this is the only way."

Hawthorne remained silent for some time. "You're going to find a way to do this no matter what I say, aren't you?"

She nodded. "You know I will."

To her surprise he smiled. "You're a big pain in the ass, you know?"

"I was just thinking the same thing about you."

He laughed. "What am I going to do with you?"

An idea came to mind. She stood and came around the table. Tammy sat on his lap and linked her arms around his neck. "You could start by trusting me to do this."

His arms came tight around her waist as he snuggled his nose into her neck. "I trust you more than anyone in the world."

With slow attention she kissed his ear, nibbling on the lobe. "Keep saying those nice things to me. I think I like it."

He shuddered and made a low sound. "Keep that up and I won't be able to talk at all. Unless maybe that's what you intended?"

With a soft sweep of her tongue, she tasted his ear again. "That's an excellent side effect, yes."

When she worked her way along his jaw, he closed his eyes. "Or you're trying to distract me."

"That's not a bad idea either."

"This isn't going to change my mind."

She tasted his chin, kissing him under his lower lip, then working her way up to smother his mouth with a lingering soft kiss. "Are you certain?"

"There isn't anything you could do—"

He moaned as she touched one place that had gone rigid with attention. "Except maybe that."

Tammy thought Joe looked perturbed, but sometimes his stony expression hid his real feelings with ease.

"I don't think this is a good idea." Joe glanced from Tammy to Hawthorne as they stood at the entrance to the shelter offices. "It's dangerous."

Hawthorne stuffed his hands in his jean pockets, his expression grim. "That's what I've been trying to tell her."

Joe looked to Tammy like an angry parent. "No way, little missy."

"It's already set up," Hawthorne said.

She lowered her voice. "Let's go where it's more private and talk about this."

They retreated to the empty office next to Mrs. Traynor's. Joe closed the door, his face a mask of uncertainty.

"What's the full plan?" Joe asked.

They explained that Tammy would wander the area and try to detect if anyone in the room matched up as the attacker.

"But what if he just doesn't come in tonight?" Joe asked.

Tammy sat on the bare desk and started swinging her feet.

"I'll come here every night until he shows up."

Joe nodded, then rubbed his hand over the grizzled stubble along his jaw. "The police know you're doing this?"

"No," Hawthorne and Tammy said in unison.

Tammy swung her feet back and forth even faster, her stomach quivering with nerves. She felt as if she might have to jog around the block to expend nervous energy. "They'll tell me it's crazy at best. They don't know about the colors and they wouldn't believe me if I told them. If we're going to catch this bastard, we're going to have to do it the unconventional way."

"Mrs. Taggert knows about this?" Joe asked.

"Yeah," Hawthorne said. "In fact Le Blanc is keeping watch on the building and Peterson is dolled up like a homeless guy. He'll be in the room at all times." Hawthorne edged closer to Tammy, and she welcomed his nearness. "No one else can know about this."

Joe pinned Tammy with a gaze. "Not even Mrs. Traynor?"

Tammy slid off the desk. "We've told her. She doesn't like it any better than you do."

Joe mumbled a curse. "This is a damn fool thing to risk." His gazed narrowed on them. "But there's a way I can help."

Tammy's hopes rose. "You can smell him."

Joe nodded. "I might be able to. If the beans don't get in the way."

Hawthorne's brow crinkled. "Huh?"

"Long story," Tammy said dryly. "Let's get busy."

Tammy could hear thunder and the beginnings of major downpour outside. The scent of rain drifted on the air. The weather acted quirky all day; bouts of rain interspersed by sunny spells.

She stood by some folding tables and glanced around the

room. Stuffing her hands inside the pockets of her jeans, she decided that loitering around looking nervous might tip off the madman. Better to mix with people and keep a low profile. The weather made her nervous, and the electricity in the air seemed more than a storm. Lately her life had dramatized like a thriller movie. She smiled as she remembered Hawthorne. She liked the man playing the hero role. Most definitely.

Tucker approached, and she almost pretended she didn't see him.

Sure, Carter. Just because you ignore him doesn't mean he doesn't exist. Kinda like this bogie man stalking you. A real monster is a real monster.

But why did he have to bother her now? She didn't need his cloying, annoying personality mucking up her color sensing abilities.

"Tammy?"

As his gravely tone rolled over her, she took a deep breath and turned toward him with the most genuine smile she could muster. "Mr. Phelps. I almost didn't see you there."

Tonight he wore sand cargo pants and a short-sleeved matching shirt designed for a safari. A pith helmet would complete the image. Maybe a big game hunter's weapon. Nah. Way too macho for him. Amusement maneuvered through her edginess and gave her relief.

"It's not your evening to be here." He lifted one eyebrow. "And it's not Mr. Hawthorne's volunteer night either."

"We decided to come in extra days this week."

He nodded, his bug-eyed gaze half humorous and half scary. Glancing around, he spotted Hawthorne and stared at him with clear dislike. "I have to apologize for saying this, but he's clearly not your type of man."

Tammy's lips twitched. She didn't know whether to laugh or growl. "What brought on that assessment?"

"The way he acted that evening I talked to you. I just wanted to have coffee and the way he reacted you'd think I was trying to attack you or something."

She shrugged. "It's in his blood. He's a bodyguard, remember?"

"Humph. There's only one reason a man acts like that around a woman. He wants her. To possess her. That's not a good thing, Tammy."

His intimate use of her first name made her want to twitch. She didn't like the way he wrapped the word around his tongue. "Hawthorne doesn't possess me. No man does."

As his eyes narrowed, she felt like a specimen in a petri dish. A fragment of red gathered at the outside corners of her vision. *Just super.* Since she'd opened herself to colors this evening she'd experienced a flood of shades from far too many people.

Tammy knew she had to learn how to regulate this flow so she could pick and chose when and how she received colors. The haphazard way wouldn't do.

She took Phelps' color into her, waiting for a signature to appear. Dabbles of green flickered along the edge. Sickly. Depressing. Could he recently have experienced a deep depression with thoughts of suicide? The idea locked on and bit into her with viper fangs. Putrid green filled her psyche with sorrow. Tammy pushed at the color, trying to shove it away. She couldn't afford this now.

"Mr. Tucker," she whispered.

"Yes?"

She inhaled deeply. "Have you...you haven't considered doing something drastic lately?"

"What?"

"Drastic. Suicide?"

His head jerked back like she'd struck him. "How did—" Phelps backed up a step.

Tammy held a hand up in supplication. "I'm sorry, I shouldn't have said anything."

Arms akimbo, his mouth open, he stood in shock. His big Adam's apple surged up and down as he swallowed hard.

"I did consider it, but it wasn't recently. A couple of months ago. I was having trouble with my dissertation and my shrink said I should get involved with something that could make me feel better about myself. My stupid security job is just a sideline. Something to keep the money coming in until I get my degree finished."

Tammy wondered if she'd misjudged Phelps. Perhaps the icky vibes she'd experienced around him had more to do with shaky mental state than true malice. Still, it seemed odd to her that a man with a master's degree would settle for playing security guard, even for the short haul.

"Is it working? I mean, the volunteering?" she asked.

Phelps nodded. "Yes." His sudden smile surprised her. "In fact, meeting you and seeing you here has been one of the highlights of my volunteer work."

She rubbed the side of her nose. "I'm flattered."

His chuckle sounded more like strangling. "No, you're not. You think I'm a creep. Remember, I've got courses in psychology behind me. That little movement you just made says you're lying."

Okay, maybe I wasn't wrong about him.

Settling in for a long chat didn't appeal to her, but she could see he meant to continue the conversation in depth. "I also know you're here for a special reason tonight, Tammy. I'm not sure what, but I intend to find out."

Tammy closed her eyes for a second as she prayed for patience. Had Mrs. Traynor told this pipsqueak about the plan?

"Even *if* there was something going on, Mr. Phelps, it wouldn't be your business." She started to turn around, but he caught her upper arm in a steely grip. She winced at the pain. "Let me go—"

"You just don't learn, do you, Phelps?" Hawthorne's steel-filled voice rang clear in the room. He took Phelps' arm and peeled his grip away from her arm. He added a slight shove to the movement and Phelps stumbled back a step. "I told you never to touch her again."

"What the hell gives you the right to tell me—"

"If you touch her one more time I'll break all the fingers on both your hands."

Murmurs rose around them. They'd drawn the attention of most people in the room. A few individuals smiled, others looked worried. Maybe they expected a fight.

Tammy wanted to cringe. Good old-fashioned testosterone had risen inside Hawthorne. She could see it in his stance; feet apart, hands clenched into fists at his sides. His actions reminded her that women and men hadn't emerged from the cave all that long ago. His eyes glittered and his lips compressed into a defensive line. Man claiming his woman. *Uh-huh.*

Embarrassment and a peculiar gratification made her look at the floor. She didn't know whether to flare with anger or succumb to the primordial side that liked Hawthorne's masculine protection.

Mrs. Traynor had witnessed the altercation, and she stepped forward. "Mr. Phelps, I think it's time you and I had a long talk. Come with me."

To Tammy's surprise Phelps followed without protest.

Cheers and clapping surrounded them, and they moved back from each other and took in the smiling faces in the room. Tammy looked heavenward as her face burned. Gradually the attention receded and everyone returned to what they'd been doing before Phelps, Tammy and Hawthorne had given them a mini soap opera presentation.

Without saying a word, Hawthorne took her arm and led her from the room and into the hallway toward the back.

"Hawthorne, where are we—"

"Privacy." His clipped tone brooked no argument, and she wondered if he was angry with her.

Her own agitation over Phelps' actions percolated through her blood. When they reached the trusty back office, Hawthorne snapped on the light, brought her inside and locked the door.

He turned and clasped her shoulders in a strong grip. The force in his eyes glowed hot, honest and so incredibly candid she ached inside. Every fiber in her body seemed to tingle.

"That was certainly interesting," she said with an even intonation. Better to keep the lion caged. "A little Neanderthal, don't you think?"

"Phelps is a bastard and I want you to stay away from him."

"You think he's the stalker? He's not. The colors I saw in him tonight don't match the signature. I'm sure of that now. I did realize some things about him...."

She trailed off as she decided it didn't matter.

Tammy expected him to relax, but instead he took a step forward until scant inches separated them. His colors overcame her with that hot, undeniable need she felt when they'd danced at the country-western bar. Each sweltering wave of sexuality surrounded her like a volcanic flow.

"Hawthorne," she whispered. "I'm getting colors from you. Lusty colors. Sanguine. Blistering."

He nodded curtly. "Yeah, and that's one reason why I brought you back here." He licked his lips. "For some reason, peeling that bastard off you has given me a rush. A very big rush. And it makes me want you right here and right now."

Her body flushed. "Oh, yeah?"

"Yeah."

He swooped in and pressed a possessive kiss to her lips. He pulled her against him with one arm. Linking her arms about his neck in an impulsive move, she returned the quick, hungry ownership of his mouth. The kiss went ravenous and she welcomed the thrust of his tongue. They battled and parried for a long minute. Hawthorne's fingers speared through her hair, caressing and kneading. His lips tortured and took as much as they gave. Finally she broke away. She bumped against the wall behind her as she stepped back and out of his arms. Tammy pressed against the cool wall, looking for an anchor to keep her from falling off the edge of the world.

"Uh, Hawthorne, that whole scene back there with Phelps drew a lot of unwanted attention to us."

"Sorry." One corner of that crazy, carnal mouth tipped upward. An amazing, little boy sheepishness crossed his features and it made her want him more than ever. "I lost control. I'm hyper with the danger I feel around you. I don't like it and it's making me crazy."

She gave him a weak smile. "You're forgiven. I think after a kiss like that I'd forgive you anything."

"Much as I'd love to explore this conversation, we've got work to do. No more altercations, Carter."

She winked. "You got it."

They left the room, but then she stopped before they reached the door to the soup kitchen. "I've got to make a stop at the ladies' room. I look like I've been pulled through a knothole backwards."

He grinned. "Hardly. You're the most beautiful thing I've ever seen."

Running her fingers through her hair, she smiled. "You're sweet. But you lie."

He chuckled and without a word went into the soup kitchen.

After she emerged from the restroom and started into the hallway, she thought she heard a noise and stopped. She looked around and saw no one. Next to the men's room down the hall another cavernous room beckoned. The music area, if she remembered right.

Yellow covered her vision, then an overwhelming feeling of

curiosity. She leaned against the wall for a moment, her balance off as the color flooded her sight.

"Damn," she murmured. Blinking rapidly, she moved toward the dark area.

Another flow of yellow filled her sight and she stopped to take a deep breath and jettison the dizziness this color left behind. Yellow with what? A coward's colors?

Green touched the corners and then increased.

Jealousy?

Jealousy coming from whom and about what? She stopped halfway to the room. Not a good idea to wander alone. *Retreat.*

Before Tammy could turn back to the soup kitchen, a hand gripped her shoulder.

Chapter 23

Tammy whirled, a frightened squeal leaving her throat.

Jeannette cursed. "What the hell is wrong with you?"

Irritated with herself, Tammy sighed in relief and smiled as best she could. "Nothing. You startled me. Why were you skulking in the music room?"

When Jeannette didn't answer, Tammy thought she could guess the answer. Jeannette had eavesdropped once again. Tammy took in the girl's appearance and noted she'd dressed like a teen, but not like a hooker. The girl's eyes, ringed by a brown sparkling eye shadow, looked almost bruised. Her short-sleeved pink cotton top hugged her breasts but didn't reveal her cleavage. Her black denim skirt clung to her rear but ended just scant of her knees. Yep. This ensemble rated a tame on Jeannette's usually eye-popping wardrobe scale.

Tammy said, "I didn't know you were going to be here tonight."

Jeannette shrugged. "Yeah, well, I was bored."

"I wouldn't expect you to come here if you were bored stiff."

The girl's brilliant red lips sprouted a sarcastic smile. "What? You think I'd just go screw a guy if I had nothing to do?"

This is starting off great. "Of course not."

"Right." Jeannette glared.

Deciding another conversation track might work, Tammy tried again. "Rainy night, eh?"

"It's a bitch. I thought I'd drown on the way here. Stupid bus was late. What are you doing here? It isn't your night to volunteer."

"I felt generous."

"Kyle was feeling generous, too?"

"He's my bodyguard, remember? We have to stick together."

Jeannette looked skeptical. "Something else is going on, isn't it?"

Mini alarms trembled through Tammy's system. "Going on?"

Jeannette glanced around. "Yeah. I'm no dummy. I can see when something's going down."

The girl's tone sounded like a line out of a television police show, and Tammy had to smile. "Nothing is *going down*."

Doubt carved the girl's face. "I...uh...talked to Kyle awhile back about what I heard. I mean you and Joe talking about that weird stuff."

"Keep your voice down, please."

The girl's trademark pout appeared, her brilliant red lipstick perfecting the result. "Give me a break. I heard you and that old man talking that night and you can't deny it."

She decided it would behoove her to reason with the girl rather than allow disagreement to jeopardize plans.

Tammy put her hand on Jeannette's shoulder, half expecting her to flinch away. "Why did you mention my conversation with Joe to Hawthorne?"

Maybe Jeannette didn't expect the question, for she looked wary. She shrugged and Tammy removed her hand from her shoulder.

Jeannette twisted the single ring on the middle finger of her right hand. "Because. Because I thought maybe Kyle needed to know. He's your bodyguard."

She could have lectured about eavesdropping, but since Hawthorne had tried that, Tammy couldn't think of a point. "Thanks for being concerned."

Jeannette looked uncertain, her bravado disappearing. She twisted the ring around again and again. At this rate she'd wear a hole in her finger. "I…um…heard something else, too. Whatever you do, don't yell."

Super. What had the girl done this time?

Slowly yellow colors filtered around the outside edge of Tammy's vision, and knew the shades of color came from the intense emotion surrounding the girl. Tammy tried to keep the yellow from encompassing her vision as it had earlier.

"I overheard Mrs. Taggert talking with Alison about you and Hawthorne. About the attack on you and your plan tonight to find the—"

"Shhhh. Someone might hear you."

Jeannette glowered and before Tammy could say another word, the girl broke away and headed down the main corridor toward the service exit that led to the back alley.

"Jeannette, wait."

"No way. I'm not taking this crap."

Lovely. Way to go, Carter.

She caught up to the teen and grabbed her by the elbow. "I'm sorry, but the plan was secret for a reason."

Jeannette halted. "You're pissed because I found out. And you don't want me to know because I'm a little nobody to you."

Tammy sighed and released her. "Did I ever say anything that could make you believe that you don't matter to me?"

"Well…no."

"Would I have gotten you the job at Taggert Security Team if I didn't believe in you?"

"I guess not."

"Have I ever acted as though I don't respect you?"

"You said you wouldn't yell and yet you did."

Exasperation ran through Tammy's veins but she kept her voice under control. "I didn't yell. I asked you to lower your voice. You understand why I wanted you to lower your voice, don't you?"

Jeannette pushed her hands through her hair and looked at the floor. In a dismissive tone she said, "I suppose."

Tammy drew on extra reserves of patience. "I'm not going to lecture you about eavesdropping, because you don't see what's wrong with it. You know that you could have put Hawthorne and me in danger just now? If the man we're looking for is here tonight, he can't know our plans."

Tammy heard a door click down the long hall. She looked back and saw the exit door on that end close gently. The hydraulic hissing sound unnerved her and she turned back to Jeannette.

Here in the dim light of the hallway, Jeannette's eyes showed clear vulnerability. "I didn't mean to screw anything up. But you're always coming down on me as if I *mean* to screw up."

Tammy could feel the girl's need to be accepted on any terms. Any disagreement called for immediate sarcasm and petulance. Immaturity ruled Jeannette's psyche, despite the progress she'd made while working at Taggert Security Team. A teen was a teen was a teen. Tammy sighed. Well, you couldn't expect perfection right away. It had taken years for Jeannette to formulate her personality. Things wouldn't change overnight.

"Would you listen to yourself, Jeannette? Your conversation is laced with a lot of 'never' and 'always.' I've noted that never and always are overused words. Rarely does something never happen or always happen."

Jeannette shrugged. "I suppose."

Tammy's body reacted to the stress of the moment, weariness creeping into her bones. She leaned against the concrete wall. "Do you understand why it was a dangerous thing to talk about my plan?"

"I didn't hear all of the conversation."

Maybe if she trusted Jeannette with a little more information, the teen would relent on her nosiness and her inability to keep quiet at the right time. "The colors you heard Joe and me talking about are a type of sensitivity."

Jeannette's eyes widened and she leaned closer and asked, "Like psychic powers?"

"You could call it that. I've had this ability to see people's colors since I was a child." She explained more about her talent and how she'd seen her sister's death and hadn't prevented it. "I know the man who killed my sister is the same one who is stalking me now. We didn't tell everyone in the office because of security. The fewer people who know about this the better."

The girl stared at the floor and didn't answer.

The notion to give up on Jeannette entered Tammy's mind. Perhaps the energy required to keep this teen on an even track required too much effort. "I'm not talking to you about this because I think it's fun. You know me better than that. I gave you a chance. Mrs. Taggert gave you a chance." When the girl looked up, Tammy said, "And Hawthorne wants you to succeed. If there's anybody in the world you admire, it's Hawthorne, right?"

"Yeah. He's cool."

"You want to keep the job at Taggert Security Team?"

Jeannette ran her fingers up over her arms as if she was freezing to death. "Sure."

"You like the money?"

"Of course."

Tammy launched in full force. "You like it better than lying on your back half the day and half the night?"

Jeannette flinched. "Yeah."

"If you won't do this for me, do it for Hawthorne. You remind him of his sister, you know."

"But she died. I'm not going to die out on the street. Not like her. She was stupid." A wild anxiety seemed to enter the girl's eyes. Then sudden sadness as tears welled. "I'm not going to turn out like her." A shuddering sigh went through Jeannette. "Besides, I don't want Kyle to be my brother. Not at all."

Conflicting emotions battered Tammy. She'd done it again and come down hard on the girl. Part of her understood one hundred percent what Jeannette felt. The other part couldn't tolerate it.

In a softer tone Tammy asked, "You really have a crush on him, don't you?"

"It's not a crush."

"What is it then?"

Jeannette's eyes grew luminous, a sweet, uninhibited glow from deep inside. "I love him."

Oh, boy. She couldn't blame the girl. She'd fallen for Hawthorne, too, hadn't she? "Having a crush isn't such a bad thing."

Jeannette cocked her head to the side. "Crushes are for silly girls who run around giggling and drooling."

Tammy laughed softly. "What's wrong with that? Having a crush means you admire someone. Hell, you might not even like everything about them. But you respect them or value certain aspects of their personality. It's nothing to be ashamed of."

Jeannette sniffed. "I thought you'd bust my chops if you knew I loved him."

"I've always known you care about him."

Jeannette cringed. "It's that obvious?"

Tammy nodded and grinned. "Yes."

A wary, almost begrudging look covered the teen's face. "And you love him, too, don't you?"

No point in denying it now. *Come clean, Carter.* "Very much."

"Does he know it?"

"Not yet."

"Why haven't you told him?"

Tammy reflected, aware that her answer carried an importance she didn't understand yet. "Because I'm human, too. I was afraid...am afraid of what he'll say."

The girl sighed. "He loves you. I can see that. Anybody with half a brain can see that. Tell him before it's too late."

Remarkable. Sometimes this young woman's wisdom sparkled from inside like a freshly faceted diamond. Tammy had to remember that life as a teenager often meant maturity and juvenile behavior all wrapped into one uncomfortable package.

Before Tammy could reply, the girl ran for the exit and outside.

Tammy muttered a curse and headed after Jeannette and into the rain. Huge drops pounded the ground, splashing upward.

"Jeannette, wait." Jeannette didn't pause. Instead she trotted down the alley between the church and the next building. "Wait! It's dangerous out here. Look, just come back inside and we'll talk some more."

Lightning sent evil shadows dancing along the walls as it illuminated both their bodies. Jeannette turned suddenly.

"I don't want to talk about love anymore. I shouldn't love him. I shouldn't love anyone. Everyone I care about leaves me." She wrapped her arms around her body as if they could shelter her against the rain.

Tammy saw alarm in Jeannette's face a moment before the significance registered. Lightning flashed at the same time Tammy's vision blurred with red. She heard Jeannette utter sounds, though the words didn't make sense.

Fear slammed into Tammy like a semi careening down a hillside without breaks. She choked on the sensation, her hand going to her throat in desperation.

Before she could turn, a strange noise, like a sibilant hiss, cut through the pouring rain. Tammy wasn't sure she'd really heard it, until Jeannette let out a soft exclamation and her eyes went wide with fear and startled pain.

Dear God!

She watched Jeannette crumble to the pavement. She turned a second too late to see more than a flash of movement in the unrelenting night. A sharp pain exploded through her skull, and she staggered, falling on her right side. Her eyesight swam and pitched, muddied by flowing red. She wiped at the water dripping down her face and her hand came away darkened by blood.

She tried to scream as a black form leaned over her, but nothing but a croak issued from her throat.

Then she recognized her assailant.

A homeless man she'd seen earlier in the soup kitchen talking to Mrs. Traynor stood over her. Rain poured off him and she saw his teeth gleam white in the darkness. She struggled to stay conscious, willing herself to rise and run.

Her body refused to obey.

Fear and pain staggered through Tammy, but before she could utter a sound, darkness descended.

As Hawthorne and Joe crossed into the dining area of the food kitchen, Hawthorne saw Joe sniff the air.

Joe had moved around the building like a bloodhound, trying to pick up the attacker's scent. Part of Hawthorne felt this was stupid. Yet he'd seen the man in action before and with Tammy's reassurance had to accept the validity of Joe's talents.

Joe wandered toward Mrs. Traynor. Curious, Hawthorne followed. He'd kept his distance from Tammy, realizing that if he remained too close the attacker would also stay away and not give Tammy a chance to detect the creep's identity.

He still didn't like this set-up. The whole operation smacked of serious flaws. Still he knew Tammy would have done this with or without him. Stubborn wench didn't even describe her. She was more than that. Brave, foolhardy, reckless, and smarter than any woman he'd known. He kicked himself repeatedly for acting the cave man with Phelps and then hauling her into the back and kissing the hell out of her. When he'd seen Phelps restraining her everything primitive within him had split wide open.

As he strolled up to Mrs. Traynor, he didn't have to remind himself of another important factor. He loved Tammy Carter more than life itself. It was engraved into his skin and into his soul.

"Joe, what's up?" Mrs. Traynor asked. "Hawthorne?"

Joe sniffed the air again and worry crossed his features. "Smells like that dad blamed sulfur. I wonder if Tammy saw any red."

Hawthorne didn't like the sound of that. He caught sight of Taggert Security Team bodyguard Peterson talking with a hooker that had stopped by to either eat or turn tricks.

Joe sniffed loudly. "Yep, I think he was here."

"What?" Mrs. Traynor and Hawthorne said at the same time.

Joe scanned the area, his gaze bouncing from person to person. "He was in the room."

Mrs. Traynor had always accepted Joe's ability as gospel. She'd seen too much evidence of how well this unusual talent worked.

Irrational fear pumped through Hawthorne. Impatient with Joe's disjointed pronouncements, Hawthorne lowered his voice. "Are you saying the stalker is here?"

Joe looked around again. "Was here."

Mrs. Traynor twisted her hands together, anxiety covering her face. "Oh, lordy. What do we do?"

Hawthorne scanned the room again. "Keep calm." Seconds later his unreasonable fear became sound. He cursed.

"Where's Tammy?" Mrs. Traynor asked.

Hawthorne looked around. "She went to the restroom. It's been awhile, though."

Without waiting for replies Hawthorne headed for the front door. Peering into the driving rain, he looked for Le Blanc's car.

Le Blanc sat in his car across the street, unmoving. Hawthorne made a hand signal for Le Blanc to approach. No movement. Hawthorne squinted through the sheet of rain. *What the hell?*

Dread encircled Hawthorne's heart.

Turning back inside, he saw Peterson approaching, concern in his eyes. "What's up?"

"I've got to locate Tammy, and Le Blanc's not moving. Check on him, *now*."

Peterson drew his weapon and started across the street. Hawthorne ignored the gasps from alarmed people as he dashed back into the building with his weapon drawn. He jogged across the room.

Something is very wrong.

Without waiting he plunged into the back area, and he heard Joe behind him. He slid to a stop. The side exit down the hall stood ajar.

Hawthorne gestured toward the restrooms, and Joe nodded as they headed that way. A thorough check of both the bathrooms revealed that Tammy wasn't in either. Hawthorne glanced back at Joe and gestured toward the exits on either side of hall. Joe nodded and motioned toward the back offices. Hawthorne ran to the nearest exit. With stealth he opened the door slowly peered outside. No sign of Tammy. His heart thumped in his chest like out of control bongo drums, powerful fear rolling inside him.

I shouldn't have let her do this. Damn it! If anything's happened to her….

Self-doubt weakened his knees, and a fine film of sweat beaded his forehead. Adrenaline raced through his system. Light-headed, he forced himself to slow his breathing. Now wasn't the time to wig out. Tammy needed him. *Stay level and don't screw up.*

He heard nothing but the rain pelting the building and the asphalt. Easing around the door he looked in both directions. When he looked to the right his heart jammed, then almost stopped.

A body lay not a hundred feet away. He couldn't see who it was.

Hawthorne wanted to rush to the body but he forced himself to look around. No one else was here. He broke into a run, skidding to a stop next to the supine figure. He crouched down and cursed.

Jeannette lay flat on her back, unconscious and unmoving. He checked for a pulse and found it weak. Blood washed away from a bullet wound high on her right shoulder. He immediately put pressure on the wound.

Rain ran into his eyes and he shook his head. "Hang on, Jeannette. Just hang on."

Right at that moment Joe and Peterson came running into the alley. Hawthorne snatched his cell phone from his belt and called 911. Joe and Peterson both cursed when they saw Jeannette unconscious.

"Oh, Jesus," Joe said, alarm clear on his face even in the gloomy alley.

"She's been shot," Hawthorne said.

Joe slipped off his raincoat. "Here, let's put this beneath her head." Joe sniffed the rainy air as he put the jacket under the girl's head. "The bastard was here. I can smell him through the rain."

"Well, you waited too damned long to find him, didn't you?" Hawthorne growled, regretting his harsh tone as soon as it came from his lips. "Here, put pressure on this wound. I've got to look for Tammy."

Joe didn't even flinch. Peterson looked grim, his dirty, ragged homeless man costume making the effect worse.

"I don't think you're going to find her here," Peterson said.

Hawthorne's head snapped up, his nerves crackling like the lightning that raced across the heavens. "Why?"

Peterson took a deep breath and met Hawthorne's wary gaze. "Le Blanc didn't respond when you signaled him because he's dead."

Chapter 24

"Sweet Magnolia, you're mine. Sweet Magnolia is so fine." He sang the name and then laughed at the rhyme.

He drove at a moderate pace. No use having cops stop him and catching sight of the lump in the back seat.

Rain battled the windshield wipers for supremacy. The weather assisted him by making it difficult for others to see. He laughed when he thought of the bodyguard in the car in front of the church. Man never knew what hit him. What a dumb bastard. Bodyguard, his ass.

He laughed again. Of course, getting close to Sweet Magnolia hadn't proved easy. Still, when she chased that little bitch outside it had almost made him laugh. He'd plotted and plotted to capture his Sweet Magnolia, and yet she made it easy for him. Fate seemed to favor him now that he'd done penance for the last mess up.

"Mother was right. Penance does take one to heaven." Proof lay in his back seat, trussed and quiet.

He heard a sound and he realized that his passenger stirred. *Hurry. Must hurry before she wakes.* Not too far now. When she opened her eyes in their sanctuary, he knew she'd smile and thank

him for rescuing her from sin and degradation. She'd drink with him from the bottle and enjoy the cleansing. The thought of the bottle made his stomach burn.
Yes, she'd enjoy it.
Or else.

A cool breeze drifted over Tammy's body.
A hum, like something mechanical, buzzed in the background. Air conditioning? No. More inconsistent than machinery. A human voice?
On the edge of consciousness, she knew she should feel fear. Instead physical discomfort dominated her thoughts.
Her head throbbed, beating in her temples with an annoying pulse. She lay on her right side on something that felt hard as cement. She couldn't move; weakness left her listless.
Seconds seemed to tick away into minutes as Tammy fought with the fog in her brain and the lethargy. She tried to move again and found her arms tied behind her back and her feet bound. Sharp pain arched through her shoulder blades. Her arms cramped and she gasped. In fact, all of her hurt bone deep. Rough material scratched her forehead, cheeks and nose.
How had she gotten here? Where the hell was here? What had happened?
The draft over her retreated and she smelled something rotten like garbage. *Nasty.* She wiggled her nose like a rabbit.
Sounds invaded Tammy's hearing, one by one, as if her body's defense mechanisms didn't want to overwhelm her. Subtle shifts occurred in her mind, and the confusion frustrated her. Scratching sounds breached the area, then a clanging.
As if a train passed nearby, the almost imperceptible rumble of a train along the tracks.

Then she heard something else.

Someone hummed a tune.

Shaking her head, Tammy opened her eyes. Blinking rapidly, she gazed through narrow slits in the material over her face. Fear glided inside her like a stealthy serpent. Quivering, she tossed her head again to try and remove whatever blocked her vision. No wonder she couldn't see well. The scratchy canvas sack covering her head barely possessed adequate openings for eyes, ears, and mouth. Beyond the eye slits the area remained cloaked in gloom. She blinked as her gritty eyes stung. Tears popped forward to wash away irritation.

Through the shadows she perceived a dingy ceiling high above. Ropes hung from one section. The ropes swung with just perceptible movement.

Fine trembling passed through her body as she remembered what had happened.

Someone had attacked her.

The stalker.

Afraid to call out, Tammy listened to the sounds around her while her breathing accelerated and her heart turned to a steady trot.

Don't panic. Must not panic.

Jeannette. What happened to Jeannette? Shot. The attacker must have shot the girl.

Turning her throbbing head to get a better view from the mask, she winced when the muscles in her neck protested. Maybe her attacker had hit her over the head. She recalled the pain, though her memory of the actual event clouded with images that seemed unreal. A dull ache spread along her right side, and Tammy dared to move. A moan escaped her.

Seconds later a slit of light appeared in a hole in the ceiling. Light? Morning? Early evening? Too much natural illumination covered the area for night. How long had she lain here, oblivious to the world?

Sweat beaded on her skin and her breath rasped as new fear nipped at her like a wild beast. Next would come the claws of lost control that ripped and tore. She trembled, aware she hovered on the cusp between holding together and certain panic.

No! Get a grip! I've got to survive and I won't if fear paralyzes me. Hawthorne will find me. He has to realize I'm gone by now.

She lay tied like a turkey ready for Thanksgiving dinner in some weird place from a horror movie. Through her stupidity and stubbornness she'd proved Hawthorne right. By engaging Jeannette in a fiery conversation, she'd allowed Jeannette's feelings to overwhelm her, and she'd picked up the girl's colors rather than the attacker. When his colors had come, it had been way too late to save Jeannette or herself from attack.

Self-recrimination tensed her muscles. She shifted again trying to relieve the pain. She must find a way to get loose. Now that she was in this mess, she must think her way out of it. Anxiety nipped at her.

What would Hawthorne do in this situation?

She heard a change in the mechanical humming and then in the voice she'd heard earlier. A shuffling nearby made Tammy hold her breath. Playing dead wouldn't work. Unconscious? No. Better to face the fear and whoever had kidnapped her.

Seconds passed in agonizing increments and her stomach knotted with apprehension. Seeing the man who'd taken her from the alley would serve to relieve her in one way. At last she'd know the enemy who had killed her sister.

A board nearby creaked. Footsteps came in her direction; they echoed in the cavernous interior. Fright skittered like ants through her veins.

A cream and velvet voice said, "Sweet Magnolia, I know you're awake. Don't move now. If you move you'll fall off the edge of the earth. And that would be a shame."

* * *

Rain continued its assault on the Denver area, but at the soup kitchen Hawthorne had worse things to worry about.

His grinding concern for Tammy made everything seem to move at the pace of an overweight elephant. One nuisance in particular came in the form of Sergeant Leopold Strasky.

Sergeant Strasky's face reminded Hawthorne of a bloodhound. Saggy jowls and small chin didn't match with the man's lean body. Hawthorne half expected the guy to start baying at any moment.

Wonderful image, Hawthorne. You're losing it.

Strasky looked bored, but Hawthorne told himself the man's stalwart expression meant concentration on the task at hand. Too bad this whole shindig took hours of investigation to arrive at the conclusion that they didn't have much to go on.

Hawthorne thought Mrs. Traynor, Joe, and Mrs. Taggert looked concerned and harried, as if they couldn't wait to spring into action. Each one of them, as well as dozens of other people in the soup kitchen, had submitted to questioning about Tammy's disappearance.

Hawthorne's impatience raged through him, and he struggled to hold back sarcastic retorts. The police were doing all they could, but his own fear made him reckless. He wanted action and he wanted it now. It disturbed him, this inability to control wild feelings. As a bodyguard he relied countless times on unrelenting composure. Now it failed him. Helplessness had no place in finding Tammy, and his impotence irked him. He prayed countless times that the stalker hadn't hurt her.

God help the man if he'd done anything at all to her. Hawthorne would hunt him down and make the bastard wish his parents had never laid eyes on each other.

"Is there anything we can do?" Mrs. Traynor asked, her face a mask of discomfort. Her hands fluttered. "It's bad enough young

Jeannette's badly injured, but poor Tammy is in the clutches of that crazy man. We've got to find her quickly."

Strasky scanned the group surrounding him in Mrs. Traynor's office. "That wraps it up for now."

Mrs. Taggert's eyes gleamed with uncharacteristic tears. She glanced at Hawthorne and Joe. "From what you've said, this man is extremely dangerous. If he killed Tammy's sister—"

"We don't know that, Mrs. Taggert," Sergeant Strasky said.

Hawthorne reached out, unable to resist giving her comfort. He put his arm around her shoulders and squeezed for a moment, then let her go. "He's right. We've got to keep our imaginations under control. If we start thinking bad things have happened, it'll only get in our way."

He knew the speech was as much for his own benefit as it was for his employer.

Officer Strasky nodded. "I understand your concern. We're on it. We've obtained the description from the girl of what the man looks like. We have more to go on than you think."

Hawthorne's attempt to be patient warred with anxiety so powerful his mind reeled. "Has there been any word on Phelps?"

Strasky said, "We sent a car to his house some time ago but there's been no sign of him."

Mrs. Traynor reached for Hawthorne's shoulder and pressed reassuringly. "I still say it can't be him."

"Why's that?" Joe asked.

"I don't think he left the building during the time Jeannette and Tammy left the soup kitchen," Mrs. Traynor said.

"But you can't be sure of that?" Hawthorne asked.

Mrs. Traynor's uncertainty showed on her face. "No. No, I can't be sure."

Strasky pushed a strand of brown and gray hair off his forehead. He consulted his notes again. "He said he wouldn't have anything to do with Mr. Hawthorne or Ms. Carter again. Said they hadn't learned their lesson yet, but they would?"

Mrs. Traynor nodded. "That's right. But I don't think he meant shooting Jeannette and kidnapping Tammy. He's had some problems but he's more of an annoyance than a danger. Believe me, I know the difference between menace and pest. I've seen enough of both over the years."

The police officer scratched his nose in a noncommittal gesture. "We don't know enough about this Mr. Phelps to be sure he isn't the one. We've contacted the security company he works for. It's the same place that covers Taggert Security Team and all the other companies in the same building." Strasky's gaze passed over the small group and landed on Hawthorne. "Everyone is a suspect."

Hawthorne managed to keep his trap shut, even though his first impulse urged him to tell Strasky where he could shove his suspect theory. Hawthorne knew that any good officer looked at a situation with an open mind.

After Strasky left Mrs. Traynor pouted. "I can't believe that Strasky said that you're a suspect, Hawthorne. That's downright crazy."

Hawthorne shrugged. "He's just doing his job. He doesn't know jack about me."

"Humph." Mrs. Traynor headed for the door. "This is worrying me something awful." She stopped at the door and sighed. "I'm staying late tonight. If any news comes in, be sure to let me know?"

As soon as she left, Mrs. Taggert turned to Joe and Hawthorne. Her red eyes looked grim. "We can't stand around here. We must do something."

Hawthorne had endured hours of waiting and it drove him half crazy. "Joe do you think you could do for Tammy what you did for Kiley when she was kidnapped?"

Mrs. Taggert almost flinched. "Don't go looking for her yourself, Hawthorne. It'll get you killed."

Hawthorne crossed his arms. "With all due respect, I'm not going to stand around here and scratch my butt waiting for something to happen. The police have evidence but the man who took Tammy has time and other factors on his side. He's way ahead of the game, and I don't like the rules."

Mrs. Taggert stayed silent.

Hawthorne continued, "Jeannette said to Millie while they were in the ambulance that the creep who shot her looked like a homeless man who had been to the soup kitchen numerous times. The police have a half-assed description of him from Jeannette, Millie and anyone else at the kitchen who happened to remember him."

Joe nodded. "With a great disguise like that, he probably dressed like a different homeless person each time he came in."

"So why would Jeannette think it was one man?" Mrs. Taggert asked, leaning against the wall as if it might hold up her flagging patience. "How could she know if he was in disguise from one time to the next?" Her eyes widened. "Unless he wasn't in disguise. Do you think he really is homeless?"

Joe shook his head vigorously. "I think he's the type who plays for keeps. He kills. This man looks like you and I. He wouldn't stick out in a crowd."

"A blender," Hawthorne said. "A difficult bastard to track."

Mrs. Taggert's horrified expression looked as bad as Hawthorne's stomach felt. "I can't believe this is happening." She shuddered. "I keep thinking how awful it was when Kiley was kidnapped. Now Tammy."

Joe's eyes turned hard and determined. "We'll find her. We'll find her."

Hawthorne stared at the olive drab wall between Mrs. Taggert and Joe. "I think Jeannette is right about the man, though. She has a talent for observation. Once my sister told me she kept out of trouble because she could tell a real John from a cop a mile away."

Mrs. Taggert's expression turned curious. "How did she do that?"

"She said it was in the eyes. She could always tell."

"But she'd have to get close." Joe's mouth twisted in disbelief. "Jeannette wasn't close to the guy that shot her."

Hawthorne nodded. "But I think she may have had him as a customer before she came to work for Taggert Security Team."

Hawthorne watched Mrs. Taggert's worn features crease with barely subdued disgust. "You're not saying Jeannette's involvement at my company brought this creep to Tammy's doorstep?"

"No." Hawthorne hastened to reassure Mrs. Taggert. "The guy might have singled her out. I think he knew about her connection with Tammy and picked Jeannette because of that."

"We gotta talk to Jeannette again," Joe said.

"I'll talk to her and then relay any information I get to you by cell phone," Mrs. Taggert said.

Joe looked at Hawthorne and nodded, as if he knew about the insidious worry creeping through Hawthorne's blood.

Hawthorne's disquiet leapt forward. "Help me to find Tammy."

Joe mimicked Hawthorne's earlier stance, feet apart and arms crossed. "We'll have to do it my way."

Hawthorne inclined his head. "Whatever it takes."

"That means using my senses to find Tammy. It may seem weird to you."

Hawthorne managed a weary grin. "Tammy proved to me that her perception of colors work. You helped Scott find Kiley and if Scott believes you...well...I've got to believe you."

Apparently satisfied, Joe started for the door. "Meet me out front."

After Joe left, Mrs. Taggert pushed away from the wall. Her eyes softened and she reached out to pat his shoulder. "I know you love her. We'll find her."

Her revelation knocked him back a bit and his mouth dropped open. "How did you—"

"I've known it for months." A gentle smile creased her weary face. "Let's get cracking Hawthorne. Tammy needs us."

Tammy quivered as the man's voice spilled over her, icy and filled with eerie mirth. Her skin rippled with goose flesh. Red popped across her vision like errant firecrackers, and she winced at the throbbing in her head.

The madman's signature bombarded her. He matched with the red colors she'd seen so many times before. His sickeningly sweet voice held a mocking tone.

"Sweet Magnolia, are you ignoring me? It's not good to ignore your master. I said don't move. You're on something very precarious. Treacherous, as a matter of fact."

She opened her mouth, but nothing came out but a croak. Trapped, her voice wouldn't yield to her mental command. She froze, wondering what he meant by precarious position. The hard surface under her felt solid.

"Water?" He took an old army issue canteen and opened it, waiting for her response. She nodded weakly as he knelt down.

He slid his hand behind her head...a hand that felt big enough to crush her skull. Swiftly he whipped the canvas mask off her head. Relief surged through her body. *Some consolation, at least.*

She hesitated to drink. What if he meant to poison her? Quickly she disregarded the idea. A man like this might plan to kill her, but poisoning wouldn't produce the excitement required. No. This man relied on thrills of another type all together. Tammy couldn't say for certain what he enjoyed, but she knew the answer would come soon.

He chuckled. "A little water to get my answer. A little water before you taste of the sacred."

She didn't have a clue what he meant, but it sounded ominous. "Sit up."

She struggled to do as he said, and he pulled her into a sitting position. Tammy groaned as pain shot through her back.

He placed the canteen against her lips. As she drank she darted her gaze around the room, shameless in her search for information. Now that the canvas didn't obscure her sight, she noted other features she missed earlier.

She couldn't see much. Then Tammy glanced to the right and realized why her captor had cautioned her. She gasped and choked on the water as she saw the floor many feet below. Nausea reared up and punched her in the stomach and she coughed.

She was on a wooden catwalk area perhaps thirty feet across with an unsound looking stairway leading to darkness below. So near the railing, if she'd rolled while unconscious she wouldn't have to worry about the stalker. She wouldn't worry about anything again after the fall took care of her.

Her huge prison looked like a factory or warehouse. A block long perhaps with scaffolding arranged in various areas. Junk and old machinery adorned the area, giving the place the creepiness of an abandoned museum with all its treasures left to rot.

Even on the catwalk time accumulated. The filth of decades, dust, bits of paper, old cans, a used condom, you name it…it was there. Lighting fixtures and several single light bulbs hung on wires from the ceiling high above. She guessed the ceiling towered thirty to fifty feet in total. To her left was an abandoned office. Perhaps this area once served as an overlook office…a way for supervisors to look down on hapless employees.

While she didn't know the building's original use, she tried to think about its location. Downtown Denver? The outskirts of the city? Somewhere entirely different? If she knew the time perhaps she could ascertain where the man had taken her. A long shot, yes, but something to strive for. After another sip of water, she looked around again.

Someone had decorated almost every square inch of the brick walls with graffiti. She couldn't help but read a phrase or two.

Fight or you die. The end is near.

For an inexplicable instant she saw Hawthorne's visage mixed among the red that tainted the corners of her vision. Maybe the graffiti held a message for her. Perhaps she saw those particular words for a reason.

Fight or you die. The end is near.

Tearing her gaze away from the cryptic words, she took more generous swallows of water, and managed to ask, "Who...who are you?"

She didn't recognize the homeless man. His grizzled, thick beard and mustache covered most of his face, and his long, lank hair served to cover his identity. Yet his voice held a familiar nuance that chilled her blood.

The voice on the phone that first time.

When he pulled back she twitched, uncertain. Had she said the wrong thing? Better to play it safe and only speak when spoken to until she knew his motivations.

Instead of answering, he lowered her back to the floor. His red colors wavered, but remained steady. She swallowed hard and held back nausea. The man grinned, showing even white teeth. No, those teeth didn't fit with a homeless man.

Reaching up, he peeled off his mustache, then his beard. Seconds later he removed his shaggy wig. Tammy didn't need to see more to recognize her tormentor.

"Oh, my God," she whispered.

Chapter 25

"God had nothing to do with this, Sweet Magnolia."

The man chuckled, grinning with a face familiar to Tammy from the complex housing the offices of Taggert Security Team. That she hadn't recognized him before now surprised and angered her.

Some would call the man handsome. Yet Tammy always believed that a man possessing the greatest of looks turned ugly if he harbored evil in his heart.

Tumbling blue-black hair covered his head, luxurious as a pelt. Almost onyx irises gave his hooded, deep-set eyes a disturbing effect. His hawk nose complemented the sardonic cast to his face. His petulant mouth, with full lips and feminine curves contrasted with his wide, masculine jaw. In a sane man the combination would have devastated. Instead it made her shudder to look at him.

She guessed him at no older than thirty-five, if that. The layers of dirty clothing he wore disguised his build. His costume made of several layers prevented her from saying if muscle or fat made up the larger portion of his size. She estimated he stood six feet tall.

What a good shell for evil. *A dark, evil angel.*

The image he presented in Tammy's thoughts made her quake and the red inside him engulfed her, sprouting like weeds in her mind. Tammy knew, with conviction, that this man had killed her sister and committed other unholy crimes against women. All his bad deeds went unpunished. His evil came either from inborn factors or a wretched environment or perhaps a combination of both. In the end it didn't matter. She could speculate later about what caused him to do this. Staying alive under his watchful eye would take finesse.

She managed to force words through the panic choking her throat. "You're a security guard at the building where I work. You haven't worked there for long."

He nodded and made a dismissing noise in the back of his throat. "About four months. Took you so long, Tammy, to see me. I'm disappointed you didn't recognize me the few times you saw me. All the time we spent together."

Her mind wrapped around his words but it didn't compute. She'd never spent time with this man. She'd barely said hello. He'd worked the evening shift at the building, and most of the time she'd seen him from a distance, if at all.

Better to play along with him, Carter. It may buy your life.

"I'm sorry. We never got to talk—"

"No!" He bent double to lean into her face, his nose almost touching hers. His clean, peppermint-scented breath wafted over her face. "You don't really recognize me." He smiled, a caricature that showed his gritted teeth. Words came from him in a great torrent. "Remember me, Sweet Magnolia. Remember. It could save your life…for now."

Tammy searched her mind for answers. "Why do you call me Sweet Magnolia?"

He laughed again, a sarcastic, guttural sound. He slapped his forehead and she noticed then that he wore a huge garnet ring on the middle finger of his right hand. Her memories flipped back to last night…or what she thought was last night. She'd seen someone wearing that ring.

The homeless man who'd talked with Mrs. Traynor at the soup kitchen last evening.

A man she saw at the homeless shelter every night she volunteered there.

He'd watched her all along. He'd stalked her as a security guard. The night she had those horrible visions of red in the parking garage, the security guard allowed Hawthorne into the underground area. And his excellent disguise as the homeless man guaranteed no one recognized him.

Before she could speak he said, "Don't you remember long ago when you were just a little bitch? I'm the one who cleansed your sister. But you don't have to worry about her now. She's in heaven where she can't sin."

Tammy wanted to cry and scream. She wanted to take him out back and shoot him herself. An execution, a justice for all her sister had suffered. Instead he held her at his mercy. For how long? How long could she keep him from killing her, too?

"I…I knew you killed her." Tammy swallowed hard, trying to keep the horror out of her voice. "I knew whoever stalked me had murdered my sister."

He uttered an odd laugh that sounded like a snake hissing. He leaned back slightly, and she closed her eyes against the sight of his self-satisfied grin.

"Yet you still don't remember my name, do you, Sweet Magnolia. Think back. Think back."

"I can't. I—"

"You lie." He sat on his haunches. "You're different, Tammy. Not like your sister. At least, you weren't. Until that bodyguard man corrupted you. I thought I could let you live until you screwed him. Then your purity was lost. Lost and gone to hell. Your polluted soul will now be cleansed by the bottle."

She didn't know what to say to his rambling. His chuckle rumbled like an animal as he shook his head. "But you refuse to remember my name."

"You seem familiar."

"I'm Allan."

Understanding rolled over Tammy. Heat seared her face, her fury and alarm potent. Memories of her childhood and teen years erupted like bad scenes from a post-traumatic stress episode.

As his next-door neighbor, she had played with him as a child. Barb joined in their games. Soon, though, Tammy had noticed strange things about little Allan. His red colors warned of his unbalanced state.

At that age his height and weight were meager. They teased him unmercifully. The first time Barb had said something mean to him he'd hit her in the stomach so hard she'd dropped to her knees. They'd never mocked him about his stature again.

While Barb had ignored his odd behavior, Tammy had experienced a bizarre sense of nervousness around him. She'd described him to Barb as unpredictable, and yet Barb had said all boys acted like Allan. After Tammy discovered that he'd killed his family dog with a baseball bat and strung the cat from the clothesline, Tammy refused to play with him...alone.

Right after that, Allan had gone away. Where, neither his parents nor hers would say. A few years later, when they reached their teen years, Allan returned. Without a word as to where he'd gone or why, he popped back into their lives and expected to be friends. Tammy heard rumors Allan had spent time in a mental institution, and her gut instincts told her rumor held truth in this case.

Off and on he flirted with both Tammy and Barb. Barb had remained cordial to Allan, but Tammy had feared him in a way she couldn't explain. They'd both refused dates with him.

Barb apparently hadn't realized how dangerous this man was. Two months before Barb's death he disappeared. No trace of him ever appeared, and soon everyone thought him dead or a runaway. Obviously he'd come back to kill Barb.

Barb had been strangled and then stabbed dozens of times. The passion of the crime had pinpointed that the victim and the killer knew each other. Still, the evidence police gathered didn't lead to Allan. None of Barb's dozens of boyfriends could be charged with her murder. They all had solid alibis.

Tammy's soul throbbed with a special hate for him, and a certain dread that he planned to kill again soon.

She whispered, "Allan Halston. You're Allan Halston."

"Yeah."

"Why Allan? Why are you doing this?"

Halston's perpetual grin lessened. "I'm your savior. Just as I saved Barb, so will I rescue you." His every syllable warned of dire punishment ahead. "And you won't fight it. At least not for long. Barb didn't fight after I squeezed her neck. When her blood mixed with water she looked red...as red as a fiery sun on the horizon over the desert."

A killer's poetic tongue.

An image of her sister's terrified face slammed into Tammy's thoughts. She closed her eyes tightly as if that would crush the horrifying picture. Instead the red hovering around the edge of her vision increased, and so did the image. Tammy shook her head.

"What's the matter, Sweet Magnolia?"

She stayed silent and concentrated on the aches and pains in her body. Maybe that would keep the terror at bay. When she dared to open her eyes his grin sent chills rolling through her.

His smile increased an iota. "Do you remember why I call you my Sweet Magnolia?"

Tammy shifted and the movement sent pains shooting through her hands. She stifled a groan. "You teased me when we were teenagers. You'd seen a movie where the hero called the heroine that name."

Halston nodded. "Very good. Perhaps you can be trusted." When she didn't say anything he continued. "Your memory of what our life was like together might stay pure. You'll remember only the good times we had. Not the crap doctors made up."

Tammy's thoughts scattered, confusing her momentarily. "Doctors?"

"They told my parents I had psychopathic tendencies." His dark brows waggled comically, and she wished she could laugh instead of experience abject horror. "The dumb bastards thought I didn't know what that meant. I could have told them I went beyond tendencies and straight into the darkness." A short, bark-like laugh left his mouth. "I researched. Researched until I realized that psychopath isn't a schizophrenic or a sociopath, or any of those *other* deviations." He gestured at the cavernous building around them. "See, I'm just like this room. I'm larger than anything you can dream. I'm bigger than any wish you've made." His off kilter grin widened, becoming more lopsided. "I'm worse than your nightmares. And I'm your only hope."

After his little speech, she froze, too frightened to twitch a muscle. She acted like a lizard caught in the sights of a bird of prey. Perhaps, if she didn't move, he wouldn't notice her. She knew this wouldn't hold true, but she couldn't stop her reaction.

When she didn't speak he went from squatting on his hunches to sitting cross-legged on the floor next to her. "My actions shall cleanse you of evil, just as the hero cleansed the heroine in the movie."

Tammy opened her mouth before thinking. "But the hero loved the heroine and married her. You don't love me. You've never loved anyone."

He smiled, as if he'd done her a great favor. "I always loved you. Since you were little. Your parents never knew what I wanted to do to you, even then. You didn't know why I killed Bucky, our dog, did you?"

"No."

"To keep from killing you." He waved his hands in a grand gesture. "You see, I knew you were destined for great things. And you were…until you hooked up with that bodyguard man." He shook his head. "Big mistake, Sweet Magnolia. Big mistake."

Fear erupted inside her, and she jerked, tugging at the ropes holding her. A sob almost escaped her lips, but she swallowed it back.

Halston's smile slipped into a demon's grin. "And I killed that hairball of a cat afterwards to keep from killing your sister." He shrugged. "Guess that didn't help for long, did it?"

Incredible. His nonchalant tone amazed her. As she dared to glance at his eyes again, she knew she'd find an empty soul.

So his compulsions existed even as a small child. Perhaps if she kept him talking, she could think of a way to survive this hellhole and the man in front of her.

"And when that was over, what or who did you kill next?" she asked.

Shrugging, he held up his hands in an odd gesture of surrender. "A few more animals. A rat. Mice. Another cat. The dogs were the easiest, though. So trusting. Even if they weren't, I could club them or shoot them, couldn't I?"

Repulsion spread spider legs over her skin. Queasiness rolled through her in sickening waves. "And when you couldn't find one of them to kill, you chose my sister?"

Halston stood and walked to a splintered wood table near the door of the old office. "Oh, no. That was different."

"How?"

He turned to face her, his expression as blank as a peaceful lake. "You have to understand. That's one of my goals. You'll understand me before the day is over. You'll know what it feels like to be me. To have my sacred needs. My mother told me I didn't understand her. That I couldn't know how hard her life had been with me to take care of. You see, she liked little boys. Not just me. But me most of all. And she made me see how life had to be. She cleansed me by making me drink of the water of the body."

Awareness inched into her brain. "Water of the body?"

He reached for a beer bottle sitting on the table. Inside the amber bottle a liquid swayed. "You know. Urine."

"Oh, God."

Shrugging, he put the bottle back on the table. "The ecstasy I get drinking this precious liquid…well…it's indescribable."

Her stomach heaved and she turned to her side and almost retched with disgust.

Halston continued. "She taught me that I could have what I wanted when I wanted. Nothing stands in my way."

I'm going to be sick. Tammy's mind rebelled, filled with pictures of how Allan must have suffered horrible sexual and psychological abuse at the hands of his mother. Had Allan's father known and ignored the situation? Horrifying, but some of Allan's behavior made sense in a psychological perspective. She pictured his mother perpetrating horrible acts upon Allan, and her piquant, smiling face didn't fit the story he told. Could she believe it?

What does it matter? He's sick and he'll kill me. Now's the time to think of escape, not analyzing his deviance.

Distracting him remained her only chance for survival. "Why did you kill Barb?"

"I told you. She needed to be saved."

Tammy thought back to Allan's mother and remembered she had red hair like Barb and Tammy. Perhaps if she knew other things his mother had done, she could make sure to act the opposite and buy herself some time.

She licked her dry lips. "Did you hate your mother or love your mother?"

The sudden question seemed to stun him. He paused, immobile as stone. Shadows entered his already dark expression and his sneer gave ugly a new name. *Evil incarnate.*

As he glared Tammy wondered if she'd made one of the biggest mistakes of her life asking him that question.

"I hated her." He laughed, then shifted his booted feet. His dirty socks peeked through the holes in the toes. He swore. "Isn't that a cliché? The man who hates his mommy." His laugh strangled in his throat, sounding more like a sob then glee. "And you're just like my mother, you know. She did awful things. So many women have done bad things to little boys."

Halston's voice wavered, and Tammy thought his eyes looked moist. A trick of the almost non-existent light? Seconds later he turned toward the splintered wood table again.

"Of course, it is my sin as well. My mother wouldn't have been bad if I hadn't been impure. Contaminated thoughts, tainted deeds. All is connected."

His cold-hearted tone made her recognize that his pathology was planted deep. Halston believed his own propaganda. She wouldn't change his mind talking to him.

He reached for the beer bottle sitting on the cluttered surface. "Here. The elixir and cleanser that will take away your sin."

If she thought it contained another poison she might have withstood this horrible sickness racing through her. Instead, knowing what the bottle really contained made her whole body tense with revulsion.

Tendrils of pure terror threatened, but she kept her wits together. If she lost control, she was as good as dead.

Hawthorne, find me.
Find me.
I need you!
I love you!

* * *

Morning moved into the early hours, and Hawthorne wondered if this dark alley between the church and the next brick building ever saw much daylight. The dank, rancid smell permeating the area seemed ripe for criminal acts. How ironic that Jeannette had suffered here, and someone had snatched Tammy. Maybe some places did draw evil.

Hawthorne forced his mind back to how to locate Tammy instead of the wrenching fear eating him alive. He turned to Joe. Joe stood in the alley next to the spot where Jeannette had been shot. Joe squatted and stared at the red spot where blood stained the asphalt. Police had taped off the entire alley, but neither Hawthorne nor Joe worried about the consequences of trespassing when Tammy's life mattered more.

Hawthorne's gut, minus food for several hours, had the audacity to growl.

Joe looked up and gave him a wan smile. "Why don't you slip into the kitchen and find some of that fried chicken they had last night? Plenty left over."

Despite his hunger, the thought of eating made Hawthorne ill. He couldn't recall the last time he'd felt like this. Maybe he never had. "No thanks. No time."

Straightening, Joe sniffed the air. "I'll be damned."

Hawthorne went on alert, looking around. "What?"

Joe grinned. "I can smell your brain roasting all the way over here. You don't get some fuel in that body, you won't be any use to Tammy at all."

Joe's sense of humor buoyed Hawthorne. "Yeah, I suppose."

"No suppose about it. Now get in there—"

Joe stiffened as if someone had shot him, and he looked back over Hawthorne's shoulder. A creepy sense filtered through Hawthorne and he swiveled immediately, his hand on the gun in his shoulder holster.

Nothing. Nothing but weak sunlight filtering through high clouds and the scent of accumulated garbage met Hawthorne's senses. He turned back to Joe. "What is it?"

"I saw it. Just a flash."

"Saw what in a flash?"

Joe shook his head, and Hawthorne's irritation slipped lose. He stomped toward his friend until he almost stood on the bloodstain. "Joe, what did you see?"

Joe's gaze flicked upward to the sky, then back down at the stain. "I saw rather than smelled. I saw the man through Jeannette's gaze."

Wary, Hawthorne backed up a step. "Does that information help us?"

Sadness traveled Joe's worn face. "Nah. I don't think so. I've got to concentrate and see where he is. Like I did when Kiley was kidnapped."

"Is there anything I can do to help?"

Joe shook his head. "I think I'm in the wrong place."

"What do you mean?"

"I need to talk to Jeannette. Be in the room with her. I guess you could say she's necessary for me to see more than the man that shot her. If I can hold her hand, maybe I can get a fix on Tammy."

Frustration burned a hole in Hawthorne. "Every second longer that it takes to find Tammy—"

"Don't think about it that way."

"Do I have a choice?"

Joe moved closer and clapped his tough, broad hand onto Hawthorne's shoulder. "Yeah you have a choice. I've never known you to give in before. Don't start now. Little Missy needs you."

Deep inside he knew Joe's words rang with truth. Nodding, Hawthorne said, "Come on. Let's go."

Hawthorne drove his Jaguar through the morning rush. Thick traffic and road repairs slowed their progress. Hawthorne drummed his fingers on the steering wheel. The sun burned high and bright without a sign of rain clouds anywhere.

He slipped on his cell phone headset and dialed Mrs. Taggert's cell phone. After a few rings she answered and Hawthorne gave her their next plan.

"Good thinking. I haven't been able to talk with Jeannette anyway. They've been running more tests and she's not back yet," Mrs. Taggert said.

Hawthorne's gut burned and now he wished he'd eaten something to counteract the acid. "What's wrong?"

"Nothing serious, they say. But I'm not sure I believe that. Wait. Here she is now. I'll see you in a few minutes."

When he hung up, Joe flashed him a dour look. "Something wrong with Jeannette?"

Pulling off the cell phone headset, Hawthorne gripped the leather steering wheel tightly. "Mrs. Taggert says she's not sure. I'm not getting a good feeling about this." He riveted his attention on the heavy traffic, hoping it would keep his mind clear. He drove a little fast, but he didn't care. "The police aren't going to find her in time, you know that. It's up to us. We've got to get to her, Joe. If we don't...." He felt her in every inch of his bones, and his heart ached. Tears filled his eyes, and this time he didn't stop them. Two tears escaped as he took a shuddering breath. "Damn."

Instead of looking his way, Joe slouched in the seat, leaned his head back, and folded his hands. He closed his eyes and sighed. "You know, I remember when Scott Danger was trying to find Kiley. You guys are cut from the same mold. Tough as old sticks but with hearts like gold. You love Tammy, I know."

Hawthorne cleared his throat. When he spoke his voice came soft with pain. "I love her more than anything in the world, Joe. If anything happened to her and she doesn't know I love her...God, Joe, I should have told her. I guess I didn't realize *how* much I loved her until now."

Joe looked at him this time, and they locked gazes for a second before Hawthorne pulled his attention back to the stoplight in front of him.

"No shame in a man admitting his feelings. If you want to talk about it, you can tell me. Hell, I lost my wife partly because I didn't say what I meant and do what I said. You'll get that chance to tell her. We'll make sure of that."

Hawthorne's tears dried at his friend's words. Tammy needed him to stay strong for her. And when he had her in his arms again, she'd know he loved her with everything in his being.

Hawthorne's stomach continued to bother him all the way to the hospital, but he ignored it. They headed straight for Jeannette's ward. As they walked through the corridors, he remembered when Tammy had come to see him after he'd suffered a bullet wound. He recalled the warm, tender kiss she impulsively pressed to his lips. Perhaps that had sparked the raging attraction he'd always felt for her. Maybe then he'd started to realize that the flirting and joking concealed a building attraction. Attraction, hell. An all-out war on his hormones and his heart. He managed a secret smile. Yeah, he'd show her hormones when he had her in his arms again.

Seconds later they found Jeannette lying in the bed, her shoulder wrapped securely under the light blue hospital gown. The white pillowcase barely contrasted with the girl's ashen skin. She looked vulnerable and Hawthorne felt responsibility weigh on him deeply. He had to jerk himself into reality.

She's not your sister. She's smarter, tougher than your little sister ever dreamed. Remembering that wouldn't be easy; sometimes he forgot that Selina had created some of her hard luck. Young, impulsive, and with a righteous attitude, she decided she knew it all. With her teen susceptibility visible for the entire world to see, she'd been snagged and bagged by predators. Jeannette owned a savvy his sister never possessed. Maybe that same know-how would help him find Tammy.

Mrs. Taggert rose from the chair next to the bed and greeted them as Jeannette opened her eyes. She looked bleary, but then Jeannette's face lit up as Hawthorne and Joe came toward the bed.

"Hey." Jeannette waved to them and when Hawthorne leaned down to kiss her forehead, she blushed furiously. "What was that for?"

Hawthorne worked up a smile. "General purposes."

Jeannette grinned sheepishly, but looked baffled. "Huh?"

Mrs. Taggert managed a short laugh. "One of his favorite sayings. Ignore him, Jeannette. He's tired and hungry, I'll bet."

Jeannette's heightened color made her look better, and Hawthorne was glad he'd kissed her. "I won't ask how you're feeling."

Jeannette nodded and cursed. "Like crap. The pills they gave me make my eyes cross." Her glance bounced from Hawthorne to Joe, altering to anxiety. "Where's Tammy?"

Joe spoke before Hawthorne could. "Nobody's told you." He tossed Mrs. Taggert a reproachful glance. "You should have told her."

Mrs. Taggert frowned. "I didn't want to upset her."

Alarm raced over Jeannette's face. "She's...is she dead? No, she can't be—"

"Easy, easy." Hawthorne touched her forearm. "He didn't kill her."

Even as he said the words, he prayed with all his heart he told the truth.

Tears trembled on the girl's lashes. "God, but that creep got her, didn't he? I wasn't sure. After he shot me he took her, didn't he?"

Mrs. Taggert put her hand on the girl's other arm. "We're doing everything we can—"

"No, you're not!" Jeannette yanked her arm from Mrs. Taggert's grip. "Why are you all standing around here?"

Hawthorne resisted the urge to scold. "We care about you. And we know you can help us find Tammy."

Jeannette's fury subsided, her wrinkled brow smoothing as tears fell on her cheeks. "How?"

Joe moved closer to the teen and took her hand in his callused palm. "If I can make a connection with your mind, I might be able to tell where the bastard took Tammy."

Jeannette's eyes widened and she looked down at Joe's work-roughened, tanned fingers. "Really?"

Joe nodded and turned her hand over. "Such a smooth palm for a tough young lady."

His melancholy expression made Hawthorne wonder if Joe would lose contact with his more rational self.

Mrs. Taggert pulled a chair up for Joe. "Let's get this show on the road."

Chapter 26

Joe pressed Jeannette's hand. "Relax, or this isn't going to work. Now let's try again."

Hawthorne watched Joe try to make a connection. Joe had explained to Jeannette, Hawthorne, and Mrs. Taggert what he planned to do. If he could make a link, however slight, to Jeannette's memory of what had occurred in the alley, Joe might gain insight to Tammy's whereabouts.

Hawthorne wanted to believe. He wanted to believe so much his jaw ached from clenching his teeth.

Mrs. Taggert sat in an extra chair at the foot of the bed, her curious gaze trained on the proceedings. "Should we maybe try something else? Maybe the drugs in her system are clogging up the works?"

Joe's eyes snapped open and he tossed an indignant look at her. "This is the only way to make it work, drugs or no drugs."

Looking chastened, Mrs. Taggert nodded. "Of course. Go on."

Jeannette closed her eyes again, and Joe gripped her hand in both of his. Hawthorne pulled the privacy curtain around as far as it would go. The illusion of isolation helped. Retrieving the information they needed to find Tammy mattered more than what others thought of the unusual proceedings.

Impulsively Hawthorne closed his eyes as if by doing so he could help Jeannette and Joe connect with Tammy. He touched Jeannette's hand in hopes of comforting her.

A minute passed. Two.

Hawthorne heard the murmur of visitors in the ward, the steady drone mesmerizing. A citrus scent filled his nostrils. An antiseptic perhaps or a woman's cloying perfume. Cold breached his polo shirt and tingled against his skin.

Suddenly the sounds around him changed. A train? Was there a train station around here? He didn't think so, and even so, how could he hear the whistle of the train through these thick walls and windows? Faraway traffic, the annoying cacophony of car horns directed by irritated drivers barely touched his ears.

He watched the snaps of light against the inside of his eyelids, wishing with everything within that Joe would make the connection. *Come on Tammy. Where are you? Joe is trying to find you. I want to find you. I love you. I love you so much. Reach out for Joe, babe. Reach out.*

Then something happened before he could move or speak or comprehend. Red obliterated his vision, sparking and then spreading. He gasped in surprise and cursed. He heard voices around him, but he didn't...couldn't respond. Instead he watched the vision in his head expand like a movie screen. The colors, the sights, the sounds, the scents burst on him so quickly his legs almost gave way. A red brick warehouse, huge, abandoned for dozens of years stood in front of him. A yellow VW Beetle stood outside near a rickety door. His gaze swept the area and he saw other warehouses, several built in the last century.

Hawthorne knew where Tammy was.

Slated for renovation in a year, the old area served now as a place for some homeless to congregate, and for not so savory elements to make drug deals. Then he heard Tammy's voice in his mind.

Hawthorne, find me.
Find me.
I need you!
I love you!

At the tremulous sound of her frightened voice, his entire body shuddered. He felt her love cover him, and at the same time her fear.

She loved him. Joy sprinted through and mixed with the urgency to find her. Oh, God. She *did* love him. He forced thoughts toward her, hoping she would hear him.

I've got you, babe. I'm going to find you. And I love you, too. Hang on, babe. Hang on!

He heard more voices, and he realized Mrs. Taggert and Joe spoke to him in urgent voices. Weakness trembled through his knees.

Hawthorne swore again and resisted opening his eyes. "I can't believe it. I've made a connection. I've made a connection. I can see the building where Tammy is!"

His eyes snapped open and he saw then that Jeannette and Joe gaped at him.

"You made the connection?" Jeannette's voice came small and weak and pleased. She pressed Hawthorne's fingers. "Where is she?"

"Where is she?" Mrs. Taggert asked as well. She'd come out of her chair and now stood next to Hawthorne.

Hawthorne smiled. "The old warehouse district. And all we have to do is look for a yellow VW Bug."

I've got you. I'm going to find you. And I love you, too. Hang on, babe. Hang on!

Tammy heard Hawthorne's voice, and it vibrated inside her like a welcome dream. Frantically, she looked around, certain she'd see him. Instead, she heard only the sound of wind and the breathing of her captor.

She wanted to cry. She must be hallucinating. Nothing else would account for hearing Hawthorne speak to her. God, how she wished he did love her and that he'd come for her. Still, the sound of his voice somehow gave her confidence. Slow, sweet warmth wrapped around her like a comfortable blanket; mentally she hugged it close.

Wind rattled the warehouse; wood inside the building creaked and groaned. Tammy glanced around the platform, wondering if the old timber would break under their weight. She pictured the staircase pulling away from the wall and the supports under them falling.

Another look at the floor far below made her shiver in reaction. She couldn't afford vertigo right now.

The warehouse groaned again. The creepy sound reminded Tammy of the proverbial haunted house. Despite her fear of Halston, she wondered how many souls wandered the landscape. Had people found their death inside these old walls? She looked up at the ceiling.

Halston paused, his grip anchored around the beer bottle. "What are you looking at?"

He glanced at the ceiling, the underside of his broad chin presented to her. Colors danced along the center of her vision. Blue. Purple. Yellow. Pink. Furious red.

Turmoil? Doubt?

As wind battered the structure, she formulated an idea. Halston was clever, but that didn't mean she couldn't manipulate him.

Tammy continued to examine the ceiling. "Can't you hear that? Sounds like mice. Or maybe…maybe someone is scampering along the rooftop. Do you think someone could be out there?"

With jerky, almost comical movements, he shifted and glanced around the area. "No way."

"How do you know? Is this a good neighborhood?"

When he turned a sardonic glance onto her, she wondered if she pushed too far. "Huh. Hardly."

"Where are we?"

"Denver."

"Where in Denver?"

He didn't answer. Even as her heart thumped frantically in her chest, she knew she had to take action. She examined the room and saw a heavy board lying not that far away. A rusted nail protruded through the board. Excellent. A possible weapon.

She kept her voice neutral. "I have to go to the bathroom. Can you please untie me?"

Indecision fluttered over Halston's face. The red hovering around her vision shifted, turning again to an uncertain shade of green. She'd mangled his thinking process for a few minutes. Good.

He smiled slowly. "Least I can do for you considering what you're going to do for me. Besides...can't have your arms and legs falling off, can we? At least, not until I'm ready."

His ice-clad words made her skin twitch with loathing. What did this gross creature have in mind? Rape? She could withstand that horrible possibility. Anything was better than death. No. Eventually he'd kill her. No doubt in her mind now; Halston was a serial killer.

Halston retreated to the table and put down the bottle. A reprieve had come, at least for a short time. Then he dug in his pants pocket and retrieved what looked like antacid tablets. He popped one into his mouth.

Suddenly, he knelt down, and she flinched. When he laughed and reached for her hands, she asked, "Is this funny?"

Halston's snicker turned to a high-pitched giggle. *You sound like a choking hyena, you sick bastard.*

He paused, and she wondered if she'd taunted him too far. Then he reached for the ropes at her wrist and worked at the knot. "Funniest thing I've seen in a long time. I love to see humans react. We're all animals, you know. No better than the beasts that eat carrion in the night. We feed on those less fortunate like the sinful creatures we are. You thought I was going to hit you. But you see, I never do anything predictable. That's why the police haven't caught me. That's why you can't escape me. I'll just kill you when I catch you."

As he released her wrists the circulation returned and the pins and needles feeling burst through her limbs. She groaned in pain. She winced as her protesting muscles allowed her to bring her arms forward. She rubbed her wrists.

Ignoring her pain, she pushed forward with the idea of distracting him. "How do you know the police are looking for you?"

He glared, his gaze opaque as frost on glass. "You ask funny questions."

Risking it all, she asked, "Have you *saved* many people?"

He nodded and scooted down until he could reach the knot at her ankles. He picked at the ropes ineffectually. "Of course. I thought about you and Barb for a long time, and I wanted to save you both so badly. But I had to save other women first. I left them in places the police couldn't find them." He heaved a breath. "At least, I don't think they've found them."

"You've looked for clippings in the newspapers, haven't you? About the authorities finding bodies where you left them?"

His eyes narrowed and he leaned forward, his hands pausing on her ankles. *Just get it over with you creep. Untie me. Untie me! Your touch repulses me.*

"How did you know that?" he asked.

She shrugged. "A good guess." Making sure she executed no sudden moves, she slowly sat up. "Is that why you hid the bodies? You didn't want other people to know you're a savior?"

"A true savior doesn't brag. Doesn't make the police notice him. And they haven't noticed me since I was a kid. People paid attention to me when I was small; they were worried I'd gone rotten like an apple. They had to fix me." His rumbling laugh echoed around the warehouse walls. "I think by that time it was too late. I knew what I was by then. Then my parents tried to blame violence on television. Like I'd gotten my idea to be a savior from some stuff I saw on T.V. That's the biggest bunch of shit. Nobody on television knows my truth. They don't know that God has sent me to cleanse evil. They don't know what I am."

Halston's nonchalant attitude and willingness to tell her about his crimes baffled and scared her. "What are you?"

Instead of answering he graced her with a disturbing smile. The ropes around Tammy's ankles gave way. Even as shooting pains erupted through her muscles and tingles leapt along her skin, the temptation to run almost overwhelmed her.

He stood and walked toward the table where the beer bottle sat. *Now or never, Carter.* Adrenaline spiked in her body as Tammy realized what she had to do. She might never get another chance. She sprang to her feet and ran for the single weapon in sight. The board with the rusty nail.

Tammy lifted the heavy board as Halston swung around and reached for his weapon sitting next to the bottle on the table. She swung with all her might, cracking Halston across the side of the head with a solid thump.

She heard the weapon's report and didn't have time to think about if she'd live or die in the next second. When she didn't feel pain from a bullet, it amazed her. The heavy board dragged at her arms and she released it and it dropped, sending a clatter throughout the building.

Halston grunted as his eyes fluttered closed. He let out an enraged cry of pain as he clutched his hands to his head and slumped to the floor.

She ran by his prone body, but he grabbed her right foot. His powerful grip sent pain rocketing through her ankle. At the risk of falling she kicked out with her left leg and landed a swift one to his temple. With a grunt he let go and she ran toward the stairs. Below a huge, partially shut metal doorway beckoned to her. Escape was near if she—

An ominous cracking noise rang through the air mingled with a roar of outrage from Halston. She cursed. The stairway would give way any second. *Hurry. If she ran fast enough—*

Ten steps from the bottom the wood split and tore. A horrendous shrieking and groaning issued from the staircase as nails released their decades old grip. She grabbed for the splintered banister and tiny pieces stabbed her hand. *Splinters or possible death. No contest.*

Tammy hazarded a glance behind her.

Halston stood at the top of the stairs, his eyes wild, hair mussed, and blood seeping from his head. He let out a roar she heard over the protesting, disintegrating structure.

"I'll get you! You bitch!"

Fear lent power to her shaking limbs as she lunged forward, jumping the last broken steps.

Seconds later the flight of steps came apart with a screech. She hit the bottom of the stairs and they broke away. A scream left her throat.

Pain enveloped her body as the scaffolding tumbled Halston from his perch and then came down upon her.

Hawthorne heard the tremendous din as they stepped out of the Jaguar in an old parking area not far from the warehouse.

"Sounds like all hell is breakin' lose," Joe said, his eyes wide. "Did you hear a scream?"

Hawthorne's adrenaline surged as he started to run toward the building. "Come on."

Mrs. Taggert had called the police as Hawthorne and Joe left the hospital, but Hawthorne wouldn't wait from them to arrive. Tammy's life could depend on swift action.

"Here!" Hawthorne reached for the first doorway and they found it locked.

Joe pointed toward the end of the building. "Try those metal doors! I'll look down at this end! There's got to be an easier way inside!"

Hawthorne sprinted toward the metal doors. When he reached them he crept to the opening and peered through. His throat tightened and his heart raced at what he saw in the murky interior. Tammy lay, barely visible, under boards from a broken scaffolding and stairway. A bleeding man crawled toward her. Gibberish tumbled from his cut lips. Hawthorne recognized the man immediately as a security guard. The one who'd let him into the parking garage the night Tammy had called in a panic.

Hawthorne drew his gun and lurched into the building.

Holding his weapon out, he aimed at the man. "Hold it right there! Move an inch and you're dead!"

The man stopped and looked up, his eyes blurred with pain, madness, or both. "I must save her." The husky voice rattled, as if the man had something in his throat.

Sweat trickled down Hawthorne's left temple and his heart hammered. He moved closer with deliberate steps. "Stay away from her or I'll blast you into the next life."

The man guffawed, then coughed, and blood ran from his mouth down his chin. "You wouldn't. You can't. I'm the savior. I'm the only one who can rid the earth of sin. You have no power over me."

"Don't do it." Hawthorne gritted his words out one by one and moved nearer yet again. "Don't."

In the distance sirens wailed and Hawthorne knew the police would arrive soon. His anxious gaze settled on Tammy for a second, then back to the security guard. As much as he worried about her, Hawthorne couldn't afford to take his attention from the other man.

A commotion behind the huge pile of collapsed stairway and walkway startled Hawthorne and the man. Hawthorne kept his aim on the security guard.

"It's me!" Joe trotted from around the side of the mess and stopped. He eyed them and then Tammy. "Oh, God. Little Missy."

"Check her out, Joe," Hawthorne said huskily, his voice sounding as if he hadn't consumed water in days. Anxiety clenched at his stomach.

As Joe pulled plywood away from her still form, Hawthorne took another step toward the security guard.

Joe's muttered cruse sounded like the groan of a dying man. "Oh, no. No. No."

Hawthorne knew in that moment what Joe would say, and his heart did stop this time. Ground to a halt and retreated deep inside to hide where no one would ever find it again.

Hawthorne dared to ask, "What? What is it?"

Joe looked up, his eyes glittering with tears. "She's...oh...she's—"

"No!" The security guard crawled toward her again. "No! Not yet! Mine to send on! Mine!"

Joe froze, his face a mask of infinite horror and despair.

Hawthorne felt a blast of pain like a physical blow hit him square in the chest. He thought everything within him would still, dissolve until nothing remained but a sorry shell. Hollowed out in seconds, he stood rigid as a pole. Deaf, dumb, and blind to everything but incredible disbelief.

Tammy. Dead.

If Tammy was dead, Hawthorne cared about nothing and no one.

"You sorry son of a bitch!" Hawthorne, close enough to the security guard to almost touch him, took a last step and grabbed the man by the shirt collar. He yanked the man up to his feet. Foul words issued from Hawthorne's lips in a stream of hatred he'd never experienced before for any human. "You killed her!"

Strength more potent than any he'd felt coursed through Hawthorne's body as he jabbed the barrel of his weapon against the man's forehead. The man's weight dragged down Hawthorne's arm. Hawthorne threw the man back against a pile of wood almost five feet high. More curses spilled from Hawthorne's lips.

The man shook his head as if realizing his life hung by a high wire and one step would send him plunging to his death. "She was mine. Mine! Not fate. Not accident. No!"

"She was never yours," Hawthorne whispered raggedly. "Never yours to touch or to hold or to love. You never had that, you piece of crap. And you never will again. Because you'll be dead!"

"Hawthorne, don't." Joe's raspy undertone penetrated the heat running through Hawthorne's blood. "He isn't worth it. Little Missy wouldn't want…she wouldn't want…."

Joe's voice broke, and so did Hawthorne's heart. A lust to kill the incredible bastard who had taken Tammy from him poured through Hawthorne.

Oh, Tammy, sweetheart, I'm so sorry.

Screeching tires and the ever-increasing howl of sirens reached Hawthorne's ears. Along came the realization that Joe was right. Tammy wouldn't want him to kill this man. Momentary satisfaction wouldn't bring her back. Nothing could bring back the only woman he'd ever love.

His grip on the man's neck loosened. His heart thumped wildly and a haze of red filled the outside of his vision. The security guard slid down the wood stack and lay gasping on the floor.

Joe moved to Hawthorne and laid a hand on his shoulder and pressed as if to give comfort. Hawthorne shuddered. Nothing would be right again. He turned toward Tammy, tears filling his eyes.

"Hawthorne?" The weak whisper filtered from Tammy's direction.

Hawthorne almost choked on his next breath. He didn't answer the ghostly voice because he was certain hallucinations had found him.

Joe whirled, his eyes wide in disbelief. "I checked her—Oh, Little Missy!"

Hawthorne and Joe converged on her. Hawthorne's knees collapsed as he settled beside her, his hand on her forehead. "Babe, don't move. We've got you. Help's on the way."

Blinking rapidly as if to focus, she gazed up at him. Hawthorne caught her hand in his and pressed it to his lips. Tears ran down his face. "Don't cry, Hawthorne."

His next breath came frayed and strangled. "Where are you hurt?"

She gave him a weak smile and struggled to sit up. Hawthorne pushed her back gently. "No. Wait until the ambulance gets here. Just tell me where you're hurt."

Tammy's grimy, scratched face managed a smile. She placed her other hand over her heart. "Here's where I hurt."

Worry stabbed Hawthorne yet again. "What?"

Her grin widened. "I heard you say you loved me. What took you so long?" Tears poured from her eyes. "If you don't tell me you love me again, I'll die of a broken heart."

Hawthorne thought he'd expire right there as joy pierced his soul. All the terror and hate and grief of the last few minutes washed away. His arms trembled, his stomach felt hollow, but his heart filled with an indescribable happiness. "I love you, more than anything on earth."

Joe stood and smiled. "Welcome back, Missy. A miracle, I say. I mean, I thought you had no pulse. A miracle."

Hawthorne had never seen a bigger smile on a woman's face. "You came for me. Just like I'd hoped. Like you said. You came for me."

"We would have gone through hell to get to you," Joe said.

Hawthorne chuckled and touched her hair with gentle fingers. "To hell and back."

"I love you, Hawthorne," Tammy said.

"Say it again."

"I love you."

He closed his eyes and whispered, "I love you, too, Carter."

Fresh tears cleansed her face. "Then everything is all right, Hawthorne. Everything's all right now."

And she drew him down for a kiss.

Epilogue

Tammy pressed her hand to her stomach and smiled. *Everything is right with the world. Indeed.*

Hot sun pressed down on her and a brisk wind blasted through her hair as she stood on her private balcony.

The cruise ship under her feet sailed smoothly over the glassy surface of the ocean. Diamond points glittered on the water as a school of fish skimmed the surface and danced with the vessel in a playful game. Their colorful scales gleamed with a thousand colors. Seconds later the fish disappeared. The splash of water sounded like music, a special heaven created for her alone.

She glanced around in contentment. Just six months ago she couldn't imagine standing on her private balcony in a deluxe cabin suite on a ship bound for Alaska. As she looked out on the sparkling water, she wondered what she'd done to deserve such happiness.

Two seconds later she laughed and said, "To hell with it, Carter. Just enjoy!"

The cabin door creaked opened and closed and she turned back to the room. Tammy's heart did a triple flip and a cartwheel at the sight of the man striding toward her with a ne'er-do-well grin on his mouth. In shorts and a T-shirt, he was the handsomest man she'd ever seen...ever would see.

Simply marrying him had changed her life forever.

Since the day she'd almost died in that horrible warehouse, she spent more time loving and living and less worrying. She looked at each day as fresh with new possibilities. No time to worry about the past. Now, much to her delight, her future looked brighter than ever. She didn't think much about Halston anymore. Hawthorne's touch did wonders for her when she remembered bad times. Memories of that horrible event lingered, but would fade like old photos as time marched forward.

Without a sound he gathered her in his arms and kissed her breathless. When he released her he looked at her intently. "All right, babe?"

"Just thinking for a moment."

He frowned. "About Halston."

Tammy sighed. "Yeah."

"You never have to worry about him again."

She knew that intellectually. Halston had died at the warehouse, his fall from the scaffolding resulting in internal injuries. His autopsy revealed he had stomach ulcers that might have killed him if gone untreated. While it couldn't be proven, Tammy wondered if years of drinking from that beer bottle and ingesting its horrible contents ruined Halston's stomach lining.

She shook off thoughts of the man. No, she didn't jump at shadows or cringe thinking someone watched her. Maybe because Hawthorne's love gave her a strength that added to the fortitude she'd always possessed.

Perhaps because together, they could fight any demons life could throw at them.

So many things had changed since the day she'd fought for her life at the warehouse.

Their lives filled with the people they'd come to love. Tammy found Joyce and Lincoln like a second set of parents. Their warmth and affection gave her a new pleasure. Joe and Jeannette thrived, proving some people just needed a second chance.

Other people passed from their lives never to return. Tucker Phelps left the area after a month, obviously not finding assisting the homeless to his liking. Tammy couldn't say she missed the man an iota.

Hawthorne no longer felt guilty over his father or his sister. Like Tammy, Hawthorne continued to find fulfillment in working with the homeless whenever he could.

Without a word he tugged her closer and indulged in a knee-melting kiss.

When he released her lips, he said, "Man, it's still incredible."

She grinned. "What?"

His sizzling perusal took in her face and drifted down to the low dip in her bikini top. His big palms traced over the barely there scrap of material covering her butt, cupping and exploring. "Four months married and my heart still stops at the sight of you."

A blush traversed her face and slid down to her cleavage. "Flattery will get you everywhere."

He nibbled on her neck. "Here?"

Tammy shivered as his hard muscles moved against hers. "No fair. Aren't you going to tell me what Mrs. Taggert said?"

Hawthorne had left their belated honeymoon suite to call dry land and tell Mrs. Taggert all fared well. The woman worried like a grandmother.

Hawthorne paused in his feasting and chuckled. "She sounded awkward. Said she was surprised I found time to make the call. I guess she thought we'd spend all our time indoors. She fumbled and stumbled over her words and finally said, 'I'm just digging myself a deep hole here, aren't I?'"

Tammy laughed. "Everything's okay there, I hope?"

His fingers cruised over her spine. "Mrs. Taggert sends love from Kyle and Scott and little Max, too."

Tammy's heart filled with a special joy at the mention of the little infant that had been born not so long ago. The thought of him made her secret more delicious.

Hawthorne continued. "Jeannette's jealous as hell and wishing us the best. "

"Jealous that we're on our honeymoon, or that we're on a cruise to Alaska?"

He waggled his eyebrows. "I think she's over her crush on me. I think she'd like a cruise to just anywhere just about now. Mrs. Taggert is keeping her plenty busy."

Jeannette worked on her GED and kept her job at Taggert Security Team. Not an easy feat, but one the girl was determined to continue. Tammy missed the girl even now. They'd grown closer over the months until she'd become like a sister to Tammy.

"She'll be fine. She's tough like me." She eased into a rueful smile. "Like snake skin."

He groaned and traced his hands across her back. "Babe, you don't feel anything like snake skin, believe me."

His fingers inched into the tiny bikini bottom and she gasped. "Oh, Hawthorne."

He kissed her neck again. "Yeah."

"If you don't stop I might explode." While it became difficult to think under his gliding fingers, she cupped his face and said, "You're insatiable."

A husky laugh rumbled in his throat and vibrated into her body. "Complaining?"

His hands found new territory and conquered.

Breathless, she managed to gasp, "Never."

Hawthorne's mouth wandered over her lips in tribute. Tammy had never felt a love stronger than his, and she cherished it beyond anything. She pressed against him and soon the world dissolved as one kiss followed another.

An eternity…an exquisite eternity later, they lay naked on

the bed cooling in the breeze from the open balcony door.

Hawthorne's hand slid over her stomach and her muscles jumped. She giggled.

He groaned. "Damn."

"What?"

"That's just about the most beautiful, flat stomach I've ever seen."

She sighed. *Well, Carter, as the old adage says, there is no time like the present.* She turned toward him and trapped his hand against her hip. "It's not going to be flat forever."

Hawthorne said nothing for a solid minute, then awareness dawned like a new sunrise. "What are you...are you saying what I think you're saying?"

She tweaked his nose playfully. "You're a pretty smart guy, Hawthorne."

He grabbed her hand and pressed a kiss to her fingers. Then awe etched his features. "When...I mean how...I mean—"

She covered his mush mouth with her hand and rolled him onto his back. "I think you know *how*."

He licked her palm and forced her to take her hand away. Narrowing his eyes, he gave her a mock frown that disappeared and changed to clear happiness.

"Oh, sweetheart. That's so beautiful," he whispered.

The happiness on his face made her ache with love deep in her heart. Rolling onto her back, Tammy placed her hands on her stomach. He put one hand over both of hers. Seconds later they both smiled.

He laughed. "Pink."

She grinned evilly. "Blue."

With a wicked twitch to one eyebrow, he shook his head. "You lie. I saw pink."

She pulled her hands out from under his and teasingly swatted him. "Just because you see colors occasionally doesn't make you an expert, bud."

His face sobered. "Yeah, but I'm damn glad I saw where you were, Tammy. I still swear to this day I heard your voice—"

She kissed him. "You know I believe you. I heard you tell me that you loved me, remember?"

Hawthorne's serene grin made her smile in turn. "How could I forget?"

"Let's forget about then. Lets think about...." She placed her hands over her belly again. "These two."

Shock crossed his face. "Two?"

"Okay, so you did see pink. And I saw blue. Warm pink and fuzzy blue. We're having twins."

His eyes widened comically. "Oh, Carter."

"Yes, Hawthorne?"

His kiss left her shivering with a sweet desire she couldn't wait to fulfill.

And they fulfilled that love. Again and again.

~END~

About the Author

Suspenseful, edgy, thrilling, romantic, adventurous. All these words are used to describe Award-winning, best-selling novelist Denise A. Agnew's novels. Romantic Times Magazine called her romantic suspense novels DANGEROUS INTENTIONS and TREACHEROUS WISHES "top-notch romantic suspense." Denise's record proves that with paranormal, time travel, romantic comedy, contemporary, historical and romantic suspense novels under her belt, she enjoys writing about a diverse range of subjects. Writing tales that scare the reader is her ultimate thrill. Snappy banter is her favorite dialogue, and she not only likes reading it, she loves writing it.

Denise's inspiration for her novels comes from innumerable sources, but the fact she has lived in Colorado, Hawaii, and the United Kingdom has given her a lifetime of ideas. Her experiences with archaeology have crept into her work, as well as numerous travels through England, Ireland, Scotland, and Wales.

Denise lives in Arizona with her real life hero, her husband. She is currently writing a romantic suspense featuring a firefighter hero.

(Watch for Denise's *Midnight Rose,* a chilling historical thriller you won't want to miss.)
—Lee Emory, Publisher